Crossfire at Bentley

by JS Ririe

Jan Hill Books

Crossfire at Bentley: by JS Ririe
Publisher: Jan Hill Books
ISBN: 978-1-7333027-6-0
Copyright 2021: Jan Hill Books
Cover Image by: deklofenak
Cover Design by: William Gensburger

Praise for: Crossfire at Bentley

"I am so hooked on this book! I am usually not a reader but I couldn't stop reading this! It's a must read for sure!"

~ Taneeca H.

Dedication:

This book is for those of you who, like me, have made more than a mistake or two when it comes to love but still believe in the joy, peace and fulfillment it is meant to bring. I have paid a bitter price for following my head instead of my heart, but I have learned some profound lessons about who I am and what matters most to me. While I am a little too old to believe love will find me in this life, I have hope that all things are possible to him or her who has faith in something greater than what mortal eyes can see. ~JS Ririe

Chapter 1

When I left Bentley, it was meant to be forever. I had carefully locked away heartache, disappointment, and the need to know things that would likely remain hidden until the day I died in an attempt to go on living as other people appeared to do. But regardless of the distance traveled—or how full each hour was filled—nightmares influenced by all I had lost haunted my dreams. And memories that had become more than a hindrance to my sanity crept into my wakefulness with such regularity that I doubted I would ever feel any less confused. I longed to erase time and go back to much earlier days when I still believed in love, devotion, peace of mind, hope for something better than what I had found and a beautiful, miraculous intervention to a life that had lost all spontaneity and joy.

I had tried unsuccessfully to escape the most debilitating parts of my past by engaging in what I had always done in an effort to survive—keeping so busy with work and trivialities that I was too tired to think about anything of a personal nature. That attitude of avoidance and strong personal resolve had kept me moving forward after college graduation when I found myself in an impossible situation of my own making. Fortunately, I had been hired as an apprentice at a clothing design firm in San Fransisco where I was given the chance to collaborate with, and help, one very temperamental, but well-established designer.

Bethany Kilpatrick knew exactly how to get her work featured in magazines, over social media and on the runway, but she could hardly be described as someone who liked people. Her voice was jarring, her attitude condescending and her appetites excessive. Still I had to give her credit for knowing how to use her carefully honed skills in advancing her career and filling the need she had for certain kinds of companionship because she had never married or become even slightly domesticated. She lived for her creations and the adulation her work brought. While I admired her flourishing career, I had no desire to become like her.

My need for autonomy, once I learned how to express an opinion vocally, did not sit well with her. She wanted a clone—created in her image —who would do her bidding without having any personal aspirations. That wasn't much of an issue while I was learning the ropes. I loved working with expensive fabrics, the latest trims and accessories and seeing exquisite creations come to life, but it wasn't long before I knew I truly had been blessed with the ability to create my own clothing line.

Miss Kilpatrick, as she insisted that everyone in the company address her, never uttered a word of thanks or praise for the tweaks I made to her designs that made them come to life. She simply claimed the glory while I remained hidden in an unfulfilling background until fate stepped in and I got my first real break after five long and grueling years. She was in the middle of one of her tantrums over what she considered a slight to her massive talent when she walked off the job one afternoon and didn't come back for nearly a month.

It was right before the spring show, and the owner of the company was livid—almost to the point of breathing out fire. He called me into his office and declared that he had no choice except to pull the entire line. Without prior warning, I had arrived at the moment when I could either take charge of my own future or become unemployed. After several moments of oppressive and calculating silence, I assured him that I could fill in during her absence. Most of the designs were complete, and I knew exactly what she was contemplating with those that weren't.

Without being entirely sure that my bravado was well-placed, I worked like a demon was chasing me until the night of the show and pulled it off with such flair that Mr. Fredericton asked me to take her place. When she returned and found that she wasn't indispensable, she retaliated by moving to the South of France to create her own empire. I didn't hear much about her after that, only that she blamed me for destroying her life. Apparently, thirty-five years at the top of the industry didn't ensure continued success for anyone.

But I was young, enthusiastic and determined to make it regardless of how my sudden rise in a very competitive and cutthroat industry had come about. I felt a tempered amount of personal satisfaction, but my promotion placed me in a position where many of the people I had been working with wanted to see me fail. It was a constant battle to keep former colleagues and friends from undermining every move, and after what seemed like a totally misspent life, my work was all I had. So I found myself pushing through every roadblock and personal attack without giving in to anger, righteous indignation or self-condemnation.

Over the next two years, I visited Italy, England, South America and Japan promoting my work. Like my predecessor, my creations were featured on the covers of magazines and in some of the most celebrated fashion shows on both sides of the continent. While I was still living somewhat frugally, I purchased a home—a wood and glass, modern edifice —in one of the heavily wooded areas outside the city.

People were starting to equate my name with my creations, but I wasn't anywhere near as happy as it thought I would be. I was grossly disenchanted with a life that had given me recognition, respect and material possessions and needed something that would provide meaning to what I considered a superficial existence.

I longed for a family, and often caught myself wishing for the financial challenges that came with raising one. l wanted my stylish home filled with diapers, childhood illnesses, temperamental in-laws, and a man whom I dearly loved demanding my time and attention. In less than a month I would be thirty, and it seemed as if that part of my life would soon disappear like the dew when the sun began to shine.

Trying to pinpoint the exact moment when I first recognized that my life was virtually the polar opposite of those of my former roommates and friends was impossible. I suppose it came about so slowly, and through such unconventional ways, that I was unaware of any huge divide until most everything in my world had become something I barely recognized. But by that point, it was too late to set a different course.

However, I was acutely aware of my first experience with loss, uncertainly and the most excruciating pain imaginable. I was seven and alone in the house with my father who had a bad heart but who took his responsibility as head of our family seriously. My mother was having her hair done, and my older brother, Nate, was playing basketball with his high school teammates.

Like any young child, death meant nothing to me, but my instincts for survival were strong. So when I heard a noisy crash while watching one of my favorite television shows, I ran to the back of the house. My father had come home from work early complaining of having a mild case of the flu. I pushed on his door to no avail and screamed for him to let me. When all remained silent, I dialed 911 on the landline phone that still hung on the wall in the kitchen. But when the paramedics arrived, and were finally able to get inside the bedroom, they only told me he was gone. Shock was instantaneous, and I don't remember shedding a single tear while they waited with me until my mother got home.

I could never recall much about my life after that. I suppose I went into my own dark place where my mind tried to shield me from things I was too young and inexperienced to understand. That was certainly a reasonable conclusion after what happened with my mother. I know she did her best, but she simply wasn't equipped to manage children, home, a job and personal grief on her own. She soon slipped into a despondency where she wasn't able to get out of bed for days at a time. And when she did, she just stood at the kitchen sink and cried. Nate left home for college eighteen months later, and I didn't see much of him after that.

I tried to be the help and support my mother needed, but while some days were better than others, I mostly stayed to myself reading books, watching television and playing games on the family computer when I wasn't at school. But then the second, irreversible tragedy struck and . . . .

My thoughts were interrupted when one of the company runners—who was assigned as an interface between designers, seamstresses and management—came hurrying into my office where I was busy sketching. She was a pretty girl with freckles, honey blond hair and big blue eyes.

"Why haven't you checked your messages?" she asked with a certain amount of indignation as her arms crossed in front of her chest. "Mr. Fredericton has been trying to reach you for the past forty-five minutes."

I turned from my art easel with a heavy sigh wondering why he hadn't come to find me himself if what he had to say was so important.

"All technology is on mute when I'm working," I told her. "Distractions break my concentration. Everyone knows that. What is so crucial that it can't wait until I finish?"

"He didn't say, only that he expects you in his office pronto."

She was gone before I had time to step away from my stool. I knew better than to keep the man who signed my paychecks waiting. While I was one of his top designers—who had helped make him a lot of money since Bethany's departure—he was the one with the influence and connections to keep me climbing the ladder of success or fall into oblivion.

So I took my latest sketch and put it in the locked safe with the rest of my designs for a fall collection. I hated securing my work for a quick trip away from the office, but espionage in the fashion industry was legendary. One click of a button on a cell phone and the intellectual property I had been working on for months would be used by someone else.

Mr. Fredericton was waiting at his cluttered desk when I entered his opulent and spacious office with massive windows that overlooked the marina. He liked admiring his yacht from a distance almost as much as he liked hosting parties on it.

"Sit down, Jada," he said in lieu of a more traditional greeting. "There's something we need to discuss."

I felt my knees go weak but did as he requested. While he was great businessman, who knew how to control every aspect of his company, his personal interactions with his subordinates left something to be desired. "I'm sorry I didn't get your message sooner, but I tend to lose track of time when there's work to be done."

"I'm not worried about your productivity right now, Miss Sloan," he countered. "I've had a request from an old friend that needs immediate attention."

"Of course, sir. I'll do anything I can to help."

"Exactly the response I was looking for because this is something I expect you to do without complaint since it involves your old alma mater."

I looked at him with confusion. I had been away from Bentley for eight years. What could I possibly do for them besides continue to send my yearly contribution to the alumni fund so other young people, without sufficient means, could experience what I had in furthering their educations?

"Chancellor Allred would like you to be part of a weeklong pilot program of lectures and practical demonstrations designed to help current students get a better idea of what the real world expects once they get their degrees. While internships have been more than helpful in the past, it's becoming increasingly difficult to find companies willing to devote the time and resources necessary to babysit someone they may never hire. He's hoping this program will help bridge that gap."

I sank back in my chair. While college had been a worthwhile experience, I had no desire to go back. But I couldn't exactly leave my boss hanging when I had already made a commitment.

"When would I be expected to leave? I am in the middle of developing a fall line."

"Three days from now. I know that's short notice, but the timing can't be helped."

"You mean I wasn't his first choice."

"While you've done very well for yourself with my backing and encouragement, you aren't the only alumna from Bentley I've known."

"We're talking about Miss Kilpatrick now, aren't we?" I asked as gooseflesh covered my arms and legs. In many ways, I still felt responsible for her sudden exit from the industry.

He cleared his throat before responding. "Bethany agreed to do it when she was in one of her more generous and compliant moods but bailed at the last minute. I need you to take her place and work your magic again. I can't afford to have my company's name tarnished and was hoping it might produce a few candidates capable of being an assistant for you."

"I thought I was pulling my own weight."

"You are, but from what I've seen of your fall line you'll be in more demand than ever when it comes out. I think it's time you had someone to help out with the more menial tasks like you once did for Bethany."

My brow furrowed unbecomingly. "Am I supposed to take that as a compliment?"

"You can take it as you like. I would never insult your intelligence by playing games. Bethany humiliated us once by defaulting on her obligations. That's not going to happen again if I have to go to Bentley myself. I have authorized a cash reward for the design you feel has the most promise when it comes to inclusion in your fall line. And if you find someone you really like, I am willing to offer him or her an internship at no expense to you."

"That's very generous, sir."

"It's how you came to my attention. I'm sure there will be time between lectures and demonstrations to get some work done. Quite frankly, we could use the positive publicity."

"Very well, sir," I replied, not daring to probe into affairs that had nothing to do with my job description. "Are there any further directives?"

He slid a thick manila envelop towards me. "I had one of my assistants make a copy of all the data we have relating to the seminars. Housing has been arranged and there's a small stipend to offset some of the expenses. Since each field is unique, I trust you will be able to figure out the necessary supplies. You can take whatever you feel is requisite from the storeroom and use your expense account for traveling. And just for the record, I know you'll be better able to relate to the students than the original choice. We need prospective designers to see that we are a company open to young people with creative, fresh ideas."

I left his office not knowing if I should feel elated or worried. Every designer was just one season away from being discarded, and I was much too young and determined for that.

Bethany's sketchy and uninformative outline left me shaking my head. But then she had always relied on her persona to take care of the more tedious aspects of her job. Just being in her presence would make any student feel like he or she had arrived at a point where greatness was almost assured. I had certainly been in complete awe the first time I saw her in action. She had been a dynamo in a fashionably cut dress and stiletto heels who almost dared anyone in a subordinate position to question even her most inane demands. I had never quit wondering what been the root cause of her dramatic fall from grace, although there had been plenty of speculation at the time.

Since there was no way I could compete with the ambiance her very presence would create, I spent the next twenty-four hours coming up with a syllabus of my own. But giving my students what I envisioned meant taking more supplies than would fit in my car, and there wasn't time to ship anything. So I was left with no choice other than renting a van if I didn't want to fall on my face and disappoint anyone.

The guys who worked in the warehouse were more than willing to help me load a dozen mannequins, boxes filled with fabric and trim, and anything else I thought I might need, but the driving would be left up to me.

It would take fourteen hours to get to Bentley, and I felt the anxiety rise as I drove out of the city. I was not at all pleased with the upcoming trip. I had never been fond of strolling down memory lane because there wasn't much in my past that I cared to remember, and each mile in the white van with tinted windows gave me more time to think. I fought back tears all through the state of Nevada and on into Utah. My father's death had led to my mother's voluntary commitment to a mental institution when I was eleven. I had tried not to hate her for leaving me alone but had never understood how she could abandon me to seek refuge in a make-believe world with no foundation. Had it not been for my Grandmother Sloan, I would have been sentenced to seven years of foster care because children in my position were seldom adopted. There was always the chance that my mother would come to her senses and want me back.

I suppose knowing what might be part of my genetic makeup was one of the reasons I turned inward during my teenage years. It was easier to act disinterested when I met new people than explain why I was living with my grandmother—a very private, hardworking and unenlightened woman who had spent her entire life on a farm—but she was the only person in my life I knew I could count on.

Excelling at school had been easy since I could get lost in the books I read, but I never learned how to trust other people or make many friends. That's why my chosen career seemed so strange, especially since taking the leap of faith after Bethany Kilpatrick disappeared. I had the creativity necessary to accomplish most anything I set my mind to doing but still lacked the cutthroat attitude and confidence to challenge anyone on the road to success.

Since I didn't want to arrive at Bentley looking like some disheveled and vacant-eyed zombie from a b-rated movie, I stopped at a roadside motel to get some rest. But that room with its papered walls, dark-colored bedcovers and leaky bathroom faucet only forced more unpleasant memories because it reminded me of the place where the last of my innocence had been stripped away by a man I wanted to believe really cared about me.

Greg Kelly came into my life after a painful relationship with the only man I had ever truly loved ended and seemed to bring out my most carefree and daring side. He was reckless and wild and longed for adventure. I needed that after a lifetime of hiding in the shadows so my self-perceived inadequacies wouldn't be quite so obvious. He raced cars on the weekends, did just enough studying to pass his classes and already had a job at his father's firm in San Francisco when he finished law school at Berkley.

Since we were both seniors headed in the same geographical direction after graduation and appeared to be compatible, becoming involved spring semester seemed like a good idea. I had never lived alone and was already having doubts about being able to make it on my own.

Bethany Kilpatrick had selected me to be her intern at *Wide World of Design*—although without the personal involvement I would have in doing practically the same thing now. It was a huge honor and everyone in my classes was jealous of the opportunity it presented to get my foot in the door without having to pound the pavement looking for work. She was a prolific, well-known Bentley graduate, only thirty-five years ahead of me. I had seen pictures of her hanging in the department's hall of fame and her antics and accomplishments were included as part of nearly every lecture.

That made her a true enigma since it was hard to separate fact from fantasy, but while I wanted to work with her I didn't like the idea of being molded in anyone's image. I had been my own person for as long as I could remember. Perhaps that was my biggest objection to my current, untimely assignment. I didn't want to mess up anyone else's life by either overstating or understating what was more than obvious to me.

I pulled the covers up to my neck before looking at the alarm clock beside the bed. It was one-thirty in the morning, and I had yet to fall asleep. I wanted to blame Greg for all my personal issues since my mother was still living behind locked doors and my brother wanted nothing to do with me. She had been diagnosed as being both bi-polar and schizophrenic, and Nate was happy with his career and family. But I couldn't exactly blame my former flame for anything since we hadn't seen each other for years.

We had married on a whim at the county courthouse with strangers as witnesses and had never lived together as husband and wife. It was too close to graduation to find a place and once I was settled in the loft where I planned to live in San Francisco, he never felt right about telling his parents what we had done. They were affluent, successful people, and I was a nobody from the wrong side of the tracks.

All of my visions for an incredible sex life, self-assurance, enduring love, beautiful home and family I could cherish forever were gone before our six-month anniversary arrived. I mentioned getting an annulment since we only saw each other on weekends, and he didn't so much as blink an eye in protest. With nothing left but my work, I gave it everything I had without ever telling anyone I had been married.

I thought about dating occasionally since I hated being alone, but the scars ran deep. It's not that I was bitter. I was more confused than anything else and often wondered why he had ever paid attention to me when he could have any girl on campus with his good looks, boyish charms and lavish allowance. Maybe he simply found me amusing because I could do things other girls found stupid, unnecessary or demeaning. I knew how to change a spark plug on a car, cook a nutritious meal and keep my mouth shut when my opinion wasn't wanted.

If I hadn't been so impatient to find love, and a reason to go on, after having my heart broken by a man who was all wrong for me too, I would have seen from the beginning that we were totally mismatched.

But doing things the hard way was easy for me. That's why I hadn't stated my true feelings about obeying my boss's latest command. The last thing I needed while trying to finish my fall line was some distasteful trip into the past where I might not be able to remain in control.

Chapter 2

It was late the next afternoon, and the sun was casting a red glow across the horizon, when I pulled the white van I had driven across three states to a stop in front of the majestic, bronze gates leading to the hallowed halls of Bentley University. How rustic, quaint and quiet the entire town seemed after the hustle and bustle of San Francisco where people flooded the streets, even when they were encouraged to stay home, and townhouses were set so close together amongst rolling hills that it was often difficult to tell when one ended and the next one began.

Despite a few rough years when thoughts of a much simpler time flooded my consciousness daily, I had grown to love the island fingers that jetted out from the mainland, the ethnic centers where it was easy to observe the clothing worn from nearly every country around the globe and the tinkling of cable car bells that could be heard almost nonstop throughout the day and night. My very surroundings had helped me dig deep into my soul and discover things about myself that I found both valuable and commendable, if not quite endearing or personally useful.

But I wasn't ready to run headlong into a bunch of students who were eager to learn what I might be able to teach them—or unload everything I had brought with me—so I turned the key in the ignition and rested my head against the back of the seat. It was impossible not to feel somewhat anxious when I was about to walk into a past I had tried so hard to forget.

While college life had its perks, there were some unresolved feelings that made me want to turn the van around and head back to the coast.

I was no longer that bashful and gullible girl whose grandmother had driven her to a municipality where police officers spent most of their time correcting unruly students and professors wanted everyone who entered their classroom to succeed. Almost a decade of trying to make it without any emotional support had left me leery of people's ulterior motives and less-than-willing to be open when it came to my personal wants or desires. That included finding someone I thought I might be able to work with.

But as I sat in the warm comfort of the van in rapidly fading sunlight, I knew I couldn't postpone the inevitable forever. I had come on this journey because my boss had made it impossible to do anything else, but I had a sick feeling that delivering a few lectures and conducting some hands-on workshops would be far easier than walking around a campus where ghosts of the invisible kind could so easily haunt me.

I released my hold on the steering wheel and pushed my hair away from my eyes. Once I passed under the impressive arch, time would move backwards and each ivy-covered building, pathway overgrown with shrubs and wild flowers, and statue that had been erected to people who actually made a difference when it came to influencing impressionable, young minds would assault me with vengeance.

Bentley had not been my first choice when it came to pursuing an education, but it was the only school to offer a full-ride scholarship as long as my grades didn't slip. Since my grandmother couldn't afford to help pay for my personal needs, and I didn't want to wait tables forty hours a week or take out a student loan that would require years to repay, I loaded my few earthly possessions in the back of a 1980s station wagon, left everything even remotely familiar behind, and set out to see what I could make out of a very unsatisfactory life.

Off campus housing was not plentiful, but it was far cheaper than living in the dorms. With the help of a lady in the admission's office, I moved into a red brick residence with five other girls who inhabited the main floor apartment. Other renters lived in the attic and basement. It was in the numbered streets just beyond the south campus border. It was also at the bottom of a long flight of winding stairs that criss-crossed their way through thick and thorny shrubbery. I had almost expected to see little, green leprechauns dancing in and out amongst the foliage the first few times I walked there. The entire campus reminded me of Ireland, a country I had never seen except in pictures, but the country that was the birthplace of both my great, great paternal grandparents.

According to what I had been told, they had immigrated to the United States after World War I in hopes of finding a better life. Living conditions in the old country had been harsh with few jobs for unskilled laborers, inclement weather most of the year and very little to eat other than cabbage and potatoes. It had taken them three years to save up money for passage on a ship, and once they arrived in America—a place they considered the promised land where opportunities for everyone abounded—they found out that the grass was not always greener on the other side of the fence. Their accents were so stiff that people had trouble understanding them and jobs in the cities were no more plentiful than they had been at home.

But instead of admitting defeat and returning to Ireland they moved west, stopping along the way to work day jobs so they would have enough money to keep moving until they found what they were looking for. Eventually, they purchased an acreage in a small farming community just a little over a hundred miles north of Bentley where they raised two sons. The youngest, my great grandfather Sloan, took care of his own family in the ancestral home. And that is where my grandmother raised me after my mother was no longer able to do so.

I was finishing my freshman year when the woman who had gotten me through adolescence died. It was unexpected just as it had been with my father, and the lawyer who had been hired to take care of legal matters—while supposedly protecting me—said it would be foolish to hang onto property that was not in a prime location unless I planned on living there one day. Since I had no idea what my future might bring, and the money I made by selling the old house where everything needed a complete overhaul would keep me from having to work while I finished college, I agreed. He gave me my share of the profits, and I was happy until I learned that he had purchased the property himself so a new community of over twenty luxury homes could be built. I had been swindled, but the law was on his side.

I missed my Grandma Sloan. She reminded me of my father with her quiet nature, sensitivity to the needs of others and attention to details that most everyone else missed. She was a simple woman who read voraciously, played the piano by ear and told fabulous stories that I often wished had been committed to paper so I could relate them to my own children when that time came. Her flower gardens were the envy of everyone in the community and the food that came from her kitchen was better than anything I had eaten in the most expensive restaurants at home or abroad. She was the only family, other than my brother and my parents, that I had ever known.

While I had seen Greg a few times over the years since our brief marriage ended, I couldn't exactly include him as family. He had attended several of the runway shows where my work was featured and always made it a point of bringing flowers and speaking to me. I knew he felt even worse than I did about what had happened from the sad and unfulfilled look in his eyes. He hadn't married again either, but despite his often impassioned pleas to give him another chance, I couldn't bring myself to do so. He hadn't exactly crushed my heart. Our love wasn't strong enough for that, but he had certainly caused me plenty of sleepless nights.

I didn't want to relive any lessons in life, love and loss just because I had been forced to return to the place where I had felt the most vulnerable. It was doubtful I would run into anyone I had previously known, except for a few old professors. That was okay. But if I saw Brett, I didn't know what I would do. Just recalling his name made the tears well in my eyes and my heart begin to thump so hard and rapidly that I thought it might explode. Wanting to get over him was the real reason I had married so foolishly.

I bit down on my lip until I could taste blood. Brett Fowler had captured my heart the moment I first saw him. He was indescribably beautiful, if that was a term that could be used to describe a very masculine man with thick, curly, blonde hair, deep-set, blue eyes that could see into my soul and a smile that lite up my world.

He had walked into the lecture hall my first week at college with two other guys—all impressively older than me. I thought I might be experiencing my first earthquake when his eyes met mine. It was as if the entire rock building moved, and I had to inhale deeply to keep from blacking out. I was sitting on the front row and tried not to stare as he made his way to the back of the room. But when he turned and smiled at me, I knew I wasn't the only one who had felt something life altering.

I don't remember a word that came from the podium. I only remember having to fight the urge to look over my shoulder to see if he was still looking at me. I wanted to touch his skin, run my hands through his hair and gaze into his incredible eyes until the day I died. I was totally and completely mesmerized, but when he sent a note wanting to know my name and telephone number I froze. I wasn't sure if he really wanted to get to know me, or if he was just having some fun because he knew I was attracted to him.

In a vain attempt to appear worldly and cool, my reply was nothing short of ridiculous.

"My name is Jada Sloan, but I think a more formal introduction would be appropriate."

The snickering in the back of the room when he read my inane reply caused me to make a beeline for the door the minute the lecture was over. I was mortified beyond belief and hoped I would never see him again. I think I would have gone back to my grandmother's house, a college dropout before I even began, if I hadn't known I would be disappointing the only living person who had a real interest in me.

It took almost a year of unexpected and nerve-shattering encounters before we were *formally introduced* by a mutual friend who found the situation highly amusing and decided we had been dodging our feelings long enough.

Brett was seven years older than me. He had spent two years in the Army and traveled extensively with the German students he taught on campus as an adjunct professor. He was also the lead singer of the most popular band in the area that played at nearly every university dance, recorded background music for commercials and wanted to make it big. Unfortunately, true success only came to a favored few.

He was totally unpredictable and disarming, and I was captivated by his outward charms and ability to make any girl feel sexy and wanted. They would follow him across campus, send gifts to his classroom and hang out in front of his loft hoping he would notice them. His magnetic appeal to the opposite sex—and his very real interest in them—kept me from making an even bigger fool of myself since I had no intention of becoming one of his groupies.

He seemed to like the fact that I didn't fall at his feet, but what he didn't know was that I did it on purpose. It was safer to have my fantasy life remain in my head where I wouldn't be subjected to being humiliated again or get dumped. After all, I wasn't exactly the kind of girl who stood out in a crowd, and I certainly wasn't some free spirit who would stoop to any kind of behavior just to spend a few hours alone with him.

But once we began spending time together, I knew just how much I really wanted to be his one-and-only. I would fantasize that all of the songs he sang were dedicated to me, and I was the only one he ever went home with at night. Unfortunately, he wasn't ready to make a commitment to anyone. He was having too much fun playing catch and release. I understood his need to be noticed but wanted to believe that somewhere beneath his desire for fame and fortune he wanted a meaningful relationship where he felt safe enough to let his doubts and insecurities show.

By the middle of my sophomore year, he had ruined me when it came to being more that casually interested in anyone else, but I would not have admitted my feelings for all the rice in China. I was afraid he would forget about me if I did, and his erratic shows of affection were better than nothing at all.

So we played our safe little games where no one could get intentionally hurt. I pretended not to care that he jumped in and out of my life like a yoyo, and he pretended not to notice that underneath all the denial I really cared about him.

That cycle of elation followed by bouts of depression and remorse because he could be gone for weeks to months at a time continued until the middle of my senior year. The power he had over me was frightening. Nothing seemed to matter when we were together, but once he was gone I started to doubt that anything we had ever experienced together was real.

Loving him or, more accurately, loving the fantasy I had built up when it came to what I wished we could have, came as naturally as breathing. My personal roommate, who was engaged to a man she adored that never looked in another girl's direction, was always warning me to leave him alone because he would eventually ruin my life. Unwittingly, I knew she was right, but I couldn't seem to let go of the make-believe life I wanted to imagine could still be mine.

I justified his childish, often insensitive and self-absorbed qualities as being part of the package. After all, everyone knew that musicians were a sought after commodity whose very natures were unpredictable and intense. So I excused his erratic behavior as nothing more than the artistic license necessary to more effectively pursue his dream, and the women who practically stalked him were his mealticket to stardom and success.

Sometimes we would meet truly by accident. Those were magical moments when my heart caught in my throat, and I knew I had found a slice of heaven on earth. His arms would encircle me with the warmth and physical closeness I craved, and when his lips found mine in an all-encompassing kiss, I would close my eyes to all the obstacles that stood between us. Those unexpected moments seemed to tell me that what we had was right and would someday lead to everything my pure and simple heart desired.

But our someday never came, and our last encounter finally pushed me over the infamous edge. I would remember those hours with perfect clarity until the day I died. He called after his usual months of absence without an explanation. I wanted to let him know just how unacceptable his behavior was, especially since I knew it would ruin yet another blossoming romance. But the sound of his voice, and the way he said my name, made all my justifiable resolves disappear.

He wanted me to attend a recording session with him at a studio in a city an hour away and needed to leave in twenty-five minutes so he wouldn't be late. I had a study date for an upcoming exam but with little remorse in my tone of voice or my heart I broke it. Then I dressed in something he had never seen before and added an extra coat of mascara. This would be no ordinary date. It was the first time he had ever invited me into his world of passion and dreams as more than a casual observer. And regardless of the fact that I knew he had likely taken many girls to just such an event, I wanted to pretend for just one night that we were a couple in every sense of the word.

The feel of my hand in his as we drove the miles towards our destination made me want to believe that I had finally been lifted from a past of abandonment, loss and self-imposed isolation because I didn't want to be hurt by anyone again. I cast a glance in his direction every few miles and was often rewarded with a warm and comforting smile. When we were together, I felt as if I could throw away any lingering fears and embrace life with the first true joy I had known since the day my father died. In many ways, Brett was just as emotionally broken as I was.

The building we entered in an industrialized section of the city had a red brick facade, tall trees in the space between the street and the sidewalk and a brightly lit entrance. It was at least fifty years old, but the interior had been renovated to include numerous office spaces, fashionable living quarters for the artistically inclined and a completely up-to-date recording studio. He introduced me to the members of his band, the producer and the group's personal manager before leading me to the control room where a man wearing a headset sat in front of a soundboard with dozens of sliders and nobs and a microphone that allowed him to make his wishes known.

Since Brett was there to work, he didn't stick around to chat. There was soundproofing material on the walls and a large window looking directly into the studio. While I sat as quietly and erect as I could in the only available chair, the man named Randy told me not to make any noise until they finished what must be accomplished in very short period of time. That was okay with me, even though I wanted to shout from the rooftops my feelings of joy for being with the man who had been in and out of my life with such frequency I often felt like my head would never quit spinning like a tightly-wound top.

But Brett had never really expressed how he felt about us, and I didn't want to jinx the evening prematurely. So I watched in amazement as he worked and soon began to understand just how completely his music governed his life. No matter how many takes the producer called for, he stood in front of his mic with a fervor no one could miss as he sang familiar melodies that brought tears to my eyes. He was in love with life and emotional release that was easier dealt with in song than mere words. Maybe his talent and fervency really was too all-consuming and intense to be shared with just one girl.

It was nearly two in the morning when we left. I had an early class but didn't want the night to end. We stopped at a convenience store for energy drinks because his vocal chords were throbbing. I knew how completely exhausted he must be and almost asked if he wanted me to drive so he could rest, but that seemed unwise. While I carried a valid driver's license, I had never owned a car and hadn't driven since leaving my grandmother's farm.

Only minutes passed until the city lights were left behind and we were on a dark, country road. It was a different route than we had taken before. I figured it must be a shortcut, but before we had gone very far, he pulled into a tree-lined lane leading to some private residence and turned off the motor.

"I'm not ready to take you home quite yet," he said. "I hope you don't mind."

The few stars overhead did little to light his features when he turned to face me, and I swallowed back a mixture of excitement and uncertainty. While I had dated a number of different guys, I had never been alone like this with a man I knew I loved. He aroused in me terrifying, yet exhilarating emotions I wanted to explore. But I had no doubt that he had experienced Biblical intimacy with many women, and I was still a virgin who wanted to stay that way until my wedding night.

"Not at all," I replied, suddenly wishing I could be completely open with my body, heart and soul. "I know how tired you must be."

"It's not just that. Something about this night seems truly magical. I'm glad you could come on such short notice. I was afraid my invitation might be disrupting some previously made plans. I know I'm not the most reliable guy in the world, but it's not because I don't care. I just get caught up in my work and entire weeks can slip by without conscious thought."

"Your music will always come first. You've never made a secret of that."

He put his arm around my shoulders, and I snuggled contentedly against him.

"I love what I do but sometimes wish I wasn't quite so driven. Between teaching classes, organizing and taking students on tours and my music there doesn't seem to be time for anything else. It's hard to believe that we've been acquainted for over three years and really don't know much about each other."

"That can easily be remedied."

"Perhaps, but time has a way of running out for everyone," he said as his lips brushed my hair. "Sometimes I wonder if the kind of love I sing about even exists. I never seem to make it past the infatuation phase, and you'll be graduating in May."

"I certainly hope so," I replied a little too quickly. "I can't see myself hanging around the university forever."

"And I don't see myself ever leaving Bentley, unless my musical career suddenly takes off. It's what I've wanted since I was six and picked up my first guitar, but there are thousands of groups just like mine who give their all and never end up with even a modicum of success."

"Tonight seemed like a huge step forward. Everyone was applauding your work."

"The guys I spend the majority of my time with are great, but the competition is fierce. You'll find that out for yourself soon enough if you want to make it big as a fashion designer. There are only so many spots at the top in any industry."

I pulled away from him. Thinking about the future when we had this moment was impossible. I wanted to cherish his nearness and the fact that he was letting me see his more vulnerable side. It was something else he had never done before tonight. But while my heart told me to throw my arms around his neck, admit that I loved him, and express in no uncertain terms that I didn't care about my own career as long I could be his helpmate and strength as he pursued his own, my head was telling me to remain cautious. So I simply placed a soft kiss on his lips.

"What prompted that?" he asked. "I just told you that I'm not a big believer in having dreams come true. You should be mad at me for raining on your parade. I know how hard you've had to work to get through school and deal with family hardships. I should have been more supportive when you needed me."

"No life is perfect, and you had your own issues to work through. Maybe I'm just glad you finally let me see that you're human like the rest of us."

His laugh was bittersweet. "Why would you even say something like that? I'm the most human guy around."

"Not to all your adoring fans. You'll always be bigger than life to them."

"What about you?"

I felt my heart skip a beat and hoped he didn't notice. "You know how great I think you are. I've waited a long time to see what goes on behind the bright lights, unforgettable songs and screaming girls."

"So watching me do my thing wasn't too boring? I was afraid I would find you curled up in a ball somewhere sleeping."

"Never!" I responded. "I could listen to you sing forever."

"Good to know since performing on stage will always be my drug of choice," he responded. "But I do need time to come down from the highs so I'll be ready to do it again. I'm glad you were able to come with me since I wanted to share this night with someone really special. Despite my tendency to downplay most everything so I won't be disappointed, I think we may have a hit with at least one of the songs on this CD. Do you have any idea what that could mean for us?"

"Not exactly," I said, wishing the *us* he was talking about meant him and me, not the group he sang with. "Why don't you tell me."

"It could mean a recording contract, J."

I loved it when he called me by the nickname he had given me when we went out on our first date. It made me feel like I was a little different than the other girls he hung out with.

"Our music could be played on every radio station in the country. We might even become famous enough to travel the world playing to sold-out crowds. I could finally buy a car that wasn't in the shop every other weekend and live in an apartment bigger than a breadbox."

"It sounds like a wonderful life," I said, trying to study his face in the dark. "I always knew you were good. You write music with your heart, and it strikes a responsive chord in others."

"You've been my inspiration for a lot of songs," he admitted with a smile. "I just didn't want to tell you because I didn't know how it would go over with anyone."

His statement was a little cryptic and my response wasn't much better. "I suppose being in a serious relationship could hamper a musician's life."

"That's not the only problem with the life I want. I've been on my own for a very long time. I come and go as I please and don't have to account for my actions to anyone—unless they're paying me. I've had serious girlfriends before, but the relationships always ended badly."

"The past doesn't have to determine the future," I said, thinking back to all the negative genes my body could so easily be carrying.

I could die young like my father, end up in a mental institution like my mother or simply walk away from the unpleasant like my brother had done. But despite some majorly bad odds, my grandmother had convinced me that the future never arrived. All we had was the day we were living, and we needed to make the most of it.

"You're right," he said, turning away from me and gripping the steering wheel. "Maybe I'm just a selfish wanderer who finds convention stifling. My mother and sisters certainly think so. They would like to see me married with half a dozen kids, but I'm not sure I would make a good father or husband. That doesn't mean I wouldn't be willing to try, but I'm not sure I'll ever be the marrying kind. My father certainly wasn't."

"You're twenty-eight," I responded and immediately regretted it.

"That's young in today's world, J. Most men don't even think about settling down until they reach their mid-to-late thirties. It's the girls who are always worried about biological clocks. Most men simply want to sow wild oats for as long as they can."

I fought to keep from saying something truly derogatory. "But doesn't that open you up to a lot of different risks?"

"If that's your polite way of asking if I've had an STD or gotten a girl pregnant, the answer is no. I take the necessary precautions and would never hurt anyone intentionally. I hope you believe that because I really don't want this night to end. I have a sleeping bag in the trunk and was hoping you wouldn't be averse to sharing it with me under the stars. I'm not sure I have what it takes to drive any further, and I promise to behave since I know you're not like other girls. I just want to hold you in my arms and feel your heart beating next to mine."

"But isn't this private property?" I asked.

"Most likely, but I don't plan on being here long enough for anyone to ask us to leave. I just need some quiet time with a girl I find completely captivating. Despite my frequent absences, a day rarely goes by when I don't envision how you looked that day I sent you a note during one of the most boring lectures I've ever attended. I only went because a colleague asked for my support. Little did I know how completely a shy, young freshman would capture my heart."

If his words were meant to placate me into doing as he wanted, they certainly worked. There was nothing I wanted more than to spend what remained of the night in his arms.

I followed him around the car and watched as he pulled a sleeping bag from the trunk. "Thank you for being so understanding, J. I have a class at nine so I'll set my cell phone for six. That should give us plenty of time to get ready for a new day."

He locked the car doors and led me to a small grotto about sixty yards away. I could hear crickets chirping and an owl hoot as he prepared to fixed a bed for us on dried twigs that crackled when we stepped on them. The night was warm, but I still involuntarily shivered because it was impossible not to wonder how often he had taken the side road and asked another girl to share his sleeping arrangements. The enclosure was secluded—almost like a private kingdom—and no one could see us from the road.

"I hope you'll be comfortable enough," he said, unzipping one side before bending down to spread the sleeping bag out. "I usually travel with our manager and the rest of the group so I don't have to worry about staying awake. But for some reason, I didn't want to be alone tonight."

"I'm glad you invited me. Like I said before, I've had a wonderful time," I replied, gazing up at the stars and hoping I would regain some much-needed clarity before I was laying next to him. All my wildest dreams could see fruition tonight, or I could end up with a thoroughly broken heart. If Brett was being honest about never intentionally hurting someone, the decision to let anything get out of hand was up to me.

"You slide in first," he said, pulling back the cover. "You can leave your shoes on if you want, but it might not be very comfortable."

Swallowing back a lump of trepidation, I looked around for a rock I could put them on. Hopefully, it wouldn't be next to some ant pile. But if Brett had been here before, he would know if I had anything to fear—other than allowing myself to be in such a compromising situation and liking it. I thought I heard a cow moo as he climbed in beside me and closed the zipper. For a sleeping bag, the one we were in was plenty big enough for two. I was laying on my side when he turned to face me and slipped his arm underneath my neck. His sigh was one of exhaustion and pleasure.

"You have no idea how many nights I've dreamed I was holding you in my arms, only to wake up with the need to take a cold shower before even contemplating sleep again."

"I've had a few of those dreams myself."

"So you're not a complete innocent."

"That depends on the definition you assign to the term. While I've dated a number of guys and know what most of them are thinking when they take me home from a date—or even in the midst of one—I've chosen to save myself for the man I marry. I suppose that sounds childish and antiquated to you."

"I think it's kind of sweet since I haven't heard it from a girl since I was fifteen, but then I always knew there was something special about you. I'm sorry for embarrassing you that first day. I had no idea the situation would escalate to the point it did."

"My stupidity caused that. I thought I was being clever with my comeback, but in reality I was just showing my naiveté because I spent my most formative years with a grandmother who believed girls should be nonaggressive around guys."

"There's a certain amount of wisdom in that."

I felt my brow furrow. "But you like assertive women."

"Only when it comes to my singing, and a few other things. They're the key to my success, and I have to do whatever is necessary to keep them coming back—hopefully with even more of their friends."

"It's a complicated life you live," I said, wishing for just this moment that I could be carefree and without a conscience that was always pestering me.

"Not all the time, J. You and I have shared some incredible times. I'm just sorry I haven't been around more. Any idea where you'll go when you graduate?"

"I'm afraid that remains to be seen. I have some of my most difficult courses to finish. Did you always want to be a college professor?"

He kissed my forehead before replying. "That was a matter of good fortune and perfect timing. I was in graduate school when the dean of the foreign language department resigned. Since I was already teaching classes for the German professor who took his place, I simply assumed more responsibility. Having a flexible, paying job that didn't interfere too much with my music was exactly what I needed to keep a roof over my head and pay the bills. And all the trips abroad with students gave me a chance to see most of Europe and parts of Asia on someone else's dime."

"So you plan on doing it for awhile."

"Nothing in my life is set in stone, but I don't want to talk about anything other than us right now. Do you have any idea how beautiful and desirable you are. Every time I come back to your door, or push the icon next to your phone number, I'm afraid you're going to tell me to get lost because you've found someone who can give you everything you truly want. I wouldn't blame you, but it would make me sad."

"You've never said that before."

"Maybe I should have. I don't want to lose you, but I have no right to ask you to wait around for something I may never be capable of giving. If we should get a contract, my time will no longer be my own, and I could be gone for more than months at a time."

It was the perfect time to tell him that I didn't mind waiting, but once again, something I couldn't define held me back.

"I hope you find everything you're looking for, Brett. But just so you know, you're not the only one with concerns about the future or unresolved issues from the past that make it hard to trust or commit. I want everything life has to offer as well, but mostly I just want to be important to someone."

"You're important to me, J. I feel like I never want to be away from you again. I love holding you in my arms and kissing your soft lips . . . . "

His words drifted off as the sound of heavy breathing began. I tried to rest as he was doing but couldn't stop myself from caressing his cheek and wishing he wasn't quite so tired. He excited me as no man ever had, and I longed for the time and place where I would feel right about giving myself completely to him. But maybe it was better this way. We had spent some beautiful moments together without pushing any boundaries, and he had let me know that he really cared.

When his alarm went off, I was still in his arms. His kiss was meant to awaken me, but in truth I had done nothing more than close my eyes and pretend that we really were at a crossroads where all of my dreams might actually come true.

"Good morning, beautiful. Were you able to get any sleep?" he asked while stretching in a very lazy and content way. "I'm sorry I wasn't better company. I must have been more tired than I thought after being in the studio so long."

"No worries," I responded, wishing we never had to leave the grotto where birds too small to easily see were chirping in the trees and tiny fingers of sunlight were breaking through the spaces between leaves and branches. "It was a long day, and you were putting every ounce of energy into your singing."

"While that's true, it's no excuse for falling asleep when I have a beautiful woman in my arms. I promise to make it up to you."

"Don't make promises you might not be able to keep," I said as he shook dry grass and small twigs from the back of the sleeping bag but didn't bother to fold it before shoving it into the trunk of his car.

"I never say things I don't mean J. But you're right, none of us can predict what the future might bring."

We were standing in front of my door when he pulled me into his arms again. It wouldn't be easy explaining an entire night away from home to my roommate who was already worried about me. But there was nothing to regret, except fact that my breath must smell awful and I looked a mess.

My heart was racing madly when he leaned down to kiss me. I should have been worried that someone might see us, but I simply put my arms around his neck and let my whole body respond to the thrill of his lips pressing against mine.

"You'll be the first to know when I hear something about the recordings," he said a few moments later as he picked a dry leaf from my hair. "You're my muse, now and forever."

I waited with baited breath and a thick knot in the pit of my stomach for him to call, but when a day turned into a week I knew he was gone. I suppose I could have sent a text asking for clarification but knew that guys only stopped communicating when they were no longer interested. It hurt deeply that he could be so callous and indifferent, but when I read in the university newspaper that he had taken another group of students to

Germany the day after we got back from the city, I knew what I thought we might have one day was over.

Nonetheless, I still listened to the radio every day for over year hoping to hear one of his songs.

Chapter 3

My mind was so lost in painful recollections of Brett Fowler's memorable exit from my life that I didn't hear footsteps approaching over the clean, black asphalt until a fist hit the top of the van. The sound startled me completely, and I had to force myself to focus on the red, pigmented sky to the west so I wouldn't say or do something completely unladylike or unnecessary.

When I was no longer frowning at having been so rudely interrupted, and my heart had returned to a more normal rhythm, I glanced through the darkly-tinted driver's window that had made the journey across deserts and along expanses of open highway more bearable. A young man in tan slacks and a blue shirt was trying to get a good look at me. I admired his courage in approaching a stranger when he wasn't wearing a badge but then remembered that I wasn't in San Francisco any longer where people avoided contact with others unless forced to do so.

I turned the key in the ignition so the window would roll down. That gave me time to make sure the door was still locked, and I was mentally prepared for a confrontation. I had no idea what I may have done to incur someone's wrath, but the young man didn't seem openly hostile. I was the one who felt ill-at-ease with my designer frames sitting on the dashboard and my clothes rumpled from traveling.

"Are you having car trouble?" he asked in a voice that seemed unusually deep since he couldn't be more than nineteen or twenty.

While the young man's eyes surveyed my appearance with more than casual interest, I found myself wondering if he was even slightly impressed by what he saw. Not that I had changed all that much physically during the past eight years, but I was hardly the girl I had been when I left. Unsavory and complicated life experiences had robbed me of my youthful innocence.

"No," I replied, inhaling the fresh, small-town air. "Is there a problem?"

"There might be if campus security gets here before you leave. Didn't you see the no-parking sign on the fence? The university chancellor has imposed new rules to make sure everyone is safe. Two girls were rapped during the spring semester and one disappeared. It's made people nervous. We've been asked to remain vigilant and report anything suspicious to the authorities."

My lips twitched of their own volition before I could respond. "I'm sorry to hear that. Bentley was always such a safe place."

This time, he was the one whose expression changed. "You've been here before?"

"Not for a long time. That's why I stopped. I needed a few minutes to reminisce and collect my thoughts before passing underneath that arch. It's like going back in time, and while most of my experiences here were positive, there are a few that have caused some sleepless nights. But I'm sure you're too young to understand that."

"I'm not that young, and you can't possibly be that old," he replied. "Although you do look out of place in that van. You remind me more of a girl who should be driving a BMW or some expensive sports car."

"There's an MR2 in my garage back home, but it wouldn't hold what I needed to bring," I said with a smile. It was nice talking to someone who knew nothing about me. It meant we could converse freely without making demands or passing judgments. "But just so you know, I'll be thirty on my next birthday. That must seem ancient to you. I know it did when I was your age."

"Age is irrelevant, especially after graduation. By then we're all searching for the same things—monetary success and personal happiness."

"It sounds as if you have life all figured out, but I suppose I should be going if I don't want to spend the night in the county jail. Perhaps you could direct me to Whitman Cottage. It must be new."

"Sure enough," the young man replied as his eyes seemed to dance with amusement. "Does that mean you're with that group of old-timers who are giving seminars this week? From where I'm standing, you're not going to fit in."

His candor made me smile. "Why not?"

"Because they're ancient and think their societal contributions make them too important to converse with anyone who doesn't have a slew of PHDs attached to their name."

"I'm sure that isn't entirely true. At least I certainly hope not," I replied. "I may not be a scientist, mathematician or an engineer, but I still have a degree."

"In what?" he asked.

"Fashion Design! I'm here from the *Wide World of Design*."

"So that's why you're driving a van. You need larger props than a marker on a white board to get your lessons across."

For the first time that day, I felt some of my concerns crumble. "What I do may not make the world a safer, more prosperous or intellectual place, but there is a need for clothing women can wear and feel good in, especially since few of us are stick figures naturally."

"I didn't mean to offend you," he said. "I like my dates to look nice and my women curvy. I guess I just never thought much about the mechanics behind being fashionable and alluring. All guys have to worry about is whether their jeans are skin tight or have a slight flare."

"I'm not sure some of the designers I work with would agree with that assessment of what the male population should be wearing. Although I have to admit that working with women's lines are more fun."

"Point taken," he replied, shifting the weight on his feet. He was an extremely good-looking with brown hair, dancing blue eyes, a ready smile and a physique that could rival any male model in the industry. It was easy to tell that he spent time doing more than just studying. "I wish I had an excuse to attend some of your workshops. All my professors wear herringbone jackets or ugly sweaters and have about as much personality as a lump of clay. It makes for a dull time in the lecture hall. But if you were standing in front of the class no one would have difficulty staying awake."

"I hope that was meant as a compliment," I replied as the transition into a world of obvious flattery suddenly hit me. No one had even attempted to flirt with me in what seemed like forever. "Can I give you a lift?"

He shook his head. "Naw! But thanks anyway. I'm heading into town. A guy has to work if he comes from a blue collar family and wants any of the extras while going to school. I only stopped to give you a heads-up about parking next to the gates. It's a no-no that comes with a rather stiff fine, or so I've been told. Whitman Cottage is clear across campus, down by the old math building in a cluster of old, thorny trees. Just hang a left here, follow the signs and you'll be there in no time at all."

"Thank you," I said as he turned to leave.

But while I was setting the gear, he swung around to face me again.

"Take care, gorgeous," he said with another disarming smile. "There are a lot of wild men loose on this campus who are looking for a good time with no strings attached. If you need anything while you're here, just ask for T.R. Everyone knows who I am."

"No doubt!" I thought as he sauntered away. A handsome flirt like him would be hard to miss.

The clock on the dashboard said it was seven-fifteen. No wonder T.R. had asked if something was wrong. I had been parked in the same place for nearly two hours. Guest lecturers were supposed to check in no later than five so they could get settled and eat before the *welcome to the event* meeting began. While I had been in no hurry to get to Whitman Cottage with any time left over to think, I was not in the habit of being late. It was sign of disrespect for the person in charge.

I passed under the arch and took the first left after a small garden where carefully tended pathways, benches, statues, trees, flowers and a fish-stocked pond was meant to set the stage for the peaceful place I had once called home. At first glance, it didn't appear that Bentley had changed even a fraction as much as I had over the years. The ambience reflected the aspirations of past leaders who wanted to emphasis that higher learning didn't always have to take place in modern, high-rise buildings made of glass and steel where computers took the place of in-person instruction. The roadways were lined with trees and low-growing shrubs. The stone buildings were covered with ivy and the lawns lush and green. The only addition I noticed were sprinkler heads moving back and forth in front of the student union building.

It wasn't long until I was passing the gymnasium where I had been forced to take such loathsome classes as weightlifting, aerobics and volleyball. I much preferred riding my bike in the country, taking long walks and doing yoga. The closest I had ever come to failing a class was when I took an introduction to swimming. I had nearly drowned as a child and figured it was about time I put my fears to rest. But every time I put my face under the water I panicked and came up choking. The instructor tried her best, but none of the threats or encouragement she gave could override my deep-seated terror. I figured I would end up living in some desert where I wouldn't have to worry about water, but my job took me the Pacific Ocean. While I loved walking along the beach and listening to sound of seagulls overhead, I seldom let the waves get anywhere near my toes.

Personally, I felt that excessive, physical exercise was just another ploy to get people's hard-earned money. It ranked right up there with fad diets, weight loss programs,   gyms, personal trainers and products and procedures that were meant to get rid anything from an unwanted bump on the nose to having large portions of fat sucked out from any offending part of the body.

Not that I wasn't concerned about the obesity epidemic in the country. It was a huge problem that put even young children at risk, but none of the programs, diets, exercises or pills I had ever heard about worked once the person using them went back to even a semblance of normalcy. And I had spent enough time working with anorexic, bulimic and drug-addicted models who had to stay a size zero in order to be on the runway, or in photoshoots, to know that looks alone seldom made anyone happy. True peace and joy came from accepting one's biological heritage and physical limitations. Along with living a life free from excess of all kinds and concentrating on God-given abilities like being kind, forgiving, genuine, unassuming and willing to express gratitude for the simplest things life had to offer.

The light breeze coming through the open van window caused a lock of hair to blow across my face. I brushed it away with the back of one hand. Why was I thinking about platitudes and societal ills when I dressed in the latest fashions and tried to live a healthy life? Maybe it was knowing I would soon be facing a room filled with hopeful students who wanted to know what the real world of fashion design was all about.

I could explain the path I had taken, but then I had been lucky when compared to most of the other hopefuls who entered the field when I did. I gave credit to my grandmother for teaching me how to recognize when remaining silent and when expressing my ideas or concerns would lead to a favorable outcome. She made it abundantly clear that the world didn't revolve around my needs or yearnings. I was merely one, small cog that kept the wheel turning, and there would always be someone more than willing and capable to take my place.

Besides, being in the right location at the right time had almost as much to do with making it big as talent. I wanted to do more than give my students encouragement on designs and let them know that having to start at the bottom wasn't a myth. I would encourage them to look deep within their souls as to whether or not they were ready for a life filled with frustration, disappointment and outright rejection before they saw even a hint of success.

It might not be what my boss wanted me to do since he expected me to scout out potential designers for his company, but what I did was exhausting and left little time for a social life or family. Not that dating had been much of a priority since my fiasco with Greg, but I still wanted that lasting kind of love I often read about in romance novels and saw on the big screen.

I drove past the library, the fine arts building and beyond a new housing complex before I saw a large, two-story, log cabin nestled amongst the pine trees that had been part of the college of forestry and conservation when I was a student. Whitman Cottage was just where T.R. said it would be. The duck pond I remembered was still there, but most of the wooded area where students experimented with new varieties of trees, shrubs and plants was gone.

The parking lot was on the north side of the building. I followed the arrows to one of the last available spaces. But when I tried to climb out of the van my legs nearly gave way. I hadn't taken a break to stretch out since lunch. That was foolish indeed, and I chided myself for not taking better care of myself as I reached for my purse and then slammed the driver's door shut before going around the vehicle to retrieve the suitcase that carried my personal belongings. Classes would not begin until the following afternoon. That would give me plenty of time to get settled and unload what I had brought after trying to get some much-needed sleep.

Despite my firm grip on reality, I half-expected to see Daniel Boone in his coonskin cap and leather breeches, or at least someone who looked a great deal like him, step onto the porch to greet me as I made my way up the steps to the front door. There were broadcloth curtains at every window and a home-crafted swing next to a freshly-stained railing.

I peered through the screen door before entering the lobby. An elderly woman was sitting behind a desk, totally absorbed in the magazine she was reading.

"Good evening," I called out as I walked through the rustic-looking lobby and placed my suitcase on the floor in front of her desk.

The lady looked up and gave me a half-hearted smile. "Good evening to you. I can only assume that you must be Miss Sloan since all of our other guests have been here for several hours. We were beginning to worry that something might have happened. Dinner was served at six."

"I'm sorry," I said, glancing at her careworn face. She had likely missed her own evening meal waiting for me. "I had every intention of arriving on time but nostalgia seemed to get the best of me."

"That's been known to happen," she replied, pulling out a guestbook so I could add my name. My lodging and meals had been paid for by the university, but it was up to me to take advantage of the amenities provided. "The other guests are in the conference room being briefed on the week's activities. You might want to join them before getting settled so you'll know what to expect. There have been a few changes to the itinerary since we sent the original packet of instructions to our presenters."

"What about my suitcase?" I asked.

"I'll see that it's taken to your room. You've been given suite 205. Just take the stairs to the second floor and turn right. I'm sure you'll be very pleased with your accommodations."

She handed me a key and then pointed in the direction of two closed doors. It appeared I had little choice other than do her bidding if I didn't want to make a bad situation worse. However, as I moved away from her desk, my stomach started to growl most unbecomingly. She pretended not to hear the undignified sound as she removed her purse from a drawer and headed down a back hallway. I hadn't eaten anything since lunch but always carried a few protein bars. I would eat one of them as soon as the meeting ended since I had no desire to go scouting for a more substantial meal.

The large, open room was nearly full, but I found a chair at the back table and sat down. A few heads turned in my direction, but no one acknowledged my presence with a welcoming smile. It was obvious I had made a very bad first impression and was not going to be readily accepted by any of the presenters who were not only much older than me but looked very serious, scholarly and aloof. Trying to find a common ground with any of them would be impossible. I had purposely chosen a field where advanced mathematics, science or logic was not required.

It was after nine when the meeting ended. I waited until everyone had gone before making my way to the front of the room to apologize for my tardiness. Mrs. Fox—the woman who had sent the invitation to my boss— gave me a packet that had been prepared for my use and said she was glad I had been able to make it. But I knew that underneath her calm exterior she was trying to hide her irritation over the fact that I had been given plenty of advance notice to make it on time.

And when she asked if I was hungry since I had missed the evening meal, I told her I would be fine until morning. Then I hurried across polished wood floors and up the main staircase without saying more than a brief hello to anyone who was still in the foyer or hall. I felt like a wayward and incompetent child being surrounded by so many men and women with several advanced degrees and long lists of academic excellence in their respective fields. Miss Bethany Kilpatrick could have pulled off this assignment with her usual flare because she was a world renowned designer, but I was nothing more than a newbie in what my colleagues must think a very frivolous field.

Not that I wasn't doing okay for myself. I was making more than enough money to provide for my needs, but I lacked the mental intellect to carry on more than a superficial conversation with any of my colleagues. I hoped my insecurities would dissipate once I was in the classroom with students who shared the same interests. If not, I would be spending my free time alone.

My room was pleasant, but it was nothing like what I was used to. The walls were made of polished logs held together with some kind of tan cement that kept the elements from seeping through the cracks. Calico curtains hung at the windows and the bedspread was an intricately-designed, hand-crafted, colorful quilt. The bed and dresser were also constructed of logs, and I had no doubt that they would bring a good price if their creator took them to the city to sell.

But while I knew I would be comfortable enough because the bathroom had a full-length mirror and both a shower and a tub, the atmosphere was too countrified, dark and confining for me. I much preferred the light walls, abundant windows and open air feeling inside my home outside San Francisco's city limits. It made me feel alive and free, and I spent every spare moment away from work overseeing much-needed renovations since it had been constructed in the 1950s. By the time I returned home, the master bathroom would have a jetted tub that looked out on the back gardens and pool I took care of myself.

I was about to slide my empty suitcase into the closet when I noticed a phone book on the bottom shelf of the nightstand. Cold chills spiraled up and down my spine as Brett's face flashed into my mind for a second time that day. After every inexplicable, heartless and mean thing he had done to me over the years, I could still recall every detail when it came to his features and the stances he so often took when he was singing in front of a crowd or hurrying down the hall in the fine arts building so he wouldn't be late for class.

But it was the way he looked at me and the emotions he aroused when we were together that were the hardest to justify after he left me alone for the last time to go off on another adventure without a word of warning or regret. I had cried myself to sleep almost every night for months as I envisioned the light blue of his deep-set eyes, the way his mustache tickled my nose when we kissed, the silky thickness of his blonde, curly hair, and the way his sensuous lips curled when he said my name. Those were the things that still caused me to believe that not everything about us had been a lie.

"Stop it, you fool," I scolded myself, while resisting the urge to take the thin, floppy book with a bright, yellow cover in my hands and thumb through the pages until I came to the right heading. "Even if his name is still listed, what good is it going to do you? He's probably married with a family he adores, regardless of what he told you."

I plopped down on the bed and buried my face in my hands, but it didn't stop my unwanted musings as my eyes closed against the shadowy images that seemed to be dancing across the walls in the lamplight.

"How can you even think about forgiving him for running out on you without looking back? And even if you can, it's highly unlikely that he would be overjoyed at seeing you again. He might not even remember your name. It's not like you had an actual relationship. You were just some girl he got in touch with when no one else was around. If your paths did cross, you would only get in his face and then all the pleasant memories would be gone. You might even tell him what his selfish antics led you to do, and you certainly don't need his pity."

Before taking a shower and climbing into bed where I hoped I would be able to sleep, I read through the packet Mrs. Fox had given me. It listed the number of the classroom I would be using in the College of Family Living building, the grading criteria for the course and a brief list of available activities I was encouraged to attend. Other than sharing the same table at meals, I had no desire to spend additional time with any of the other presenters. If I felt the need for company, I would ask around campus about where to find T.R. He seemed amenable to my company and was much closer to my age.

The next day was demanding, but it was also one of the most pleasant I had spent in a very long time. All the displays and supplies I had hauled from the coast were unloaded and set up by noon, and I welcomed my students at one. We spent three hours in lively conversation and began work on the rather daunting project I assigned to create a design with the potential of being included in my fall line. I knew that would only happen if they were thoroughly familiar with my work, but I couldn't exactly hire someone to assist me if it meant adding more friction to an already chaotic life. Unlike my predecessor who liked to create havoc, I needed both quiet and peace to survive.

The fifteen attendees were filled with the innocence of living a life virtually controlled by personal aspirations, moral constraints and university guidelines that were meant to keep them both productive and safe. It brought back memories of the years I had spent believing the same things before I discovered that no one is truly indispensable and sometimes clawing the way to the top is the only way to get there.

It wasn't in my lecture notes, but I told my students about my own dreams of grandeur as a recent Bentley University graduate—minus the unfortunate nuptials— who managed to snag an entry level position at *Wide World of Design*. I thought I had it made working for Bethany Kilpatrick, but she owned what I produced, and all my frustration and disappointment was just part of the learning curve. It was like the old adage my grandmother always proclaimed when I got out of sorts as a child—*if you can't stand the heat, then get out of the fire.*

Since I was on my own in a big city and could end up living on the streets just as easily as making it to the big-time, I began paying attention to everything that went on around me from the gossip around the water cooler to what was happening in the boardroom and on the runway. I even took online courses in finance, marketing and human relations to make me more marketable and learn how to make my voice heard.

They seemed to listen with interest, but it wasn't until I told them how my big break came that they truly seemed to come alive. I knew then that what I taught them about design would be forgotten the moment they walked out the door, but unadulterated, solid advice on how to make it in a very complex world might give them the edge they needed to not only survive but thrive.

I just didn't want a single one of them harboring unrealistic expectations. Fashion design was like any other industry. People got trampled, people made it big and being in the right place at the right time was just as important as anything that could be learned at school.

The food in the dining room that evening was excellent. I tried to pay attention to the discussion going on at the table and make an intelligent-sounding comment or two, but I couldn't stop thinking about Brett.

Everywhere I had gone throughout the day there had been reminders of him. The birds singing in the treetops reminded me of walks we had taken in the arboretum. The water in the ponds brought back memories of the coins we had thrown into them while making wishes that never seemed to come true. And the closing of each classroom door made me recall the expectancy I always felt when I knew we might be in the same building. Even the food reminded me of him since I was almost certain that the plates sitting on the table in front of us were the ones we had used in the cafeteria so many years ago.

I found it incredibly hard to understand that while little had changed at Bentley, so much had changed in me. Despite garnering a certain amount of fame and respect from my associates and being able to afford my own home, my life seemed empty. I had never met another man who could tug at my heartstrings the way Brett had done—not even Greg. I regretted my involvement with him almost as much I regretted not having the courage to chase after Brett while there was still the chance of catching him. Through bitter experience, I had discovered that falling in love was a miracle that should never be taken lightly, and falling out of love—even when the relationship wasn't practical or even possible—was never as easy as people liked to believe it would be.

But despite my lack of interest in what was being said, I managed to hear the request when someone at the table asked for the salt. Otherwise, I might have been chastised for not paying attention to my colleagues who were explaining how stimulating their days had been filling receptive minds with sage advice, wisdom and academic knowledge. My experience had been far less laborious and pedagogical, but that was okay with me. They'd had years to create the lives they wanted, but I wasn't even close to where I yearned to be. And Brett Fowler was responsible for that.

It was as if his very soul was reaching out to mine even now and causing a sort of delirium that wasn't normal for a rational human being. I feared that meant I was either becoming mentally ill like my mother or assuming the role of a hopeless romantic like my father since it seemed totally ludicrous to believe that we were really soul mates whose stars had yet to align.

Back in my room, I removed the dress I was wearing and hung it in the closet that smelled like varnished lumber. Then I put on a long, cream-colored, silk bathrobe with delicate rose stitching around the edges, that I had made during a weekend at home, and secured the belt around my waist. I was dead tired. The drive to Bentley had been grueling, and even though I had enjoyed lecturing with the intent of coming away from the experience with several names I could give to my boss as potential interns, a part of me was filled with restlessness and sadness.

I almost wished I had run into T.R. somewhere during the day. He was a charming young man who made me feel desirable as a woman again. That was quite a feat after all the years I had spent being anything but feminine and pliable as I tried to make it in a very complex and often frightening world without having someone around to turn to when times got rough. At least seeing him would have been a pleasant diversion from all the self-denigration I seemed incapable of not hurling at myself.

Since I was still too wired to even lay down on the bed, I crossed the room to the handcrafted dresser and began running a brush through my hair. My goal was a hundred strokes each night. According to my grandmother, that's what brought out the shine and kept it healthy.

"Well, Jada, old girl," I addressed my reflection as the brush ran up and down through my tresses. "How does it feel to be a semi-honored alumna of this prestigious university and have students look up to you for guidance when you're still trying to figure out what you're going to do with your own life? You may have learned a few things after leaving these hallowed halls, but your emotional and spiritual life is a wreck. All you ever really wanted was a husband and children so you could be part of a family that wanted to be together, but here you are on the eve of spinsterhood with no prospects for anything better than what you have right now? You may even end up with a cat."

My brush stopped in mid air, and I involuntarily shuddered as someone knocked on the door. I wasn't sure if I was relieved or irritated at having my miserable thoughts interrupted. A healthy dose of reality often prompted me to make a change, but I wasn't in the mood to talk to another stranger. Maybe if I pretended I wasn't there the person in the hallway would go away.

"Miss Sloan, are you in your room?" a timid voice called out as I sat on the stool trying not to notice the deep frown lines forming between my eyes. It made me wonder what my colleagues and students really saw when they looked at me. Every ounce of spontaneity and joy seemed to be gone from my face. "I know this may be an imposition since we just met, but I could really use a friend."

Her reference to one of the things that was sorely missing from my life aroused a spark of curiosity. All of my friendships had spontaneously disappeared when I left Bentley and finding new ones in the city had never been a huge priority since I couldn't afford to look distracted or emotionally fragile around anyone.

I took a deep breath before responding. "I'm here, but I need to know who it is before opening the door."

"Annabelle Little. We were sitting at the same table during dinner."

I tried to remember what she looked like as I made my way across the floor, securing my robe more tightly around me. I vaguely recalled an older woman in a gray suit but had done little more than acknowledge her presence since my thoughts were in such disarray. The door didn't make a sound as I drew it open.

"I hope I didn't awaken you?" Annabelle questioned as she looked at my robe and bare feet. She was about my height but it was impossible to tell her age. Her hair was pulled severely away from her face and she wore no makeup. She looked a little frightened at her boldness and stood so erect that it made me wonder if she was wearing a corset.

"Not at all. I was just thinking and brushing my hair."

"It's lovely," she said, lowering her eyes towards the braided rug that covered the majority of the wood floor.

"Thank you," I replied, not quite sure what I should be saying to the reserved woman since I had no idea what she wanted. "I used to be a student here. Of course, that was a long time ago."

"Not that long," she responded. "You're the youngest woman in the group. The men had trouble keeping their eyes off you."

"That's because I made such a bad impression last night by missing dinner and being late to the orientation meeting, and my comments while we ate just a short time ago were more than lame. I'm afraid my field of expertise is far from academic. I would imagine most everyone's thoughts, when it comes to me, are centered on why I was even invited."

She gave me an exasperated look. "Many different fields are represented. You would know that if you had read all the materials we were given in our packets—including the life sketches. That's really why I hoped you would have a few minutes to talk."

I was at a complete loss as to what she could possibly want after such an unfair rebuke but something compelled me to stand back so she could enter my room.

"You're right, Miss Little. I should have paid more attention to the reading material, but I was feeling a little disconnected and out of place."

"Is that why were you late?" she interrupted, regardless of the fact that I had more to say. "I know how frightening it can be for a woman traveling alone. I was hoping you hadn't experienced any real difficulties."

"Everything was fine. I just stopped to reminisce and lost track of the time."

"That must have been pleasant for a girl as pretty as you. My professor's couldn't remember my name even when I was sitting right in front of their noses. Of course, that was to be expected since I've always been plain. I suppose that's why I became a research scientist. Since I never went out on dates or had many friends, I turned to books, experiments and laboratories rather than taking the risk of being accepted by people."

Her openness made me realize that we did have something in common when it came to feelings of self-worth, and a slight smile lifted the corner of my lips. "I happen to be a great fan of reading, but the knowledge I possess about scientific research is almost non-existent."

"Maybe I could teach you something about it while we're here. If you have the time, that is."

"Thank you, Miss Little. That would be nice. I like to learn new things, but my work keeps me very busy."

"You must be very successful. You look like a fashion model."

"Hardly," I laughed. "I'm neither tall nor thin enough. Besides, I've never been one who enjoys the limelight. Like you, I prefer working behind-the-scenes."

"Wow," she said. "I sort of figured your life would be nothing short of perfect and glamorous."

"Well, it's not. Most of my evenings are spent working."

"You mean you're not married?"

"Not any more," I said without thinking.

She gave me a compassionate look as I dropped to the side of the bed. I had just broken a very sacred promise about keeping my relationship with Greg a secret and for no other reason than being caught off guard. I should have told my boss that I couldn't come. The past I had tried so hard to bury was already trying to destroy me.

"I am so sorry for bringing up something painful, Miss Sloan," she said as I sat without moving, staring at the cracks in the floorboards. "I should have realized that any topic you felt comfortable discussing would be included in your bio."

My head was still spinning, and I longed for the freedom to be ill. But I couldn't let a stranger know what a great blunder I had made. It would only fuel further questions and more speculation.

"That ill-fated marriage was a horrible mistake, and I would appreciate it if you didn't mention it to anyone. I am not in the habit of discussing my private life. But you mentioned something about needing a friend. I think that could be arranged if you'll just tell me what I might be able to help you with."

Annabelle Little wrung her hands together in a gesture of helplessness. "I really am sorry for speaking out of turn and causing you any distress. I don't always know what to say when I'm around people, but I thought with your background that you might be willing to give me a few pointers about being more attractive to men."

Her eyes held a kind of expectancy and hope that made me want to forget everything that had already been said between us, but I had no idea what I could do. I was a clothing designer, not a magician. And while her features were good, and she must obviously had the money to buy quality clothing, there wasn't time to give her a lesson on style and take her shopping.

She was the epitome of what I had always supposed a research scientist would be—reserved, studious and totally oblivious to anything but her work —and I felt sorry for her. No woman should have to go through life believing she had nothing of value to offer a man. But in many ways, I was as crippled in that regard as she was.

"I'm not sure what you have in mind, Annabelle," I said, using her given name in hopes of bridging some of the expanse that still existed between us. "It's late and all the stores are closed."

"That's okay because I'm not looking for a complete makeover. I mostly wanted to know if you would you go to the orientation party with me tonight. It is being hosted by the student groups we're working with. I seldom go out in the evening but felt like this was one event I didn't want to miss."

"Oh, I don't know," I said with a rapid shake of my head. "I need to get ready for my lecture tomorrow."

"I understand the need to be prepared, but you wouldn't have to spend the entire evening with me. I just need a few minutes of your time so I won't feel so out of place. Besides, it might be fun. There will be a dance and refreshments. Professor Price will be there, and I know he's interested in you."

"Professor Price," I thought to myself as I tried to recall the face of the slim man who had the nervous habit of clearing his throat in the middle of every sentence he spoke. He taught botany at some prestigious university, wrote articles for scientific digests and secured grants for further experimentation with plants. There was little chance he had any interest in me, and the feeling was mutual.

"I'm sure he's a very nice man, but he must be over fifty."

"He's fifty-eight," she flatly replied. "But you're right in saying that he is very nice. We had a rather lively discussion before you arrived at the table."

The light suddenly clicked on like an incandescent bulb in a dark room. Annabelle was interested in Professor Price for herself. That would have been clearly evident before now if I had been paying attention to her body language and the meaning behind some of her rather peculiar statements instead of allowing my mind to slip into the past where it would only be bring more confusion and regrets.

For that reason alone, I paused before responding. A woman who felt a strong attraction to a man needed to know she at least stood a chance.

"I find it very interesting that you would mention him since I was thinking all through dinner that I could definitely see the two of you becoming very good friends. You have so many of the same interests and seem to be very compatible."

She blushed most becomingly. "Am I that obvious? I doubt he sees me as anything more than a temporary colleague."

"You'll never know unless you give it a chance. Are you sure he's going to be there?"

"He didn't exactly tell me he was going, Miss Sloan," she admitted while I tried not to stare at the ball of hair that was tightly secured to her head just above the nap of her neck. It was thick and sleek with just a tiny sprinkling of gray, and I couldn't help but wonder if she ever wore it down. "I overheard him talking to someone else."

I pulled my thoughts back to the present. She was asking for a few minutes of my time, not my opinion as to what she could do to help enhance her assets.

"That's good enough for me, Annabelle. What time did you want to leave?

Her return look was one of almost disbelief. "Are you saying that you'll really go with me? I know it's not how you wanted to spend your evening."

"There's always time for work, but you have to take advantage of an opportunity for romance when it arrises because second chances are rare. Maybe I'll find someone as nice as your Professor Price for myself."

"Thank you for being so understanding," she said with a relieved smile. "Could we go right now?"

I looked down at my robe. "Perhaps it would be best if I took the time to change and touch up my makeup. I'm not exactly ready for an evening out."

"I'm sorry," Annabelle replied as her eyes found the floor again. "I was so excited I forgot you were ready for bed. You must think me rather pathetic, but the truth is that I've never given much thought to men until now. Maybe you could give me a few pointers about capturing Professor Price's interest on the way to the student union building."

"My advice may be less than useful since I haven't dated that much either, especially during the past few years, but I'll do everything I can to make this excursion into the unknown count. Now, go back to your room and put on your prettiest dress. I should be ready to leave in half an hour."

I watched the rather mousy-looking woman shuffle off down the hall and wondered if I was making a huge mistake by encouraging a relationship that had very little chance for success. In five days, we would all be heading back to our normal lives. But then I reminded myself that everyone deserved a shot at love—even those who seemed the most unlikely to find it.

With that thought in mind, I selected a summer dress from the closet and placed it on the bed. The design was one of my own, but I had never felt it belonged in any of the lines I created. It was too frilly and feminine for that, but when I was wearing it, I almost felt like the girl who had once believed in the magic of romance. Perhaps it would help put me in a better frame of mind so I could be of more help to my new-found friend in her quest for finding love.

It astounded me that I could even think about Annabelle Little in those terms after such a brief encounter, but she had been willing to lay her heart at my feet. And in an odd sort of way, I had been more honest with her than I had been with anyone in the past. I just hoped she would keep my secret because losing control in even the most trivial matter did not sit well with me.

I did what I could with my makeup and hair and then let the folds of the dress fall in ripples around my body as I slipped it over my head. Like Annabelle, I wanted to make a good impression on someone special, but my eyes showed the fatigue and disenchantment that had not diminished since I had taken over Bethany Kilpatrick's role at the firm. I wished I had an hour to lay on the bed while cucumber patches made some of the puffiness and tension lines less noticeable. But that was my vanity speaking. No one was going to care how I looked, and making an impression on any man was a waste of time since I would likely never see him again.

By the time my sandals had been secured around my ankles, Annabelle was knocking on my door for a second time.

"Do I look all right?" she asked with tempered interest. "This is the only dress I own that isn't meant for work."

She was wearing a black, floor-length gown with long sleeves and a simple round neck. It seemed a little formal for a student-sponsored party, but it was definitely something I could work with.

"The fabric is lovely," I responded while motioning for her to turn around slowly so I could get a good look from every angle. It was something that came naturally to me by now.

"It's too drab, isn't it?" she countered as her shoulders dropped with defeat.

"Not at all," I assured her. "The lines are classic, and I always carry a few accessories when I travel. I'm sure I have exactly what is needed to make Professor Price sit up and take notice."

Before she had time to respond, I retrieved a box from the corner of the room and placed it in the middle of the bed. I had come prepared for my classes. Once my students had their designs ready for critique, I would show them how a few minor changes could make any outfit pop. I selected three, thin gold chains, a red rose and a unique belt from among the accessories I had chosen for this assignment. When I had them in place, Annabelle looked stunning.

"What do you think?" I asked, standing back so she could see her reflection in the mirror.

"I think it looks like something that doesn't belong on me."

"That's only because you haven't worn anything like this before. In my humble opinion, I believe the real Annabelle Little has finally decided to come out and play."

She twirled around in front of the mirror with the animated look of a delighted child, but the sensation she was feeling didn't last long. "I love what you've done with the dress, but it doesn't look anything like the rest of me. I've never had the nerve to try makeup."

"Why not?" I asked, knowing that all girls did not take naturally to trying to improve their appearance.

"Because I never believed it would do any good. My parents always told me what a disappointment I was. They were very attractive people who lived an active social life and had been stuck with an ugly duckling for a child. That's one of the reasons I turned to science. I knew I wouldn't be judged by a test tube."

"Nonsense," I said, appalled once again at how completely parental attitudes and behaviors could destroy the confidence of a child. "I happen to think that you have very beautiful eyes."

"You do?"

The tone of her voice let me know how genuinely shocked she was.

"Why is that so hard to believe?"

"Because you are the first person who has ever given me a compliment that didn't have something to do with my mental prowess. Do you really believe there is something that can be done about my appearance?"

"Absolutely," I responded. "I may not have exactly what you need since our skin tones are different, but I think you'll be amazed at what a little color on your lips and cheeks can do. Have you ever tried mascara?"

She shook her head. "There never seemed to be a reason for that. I've always had allergies and the ophthalmologist told me as a young girl that leaving my eyes alone was the best thing I could do to keep them from leaking and burning all the time."

"While I would never refute what a doctor said without getting a second or third opinion, there have been vast improvements in the cosmetic industry over the years. There are brands of mascara that are both hypoallergenic and waterproof. I use them to keep my very dry eyes from bothering me quite so much since I spend most of my time abusing them. I might even have a new tube you could have. I always carry a spare."

Her head was moving back and forth by the time I finished speaking. "I don't want to be a bother, Miss Sloan. And I really want to go to the party tonight, not that Professor Price will even speak to me."

"Of course he'll speak to you. I'll see to it myself. And the party is just starting. Give me your trust, and I'll have you there within the hour."

"If you're sure," she stammered, but I could sense that her resolve was weakening.

"I am, and I would like to see how your hair looks when it's down."

"But I haven't worn it that way since grade school," she responded as the fear rose in her voice again. "I wouldn't know how to act if I looked too different."

"You wouldn't have to act any differently," I said, wondering if she had ever thought of herself as being anything but a mouse. "Just be yourself, and let people love you for the person you are both inside and outside. But I can promise you one thing."

"What's that?" she asked.

I crossed my fingers behind my back before pulling the chair away from the desk and placing it in the middle of the room. If Annabelle didn't believe what I told her, nothing I did to change her appearance would matter, and she would go right back to the only personal life she had ever known—one filled with uncertainty, doubt and truly painful loneliness.

"When we get through with you, you'll not only look like a new person, but you'll feel like one too. And that feeling will let you know how to act and what to do."

While I got my makeup kit and brush from the bathroom, she sat down and clasp her hands tightly together in her lap. I almost felt bad for putting her under so much duress but truly believed we were heading in the right direction. Men were visual creatures who each had something about the female form they admired. It could be any feature from the top of the head to the bottom of the feet. That's why it was so important to cover everything.

I could tell Annabelle was scared as I began to work, but she deserved a night to remember with what I hoped was fondness, and I was going to make sure she got it. Applying foundation was unnecessary since I didn't have what she needed, but I had pallets filled with different shades of eyeshadow and blush and an extra tube of mascara. My fingers knew how to move rapidly since I was always in a hurry, and in this case it was a Godsend since I could visibly see how nervous my new friend was becoming.

When I finished with her makeup, I loosened the bun at the nap of her neck. To my utter delight, her hair fell in cascading ripples down to her waist.

"Your hair is beautiful, Annabelle," I said. "It's hard to believe that you've never let anyone see it."

"My parents taught me that it was both prideful and useless to fuss with my hair when no one was ever going to do more than glance at my face. They encouraged me to use my brain so I could support myself since it was doubtful I would ever find a husband."

I had to bite my lip to keep from expressing anger in regards to the people who had given her life. There was no excuse for the damage they had done to their daughter.

"Were your parents religious people?" I asked, hoping the question would give me a better idea of how deeply her scars ran. My childhood had been far from ideal, but at least I'd had a grandmother who encouraged my mostly far-fetched dreams. She just hadn't lived long enough to see me achieve anything.

"Extremely, Miss Sloan! When I said they had an active social life it was due to almost constant church activities that were meant to keep the parishioners coming back when there were so many other options for Sunday morning worship. We read the Bible every night before I went to bed and prayed several times each day."

"Did you attend church?"

"With great regularity! We were Southern Baptists, but I never felt comfortable with all the hell, fire, and damnation sermons. I wanted to believe that God truly loved me, despite my many flaws."

"He does love you, Annabelle," I said. "God loves all of his children and wants them to be happy."

"But being happy isn't being humble."

"In what way?" I asked, surprised by her candor when she seemed like the epitome of meekness to me.

"No idea really. It's just what my father used to tell me when I asked for something he thought was frivolous for such an unattractive girl."

"No one should have told you that because it simply isn't true, Annabelle. Doesn't it say in the Bible that man is supposed to have joy?"

"It says a lot of things that don't translate into how people are able to live in such a dismal, complex and often terrifying world. There was never much joy in our home because we were too busy being meek, dismissive and respectful. I forgot to mention that my father was a preacher who believed his family should set an example for the rest of the congregation. All the girls who came to church with makeup and pretty dresses were lectured about the sin of vanity that could so easily lead to something more offensive to God."

My brush slid easily through her hair as I thought about my own experience with religious training. I had been taught about a God who genuinely loved the children he had created and wanted them to use the agency they had been given as part of his plan. It was the only way they would learn how to truly follow the Savior and pray with enough intent to change course when they were headed in the wrong direction.

"Did his lectures give them reason enough to change?"

"Hardly," she replied. "They simply quit coming."

"And I suppose you weren't allowed to go anywhere with them."

"Most certainly not! That would have put me on a direct path to hell since so many of them were doing things no self-respecting girl would. I did what my father asked because I was too scared to do otherwise, and it was easier than making him mad."

"What would happen when he got angry?"

"He was a firm believer in using his leather belt across my legs or my back. That's how most parents in the hills of Arkansas where I was raised disciplined disrespectful and disobedient children."

Sorrow for what she had endured at the hands of a merciless father who wanted others to believe he was doing God's will made the muscles in my jaw quiver. While I often believed that modern-day parent's leniency was the root cause for the significant rise in juvenile crimes, any kind of abuse should not have to be tolerated.

"I mean no disrespect, Annabelle, but parents have no right to beat their children, and the idea that you were ever overtly disrespectful is hard to believe."

"I wasn't openly rebellious, Miss Sloan. That isn't in my nature. I just did little things that aggravated him and had an occasional impure thought."

"Like what?" I asked.

"Wanting to run away from home, or wanting to know what it was like to have a boy kiss me."

"But those things are very natural for most girls."

"I understand that now, but my father always told me that children were required to do exactly what their parents said and everything they got needed to be earned."

"Not love," I said with a shake of my head as I tried to keep my brush strokes even and gentle. Her hair smelled like lilacs and was clean and shiny. To me, that meant she had a desire to be accepted by others and feel pretty. "That should be automatic."

"Did your parents automatically love you?"

"Absolutely, but we didn't have all that much time together," I replied. " My father died unexpectedly when I was young and my mother had herself committed to a mental institution not long after it happened, but I never doubted their love. We were just forced to live through circumstances beyond our control."

"I'm sorry for all your loss," she said. "That must have been a hard way to grow up."

"It was, but my grandmother stepped in and basically saved me. She told me stories, played songs on the piano and fixed the most fabulous meals. Unfortunately, she died my freshman year at Bentley."

"And you have no other family?"

"A much-older brother that I rarely see."

"I was an only child. My mother was forty and my father forty-five when I was born. They hadn't planned on having a family, but when they found out I was on the way they hoped I would be a boy who could carry on the ministry they had both dedicated their lives to. I was a disappointment in every way. They're both gone now. They died in an automobile accident a few years back."

"Maybe their hearts will have changed by the time you see them again."

"I'm not sure I believe in anything beyond this life. Science is so much easier because outcomes can be predicted with a certain amount of accuracy."

"But you're also a religious person. You said that yourself."

"I said I went to church as a child. I didn't say I believed what my father taught. There is a difference. Do you think I would look good with short hair?"

It was her way of changing the subject, but I wasn't sure what my reply should be. "I think you have the bone structure for it. But since a woman's hair is her crowning glory, I think what she does with it is a personal decision."

"That's why I've never done anything but trim mine," she responded, winding a strand lovingly around her finger.

I stood to one side, feeling somewhat disappointed as she remade the bun and pinned it back to her head without even glancing in the mirror.

When she had finished, she rose to her feet, allowing the towel that had been covering her dress so nothing would soil it, to fall to the floor.

"I hope I haven't offended you by not letting you do my hair," she said as I picked it up and returned it to the rack in the bathroom. "It's just that I've worn it like this all my adult life and change is hard."

"You haven't offended me, Annabelle. Quite the opposite, you've given me a compliment by trusting me enough to ask for my help."

"And I do appreciate it, Miss Sloan. I still can't believe that someone like you would care about someone like me."

"That makes no sense. You're a very special person, and quite perfect just the way God made you."

"I do like your God much better than the one I've always known."

"He's the same being," I countered. "We've just learned to know him differently. But I do wish you would call me Jada. All my friends do."

We were about to step into the hall when Annabelle suddenly hung back.

"I'm scared, Jada! Maybe this is a huge mistake."

I understood her concern but wasn't about to give in to defeat just because she was having second thoughts about attending some party I would gladly have missed if she hadn't come to my door.

"Nonsense, you don't want Professor Price to find someone else, and there is no way of knowing who might be there tonight."

A look of complete terror crossed her face. "Do you really think that might happen? I must be a bigger fool than I thought to entertain the idea that he could ever be interested in me. What have I got to offer an attractive, virile, intelligent man who must have dozens of women captivated by him?"

"Let's start with the fact that he doesn't have a ring on his finger," I replied as a smile slid across my face. I needed to calm her fears without sounding patronizing, or she would bolt. "That means he hasn't found the right woman yet. And while I've only known you for a couple of hours, I think you share many of the same characteristics. You're equally as intelligent, attractive and virile as he is. You also have a very kind heart and the desire to love and cherish someone. It would be a privilege for Professor Price to get to know you better."

"You're not just saying that to make me feel less unsure of myself?"

"No! I mean it sincerely. You look absolutely stunning."

"Even without changing my hair?"

"Most men are oblivious to the things women find important. While they dress to please other woman, men have other criteria for what they find attractive. My grandmother always told me that a smile is the only thing a girl ever really needs on her face. Now, let's give the men at the party a chance to see real women who have had enough life experiences to be interesting. I didn't get all dressed up to spend the night in my room."

I took the older woman's arm and escorted her down the hallway, through the lobby, and out into the warm, night air.

"Should we drive?" I asked when we got to the parking lot.

"I would rather walk, if that's all right with you."

Some of the dread was gone from her face, but it was easy to see that she needed more time to prepare before stepping into another new situation.

"A walk would be nice," I replied. "I haven't seen much of this part of the campus. Would you believe it was an alfalfa field when I was a student here."

She laughed. It was weak and faint, but I knew then that Annabelle Little would make it through the night.

Chapter 4

We crossed the terraced lawns in silence, each absorbed by our own thoughts. I could hear crickets making their unique clicking sound somewhere in the distance but wasn't sure that going anywhere alone on campus after dark would be a good idea. The fact that two young women had been raped and another one abducted during the past few months worried me. I had always thought of Bentley as being a place of safety where students could go where they wished without having to be overly bothered about anything.

But that was just another misconception left over from my youth. The world had become a place of violence, unrest and anger where people did what they wanted without concerning themselves about consequences unless they were caught. And even then the laws, and many of the politicians who made them, seemed to favor the criminal. Nothing much was ever said about the victims, the suffering of the loved ones left behind, or even the cost to rebuild, replace or simply live with something that had been destroyed by force or intent.

No music coming from inside the student union building where I had spent hours walking through the bookstore and sitting at a booth in the cafeteria while studying and talking to friends. I could remember most of the hallways and the phone numbers of many of the people who had helped me survive my education. But while I was proud of what I had accomplished, I had little desire to talk to anyone from my past. I had spent the last eight years trying to forget much of what had transpired because all it did was reduce me to tears.

"Are you sure this is the right place?" I asked Annabelle who looked even more uncomfortable than I did now that we were so close to our supposed destination.

Her brow furrowed, and I could see tears forming behind lashes that now made her eyes look brighter than ever. "I couldn't have been that dense, could I?"

She looked so miserable that I placed my hand on her arm. "I didn't exactly look at the program, but let's not worry until we've gone inside. It's too early for the party to be over."

"But everything is so quiet, and when we passed the parking lot only a few cars were there."

"That's only because most everyone who might come can walk. If the party is being held at a different location, someone inside will tell us."

"Maybe we should just go back to the cottage," she replied. "It was foolish for me to believe that Professor Price would have any interest in me."

"Not so fast," I said as she spun around on black, leather shoes that were much more practical than the stiletto heels I was wearing. "We've come this far. It would be a real shame if we didn't at least go inside. If nothing more, we could get some ice cream, my treat."

I saw her shoulders move upright as she turned to face me. "Are you really sure we're doing the right thing? There's no fool like an old fool—or so the adage goes."

"In the first place, you're not old," I responded. "And in the second, since we've both taken the time to get dressed up it would be a real shame if no one saw us. Now put your fears aside and let's go up those stairs. We'll never know what might be waiting on the other side of the door unless we're willing to open it."

Something in the tone of my voice must have given her the courage to put one foot on the first step that led upward. I wasn't overly confident that we would meet with success, but if Professor Price was there, I would keep my promise about making sure they were properly introduced. It brought back memories of the way I met Brett, but I pushed them aside as we entered the brilliantly lit foyer.

"Where do we go from here?" she asked.

"Just follow the music," I replied, quite relieved that we could now hear a band starting to play.

But when we got to the ballroom door, I was the one to hang back. No one was there to check off names from a guest-list, and the large, dimly-lit room was literally filled with students—few of whom could be part of the workshops we were giving. But then most everyone attending college during the summer would take advantage of each excuse that kept them from studying, even if it meant crashing some party that would likely be excruciatingly boring without their presence.

Annabelle must have had many of the same thoughts as we watched a sudden flood of young people move to the center of the floor.

"Where did all of these kids come from? I thought this party was meant for the lecturers and their students as a way of helping them become better acquainted."

"The word must have gotten around." I replied, suddenly realizing that with a packed house it would be much easier to disappear once I had fulfilled my promise. "But try not to worry about how many people are here. We came so you could get better acquainted with Professor Price. If he's here, that's all that really matters."

"Oh, I do hope you're right," she whispered as she looked searchingly around the sea of faces. "I really want this evening to be special."

"While I am no predictor of future events, I can tell you that Professor Price will be impressed when he sees how truly lovely you look."

Annabelle hung her head becomingly. "Do you really believe that?"

I swallowed back my own doubts before responding. Looks were only part of the equation. There had to be some undeniable chemistry before any man would make an overt move towards a woman.

"He'll notice you, and I'm sure you'll have a very pleasant evening together. Do you see him anywhere?"

While it occurred to me that I might be doing her a disservice by prodding, I couldn't seem to help myself. I liked the idea of being a matchmaker again. I had brought several couples together during college and had the bridesmaid dresses still hanging in my closet to prove it. I would keep an eye on her during the evening and perhaps even minimize a few lulls in a conversation, but I couldn't undo a broken heart.

"No, but I'm sure he is a man of his word," she said, bringing me out of my musings so quickly the lines between my eyes didn't have time to relax. "If he said he was coming, he'll be here."

"In that case, why don't we walk around the edge of the dance floor. If we see him, all we have to do is act surprised."

"I couldn't do that!" Annabelle exclaimed. "It would be dishonest since he's the only one I want to talk to."

Her level of commitment to childhood teachings she no longer valued was baffling. But we couldn't remain where we were indefinitely without someone noticing, and we were both too reclusive and old for that.

"I'm afraid that's how this game of love is played. You will be surprised when you see him, won't you?"

Her giggle was a little unnerving. "When you put it that way, I suppose it isn't too great of a sin."

"Then let's do it."

I gave her a slight shove in the direction of the ballroom, regardless of the fact that it seemed highly unlikely that the Professor Price I had seen at dinner would voluntarily put himself in a social situation where the music was loud, the crowd made up mostly of students who had yet to reach their intellectual capacity and the refreshments had no nutritional value. But then perhaps he had been sent to recruit students to his program just as I had been told to find and intern I would be able to train.

"Are you really sure I look okay?" she asked as we inched our way into the overcrowded ballroom.

"You look terrific," I said. "But I think we might have better luck finding him if we checked out the tables on the upper level first. That's where people always congregated to talk since the music is less intense."

We circled the parameter of the ballroom trying not to bump into anyone. Walking the familiar pathway forced both pleasant and disagreeable memories to resurface. It was impossible to count the number of times I had been in this ballroom when Brett was singing. His band was the most popular one on campus, and I had nearly floated to heaven each time he took center stage. His voice was clear and penetrating, and each song he sang left me believing that someday he would understand just how deep our connection really was and forget about all the groupies who practically salivated whenever he glanced in their direction.

It had taken a long time before I realized that the bright lights he was facing made it impossible for him to see anyone who was even a few feet away from the stage. His warm and captivating smiles were meant to enhance his persona when it came to being a man who knew how to love a woman and give her everything she thought she wanted.

"There he is." Annabelle was tugging on my arm as my visions dissipated, and I followed her eyes upwards. "What do we do now?"

"We walk up the stairs and say hello."

"I can't do that," she exclaimed for a second time. "It would be too forward."

"You can and you will if you want him to notice you as more than a colleague. I'm sure he is used to meeting people, and you never know what might happen unless you're willing to let go of some of your preconceived notions. Life is too short to remain in the background forever, especially when you see something you want."

She was wringing her hands together as she had done when we talked about wearing makeup but still followed me to the north end of the ballroom and climbed the stairs that led to the same round, wooden tables and high stools that had been there when I was a student. Even the same paintings of scenes around campus were hanging on the walls.

"Professor Price, I believe," I said, addressing the slightly-build man with gray hair and glasses who was seated alone at a corner table. The rest of the balcony was sparsely populated, but that only meant a conversation could be maintained with relative ease.

"Do I know you?"

The quizzical look on his face let me know that he had no idea who I was, but being a gentleman, he rose to his feet.

"You may not remember me, Professor Price, but I'm Jada Sloan," I hurried on before he dismissed me as being nothing more than a nuisance. From what I could tell, we had arrived long past the time for socializing. It made me wonder why he had not returned to the quiet of the cabin where he could finish out his evening in peace. "I saw you last night at orientation and again this evening at dinner."

"Of course," he quietly responded.

I felt as awkward as he looked. If it weren't for Annabelle, I would be down the stairs and out of the building as fast as my feet could carry me. But I couldn't abandon my new friend until I had made that proper introduction and was sure they could continue a conversation without me.

"Do you mind if we sit down?"

Without waiting for him to respond, I took the chair across the table from him, and literally pushed Annabelle into the one on his right where the light was the better. "You remember my friend, Annabelle Little?"

"Most assuredly."

He rose slightly from his chair again as she nodded her head and tried to smile.

"What now?" I silently asked myself between clenched teeth while my lips retained their outward position. Getting these two people together would to take a small miracle.

While we sat there in strained and labored silence, I felt like the gears in my brain were literally forcing themselves through the rusty cogs of a wheel. My own experience in the art of seduction, or even causal conversation, had been severely neglected while trying to get ahead in the business world and keep my heart from being crushed again. But without a push in the right direction, the evening could easily turn into a dismal failure since neither of my companions seemed inclined to say anything more to each other.

"Professor," I absentmindedly began since I had no clear idea of what I could say that wouldn't sound lame to people who were so much smarter than me. "It's too bad there isn't time to attend each other's lectures. I've always been interested in flowers, and Annabelle tells me you're a botanist of some renown."

"That I am, Miss Sloan."

When he offered no explanation, I hurried on in hopes of finding something that would lead to even a brief conversation.

"Annabelle is in research too. I'm sure she would be delighted to tell you all about her work."

She was staring at the tabletop but glanced quickly in my direction when I reached my foot underneath the table and touched her ankle.

"I'm afraid my work isn't exactly interesting to anyone who is not into microbes, bacteria and viruses since there are far more failures than successes."

"Why don't you let the professor be the judge of that? I'm sure plants get sick too."

I was more than happy to help move things along, but I didn't want to be the only one talking. I wanted them conversing with each other so I could sit back and relax before leaving, but Professor Price appeared to have little interest in either of us. Maybe he had come to the balcony merely to think before returning to his room.

"Do you like flowers as much as Miss Sloan would have us believe she does?" he suddenly asked Annabelle.

"Oh, very much, Professor Price," she almost purred. "Gladiolus are my favorite. They come in so many rich and vibrant colors."

"How particular, Miss Little. They're my favorite too. Some colleagues and I have developed a strain that seems almost indestructible. They're nearly as black as the lovely dress you're wearing."

Annabelle's eyes were wide with genuine interest now. "How perfectly wonderful. I would love to see them."

"Any time you like. They're in my greenhouse back home. Do you have a greenhouse, Miss Little?"

"Not really," Annabelle said with a shrug of her delicate shoulders. She was tall and willowy, just as I imagined a garden nymph might be. "I just have a small vegetable and flower garden in my back yard."

I couldn't believe what was happening. Two of the mousiest people on the planet had found something in common that they loved. I settled into the backrest of my stool and folded my arms. Life truly was amazing.

"Where are you from, Miss Little?" Professor Price asked.

"My home is in Alabama. In fact, I live in my parent's old house. They're both gone now."

"How peculiar," Professor Price marveled. "I'm from Kentucky, just a stone's throw away as the old saying goes."

Peculiar is just the word I would use to describe what was happening between the two people who sat at the table with me. I had done my share of matchmaking, but nothing had ever gone quite so smoothly. They were talking about the soil contents when I felt someone lean in close to me.

"Hey, gorgeous, I didn't expect to see you here."

I jumped in alarm, but when I turned my head I saw T.R.'s smiling face. He was dressed to make an impression on most anyone.

"Hello yourself," I said, willing my heart to quit racing. I wasn't accustomed to pleasant surprises. "I didn't expect to see you here either."

"And here I was hoping that you had been unable to get me off your mind."

He was a delectable young man, even if everything he said was just part of some game he played with the young girls around campus. I could either go along with it and have a little fun or continue to sit at the table where my presence was no longer needed.

"Do you want to know the absolute truth, T.R.?" I asked, tilting my head to one side like I had often done so many years earlier when the world still felt like a safe and happy place.

"Lay it on me, but please be gentle," he replied. "My ego is vey fragile."

"While I doubt that, I was secretly hoping to see you again. You made my day when we met."

T.R. almost beamed. "I did?"

"Without a doubt. I was feeling like I didn't belong and seeing a friendly face really helped. It also kept me from having to explain some parking ticket to my boss. He's a stickler when it comes to details."

"I can't imagine anyone getting mad at you," he replied. "Those amazing, blue eyes could soften any heart. By the way, who are your friends? I saw you walk in but couldn't extricate myself from what I was doing fast enough to catch up with you before you got to the balcony."

Our companions had stopped talking to each other, and I hoped our frivolous banter hadn't ruined what might be happening between them.

"T.R., I would like you to meet Annabelle Little and Professor Price. I'm sorry I don't know your first name, professor."

"It's Russell, Miss Sloan, but I've gone by the name of Professor Price for so many years that it's hard to remember I even have a given name. And what is your last name, young man?"

"Baker," T.R. said. "Timothy Russell Baker. It appears we have something in common."

Professor Price gave him a look that would have made me wince.

"Russell's a good name, young man. Never make light of it. I'm sure your parents gave it to you for a good reason."

"I guess," T.R. said. "I was named after both of my grandfathers. They're neat old men. I wish I could spend more time with them."

"As well you should," Professor Price said. "We never know when someone we love is going to be taken—especially from the older generation. Life is too short for all of us. You should recognize that even at your young age."

"Thanks for the advice, Professor Price," he said, giving me a look of bewilderment. "It was nice to meet you. You too, Miss Little."

Instead of saying anything, Annabelle merely inclined her head. It appeared she was back to being her former, shy self.

T.R. took two steps away from the table and then turned back to face me. "Would you care to join me for a glass of punch or a drink of water, Miss Sloan? It's awfully hot in here, and I didn't mean to intrude on a private conversation."

My smile was one of relief, and I offered a silent prayer that my companions would have no objections to me going.

"Only if it's okay with Annabelle and Professor Price."

"It's fine by me, young lady," Professor Price said in his most authoritative tone. "I'll see to Miss Little's needs. I'll even escort her back to the bungalow so you young folks can do whatever suits your fancy. All this noise and hopping around is a little too much for me."

"In that case," I said, sliding my stool away from the table. "I guess I'll see both of you later."

"Thank you for everything, Jada," Annabelle said, glancing in my direction as if she had been given the most spectacular gift ever. "Just promise me that you won't go anywhere alone."

"She's not going to be alone," T.R. told her. "I'll see that she gets back to Whitman Cottage safely enough."

We left them sitting at the table. As we walked down the stairs to the ballroom, I couldn't help but be pleased with how well the evening was turning out. I would talk to T.R. for a few minutes and then make my way back to the cottage without anyone's assistance. I always carried mace in my purse, and the self-defense class I had taken after moving to San Francisco would keep me from getting into any real trouble. Besides, I wasn't exactly some young thing that was likely to run into a predator on a college campus.

"How did you get to be such good friends with those two?" T.R. asked as we came closer to the ballroom floor. "I know you're with the same group, but you're nothing like them."

"Is this where I'm supposed to express my thanks for such a gallant rescue?" I asked.

"Not unless you want to. I'm only telling it like it is. One of my friends nearly slept through a Professor Price's lecture this afternoon. Do you think it's the same guy?"

"Could be?" I said. "Professor Price is a botanist."

"Then that's the guy with a thousand slides and a monotone voice that made everything turn into a blur before the first hour ended. But it was an honor to be chosen as part of the program, so my friend tried to act like he was enjoying the experience. Besides, it's a relatively painless way to earn a few credits since there are no massive tests involved."

"I hope that's not how my students feel about me. I'm doing my best, but I've never stood in front of a classroom before. That puts me at a definite disadvantage."

"Not you," he said with another disconcerting smile. "You have passion. Anyone but a blind man could see that just looking at your face. Almost makes me wish I was in a more artistic field."

"Exactly what is it that you're studying, besides girls?"

He laughed. "I'm going to be a veterinarian. I thought about being a doctor but grew up on a farm. Somehow working with animals is more appealing than cutting people open. I prefer my women with clothes on— unless we'e engaged in a less formal activity."

"You ought to wear a sign around your neck that tells unsuspecting girls to beware," I replied.

"And spoil all the fun? I've never pushed a girl to do anything that makes her feel uncomfortable. But that doesn't mean I don't enjoy it when certain defenses are down. After all, I am a red-blooded, American male."

"You certainly are," I replied. "Maybe I should rethink hanging out with you. I haven't been in a serious relationship in a very long time."

He suddenly put his arm around my shoulders. "I would never hurt you, Jada. I hope you get that. While I enjoy the chase and most everything that comes after, I know you're way out of my league. I'm just hoping you'll spend some time with me. It would be a huge boost to my self-image and let the girls know just how much I have to offer."

"You're shameless," I replied.

"But adorable," he countered. "I saw the way your eyes lit up when you saw me standing behind you."

"Only because I felt like a third wheel. My sole reason for coming tonight was to give Annabelle support. She came to my room earlier to ask if I would come with her so she could meet Professor Price in a less formal setting. I think it is kind of romantic, especially since they seem to have hit it off. They're both into flowers."

"Go figure," T.R. said. "I guess there really is someone for everyone. But you can't tell me that you would rather spend an evening with them than with a handsome, young man like me?"

"Maybe that's part of the problem," I responded. "I'm a woman, not a girl anymore. But I do thank you for the all the compliments. They make me feel like I'm not quite over the hill yet."

"Then dance with me?" T.R. said, extending his hand towards me when we got to the bottom of the staircase. "The band promised to be back on stage after intermission, and it's about that time now."

I was shocked by his invitation since there were dozens of girls in the ballroom who would absolutely melt at the chance to be held in his arms.

"What about your friends? And don't try to tell me that some of them aren't here. I know they would like to spend time with you, and I have plenty of preparation work to do before morning."

"Just one dance, and I'll take you back," he pleaded. "My friends see me everyday. Tonight I want to spend time with someone new."

"Someone who is a lot older than you?

"Age is relative. Besides, I'm not asking you to marry me, and no one would guess that you're one of them."

He nodded toward the balcony where Annabelle and Professor Price had resumed what I hoped was a pleasant and long-lasting conversation.

"You really are just a kid, aren't you?" I said with a shake of my head. "Just wait until you're my age, and then their age doesn't seem that far away."

"You may be right," he conceded. "But I happen to like you, even if you do consider yourself an older woman. What I can't understand is why some guy hasn't slipped a wedding ring on your finger."

"Because marriage and I don't seem to be a very good fit."

"Why not?" he asked. "A guy would have to be crazy not to want to be with you."

"You say that because we've just met, and because you're a very nice young man."

"It doesn't take a genius to know that you're a bright, beautiful and successful woman who also has a tender heart and a genuine concern for others."

"Wow!" I said. "You could tell all that about me in two brief meetings. You should go into psychology instead of veterinary medicine."

"Maybe I will," he said. "A woman like you could inspire a guy to do most anything."

"Now I know you're being facetious, but I really don't mind. There aren't many opportunities for playfulness in my chosen field."

"Just what is it you do, Jada, besides designing clothing that makes women look great?" he asked, not the least embarrassed to use my first name without asking permission first. "With your figure, you could be a model."

"Hardly," I responded. "I've often believed I should have been born in the Golden Age of Hollywood when actresses had real curves like Elizabeth Taylor, Marilyn Monroe, and Rita Hayworth."

"I've heard some of those names from my grandmother, but I doubt being born in the wrong era has stopped your success. You look like a woman who has it together in every way."

"Looks can be deceiving," I responded since I had no interest in becoming anyone's sugar-mama. That's why I decided to caution him about making assumptions. "While you're very astute and charming, I would be careful how you phrase certain things around older, unmarried women. They may seem altogether on the outside, but most of them have plenty of insecurities."

His crestfallen expression let me know I had gone too far.

"I didn't mean anything sleazy by what I said. It was meant as a compliment. You are the first beautiful, young and successful business woman I have ever known."

I decided to leave his second blunder alone. I wasn't a streetwalker, and he was just a guy trying to impress someone he liked.

"Thank you, and I didn't mean to sound like an old crone, but money and nice things don't always compensate for having someone special to go home to at night. It's the human relationships we take for granted that have the most value."

"I get that, but having nice things couldn't hurt," he replied. "I wouldn't mind driving a car like the one you said you have."

"I would gladly trade it for a mini van filled with children if that was an option. But if a nice car is something you really want, then you'll have it one day. From what I've seen, you're a very optimistic, goal-oriented and nice young man."

"Ouch," he replied as the movement around us intensified. "Don't you know that no man wants to be known as nice—sexy, irresistible, exciting, or maybe even a playboy—but never nice. That just means he's too boring to be taken seriously when it comes to romance."

"Not in my book, T.R. I've met plenty of guys that could be describes in those terms, but they were always here today and gone tomorrow. It's hard to find a genuinely good guy—one a girl could envision spending the rest of her life with."

"When you put it that way, maybe nice isn't such a bad adjective, as long as we have some of the other qualities to go with it. I like my women to think I'm unpredictable and even electrifying."

"I'm sure they do. That's why I find it so perplexing that you don't have some arresting, young thing on your arm tonight."

"But I do. I just have to convince her that sharing a dance with me wouldn't be such a bad idea."

His sudden smile after a few words that should have been left unsaid could have melted an iceberg it was so warm and inviting.

"Too bad you're not a few years older. I might be tempted to give the young ladies at Bentley a run for their money."

He swept me into his arms, and I was surprised to find that I was actually enjoying myself. It didn't really matter that nothing would come of our pleasant encounters. I needed a brief respite from a life that had become much too intense and somber.

While a popular, instrumental song played in the background, I found it easy to fall into the rhythm of the music. I had always loved to dance, and T.R. was an excellent partner—confident, graceful and charismatic. He was the type of guy most any girl could fall for—even one who was significantly older than him.

I glanced at the couples surrounding us as my feet, hips and arms moved. They looked so happy that it was hard to keep my mind from drifting back to the unpretentious days when I had danced to Brett's music without the fear of lost dreams and absolute misery causing the tears to fall. Maybe if I kept my eyes focused my partner's face I could keep that from happening now.

It was certainly not the time or the place to let anyone else know about the follies of my youth. In a few days, I would be back to the security of the life I had created to insulate myself from things that could not be changed, and this brief excursion into days gone by forever would be over.

"Hey gorgeous," T.R. said, leaning his face very close to mine when the song ended. "What happened to that smiling face? I tried to make sure I wasn't treading on your toes or doing anything else that might embarrass you."

I touched his arm in what I hoped wasn't an inappropriate way. "It's not you. I was just having some unexpected flashbacks."

"You mean your time here wasn't all sunshine and roses?"

"Hardly," I responded while trying to keep a real frown at bay. "Is anyone's?"

"I suppose not, but a person's past should not determine his or her future. It's merely something to be learned from."

"Did you learn that in one of your psychology classes?" I asked.

"Only theoretically. I may have been born a few years later than you, but I've had my heart broken plenty of times."

"Is that what you think I'm suffering from?"

His fingers closed over mine. "Far be for me to make another assumption, but only a lost love could make a woman like you look so sad."

"You may be right, T.R. Everyone needs love, and only a very fortunate few seem to find it. Perhaps we should call it a night before I bring you down too."

"I'm not worried," he responded. "Being here again was bound to dredge up a few unpleasant memories. After all, it is a college campus. But if you give me a chance, we could easily make a few pleasant ones."

"You've already given me a new lease on life, but what we have isn't real."

"It could be," he challenged.

"How? My life is in California and yours is here."

"We could see each other on weekends and FaceTime each other every day. When I finish my undergraduate work, I could move closer to you while I'm in Veterinary school. It would only be another five years until I was contributing to our livelihood."

"Now I know you're delusional," I said with a smile. "Long-distance relationships seldom work, and we know nothing about each other. Let's just enjoy the moment and not be concerned about anything else."

"Does that mean you'll dance with me again?"

"Just one more," I responded as the music flowed into a soft love ballad.

T.R. drew me into his arms, and I felt a sort of peace and sense of security just being there. The music seemed hauntingly familiar, but when he pulled me closer like a lover would and lay his cheek against mine, I didn't resist.

I was too far away from the band to know that the soloist had taken centerstage until a familiar, melodious voice filled the room. The nausea that rushed to my throat was instantaneous, as was the rapid increase in blood flow to every extremity and weakness in every joint.

"Hey, are you all right?" T.R. asked.

I gulped for air hoping to stop the lightheadedness from making my world go black. But willpower alone would not reduce the jolt to my system that made my hands icy cold and my heart pulsate so forcefully that T.R. had to feel it.

"I think a ghost from my past has just reappeared," I said, fully aware of how heavily I was leaning on him for support. "Do you know who the band is?"

"Sure! They're the *Sound Generation*. You must have heard them play back when you were in school. They've been around forever, but they're still the best."

"Yes, I've heard them," I said, finding it impossible to even glance in the direction of the stage. "Do they still have the same band members?"

"I guess so! But you could see for yourself? We could dance right up to them."

"No!" I said, gripping his arm so tightly I was afraid my fingernails might dig into his skin. "I need to leave right now."

The sudden stiffness in his body gave me cause for concern since we were standing in the very center of the crowd, but something in my voice must have told him that I was through playing games.

"Okay, but it's going to take a little maneuvering if we don't want to cause a scene."

I didn't care what it took to get me out of the room. Tears were stinging the insides of my nostrils, and I knew a huge meltdown was coming. I should never have allowed Annabelle to talk me into doing something when I had even the slightest reservations. This was Brett's domain, and the only place on campus where there was even the slightest chance that I would run into him after dark.

"Here we are," T.R. announced with a heavy sigh once we were standing in the doorway. "I'll have you back to Whitman Cottage before you know it."

While I appreciated his chivalry and was trying very hard to be polite, I didn't need an audience when I started blubbering, and I was almost to that point now.

"Please go back to your friends and forget about me," I said, biting down on my bottom lip in hopes of stopping some of the trembling. "I know the way back."

"You're crazy if you think I'm that kind of guy. Don't you remember what I told you yesterday? That rapist has never been caught."

"I know how to defend myself, T.R. If someone tries to hurt me, they'll wish they hadn't. Besides, it's not that far, and I could use the air."

"Then I'll join you. I promise not to get in your way, but you really shouldn't be alone."

"You just don't get it, do you," I responded with a brisk shake of my head as moisture gathered in the corners of my eyes. "I'm not some sweet, young thing who needs protection. I've lived in one of the most violent cities in the country for nearly eight years and have managed just fine. Go back to your life and forget you ever met me. You'll be much happier, and I'm used to doing things solo."

He moved towards the dance floor a far different man than the one I had met outside the gates or even earlier tonight, and it caused a spasm of regret. I had never been intentionally cruel before, but T.R. deserved a few more years of uncomplicated existence. Being around me would only force the line that existed between reality and dreams to blur before the need arose.

But before he disappeared from sight, I heard myself call out to him. "There is something you could do, if you wouldn't mind."

There was an upward movement of his shoulders before he turned around. "Fire away! I guess I really am nothing more than a sucker for a damsel in destress."

"My distress has nothing to do with you, and the world would be a far better place with more men like you in it."

"Does that mean you've reconsidered my offer?"

"Only if you don't mind being around someone who has an insatiable need to be in control?"

"My shoulders are broad, and I'm used to girl's tears. I have three younger sisters."

"In that case, maybe you wouldn't mind telling my friend that we're going."

"But Professor Price already said he would make sure Miss Little got home."

"I know, but I would feel better if she knew I wasn't staying. I'm her wing-man, so to speak."

"Been there, done that," he replied. "Just don't leave before I get back."

My eyes darkened. "I'll wait in the lobby. That way, she can come with us if things aren't going as well as I hope they are."

"Be back in a flash!" T.R. said with a little boy grin.

I was watching his retreat when the crowd suddenly dispersed and I caught a glimpse of the man I had once loved with every fiber of my being. He had his back to the crowd, but his microphone was in his hand and his foot was tapping to the opening beats of his next song—one he had so often dedicated to me.

The heat rose to my cheeks as a feverish excitement I couldn't restrain moved my feet back into the ballroom. I brushed past people without seeing them. My mind was ablaze with remembered passions, soft touches and irrepressible dreams. His actions had shattered my trusting heart, but instead of reaching out for the right kind of help, I had sought comfort in the arms of another man.

I was standing directly below his microphone when he turned to face the audience. The years appeared to have been much kinder to him than they had to me. He was now thirty-seven years old, but he looked just as he had that morning when he left me on the front steps of the rental I had shared with so many different girls.

His introduction began as he always had. "I would like to dedicate this song to . . . . "

My breath caught in my throat when his eyes met mine. I would have given all I possessed to know what he was feeling, but his glance paralyzed my faculties, and I could neither move nor speak. His eyes stayed riveted on my face like the hot coals of a blazing fire.

"Excuse me," he said before lowering his head and clearing his throat.

That moment was all I needed, and while my eyes brimmed with tears, I knew I could never endure another meeting. He was no longer my man, and no amount of pretending would ever change what had been lost. He could even sing our song to someone else.

I ran blindly. The pain was overwhelming, and I needed it to stop before every part of my soul was consumed. I gave no thought to Annabelle, Professor Price or even Timothy Russell Baker as my feet carried me over pathways where I could have been easily injured or even killed.

By the time my legs quit moving, I was halfway across campus and the mostly rock buildings had turned to spacious lawns and a maze of sidewalks leading to the small town where students often went to let off steam. I stopped on the edge of the hill. Behind me was the man who had stolen every dream for as far back as I could remember. Before me was the staircase that lead to the brown, brick house with the wrap-around front porch where I had spent many blissful hours dreaming about a future that was not meant to be.

I was puzzled by my irrational actions. Why hadn't I run back to the safety of the bungalow where my present life could protect me from the past? I knew this staircase like the back of my hand—every chipped piece of concrete, every worn step and every statue on every landing. I had climbed it every day for four years going between the house where I lived and my on-campus classes.

"Why can't we go back in time," I called out to the night air as I started my descent. My teeth were clenched, but the agony behind the words still broke through. I folded my arms tightly in front of me, as if I could close off my heart from each recurrent onslaught of pain.

It was dark, except for a street light a hundred yards away. I stopped on the second landing where the staircase divided. A concrete wall spanned the area in front of me. Below it was a lush forest of shrubs, ground-cover and trees. I walked to the barrier, kicked off my stiletto heels and hefted my body to the top of it like I had done so often when a problem arose that needed my undivided attention. Then I swung my feet onto the wall, drew my knees underneath my chin and tried to make sure the skirt of the dress I was wearing covered everything I didn't want to be seen.

Not chiding myself for making stupid mistakes was impossible, and I knew how to do it with unbridled flare. My words were bitter as they spewed forth like ash and cinder from the top of a raging volcano.

"When am I ever going to learn that caving in to someone else's wants never turns out well for me? Mr. Fredericton knew I didn't want to come but because he basically owns me I was afraid to cross him. And Annabelle came at me with such a sob story that denying her request would have made me feel like a monster. As for Brett, I've spent all these years holding onto the moronic illusion that he was just waiting for me to return. Never once did I force myself to accept the probability that he had found what he was looking for with someone else. But he doesn't appear to have suffered any emotional damage. I'm the one who is so tightly wound by all of life's disappointments that I can't even be civil to a good-looking young man who was only trying to help me feel less like failure."

I brushed the tears away as I leaned back until my head came to rest on the concrete pillar that formed one corner of the landing. It was cold and a little damp, but the wall was wide enough that I wouldn't fall off unless I was pushed. So I closed my eyes and listened to the sounds of the night—the hoot of an owl, the chirp of an insect and the light breeze rustling the leaves of a nearby tree—as I recalled how often I had turned to God for help over the years.

He had gotten me through my father's and grandmother's deaths, my mother's mental illness and my brother's lack of interest in ever seeing me. He had even helped me through the mess I made when I married Greg, and he would help me through the plight I was in now. I just needed to get a grip, decide what my next move should be and leave everything else to him.

I breathed deeply and methodically like I had been taught to do in a Yoga class. I had known seeing Brett again was possible, but I had expected it to be on my own terms, not in some ballroom where the last of my fantasies were shattered the moment he opened his mouth.

Had I been thinking the least bit rationally, I would have waited until he was through with his set to leave instead of running away like some love-struck groupie who knew she had been discarded. He needed to know that I had done just fine on my own, but there were not enough words in the English language to convince him that he no longer held any power over me after what I had done.

Emotional fatigue must have caused me to lose full consciousness of my surroundings because I was suddenly aware that I was no longer alone. But instead of opening my eyes, I reached for the purse that was dangling over the wall and tried to slide the zipper through its notches. I needed the pepper-spray to defend myself or my body might never be found if someone decided to discard it in the dark recesses below the landing.

When I had what I needed, I opened my eyes just far enough to see that a man was sitting on the opposite end of the wall. His face was shrouded in darkness, but I knew if he meant me any real harm he would have made a move by now.

He must have noticed what I thought were subtle movements because he stood up and closed the distance between us before speaking.

"Are you awake or still pretending to be asleep so I'll leave you alone?"

My heart leaped to my throat again as total recognition hit me.

"Why are you here, Brett?" I demanded. "If I wanted to talk to you I would have remained where I was."

"You don't really mean that. You're just upset."

"That's an understatement! You should have let it be known that you were still around?"

"No need to since I wasn't the one who left. But I think you might have a little explaining to do?"

"I don't owe you anything. How did you know I would be on the stairs?"

He sat down on the wall near my feet. "Because this is the place you always came when you were troubled."

"So you haven't forgotten everything about me. What a relief! But my being here doesn't mean that I'm upset by seeing you again. I do have other things going on in my life."

"I'm sure you do. While I may still be a little obtuse, I'm not blind. You looked like you had seen a ghost. Didn't you know I would be playing at the dance?"

"The itinerary I glanced through didn't give any specifics. Why didn't you contact me if you knew I was in town?"

Not turning away from him was one of the hardest things I had ever done, but I would not allow him the satisfaction of having the last word this time.

"First of all, I didn't know you were here since I don't pay much attention to things that don't concern me. And even if I had, I would never make a move on another man's wife."

"What are you talking about?" I demanded as my hands flailed so helplessly in the air that the pepper-spray canister slipped from between my fingers and went crashing to the ground.

"Don't look so shocked," he replied after returning it to me. "I've had eight, long years to get used to the idea that you found someone else almost the moment I left you at your front door. Your roommate was overjoyed when she told me that you had married some guy named Greg and were living your dream life in San Francisco. I didn't even know you had a job lined up."

My brow furrowed as the nausea associated with having some huge secret exposed rose to my throat. I had never told my roommate what happened the day I decided to ruin my life, but then we had shared the same bedroom for nearly three years. And it must have been easy for her to see that things had drastically changed between Greg and me since I disappeared every weekend after we were married until graduation. My change in behavior—when I had never done anything remotely like it before —gave her ample opportunity to draw some very accurate conclusions and even find the marriage certificate I had hidden at the bottom of a dresser drawer.

"Only because you never asked. You just left town and never looked back."

"That's not fair! I had every intention of making good on all my promises, but on the way back to my loft I got a call telling me that I needed to leave at five that afternoon for a six-month program abroad. One of the faculty members who was scheduled to go with the students had a family emergency and couldn't leave town."

"And you lost your cell phone so you couldn't make a simple call?"

"Come on, Jada. I had arrangements to make and packing to do. By the time I was on the plane, I was too exhausted to do anything but sleep."

"I get that, but why didn't you call when you woke up? Maybe I was just at the bottom of a long list of girls who had been important to you, and by the time you came to my name you were tired of making excuses."

"You know that isn't true. Cell phones work the same going each way. You could have made that call just as easily as me."

The laugh that escaped through my lips was hollow. "I have never overtly pursued a guy in my life. You knew that about me."

"Maybe I thought you had changed. Most everyone does while attending college."

"I did change, just not in that way. How could I when your appearances were so sporadic and short-lived? We never spent enough time together for me to feel secure."

"And you never gave me any indication that you wanted something more."

I felt the air go out of my lungs as I swung around and let my legs dangle over the wall. Casting blame and making false assumptions was getting us nowhere, and it would turn into a shouting match if one of us didn't walk away.

"Listen, Brett," I said while trying to locate my shoes. "This conversation isn't going well. Maybe we should just leave things alone and pretend tonight never happened. I'll be gone by the end of the week anyway."

"So you are with that group of presenters staying at Whitman Cottage. I knew the university was trying something different to help students understand what working in their respective fields would be like, but I thought Bethany Kilpatrick was slated to take care of fashion design. Her picture was on every poster around campus. She's one of the few celebrities to graduate from here."

"I've seen some of those posters, but I was a last minute recruit since she decided not to come. I'm sorry I showed up at the party tonight. I only went because a new friend asked for my help. I had no idea you would be there."

"So you really were surprised to see me."

I rubbed my hands together before interlocking my fingers. "I had no idea you were still at the university. I lost contact with everyone the day I left."

"Are you telling me that your roommate never told you I called the house on the old landline several times. After a few weeks of being away, I was too embarrassed to call you directly, but I needed to know you were okay."

"That makes no sense," I replied.

This time, he was the one to frown. "Why not? She never liked me. She thought I was messing with both your head and your heart and had no intention of ever settling down."

"And I thought she was just concerned about my welfare. Musicians have a reputation for being unreliable, and I shed plenty of tears every time you disappeared. The last time was exceptionally hard."

"Is that why you married someone else?"

"Yes," I admitted without hesitation. "But you need to know that we never lived together as man and wife. It was a spur of the moment decision that seemed like a good solution to some very pressing problems since he was going to law school at Berkley, and I was afraid to be on my own in a big city. We were married by a justice of the peace a month before graduation and then went back to our own apartments since we had no other place to go and still needed to make it through finals."

"Are you telling me you weren't in love with him?"

"I cared about him a great deal and thought we could make it work once we had to rely on each. I had already put a deposit on a small apartment in San Francisco, but he never moved into it with me or even suggested we find something more suitable for a couple. He was afraid to tell his parents that he had married a girl without their permission."

"We aren't living in the dark ages, Jada. People are allowed to decide whom they are going to marry."

"That's what I thought, but his parents wanted to consolidate family fortunes. That put me in a no-win situation since all I had to my name was an old car and a few personal belongings."

"You were just starting out. What did they expect?"

"Quite obviously, someone from a wealthy family who would feel at home when it came to going to the country club and attending fashionable parties. But I can't blame Greg for everything. He paid my rent until I was making enough to do it myself and stopped by when he could. But it wasn't long until we both accepted the reality that he wasn't in a position, either emotionally or financially, to stand up to his parents, and I couldn't change my family of origin. I suggested an annulment since it would save us the embarrassment and cost of a divorce, and he made all the arrangements. All I had to do was sign a few papers."

"And you haven't seen him since."

"He came to a number of my shows bearing flowers and candy. He even asked if I would give him another chance, but I had been reading about his escapades and romances in the society section. Being a lawyer suited him, and he wasn't ready to give up certain addictions and behaviors I found unacceptable so my answer was no. I guess I was finally to a point where I could stand on my own."

"You were always able to do that. You were the only girl I ever knew that was so committed to her goals and beliefs she couldn't be swayed. I tried to find you several times but had no idea where you had gone or even what last name you were using."

"I never changed my name, and the only person who knew where I had gone was my roommate."

"And she wasn't about to tell me. Why didn't you just wait for me to come back?"

"I waited for three months, but then I heard through the grapevine that you had run off with some girl."

"And you didn't check to see if there was any truth behind it?"

My eyes sought refuge in the shadows that seemed to be dancing playfully in the moonlight. "No more recriminations or questions that have no clear answers, Brett. The past can't be changed."

"So you really are still as naïve as the day we met," he replied, looking at me from the corner of one eye.

"Hardly!" I countered. "Although I'll be the first to admit that I don't know how to play games any more now than I did back then."

"Would it help if I tried to explain?"

"Not really! I've already done enough hurting to last a lifetime."

"What about my hurt?" he asked with such vehemence that I felt a moment of fear. The night was so quiet, and I doubted anyone would hear me if things took a real turn for the worse. "Don't you think it was a shock for me to see you tonight?"

"I'm sure it was, Brett, but how could you dedicate our song to someone else?"

"I have never dedicated our song to anyone else. You left before you heard my complete introduction."

My eyes blinked open much wider than normal as I jumped down from the wall and picked up my shoes. I could feel him watching me. "You really expected me to stay?"

"I've learned never to expect anything outside of my control. I dedicated that song tonight just like I've always done—to the woman I let get away from me."

"You didn't," I said, returning to an upright position.

"Just ask anybody. I've been playing at these dances on and off since the day you left. You must really think I'm some lowlife that needs to crawl back underneath a rock."

"Not really," I said.

"Then sit by me for a moment so we can have a conversation like we used to do."

He extended his hand and every part of my body shouted for me to take it. But I knew what his touch could do, and I wasn't about to let him crush my spirit again. So I brushed it away, sat back down on the wall without his assistance and folded my arms defiantly across my chest.

"You're just as stubbornly independent as always, aren't you?" he said, joining me. "We were both so afraid of missing something, or someone, that personal commitment wasn't even part of our vocabulary."

"What do commitments have to do with anything now? We've both moved on in all the ways that really matter."

The look on his face let me know that I wasn't entirely wrong. He still had his music and his groupies. I had my independence and my pride.

"Because I've regretted the decision to leave you behind since the day I made it. I was feeling too much, and the thought of being with just one girl for the rest of my life scared the hell out of me. I figured if I got away by myself for a while I could figure things out, and maybe even learn how to quit running. I came back believing I was ready to ask you to marry me, but I didn't have a chance because you were already gone."

"You really expect me to believe that?" I responded, wondering why it always took so much energy to be angry.

"Why would I lie about something like that now? Whether you choose to believe it or not, I really did love you."

"How convenient," I retorted. In all the ways that really mattered, he was still little more than a stranger. Our mutual desire for emotional safety had seen to that. "Maybe all we were ever meant to be was star-crossed lovers like Shakespeare's Romeo and Juliet."

"While that thought has crossed my mind, somewhere deep inside I never gave up believing that you were the girl I was supposed to marry. You always brought out the best in me."

"That's a little hard to believe. Did you ever get married? I noticed that you're not wearing a ring, but few married men do."

"No!" he said after a much too-lengthy pause. "I considered the possibility a time or two because I didn't want to be alone, but something always pulled me back. Perhaps it was nothing more than a guilty conscience because of the way I treated you."

"I'm sorry to hear that. One of us should have been allowed to be happy."

"I thought you were. As for myself, I figured being single for the rest of my life was just retribution for playing too many games with young girl's hearts. Have you given up on all men or just me?"

Now that I was over the initial shock of seeing him again, I figured it might be best to let some of the repressed anger, resentment and pain go. Nothing would be gained by casting more barbs, and this might be the last conversation we ever had.

"All men, I suppose. But in truth, I've been too busy the past few years to give personal relationships much thought."

"You do look like a vision of success. You deserve that after all you went through with your family and having to walk away from an unsatisfactory marriage. At least I still have my parents and sisters. I don't see them as often as I should, but I always know they're around if I need them."

"You don't have to feel sorry for me, Brett," I replied. "I've actually done quite well for myself professionally. My fall line will be ready in a few weeks, and some of my designs have been featured on the cover of the company online magazine and the runway. I moved into a beautiful house in the suburbs a little over a year ago, and I drive a very nice car."

"That's quite an accomplishment, but I know you, Jada. All you ever really wanted was a home and family of your own."

I let the air out of my lungs slowly. "I've discovered that it's not all that bad to be alone. God knows the kind of lousy decisions I make when it comes to men. I've decided to leave that part of my life in his capable hands. I'm just working on becoming the kind of woman he meant for me to be."

"From where I'm sitting, the woman you are right now is just about perfect. Is it too lame to ask if you've thought about me over the years?"

I tilted my head and smiled at him. "I've thought about you more than I wanted to—and dreamed about what might have been—but then I had to remind myself that we both made decisions that seemed right at the time. I just wish I hadn't been left with the belief that I was nothing more than a placeholder between conquests for you."

"Four years is a long time to be stringing anyone along."

"But we still spent far more days apart than we did together."

"That wasn't entirely my fault," he responded as a movement in the eerily dark space behind us made the hair on my arms stand erect. I was back in the country where nocturnal animals ruled, and humans needed to be careful. "You were dating other people too."

"Only because I saw how the girls fought to get your attention, and I refused to become one of your groupies."

His laughter made the underbrush move in a noisy way. "What can I say? I'm irresistible!"

"So it would seem, especially when you're singing."

"Is that a compliment, Miss Sloan? I do believe it's one of the few you've ever given me."

"Then I apologize for my oversights. You are an amazing and talented man."

"But my talents have never kept me warm at night."

I covered my mouth to stifle a chortle, but the sound came through anyway.

"So you think it's funny, do you?" he asked, reaching over to tickle my side like he used to do. It was still one of the most sensitive spots on my body.

"Not exactly!" I replied, trying to brush his hand away. "But you always told me how much you hated sleeping alone."

"Still do. You must think I've made love to every woman I've met."

The smile on my face disappeared as rapidly as it had formed. "Not everyone, Brett. You never made love to me."

He looked at me so intently I wished I could take back what I had said. Women who were trying to be virtuous didn't talk like that. "But I always wanted to, Jada. You were my ideal woman."

"Were?" I asked.

"Were, and still are. My feelings for you have never changed."

"You don't have to explain anything. Our relationship was pretty much a *Comedy of Errors,* even if I did just refer to us as being star-crossed lovers."

"Those errors stole a good portion of our lives."

"Maybe they have," I admitted, looking at the way the distant lamplight played on his hair. I so much wanted to touch it, but that would only lead to other things I might not be able to control.

"Still, something brought together again, and I doubt it was only a matter of fate."

The electricity in the air seemed to be gathering around us, and when he reached for my hand, and I let him take it. I needed to feel important to someone again, and the warmth of his fingers as they slid between mine were nothing short of intoxicating. I was disappointed, but somewhat grateful, when his next question brought me back to reality.

"Why did you marry that guy named Greg if you really loved me?"

I bit down on my bottom lip before responding. "I think I've already answered that. Like you, I wasn't fond of being alone and couldn't see where it would really matter since I had already lost you."

"And just like that." Brett snapped the fingers on his free hand together. "You were there."

"No, it wasn't just like that. I cared about him and maybe even loved him. But it was never anything near what I felt for you. I think he knew that on our wedding night. He said a few things that really hurt right before he made love to me."

Brett bristled but didn't pull away. "If that's the case, why didn't you end the marriage right then?"

"Because I was scared and didn't want anyone to know what I had done, especially you. I lived in fear that Greg would take me to a dance where your band was playing before we were able to leave town. I could so easily envision the look on your face when you saw the ring on my finger and knew exactly what you would say."

"And what might that have been?"

"The words that kept ringing in my ears were, 'I don't know if it's congratulations or condolences', and then you would have turned and walked away."

"Unfortunately, that sounds like something I would have said and done back then. I know we had our share of problems, but I always figured we would eventually get past everything that kept us apart."

"Me too, but it never happened. You had your career and your admirers. That was a lot to give up."

"I suppose I thought it was at the time, but I really had nothing of value to offer a woman. I was a mostly an out-of-work musician who taught a few German classes so I would have a roof over my head."

"None of that mattered to me."

"It would have if I had turned you into the barefoot, pregnant wife of a musician who didn't want to grow up. Just look how successful you are."

"I've worked hard to get where I am, but you are the only man who has ever made me feel sexy and beautiful."

"Wow!" he said. "Why couldn't we have talked like this eight or ten years ago. I threw away what I could have had because I didn't want to deflower an innocent."

"I wasn't a saint, Brett. I was just a confused, mixed-up girl who knew nothing about life. I suppose that's one of the reasons I turned to Greg. I wanted to feel the kind of love you sang about but couldn't do it without being married. I'm guessing we both got the lives we were meant to have, but it would have been nice to remain friends."

"You and I were never meant to just be friends," he responded. "But we don't have to talk all of this out tonight. You said you would be here for a few days."

"Until the end of the week. Then it's back to San Francisco."

"One of the great cities of love," he said with a half-hearted smile. "I've spent a good portion of the last eight years wondering where you were and if you were truly happy in another man's arms. You'll never know how much I hated him for taking you away from me."

"And now you know that he didn't. Any idea where we should go from here?"

"I'm not sure, J."

I might have been thoroughly disappointed at his response had he not used the pet name he had given me so many years earlier. It let me know that he hadn't forgotten everything about us either.

Chapter 5

"Miss Sloan."

I turned from the whiteboard where I was writing down the steps I went through each time a new design started to form in my head. A young woman with large, brown eyes and a captivating smile was staring at me with a very perplexed look on her sun-bronzed face.

"Yes, Amber," I said, grateful that memorizing names had always come easy to me. Of all the students attending my seminar, she seemed the brightest but also the most intense. In many ways, she reminded me of the girl I had once been. "Is there something you would like to ask? I know I have a real tendency to rattle on when trying to get a point across, and this teaching gig is a first for me."

A snicker went around the room as I hoped it would, but she seemed to miss the point of my attempted humor. Something was really bothering her.

She glanced around the classroom where all the tools I had brought for their use were displayed instead of answering me. I had given them the assignment to come up with something they thought might be compatible with my fall line the day before, and most of them were already sketching designs—some of which had great promise. But getting a product on one of the mannequins by the end of the week wouldn't be easy, and the cash prize and possibility of an entry-level position at *Wide World of Design*—if I felt their work ethic matched their talent—was only adding to the pressure the ones who wanted a real shot at success were already experiencing.

"Yes, Miss Sloan, but I feel kinda foolish about it," she finally replied, pulling her bottom lip into her mouth as the lines between her eyes deepened.

"There are no foolish questions," I told her, trying to push back the headache that was making my own concentration hard. There had been very little sleep after my unexpected meeting with Brett. He had walked me back to Whitman Cottage and told me goodnight, but there had been no kiss or plans made to see each other again. I felt as if I was reliving our last encounter while I was a student at Bentley, and all I wanted to do was cry. "That's how we learn. Besides, you're among friends."

Every set of eyes in the room was on her, but the looks I saw were ones of empathy and interest, not contempt, indifference or mere curiosity.

"I don't quite know how to begin, Miss Sloan. I don't want to look like I'm copping out after being given the opportunity to be part of this program."

"Why would you feel that way, Amber? You're here because the dean has great confidence in you—just as she has for everyone else who is here."

"That's just it, Miss Sloan, I'm a senior and will finish my classes in December. Up until a few weeks ago, I was so excited about graduating and moving to a big city to start my career. But the closer I come to leaving Bentley, the more scared I get. I've been listening to you for nearly two days now, and I'm more confused than ever."

I smiled compassionately. How well I remembered those days of fear, uncertainty and making the most horrendous mistake of my life. If she needed a little guidance, I would try my best to give it. But no two lives were the same, and I wasn't about to disclose my personal catalyst for success. No one else needed to know about my marriage to Greg or the truly horrible things that had led to its demise.

"What is it I've said that has caused so much confusion?" I asked, leaning into the edge of the teacher's desk for the support I might need.

"I guess it's a little bit of everything," she shyly admitted. "You see, I'm from a very small town, and I have no family or friends in any city. I'm just not sure I can cope with all of the problems and stressors you've alluded to."

"I see," I replied, not wanting my answer to stop her career before it had even begun. "While I would very much like to address Amber's question, I don't want to detain any of the rest of you since it's almost time for the class to end. I'll be here at seven in the morning and have made arrangements for the room to be left open until midnight the next three nights so you can work on your projects. I'm very excited by what I've already seen. You all have my cell number if you need anything when I'm not here."

Two students hurried to the back of the room, but everyone else stayed where they were.

"Thank you for wanting to hear more of what I have to say," I responded after the door had closed behind them. "I can't speak for the rest of fashion design community. I can only tell you what it was like for me. But this has to be an informal conversation—just friends talking. Is that okay with everyone?"

I needn't have asked. I had my class's rapt attention—probably for the first time—because so much of what I told them had already been covered in previous courses.

"I just want to know if I stand a fighting chance," Amber said. "I love designing clothes, but I've never been good at confrontations, and there is someone rather special back home. Everyone here, but you, already knows that."

The room was silent as I waited for another round of snickers, but it didn't happen. Everyone sitting in front of me was at the same point. They were about to graduate and filled with the hope that all their dreams would come true—despite some very real concerns—but no one could promise them anything more than the fighting chance Amber had mentioned. I would do what I could to assuage some of that fear without making it all about me.

"It hasn't been that long since I was sitting where you are, and there were many times when I wished someone could have told me what a fashion designer's life was really like before I headed away from the classroom. I had so many stars in my eyes and was ready to pay my dues, but reality seldom meets expectations—even when they're not that high. I figured if celebrities could make it big without any professional training, then I was a shoe-in for success because all my professors told me just how great I was going to be."

When no one said anything, I sat down on the top of the desk and crossed my legs at the ankles like experience in the real world had taught me to do. "Perhaps one of you could ask me a question to get us started."

A hand in the back of the room shot up. It belonged to a girl with strawberry-blonde hair who had already shown me an entire portfolio of sketches. Her name was Clarice Thompson.

"I have one, Miss Sloan. You say you understand where we're coming from, but you look and act so sophisticated and self-assured. You make it hard to believe that you were ever one of us."

"Oh, but I was, Clarice. Much like Amber, and possibly even some of the rest of you, I grew up on a dirt farm a little over a hundred miles north of here. My father died when I was a child, and my mother couldn't deal with it, so I was raised by my grandmother. She was wonderful, but she didn't even graduate high school. I came to Bentley the most scared little girl on the face of the earth. I had big, unrealistic expectations, but that was the only thing I had going for me, other than sheer determination and an academic scholarship. You see, I studied hard because I lacked the confidence to make any real friends. I wore clothes my grandmother made and spent my free time helping her with projects around the farm. She had been a widow for over thirty years and was too self-sufficient to ask for help."

I saw a few heads nodding, so I continued. "She thought I should be a teacher. I wanted her to be proud of me, but standing in front of a classroom repeating the same information day after day sounded like a dismal existence. I wanted the kind of life I saw in the few movies I attended and on TV. How many fabulously dressed and alluring teachers do you remember having?"

Everyone in the room laughed.

"I see you feel the same way I did. My grandmother died during my freshman year. It nearly broke my heart since she was the only real family I had left. But it gave me the freedom to look at different careers. I thought about different options for over a year, and even took a few very strange and eye-opening electives. But nothing seemed like the right fit. At the end of my sophomore year—when my counselor was hounding me about selecting a major if I ever wanted to graduate—I met a girl who was going into fashion merchandising. It sounded like an exciting field. So without a great deal of thought, I changed my major and plowed through some classes that made my head spin. Since my grandmother had taught me how to sew, my dolls were some of the best dressed in the county, but that was a far cry from coming up with something unique that actual people would want to wear."

"That's basically how I got started," another girl broke into my narrative. "I made all my clothes in high school and figured that with a little luck I could make it big. Being rich and famous has always been my major goal."

"I think that's the tipping scale for most everyone," I replied. "Without a dream, however unrealistic it might seem at the time, few of us would leave our comfort zone and learn what we're really capable of accomplishing."

"Did your success happen the way you planned?" Amber asked.

"Not exactly. I may have been given an internship to work with the illustrious Bethany Kilpatrick after graduation, but it wasn't exactly the dream job I had envisioned."

"I was really bummed when she blew us off, but I'm not sorry you're here," a student by the name of Ted Atherton said. "You make it sound like she just wanted a protégé she could mold into a clone of herself and figured she couldn't go wrong with someone who had studied at the same school."

"Pretty much, but I mean no disrespect to either her or her vast accomplishments. Her financial gifts to this school have allowed many students to live their dreams, and her work over the past thirty years is legendary. However, her own bumpy road to success, shrewd business dealings, lack of cooperation with most everyone and unwillingness to play by society's more acceptable rules are no secret. The only reason she agreed to take me on was because her publicist felt it would be beneficial to her career if others saw her more human and compassionate side."

"Did it work?" Ted asked.

"For her, but I had to sign a non-compete clause. Five years didn't seem like such a long time at first, but after a few months I was doing all the hard work while she got all the credit."

"But you knew that could happen," Clarice said.

"I did, but I was young and naïve and thought I would have it made if I could just get my foot in the door. I gave her my best without relinquishing personal or professional integrity—or all the ideas in my head. I wanted something fresh to work with once I was allowed to come up with a line of my own."

"So how did you get out from under her control?" Amber asked.

"I put in my time, learned what I could from her and was ready to step forward when the owner of the company decided to give me a chance."

"I read about her walking away before one of her biggest shows during my first year in the program. It was quite the scandal since she was sleeping with one of the male models, who was half her age, and neither of them showed up for the main event," Clarice interjected.

"That's because they were in the south of France, where to my knowledge they still reside. One of the other things you need to understand is that most people in the industry are highly temperamental—especially when they're at the top—and know how to maintain a grudge. Since I was her assistant and basically asked to replaced her, she blamed me for ruining her life."

"But she brought it on herself," Ted said. "You couldn't walk away from such an amazing opportunity because, from what I've heard, they only come once."

"That's true, but it hasn't been easy dealing with all the people who were on her side and wanted to see me fail. That's one of the reasons being asked to take her place here was so hard. My boss wants me to bring someone new into the firm and help mold him or her into a competent and visionary designer who is ready to create a new line, but there are still rules and a chain of command. The one at the bottom has to learn how to navigate some tricky waters on the way to success."

"I think it's exciting that one of us might get that chance, but I don't want someone else taking credit for my designs. They're my babies, and I'm pretty much committed to maintaining my integrity. My family would be devastated if I didn't."

"Good for you, Amber," I said. "Fortunately, not everyone in the industry wants the same thing. Some of the people I work with are happy sitting at a sewing machine, running errands, planning fashion shows, answering the phone or ordering supplies. I've come to the conclusion that as long as we're true to our personal convictions things will work out, even if there are a few lean and lonely years."

"I could go hungry for a long time but draw the line at being lonely," Clarice said and everyone laughed.

"I didn't mean that literally," I responded. "We always have to eat, and it's nice having someone in our corner. But part of all success is being in the right place at the right time, and not being afraid to take a chance. Does that answer most of your questions?"

"The ones that have been asked so far," Becky Collins, an exquisite and talented African-American girl on the far left side of the room, said. "You've told us how you got to where you are as a designer, but what about the rest of your life? Is it all just one big, fashionable party after another in the evenings like the media would have us believe. I can't think of anything better than being dressed to kill all the time and hobnobbing with the rich and famous."

My laughter was hard to suppress. "I can hear myself saying much the same thing a few years back. But if that's the kind of lifestyle you really want, I would suggest marrying a multi-millionaire who loves being in the limelight because very few in our field will ever live like that. I could probably count the number of lavish parties I've attended in the past eight years on one hand. Mostly, it's just a lot of backbreaking and mind-boggling work. I'm at my drawing board ten to twelve hours a day. I live, breath and dream designs. And that's just the beginning. When I've finished my sketches, I have to work through mountains of fabrics to find exactly the right one. Then it's on to the cutting board, the sewing machine, the mannequins and the fitting room. Sometimes it seems like my designs will never look as good on a model as they do in my mind."

"That sounds absolutely grueling, Miss Sloan," Becky added. "Why do you even stay with it? It must have a devastating affect on your social life."

"What social life?" I threw back at her. "By the time I get home from work, I'm too tired to go anywhere."

"Well, you've certainly cleared up a few things for me," Clarice said as she sank back in her chair. "I'm changing to political science first thing in the morning. I want a husband more than I want a life of celibacy just on the chance that I could become even semi-famous one day."

"I didn't mean to discourage anyone," I told her. "But I have to admit that a husband and family would have taken precedence had things been different. Mediocre designers are a dime a dozen. If you really want to be successful, you have to pay the price, and sometimes it simply isn't worth it."

"Do you wish you had made different decisions?" Amber asked, interrupting whatever else I might have felt inspired to say.

"Of course, but you know what people say about 20-20 hindsight? It's not going to change where we're at."

"I get that, but I need to know if you would have given up your career to be with the right man?"

I felt the heat rush to my cheeks and was glad I still had the support of the desk to keep my knees from buckling. Things might have turned out quite differently if Brett had never left me behind the last time, but I couldn't talk about the most emotionally charged years of my life with a group of kids. I was here as a representative of the company I worked for, not some life-coach who wasn't the least bit qualified to offer personal advice.

"That's something I'll never know since it didn't happen. But I can tell you one thing, it's always best to think carefully before you act. You'll end up with far fewer regrets if you do."

It was too late when I left the classroom to make it back to the cottage for dinner. I felt bad about not seen Annabelle all day. I wanted to hear how her evening with Professor Price had gone but didn't want to tell her anything about mine. I was deeply troubled by the way Brett had left me. After so many years, I wasn't sure what I thought would happen if we saw each other again—certainly not some torrid one night stand like people in the movies seemed to have without any regrets—but I had expected him to say something about seeing me again before I left.

Maybe his curiosity about what had happened to me, and having the chance to clear the air between us, was enough for him. But I needed a more fitting closure and didn't know how to reach him. I couldn't even hang around the building where German classes were taught hoping to run into him because I had other responsibilities until my time at Bentley ended. But the fact that he had even remembered where I usually went when I needed time alone had led to a restless night of remorse and speculation.

Most of the people I had met over the years claimed that one never really got over his or her first love. It clouded what could be found with anyone else. That was definitely the case with me. Looking back, I hadn't tried all that hard to make things work with Greg after our wedding night. I let one callous remark, and the almost debilitating pain it had caused, keep me from making any overtures when it came to getting to know his family or even planning evenings that would make him want to be with me. And on the rather sporadic occasions when he tried to get close, I let my disappointment and insecurities keep me from responding the way I knew I should. Maybe Brett sensed what lay behind the outward facade I presented to the world and decided I was no longer the woman he remembered. I certainly wouldn't want to spend much time with someone as mixed up as me.

Since I knew I couldn't go to bed on an empty stomach, or even make it through the long evening ahead without eating something, I let my feet carry me across familiar sidewalks towards the student union building. Most of the food in the cafeteria was barely tolerable it was filled with so many carbs, but the chef salads had always been good. I selected one from the cooler, along with a glass of non-sweetened lemonade, and sat down at a counter near the window that overlooked a truly beautiful part of campus.

There was a round, marble fountain where cool water shot high into the air before cascading back to the ground and casting refreshing droplets on anyone standing too near. And ancient trees with their bright, green foliage that offered plenty of shade during the summer and a brief respite from the wind, rain and snow during the winter. But I was mostly drawn to the colorful flowers that changed with quiet regularity from spring to fall and the well-preserved benches for resting or visiting between classes because people watching had always been one of my hobbies.

It gave me a reason to contemplate life and provided a superabundance of ideas for new creations I could bring to life on my drawing board. But for some reason, the students passing in front of me during those bewitching, late afternoon moments when the sky was filled with the most glorious shades of pink, purple, blue and gold reminded me so much of the past that any inspiration was lost in recollections of what I had let slip through my fingers because I was too unsure of myself to make a stand.

I allowed the tears to form but not fall as deep-colored greens, boiled egg, cucumber slices, cherry tomatoes and cubes of ham moved back and forth between my teeth. I would make it through the next four days simply because I had to and deal with the fallout of my return to Bentley when I was back in the safety of the life I had learned to handle. Anything less was unacceptable since it appeared that my work was all I would ever have.

Since I wasn't ready to return to my room after eating, I went to the second floor of the fine arts building. Like I had done so many times in the past, I rested my elbows on the wooden railing and cradled my chin in my hands. My eyes were fixed on the exhibit of statuary on the floor below. Various professors showcased their students work during the spring and summer each year. It was a great way for presenting the most creative pieces, garnering additional public support and helping deserving scholars get noticed by someone who was willing to invest in their future. Some of my own designs had been featured there. Seeing what I could do in the alumni magazine was what had prompted Bethany Kilpatrick to give me a chance.

Expectancy and dreams had captivated my life back then, just as they were doing now, and tears clouded my vision again as my mind returned to thoughts of Brett. Had last night really happened, or was it all the delusions of a tormented mind?

Oh, how I wished he would come up to me now as he had so often done when we made plans to meet in this very spot between classes. He would always say something corny like *a penny for your thoughts* as two strong hands were placed on my shoulders. I would turn my head just enough to catch a glimpse of him before allowing my body to savor the electrifying sensation of his touch.

I could feel his caresses now and wanted to scream out in anguish, but I was much too practical for public displays of emotion so I left the building and hurried along the pathways to Whitman Cottage where I would make preparations for the coming day. There were notes to be made that would help some of my students with the designs they were creating. I needed them committed to paper before delving any further into my disillusionment or frustration.

Making it to my room without having to speak to anyone was my goal, but when I pulled open the front door I saw Annabelle and Professor Price sitting next to the fireplace. They were deep in conversation. I figured I might be able to avoid them if I was quiet enough, but I had barely crossed the threshold when the same woman who had greeted me the night I arrived called my name. I put up my hand in hopes of keeping her from saying anything more, but Annabelle was already on her feet.

"What happened to you last night?" she demanded while closing the distance between us. "You really had us worried, especially when we got back to the cottage. I knocked on your door several times before going to bed, but you never answered. I was afraid you had become the next victim of the campus rapist. Professor Price told me all about him. You should never have gone off alone."

"How did you know I was by myself?" I asked.

Her eyes were nearly blazing with anger. It was hard to believe I was speaking to the same woman I had met only twenty-four hours earlier.

"Because that young man you were with came back a second time to say that you were not where you said you would be. He seemed quite upset—as rightly he should be. Don't you know it isn't polite to leave an escort stranded."

"He wasn't my escort. He was simply someone who befriended me when I first got here."

"That's beside the point. You made all of us believe you wouldn't take any chances."

"I was in no danger, Annabelle," I replied. "I know how to defend myself. I've taken several self-defense classes and always carry pepper spray or mace. Regardless of what you might think, I have no desire to end up as some ill-fated statistic."

"You took an unnecessary risk and had people worried about you. I know how important it is for single women to feel in control since they seldom have anyone to turn to, but there is little to stop a remorseless predator who carries a knife or a gun. I was really scared. And that poor boy, who really likes you, felt just awful about being stood up. You told him he could walk you home."

"I'll apologize the next time I see him."

By this time, Professor Price was standing next to Annabelle. He looked less formidable than he had the night before, but his words still let me know that he wasn't impressed by what he had seen of me thus far.

"Miss Sloan, I hope you realize that Annie's sentiments are genuine. While I will admit that the atmosphere at the party last night was less than ideal with all the loud noice, sweaty bodies and tomfoolery, there is no excuse for worrying people who care about you. We left right after you did believing that we would run into you on our way back. I'm not sure where that young man went, only that he was heading out to look for you too."

I took in some much-needed air before replying. I hadn't done anything with malicious intent. They would know that if I explained the situation, but it was too embarrassing knowing that Brett may have simply been toying with me again.

"I decided to take a short walk. The night was beautiful. One doesn't see skies like this in San Francisco."

"I don't blame you," Annabelle sighed. "Last night was the most beautiful ever. Don't you agree, Russell?"

"Annie and now Russell," I said to myself. More had happened to them last night than a mere walk back to the cottage together.

"Miss Sloan, would you care to join us at one of the tables for a card or board game?" Professor Price asked, interrupting my unspoken thoughts. "I'm sure Annie would like it, and refreshments will be served later. I couldn't help but notice that you were not here for dinner again."

I watched Annabelle smile at him, and my heart did a double-take. He was asking me to spend time with them because he knew it would make her happy. It was one of the most selfless acts I had ever seen.

"My class ran longer than expected so I stopped by the student union building for a salad. While I have a number of things that need to be done before morning, I would be happy to join you for one game—on the condition that you call me, Jada, Professor Price."

"Only if you'll call me, Russell."

I stifled a chuckle. Calling the professor by his first name seemed absurd. He was nearly thirty years my senior, and we had absolutely nothing in common—except our obvious fondness for Annabelle Little. And after a lifetime of feeling like a person no one would ever love, she was blossoming like a carefully tended flower.

"I can do that," I responded. "But the lady at the desk was trying to get my attention, and I need to see if it is anything important first. My students have a big project due at the end of the week and some of them require more help than others."

"We would never stand in the way of your responsibilities," Professor Price said. "Annie and I will be in the conference room with the others when you're ready."

Before I could think of a return response, he was leading her away. But it was just as well. I needed a few minutes to get used to the idea of spending any time with my highly-esteemed and intellectual colleagues. Playing even a single game with them spelled nothing short of disaster and humiliation for me.

When they were no longer in view, I approached the desk where I was handed a letter.

"It came right after you left this morning, Miss Sloan. I was going to slide it under your door when I left."

"Do you know who sent it?' I asked, glancing down at the surface of the envelope where my name had been scrawled in large letters with a swirly line placed underneath.

"A messenger brought it. I can only assume it came from somewhere on campus since there was no return or forwarding address."

"Thank you," I replied as the blood rushed to my head.

I needed to get to my room where I could read what had been written in private so I hurried up the wooden staircase as fast as my shaky legs would carry me. It took much longer than I would have liked to rummage through my bag for the room key. But once the door was closed behind me, I turned on the overhead light and sat down on the edge of the bed. The letter in my hands was thick and heavy. I slid a finger underneath the flap, grateful that it hadn't been fully sealed.

"*Dear Jada,*" it began. "*So many thoughts have been rushing around in my head since last night that it's hard to know where to begin. Seeing you again was so unexpected that I'm still having trouble believing it really happened. I'm sorry for all the unfair accusations and insensitive remarks. The idea that you didn't care enough to wait for my return—even though I should have included you in my plans—has been festering since the day I found a picture of Greg Kelly in one of the university yearbooks. I've known hundreds of guys just like him—charming, charismatic playboys who took advantage of every girl they met. I couldn't believe you had fallen for his good looks, inflated ego and massive amounts of family money that he lavished around like penny candy.*"

I stopped reading long enough for my heart to quit thumping quite so fast. I didn't need another lecture on the foibles of my youth. I had paid an enormous price for not wanting to be alone.

"*It's still hard for me to accept the fact that we were both too stubborn, or scared, to make a simple call or even send a quick text when it might have made a real difference in both our lives. So much of what you alluded to about my character made me realize that I wasn't all that different from the guy you married—only minus the money and fancy toys. I was afraid that settling down would destroy my career, especially after we signed that first contract. I needed the girls to believe in the mystique we were trying to sell so they would keep coming to the dances and concerts. The adulation I felt kept me on a perpetual high until most everyone in the group decided that chasing some mostly-elusive dream wasn't worth losing their girlfriends or family over. We were all indulging in activities we shouldn't from excessive drinking to one-night stands, but we never got involved with drugs. You have to believe that.*

"*My life was filled with all the things I thought I wanted—passion, excitement, travel, lavish praise and beautiful women coming on to me everywhere I went. I was afraid to give any of it up, but our music didn't produce the revenue the investors wanted so the out of town gigs became less frequent. I thought about striking out on my own, but I was nearly thirty-five—well passed the age of acting like some over-sexed teenager. I came back to Bentley for good two years ago when I was offered tenure as a German professor. I teach a full class-load and do occasional engagements in the evening. My life is pretty much routine and boring like that of any other man my age, but it seems to suit me. The only thing missing is having someone to share the ups and downs with.*

"I'm not telling you any of this to garner sympathy because you've made such a success of your life, and I haven't. I'm happy for you and proud too. I always knew you could do anything you set your mind to. I'm just sorry I was too immature to see what I had before I lost it."

I stopped reading again and looked into the dark recesses of the room with its highly-polished log walls, gingham curtains and rustic prints hanging suspended just above my head. Shadows seemed to be coming out of the woodwork—moving spasmodically back and forth as if they had something disturbing to say.

So far, Brett's letter had given me a great deal to think about—especially when it came to the number of women he had slept with and why. But I was no longer that wide-eyed innocent who believed in love at first sight and fairytale endings. I was an adult woman who had seen more of life than I wanted to. If Brett wanted my trust now, he would have to earn it.

I picked up my reading where I had left off.

"I know what you're thinking, J. Anyone can give lip service, but it's a little harder to walk the path of true change. I'm not saying that I have all the answers I was looking for yet. I'm definitely a work in progress, but I charted a different course knowing I might never see you again. A guy should have to work for what he wants. Anything that comes too easily is fluff. That's why I moved back into my old loft and put what money I had left in the bank. I wanted to believe that true love would eventually find me. And when it did, I wanted to have something of value to offer.

"Treating you the way I did is inexcusable, even though I knew you dated different guys while you were at Bentley. I would see you with them on campus but never said anything because I didn't want you to know I was jealous. Maybe that's why it never seemed so wrong for me to chase other girls. After all, I had been doing it for nearly two decades before I ever saw your face. But with advancing age, a certain amount of wisdom

has finally surfaced. I wouldn't go back to being young again for all the money in the world, but I do wish I had been a little smarter.

"You were the cutest girl I had ever seen—not much more than a baby really—so I figured I still had plenty of time to play the flirting game when I should have been building a firmer foundation."

"Nice to know," I said aloud as I turned another page. "But I am no longer that baby who sees life the way I wish it could be, and Heavenly Father didn't send me here to be a fashion designer any more than he sent you here to be a singer. He had much bigger things in mind for both of us, and we obviously failed him."

But instead of continuing with that line of thought, I started reading again.

"I never meant to betray you or anyone else. I was weak and bought into my own idea of what a singer's life should be like. But after some dismal years of self-reflection, I now know what I really want, and it's not so different from what we once talked about. You were my ideal woman— the one I always wanted to marry—but you scared the hell out of me. I know we don't have much time to get reacquainted since we're both busy with classes during the day and most of my nights have been booked in advance. (It's easier to keep busy than being left with time to rehash the past.) But I don't want to leave so many things unsaid. That was always our biggest problem, putting the serious discussions aside for a more convenient time. I'm doing a gig at the student union building again tonight and hope you'll come because there is something else you should know that might help you see me in a little better light. Brett."

Critic messages put my nerves on edge. That's why deciding if I should go or spend a few minutes with Professor Price and Annabelle before turning out the lights and trying to sleep was so hard. I didn't want to give up on life, but I didn't relish the idea of having mine turned into rubble again either. Even if we decided to give our relationship another chance, it didn't mean things would turn out any better than they had the first time.

I had finished taking a shower before making up my mind. Brett was offering me an olive branch of friendship, and I would be a fool not to take. If nothing more, it might offer the closure I so desperately needed. So I redid my makeup and curled my hair. Then I put on another dress that made me feel both attractive and confident. I was on my way down the stairs in stiletto heels before I realized that I had to come up with something believable that would keep Annabelle or Professor Price from asking any pointed questions.

They were playing a less-than riveting game of Bingo with all the other guest presenters when I walked into the assembly room where all of our meetings were held and our meals eaten. An assortment of prizes sat on a nearby table—some of them quite good. I felt a moment of guilt before approaching them.

"I take it you won't be joining us," Annabelle said, looking up from the card sitting on the table in front of her. Round, plastic markers were piled everywhere, and the host was calling out a new number.

"I'm sorry, but something has come up."

"From the way you're dressed, I'm assuming it has nothing to do with your students."

"It doesn't," I replied, trying to my face as blank as possible so she wouldn't be able to read anything into what I was about to say. "An old friend would like to see me, and we'll be in a very public place."

"Then I won't press," she responded. "I trust that you know what you're doing and won't put yourself in another bad situation."

"I won't," I promised, showing her the keys in my hand. "I'm taking the van."

"Then Russell and I won't have to come out looking for you. I'll check your room around midnight to make sure you've made it back."

She was treating me like a child, but in an odd sort of way I found it almost comforting. It had been a long time since anyone had worried about me.

"I'll be there as close to the bewitching hour as possible, but don't fret if I'm a few minutes late. The function we'll be at won't be over until then."

"And sometimes goodnights take time," she responded as a becoming blush rose to her cheeks.

I was happy for her. I just hoped my own evening was half as pleasant as the one she appeared to be having. Professor Price didn't speak to me, but I noticed the look on his face when he glanced in Annabelle's direction. He was definitely a man who knew what was good for him.

The big, drafty van was the last thing I wanted to drive, but I recognized the danger in crossing the campus alone. So I backed out of the parking place and made my way towards the center of campus. It was almost ten, and I was afraid Brett may have decided I was standing him up, but circumstances precluded me leaving any earlier. I hoped he would understand.

A disco ball was sending tiny fragments of light dancing across the ballroom floor when I got there. I was suddenly worried that I might see T.R. and have to explain my rude behavior from the night before. But any conversation with him would have to wait until Brett knew I was there. He was standing in front of the band, microphone in hand, and his his face lit up when he saw me walking towards him.

I returned the smile. It hardly seemed possible that close to eight years had elapsed since we had been in this room together—except for last night—and that didn't count because we had both been caught off guard and reacted quite badly. He started to speak the moment my feet quit moving.

"Ladies and gentlemen. We hope you're ready for the second half of the dance. If you have any requests just let us know, and we'll see what we can do. But before we go any further, there's a very special lady in the audience. Someone I love dearly . . . ."

My temperature must have elevated ten degrees in less than a second, and perspiration broke out on my forehead as eyes began scanning the room. But Brett went right on speaking.

"The sad part is that I've never had the nerve to tell her so in public until now. That's why I'm dedicating this song to her. It's an old one by Jack Wagoner that I'm sure few of you will recognize, but it expresses better than I ever could just how much she still means to me."

I knew the song he was referring to by heart. I had let the words wash over me like a warm, comforting blanket each time I heard it on the oldies station I listened to on the radio while driving to and from work.

"Hello, love, it's been way too long since I realized that you're the most important thing in my life. I've got a need to tell you I know that I was wrong; show you how I feel about what's going on. I don't know what to say, except I loved that girl so much but I didn't show it. Started spreading myself too thin, fooled around, thought she didn't no it. Such childish

games I played; I fooled her with my touch, but time has taught me so much. I'm old enough to say, I was too young but that's no excuse, I had too much too soon; I wanted more room to please my restless youth . . . ."

Each syllable pounded in my heart. I had dreamed these words endlessly as I thought about the possibility of meeting Brett again. Couples were moving about on the dance floor. His rendition of such a powerful love ballad had no doubt sent everyone into a world known only to lovers.

I was unable to move until the song ended. A round of applause echoed in the room as Brett bowed his head and stepped backwards. In less time than it took for me to reagin my bearings, his foot was lightly tapping on the floor. He had his saxophone in his hands as the drummer beat out the rhythm to their next number.

"That girl he sang to is one lucky lady," someone standing close to me said. "I've dreamed of him acknowledging my presence since I first heard the Sound Column play. He may be older, but he's still the sexiest guy I've ever seen."

I moved away from the girl who was looking at the man I still loved with so much lust that I suddenly understood why Brett had never been able to commit to me—or anyone else—apparently. Each year brought a new crop of beautiful and desirable young women to the university, and he could have his pick. That's just how powerful his stage presence was.

But when I found a new place to stand at the edge of the crowd and looked back at the band, Brett was nowhere in sight.

"Where did you go?" I whispered as my eyes began scanning the room. I was used to him disappearing but not in the middle of a performance. And then I felt the air move behind me.

"Well, my love," a soft voice said. "What did you think of my surprise?"

The man I had never really forgotten was standing so close that I knew he could hear my heart thumping. "I think you nearly scared the living daylights out of me. Why did you sneak up on me?"

His arms found their way around my waist. "I didn't do any sneaking, J. You were lost in your own thoughts again."

"I guess we all have our issues," I replied. "Thank you for inviting me. That song brought back a lot of memories. It was always one of my favorites."

"That why I chose it, but you had me scared. I was beginning to think what I had written had driven you away for good. I can sing about what I feel, but I'm not very good at expressing it in words."

"I know what you mean," I said, turning in his arms so I could see his face. Life had always seemed simple when we were together. It was all the days, weeks and months when we were apart that caused all the problems. "I guess that's why we never got together. We were both too afraid of being hurt, or missing out on something, to express how we really felt inside."

"Not you," he responded. "You're the most together girl I've ever met."

I was suddenly aware that more than a few people were watching us. I had never known Brett to leave the stage during a performance before, but he didn't seem to be the least bit uncomfortable. "I had to be that way. There was nothing to fall back on if I didn't make it."

"Well, you certainly don't have to worry about that now. I did a little sleuthing between classes. You've made quite a name for yourself in the fashion industry. By the way, you look incredible tonight."

"You don't have to say that," was my inane response.

"Yes, I do. I've been remiss about a lot of things in the past, but it's impossible to miss what a knockout you are, and always have been. I can't believe what a fool I've been."

"No more talk about unpleasantries. I didn't get dressed up after a long day with students for that."

"In that case, perhaps I could interest you in a dance, Miss Sloan? That's really my reason for leaving the stage."

I covered my mouth to keep from crying out. Miss Sloan was what he had called me for over a year after our unfortunate meeting. I had been such a nerd, besides being young and inexperienced, but he had never given up on me.

"You could, Mr. Fowler, but don't you have to be back on stage?"

"I think the rest of the band can handle it for a few numbers. I would like to spend some time with my lady."

His term of endearment cheered my heart as he took my hand and led me to the middle of the floor. It was a slow dance, and when he swept me into his arms I could feel many of the old emotions return. I knew it was just the ambiance and the need to feel important to someone again but decided that for just one night I would allow my life to be ruled by more than just my head. So I carelessly threw my arms around his neck and rested my head on his shoulder.

With all the pairs of eyes watching us, I should have been appalled at my behavior. I was twenty-nine—too old for bear-hugging around a group of kids—but I simply didn't care. No one in the room knew who I was, and even if they did, I would be back in my own element come Sunday or Monday morning. It was Wednesday night, and I had little more than seventy-two hours to see if the past was really gone forever.

"I asked you before, but I guess you didn't hear," Brett whispered in my ear, sending chills up and down my spine. "What did you think of my surprise? I thought hearing our song might arouse some of the better memories we shared."

"It was perfect. Do you still mean all the things you sang about?"

"I do and more. I've done nothing but think about you and me being together since last night. I can't believe I allowed you to disappear without a fight. Greg must have far more issues than anyone at Bentley knew about, or he would have moved heaven and earth to keep you by his side."

"Our relationship was complicated. We barely knew each and got married on a whim. I knew I was making a mistake when we stood before the justice of the peace, but I couldn't exactly stay here after graduation on the slim chance that I might see you again. All the months I waited to hear from you seemed to be proof enough that you really had moved on with someone else."

"You do believe that wasn't the truth now, don't you?"

"I've had moments of doubt, but trust has to start somewhere. Thank you for being so honest with me in your letter."

"I knew I had to start somewhere, but I'm sure you have questions. It wasn't easy admitting that I had willingly given in to so many temptations. And despite what the supposed professionals say, it's not nearly as easy to change course as they would have one believe."

"No, it's not," I responded while glancing up at his profile. "I spent years denying my feelings for you simply because I couldn't endure more pain. It never dawned on me that my actions would have the slightest effect on you since your life seemed glamorous, fulfilling and exciting without me. In all honesty, I was only trying to salvage what I could of my heart."

"I know I was a jerk, J. But when I came back and found out you were not only gone but married, I felt like I had been gut-kicked so hard I wasn't sure I would ever recover. I had never been dumped before. I actually came to your front door hoping to work things out, but your trustworthy roommate told me to get lost."

"She really said that?" I asked, pulling far enough away from him that I could see his face. His eyes would let me know if he was telling the truth.

"I think her exact words were *get the hell out of here. Jada's gone. She married a guy who really cares about her and isn't crying all the time like she did when you were hanging around the fringes of her life.* When I asked her where you'd gone, she slammed the door in my face. Since I didn't know any of your other friends I was left with few recourses, other than going home and licking my wounds. Did I really make you cry?"

"Do you want the polite answer or the truth?"

"There's a difference?"

"Sure! If I tell you I cried all the time wondering what I kept doing to drive you away, it could make matters worse."

"I highly doubt that. No relationship—good or bad—is entirely one-sided. If I made you feel unimportant it was only because I was used to girls throwing themselves at me. You never did that."

"Maybe I didn't know how."

"I get that now, but I needed you to fight for us since I was too big a coward to do it myself."

"Doing that was always in the back of my mind. I would come to every dance filled with a kind of expectancy that was terrifying to a country girl who had dated very little during high school. I could envision myself standing right in front of the microphone with all the other girls, clinging desperately to the belief that your eyes would somehow meet mine and you would know that I was the only girl you could ever truly love."

"So why didn't you do it? You were almost always too far away to be seen unless the lights were turned up. I seldom did anything more than smile into the darkness since the lights were so blinding."

"I remember you telling me how hot they were."

"Is that your way of avoiding another one of my questions?"

My lips slid into a smile. "Probably! I had never met a guy before who could make me feel all gooey inside, and I didn't want to be seen as just another groupie. Besides, I've never been any good at flirting, and I'm not exactly the kind of girl guys pick out in a crowd."

"That belief is only in your head, J. Guys noticed you! I watched them watching you. I don't think you ever understood how truly innocent and incredible you were."

"Were?" I asked with amusement.

"And still are," he said, swinging us around in a circle. "You haven't changed that much, even if you are a big-time clothing designer whose brilliance can light up any runway. I was literally blown away by some of the reports and videos I saw about your work on the Internet today."

"Sweet-talker," I told him. "Don't you know it isn't wise to believe everything you see or hear."

"I'm just telling it like it is," he responded. "You've made a real success of your life. My accomplishments pale in comparison to yours. I know you feel bad about your marriage, but I still bet I come out on top in the regrets department. I've never even given what I thought might be love a real chance."

"Don't sell yourself short, Brett. Everyone has regrets. I hate thinking about all the time and tears I've wasted over stupid pride and unfulfilled expectations."

The music came to an end and Brett placed a kiss on my ear. "Will you wait until I'm finished so I can take you home?"

"I'll wait," I said.

"And you won't go running off with some other guy if I'm detained?"

"Why would I do that?" I asked as the lines between my eyes deepened. "Besides, no one here is going to want to dance with an older woman who was brought here to lecture?"

"That's not true and you know it. You seem to have gotten underneath T.R. Baker's skin. I watched him run out of the ballroom right after you did. He was obviously a man on a mission since he didn't come back."

"He's just a boy," I replied, unable to deny his suspicions.

"He's a man, Jada, and knows a good woman when he sees one. I'm surprised he's not here tonight to give me some competition."

"We're just friends. I met him on my way through the campus gate on Sunday evening. He told me how to get to the cottage."

"And he just happened to show up here last night."

"I didn't ask him why he came. I wouldn't have been here myself if Annabelle Little hadn't needed my help in getting better acquainted with Professor Price. I was perfectly content confining myself to my room."

"You would have left Bentley without even trying to find me?" He sounded more than a little surprised.

"That was the original plan. I couldn't see dredging up more heartache."

"I hope I'm starting to convince you that fate has other ideas, but I really need to get back on the stage. I've never done anything like this before."

"Then go," I said. "Even if T.R. shows up, he knows I'm not into him."

Brett bent down and placed a kiss on my forehead. "All of my songs will be for you. Just remember that if any handsome, young man comes your way."

I knew that few eyes were looking in a different direction when he left my side. But for the first time ever I didn't care that I was the center of attention. I wanted to tell anyone who would listen that I was falling in love with the same man for a second time. I crossed the dance floor and climbed the stairs to the refreshment area where I had sat with Annabelle and Professor Price the night before. After selecting a table where I would have a clear view of the stage, I sat down to wait for my special knight to carry me safely home.

Brett was halfway through another song when I heard footsteps on the stairs. I turned my head in time to see Amber Bills from my class step onto the balcony. The jubilant look on her face let me know that she had seen at least part of what had transpired on the dance floor.

"I thought that was you, Miss Sloan," she said, plopping down on the stool beside me. "Why didn't you tell us that you're the girl Professor Fowler has been pining for all these years?"

"What makes you say that?" I asked, wishing she wasn't quite so bold. I might want to tell someone how I felt but a student might not be the best person to confide in. Besides, I had no idea what was going to happen beyond this moment.

"Because he's dedicated that song to the girl he let get away at every dance I've been to. I thought it was just a ploy to keep all the coeds who congregate in front of the stage and follow him from class to class from throwing themselves at him quite so brazenly. He might be older, but he's still a hunk."

"That he is, but it's been a long time since we've seen each other," I said with a heavy sigh. "Things didn't end that well for us."

"But he's never forgotten you. Were you really surprised when he said he loved you before singing one of the most romantic songs I've ever heard? What girl doesn't want to know that a guy feels that deeply about her? I know I was jealous out of mind until I saw the two of you together."

"Why would that make a difference?"

She laughed. "Don't be silly, Miss Sloan. I may fantasize about being with him like most every other girl on campus, but my boyfriend back home is the only guy I'll ever love. Besides, I like you and know you haven't had an easy life, despite your success. What you said about wanting a family still applies, doesn't it?"

"Yes, but wanting something doesn't mean it's automatically going to happen."

"But it could," she pressed. "I saw the way he was holding and talking to you. Men never allow themselves to get that close to a woman unless they want something more than a one-night stand."

"That may be, but he broke my heart once, and I'm not about to let it happen again. A song is just a song, however romantic it might be."

"Please don't let your past determine your future, Miss Sloan," Amber said, placing her hand over mine in what might be considered an inappropriate gesture since I was a visiting VIP. "I know things will work out if you want them to badly enough."

With that, she was gone, and I was left to enjoy the remainder of the evening alone. I waited where I was until the ballroom was nearly empty, and Brett and his band were securing their equipment. I had met several of them when I was a student but doubted they would remember me, even after his lavish introduction.

My heels made a loud, clicking sound as I walked across the ballroom floor, but I only paused long enough to let Brett know that I would wait for him outside the stage door. That was the exit he always used. It was close to his car, always well lighted and saved him from unwanted delays. He joined me only moments after I made my way around the corner of the building with my can of pepper spray. I was truly grateful that he hadn't kept me waiting because every unrecognizable sound made my heart race. I wasn't sure if it was fear that something unsavory might be lurking in the bushes or the sheer anticipation of being near him again.

I had pondered Amber's words about being the author of my own future as I listened to him sing more songs about love and longing. I knew I was taking another huge risk with my heart. But if I went home without seeing where things might lead, I would be in a truly desperate situation— too frustrated and scared to even think about the possibility of finding a worthwhile relationship again.

"Why didn't you stop long enough to say hi to the rest of the guys?" Brett asked after the door closed behind him. "I didn't want them believing you were some mirage."

"I'm sure they knew I wasn't, and I didn't want to interrupt should you feel the need to talk to someone who was still there."

He put his arm around my shoulders. "Those girls who hang around until I leave are part of my retirement plan. If I lose their support, I won't have an audience to play to."

"I get that," I said as he leaned against the side of a very nice car and pulled me close. I wasn't sure of the make or model, but I knew it was his. "I was just trying to give you the space you needed."

"There's no need for that anymore. The kids on campus are great, but I'm twice their age."

"You don't look it," I said.

Before responding, he lowered his head and allowed his lips to brush the side of my neck. The spasms of delight it brought made me feel lightheaded. Without ever crossing some well-defined boundaries, he seemed to intuitively know where the most sensitive parts of my body were.

That it came from years of experience in pleasing other women, I had no doubt, but tonight was about us.

I clung to him more forcefully than intended, not wanting the sensations to end. He seemed to enjoy my discomfort and applied a few more caresses before raising his face to mine.

"Was that a compliment?" he asked. "I'm not sure you've ever given me one before."

"Then I should have because you really are an amazing guy."

His eyes seemed to sparkle, as if he was entertaining many of the same desires I had—none of which were particularly wholesome.

"If we keep this up, I might not be able to control myself, J. I really am trying to be good since I don't want to drive you away again, but you're making that incredibly hard. Maybe we should head some place for a soda? I do my best to stay away from the hard stuff because I don't like what it does to my head."

"I've never experienced that kind of a buzz," I said without thinking.

The look he gave me was one of complete astonishment. "Are you telling me that you've never had so much as a single glass of the bubbly to celebrate one of your many accomplishments?"

I shook my head. "The opportunities for wanton behavior are endless, but that isn't my style. I kinda like being known as a teetotaler who has no desire to sleep her way to the top."

"But the speculation about your private life must be endless."

"I'm not some movie star, Brett, although I have designed costumes for the female leads in a motion picture or two. I can usually be found sitting in front of the drawing board with my head in the clouds somewhere."

"That doesn't sound like such a bad life to me, as long as it's what you want."

My heavy sigh was long and deliberate. "Life has been good to me in that area, but there has to be more to living than working all the time. I miss spending time with people I really care about."

"Me too," he said, kissing the top of my head. "That's why I don't want this night to end. My offer is still on the table about grabbing a soda in some quiet place where we can continue this conversation."

"I'm not sure there is such a place in this town, and it might not be a good idea anyway. I'm still running pretty high on adrenalin after hearing you sing our song, and I don't want to head down that same rabbit hole I did in college."

"We're not the same people, J. I'm tired of playing games and running from girl to girl because I can't make up my mind. We've been given another chance, but it's up to us to decide if we're going to take it."

"What makes you think things would be different this time?" I asked, taking a real risk and running one hand down the side of his face.

This moment underneath a blanket of stars was intoxicating, and I wanted nothing more than to kiss his lips with all the passion that was rushing so rapidly to the surface. But we were trying to recapture a time when neither of us was capable of making the best decisions, and there was great danger in that.

"I guess we can only hope that we've grown past our insecurities and fears," he said, placing his hand over mine. "We were both so young before —at least you were. I was old enough to know what I wanted, but emotionally I was still an adolescent boy with raging hormones. But the irony is that throughout all the years of trying to erase you from my mind, I've never been able to do it."

"And why is that?" I asked.

"Because my feelings for you have never changed. I still love you, and I would like to give us another chance."

I looked deep into his eyes to see if he was telling the truth. He didn't flinch which meant he was still adept at withholding the truth, or he no longer had anything to hide. But I would never know which it was if I walked away again. So I took a deep breath and smiled at him.

"I'm willing to give it a try. How about shaking on it?"

"Are you kidding?" he asked as I leaned back and extended my hand. "How about sealing it with a kiss?"

My reaction was automatic. "I can't do that."

I was in the most vulnerable place of my life, back with the man I had never quit loving and my desire to give my all to him was threatening to destroy everything I had tried so hard to protect.

He looked crestfallen, but with only three days left before heading home, I couldn't afford to lose control. It was several, long and agonizing moments before he spoke.

"You really have changed, J. The girl I once knew would never be so hurtful and blunt. Maybe I should have left things the way they ended last night, but I thought you were open to exploring possibilities. I'm sorry if I've offended you. That was never my intention."

"It's not that," I said, hoping I could undo some of the sting my words had inflicted. "I have to see for myself if we can really be honest with each other before anything gets physical. That may sound childish and immature to a man who has had many lovers, but I've only been fully intimate with one man—my husband—and that was a disastrous mistake. Is keeping it simple for now something you're even willing to consider?"

He didn't turn away as I suspected he might, but he didn't look any any happier either.

"I can play by any set of rules you make as long as you don't disappear again without telling me."

"I'm not going anywhere until after my classes are over."

"That doesn't give us much time. Couldn't you postpone your return trip for a few days?"

"I suppose that could be arranged since I don't have to be in my office to get most of my work done, but I really should be getting back to the cottage. Annabelle intends to check on me before turning out her lights. She was pretty upset over my behavior last night."

"Do you need a lift?" he asked. "No girl should be walking around campus alone until the rapist has been caught. You have heard about him?"

"That sad reality has been brought to my attention, but I'm not traveling by foot tonight. I have the van I rented in the front parking lot."

"Then I'll take you to it."

I didn't linger in his car as I so much wanted to do, and he didn't exert any undo pressure. He simply waited by the van door until I had my seatbelt secured and turned the key in the ignition. It was warm outside, so I rolled down the window while we said our final goodnight.

"I was hoping the evening would end a little differently," Brett admitted while closing his fingers over mine as they rested on the edge of the window frame. "But I see the wisdom in being cautious. I know my checkered past would give any girl cause for concern, but I really am a reformed, one-woman man. I want a wife and a family before I'm too old to enjoy the experience."

"So do I, only mine would be a husband and family. It's the only thing missing from my life, but I'm glad you understand why I need to take things slow."

"I'm trying, J. But you have to know that my body isn't cooperating. It wants what it obviously can't have right now. Would it be okay if I called you tomorrow?"

"That's what I was hoping you would say, but I have a new number."

"I figured as much since the old one wasn't working."

"You still had it?"

"Certainly did, not that I had the nerve to use if after your old roommate did such a number on me."

"I'm sorry she was so unpleasant, but she was the only one who seemed to know just how deep my feelings for you ran."

"And she was trying to protect you."

"Mostly from myself. We both claim to be victims of circumstances beyond our control, but the truth is that we were always free to make any decisions we wanted. We just made some very poor ones. At least I certainly did."

"Let's not get into that again, J. I want to move forward. I hope that doesn't sound too insensitive since I know you still have plenty of justifiable reservations."

"You're putting many of those to rest, but I really need to be going."

We exchanged numbers and I drove away. The temptation to keep up with the pleasant banter was intense, but I knew where my safety lay. For the time being, I would keep a respectable distance between us. When, or even if, our time for being together arose I wanted it to be as perfect as humanly possible.

I knocked on Annabelle's door to let her know I was back. She was already trying to sleep, but that was perfect for me. I didn't want to discuss my evening. I needed time to replay what had happened and decide where I wanted to go from here.

Chapter 6

I awoke to the sound of my cell phone ringing. It was five o'clock in the morning. Startled by being taken from the tantalizing dream I was having, I answered without checking to see who was calling.

"Hello, love," a voice I would never get tired of hearing said. "I'm sorry for calling so early, but I didn't want to inconvenience or miss you in case you needed to be out of the door early. I haven't been able to stop thinking about you since I got home."

"Same here," I responded as an extraordinary feeling of warmth swept over me. "Were you able to get any rest?"

"I would be lying if I said I had, but I'm not complaining. I haven't felt this invigorated for years."

"And I haven't heard a salutation that could make my heart race since you last said that to me."

"And you will hear it at least a million more times during our lifetime."

"Our life?" I questioned. "You make it sound so real."

"I have never been more certain of anything. We were meant to be together."

"That's how I feel too, Brett, but I still can't help being a little afraid. You know what they say about things being too good to be true."

"It's funny how no one has ever figured out who *they* really are. But in our case it doesn't matter, J. I believe in fate, karma or whatever other name it goes by. We would never have seen each other again if the universe didn't have alternate plans in mind for us. I'm thoroughly convinced that you would never have come back to Bentley by choice."

"Unfortunately, you're right about that. I only came because there wasn't time to find anyone else. My boss can be very persuasive when he wants something."

"So can you," Rick responded with just a hint of something I couldn't quite put my finger on in his voice. "That's why I came home last night and took a cold shower instead of pressuring you into going some place quiet with me. All the signs for wanting more were there in your beautiful eyes, but I know how you feel about reserving sex for marriage."

"You've always been able to seduce women without even trying, but I never wanted to be one of your conquests and still don't."

"I can see why you feel that way, especially after what I wrote, but I'm hardly the man you once knew. I'm ready for a lifetime commitment. No looking back, or around, anymore."

"You say that because nothing ever really happened between us so the excitement of conquest is still there."

"That's true," he admitted. "The chase is exhilarating and often mind-blowing—as is the act itself—but I'm ready for something more."

I swallowed back a lump of trepidation before responding. "Maybe you are, Brett, but long term commitments are hard, and I'm terrible at them."

"Only because you were with the wrong guy," was his cheerful reply. "I'm not saying we don't have a ton of baggage to work through, but nothing is impossible if we want it badly enough. Things are going to work out for us this time. I'm sure of it."

"You don't know how much I want to believe that. Last night was like a dream I never want to wake up from, but I've already spent nearly a decade trying to get over you. Doing it again would be impossible."

"You won't have to, J. I promise. How about instead of worrying about what's going to happen tomorrow, or even a week or a year from now, let's pretend we have all the time in the world to rediscover each other? That way the pressure will subside, and we'll be less likely to make any serious mistakes."

"Life is full of mistakes, Brett, and I'll only be here a few more days at best. How are we going to find time to see if what we feel now is strong enough to build on? Our schedules aren't exactly compatible."

"I'll take care of that."

"How?" I was wide-awake now. "You aren't planning on coming to my classroom, are you? My students have important projects to complete, and I may have to stay late the next couple of nights to see for myself what they're really capable of doing. My boss has given me license to offer one of them a paid internship after graduation. That's a lot of pressure since I don't want to pick the wrong person."

I was feeling almost sick to my stomach now. The last thing I needed was a total distraction when I had already managed to convince one of my students to switch careers.

Brett's laughter didn't ease my distress. "I hadn't thought of making a trip to your classroom, but it sounds like an idea with promise."

"You're not serious!" I exclaimed, sitting upright in bed.

"I could be, but unfortunately I'm leaving for the city in a few minutes. That's really why I called so early. We have a recording session at eight. It's just the background music for a commercial, but the pay is good. I was thinking we could grab a late lunch and see what happens from there. I've already asked one of my grad students to cover my classes for the rest of the day."

My lungs took in all the air they could. While I wanted to spend as much time as possible with Brett, he was right about both of us wanting more.

"Why don't you call when you get back, and I'll see where we're at. With so little time left, I need to be available to answer any questions."

"I can do that," he replied, but the disappointment in his voice was evident. "Do you realize that we have yet to see each other in the daylight?"

"Why is that a problem, unless you're afraid I turned into some man-eating monster when the sun comes up?" I asked.

"Never," he said. "From what I've seen, albeit only in the semi-dark, you're even more beautiful than you were as a student. Life's heartaches and struggles have given you a depth of understanding and self-awareness that is impossible for any man to miss. I'm just sorry you haven't experienced more personal joy."

"Would I be remiss if I said the same thing could apply to you?"

"Not at all. My inability to make a long-term commitment when it comes to the fairer sex is the basis for most of my unrest, but I am learning that God doesn't expect perfection from any of his children in this life. He's just interested in whether or not they're trying to live a better life. But it's too early to get into some theological or philosophical discussion, and I really don't have the time either. If lunch doesn't work for you today, how about tomorrow?"

"Tomorrow would be great," I said.

"Then I'll schedule it in, but there is one more thing. I don't have to work tonight. Is there a chance you could break away from your students for awhile."

"I think that could be arranged. What did you have in mind?"

"Nothing fancy, just a quiet dinner at my place. I've turned into a decent cook since you left."

"That's good because I've gotten worse. I hardly trust myself to boil water any more."

"You mean no more lasagna or fried pork chops and gravy?" Brett sounded disappointed.

"Afraid not! I wouldn't want to ruin your digestive system."

"I doubt that could happen, but tonight's my treat. And I promise there will be no hanky-panky unless we both decide the time is right."

"Good to know! Is there anything I can do to help?"

"Not a thing, except maybe drive yourself over in that big, white van you rented. I would come for you, but when I'm in the kitchen . . . . "

"Say no more. Just tell me when and where."

"You already know the place, but in case you've forgotten the address, it's 400 South, 560 East. How about seven-thirty?"

"I'll be there. I'm sure my students can live without me for a couple hours since they have my number. Good luck in the city. I hope it turns into a very profitable and fun day."

"The same for you, J. I know you have a lot riding on this. Just don't forget that I love you."

It was the second time Brett had said that he loved me, and it was impossible to keep that thought from running through my head as I made preparations for the day. However, I still needed to be careful with my heart. Words were easy to say, but it took a lot of hard work to make them count. I knew that because he had said the same thing that night in the grotto before walking right out of my life.

I locked the door to my room much earlier than intended. It was just a few minutes after six, but instead of joining my colleagues for breakfast I needed to be in morning sun where I could literally bask in the warmth of still being loved by the only man who had ever held the key to my heart.

"Where are you off to in such a hurry?" Annabelle asked I hurried down the stairs with a surprisingly light bounce to my step. She was standing in the lobby and appeared to be waiting for someone.

"I just felt like getting an early start."

"Did you now," she replied, giving me a look that made me feel much like a child who had a huge secret to hide. "You look more like a woman who had an exceptionally good night. I could tell that you didn't feel much like sharing when you came in. That's why I didn't push for details, but it's morning now. Why don't you join Russell and me for breakfast? He should be down any moment."

I looked at her in complete surprise. What had happened to the self-effacing, browbeaten woman who had come to my room seeking assistance in having a simple conversation with a man she found attractive? While I found her offer of friendship refreshing after the cutthroat world I was used to, I didn't want to share what I was feeling prematurely. Lady luck was a fickle being. She could bring despair as easily as jubilation.

"I'm afraid breakfast is out of the question since I need to be in the classroom by seven."

"So you really don't feel like talking about your evening?"

I put my hand on her shoulder. She was still wearing her hair in a bun at the base of her neck, but it appeared she had gone shopping. I could see a pink, silk blouse underneath her dark, tailored suit jacket.

"I don't mean to sound evasive, Annabelle. I saw my old friend like I said, but he was busy with a prearranged engagement. I was mainly there to watch. It was nothing earth-shattering like what is happening between you and Professor Price. There's a sparkle in your eyes that wasn't there the night we met."

"So it really shows?" she asked, almost apologetically.

"Of course it does, and I couldn't be more thrilled. Have you talked about how you feel?"

Annabelle looked shyly at the floor, but people often fell in love in a very short amount of time. That's exactly how it had happened with Brett and me, only we had been too caught up in other things to acknowledge it.

"We have. In fact, we're going directly from here to his home in Texas. He wants me to meet his mother."

"Wow!" I said as the tears brimmed in my eyes. "That sounds serious."

"Oh, I hope so, but I didn't mean to cause you any distress since you've been so very kind to me."

"You haven't, and I couldn't be happier for you."

"It truly is a miracle," she responded. "Russell is the first man who has ever really looked at me. Most men pretend that I'm nothing more than a fixture in the room who can take whatever is dished out."

"Then it's about time you found someone who appreciates what you have to offer to more than just the scientific community. You really are a wonderful person."

Annabelle smiled. "That's what Russell told me last night. He thinks I'm wonderful too."

"Then there's no room left for doubt since two people noticed it at the same time."

"That's only because you both like me. I'm still a mouse. I always have been and always will be. But it doesn't matter anymore because Russell likes me just the way I am."

"Then I'm thrilled for both of you. Relationships never work out when people pretend to be something they're not."

"But I want you to be just as happy as I am. I know that young man at the party wasn't what you were looking for or you would never have run away from him. I still don't know why that happened or where you went."

"None of that is important now."

"It is to me. I was hoping your date last night would turn into something equally as glorious as what Russell and I have found."

"Do I hear wedding bells?" I asked, hoping my question would divert her from asking anything more about me. If things went well with Brett tonight, I might be ready to admit at least a portion of what I was feeling.

"Maybe," she said with another girlish smile. "I'm too old to live in sin."

Her statement shocked me, but it was still nice to know that I wasn't the only person on earth who still believed that sex should be saved for marriage.

"I didn't mean to say that," she replied while my thoughts continued to roam elsewhere. "I'm not in the habit of being vocal about such things."

"There's no reason to apologize. I feel the same way. I hope you'll invite me to the wedding since I do have a vested interest."

"You'll be the first name on our list. Without your help, I would never have had the courage to approach him in such a personal way. He's such an accomplished man."

"Never doubt your own achievements, Annabelle," I responded, hugging the once timid woman who had been transformed into a swan. "Professor Price had his eyes set on you from the very beginning. But I really have to be going. I promise we'll talk again before Friday."

"I hope so," she said, returning my hug. "You're probably the only real friend I've ever had until Russell."

"That doesn't seem possible, but thank you," I said before hurrying away.

I wanted to give all my students the attention and help they deserved since that was what I had been commissioned to do. But I already had a pretty good idea which of them had the personality, willpower and drive to succeed. They were the ones who were constantly sketching, even during my lectures, and were non-committal when asked to give the rest of the class a preview of what they were working on. They were also the ones who picked out the fabric and trim they planned to use almost the moment it was taken out of the box and left the classroom early each day so no one could watch their progress.

That's why I realized by the time the day was half over that my constant supervision was doing more harm than good for the ones who were fully committed to having a career. They had learned the basics of design and clothing construction in their university classes, and I had given them an idea of what they could expect when they graduated. What they wanted now was time to complete the assigned project without unnecessary interruptions and then get an honest appraisal about the quality and uniqueness of their design.

Without a doubt, that was the part of my assignment I truly dreaded. There was often a fine line between giving constructive criticism and destroying someone's dream, but giving false hope was worse because it could lead to a shattered life. So when five o'clock rolled around, I got up from the desk where I had been sitting most of the afternoon and asked if anyone needed my assistance for the next few hours.

I waited to see if any hands went up. When they didn't, I figured I was good to go. The building would be open until the security guard made his last round, but I suspected that few would take advantage of it.

Amber followed me out of the classroom. I was worried about her. She had spent most of the afternoon in what appeared to be a daze while everyone else was scurrying around like mice in a maze.

"Do you ever feel like packing it all in and going some place where no one will ever find you, Miss Sloan?"

"Who doesn't?" I responded as we walked from the air-conditioned building into the warmth of the late afternoon sun. "I have often contemplated leaving San Francisco, but there is no other place for me to go, unless it's to another big city."

"But there could be if you were looking for a change. Mrs. Adams, the department chair who keeps poking her head in and out of the classroom, is leaving at the end of the summer. I'm sure the university would give you her job. You're a wonderful teacher."

"Thank you, Amber, but no one has mentioned an upcoming vacancy to me. Besides, I don't have the credentials."

"That's stupid! Most of the professors in this department just kept going to school until they had the right number of credits and could write and defend some lengthy dissertation."

"I think it's a little more complicated than that."

"Maybe, but not much. I guess asking someone like you to leave a glamorous and successful career to come to a small university like Bentley without a very compelling reason is a bit of a stretch."

"Not if you think I really have one?"

"Oh, I know you do. And like you told us on Monday, personal happiness is more important than money and fame. I'm sure Professor Fowler would agree. I could sit in one of your classes forever because you're not just a textbook teacher. You know what kind of life we're only hoping to have from experience, and you're not afraid to tell us the truth."

"I'm not sure that's a good qualification for a staff position. Some of my experiences may have clouded my better judgment."

"But you make it so real. Why not let students know what they're up against so they can make a more informed decision? I love studying design, but I'm not sure it's a lifestyle I can live with. From what you've said, people expect you to wine and dine them to get new accounts, and there are those who expect a whole lot more. I could never do anything like that."

"Nor could I, Amber, but we're still allowed to make our own decisions."

"Unless they're made for us," she responded. "I don't know how you could let someone else take credit for your designs."

"It's all part of the process. But I never even tried to take my career to the next level where what I created could be put on the runways in cities like Paris or Rome. I'm much too conservative, and there is a reason stick-figure models are used in what is considered high fashion. The average woman could never pull off the skimpy and outlandish ensembles that make the covers of the most coveted magazines, even if she could afford them. My goal is to help ordinary women feel good about themselves."

"That's how I feel, but jobs like that have to be scarce."

"They are, but no more so than opportunities in any specialized field. I had to make a go of it because there was no one I could turn to if I got into trouble. But once again, I was lucky because *Wide World of Design* caters to the average man or woman on the street. My boss even accepts my rather out-of-fashion personal beliefs and standards. In a way, I think he even admires them. He knows he doesn't have to worry about me stabbing him in the back, or becoming involved in a compromising situation that makes him look bad or costs him any revenue."

"Do you mind if I tell you something very personal?" Amber asked, effectively changing the subject

"Not at all, if you feel like I'm the person you should confide in."

"You're the only one I dare confide in. My family has always believed I was crazy to pursue a career that would take me so far away from home."

"That's understandable. I'm sure mine would have felt the same way if they had been alive, or even in a position to say anything about it."

It was hard not thinking about my mother who was still living within the confines of the mental institution, or my brother who didn't even bother to contact me on holidays any longer. But at least my grandmother had taken me in so I wouldn't end up in some orphanage or group home. My difficulties had made me strong in some ways, but in others, they had been crippling.

"Maybe," she replied as we made our way past the science building. "But I'm beginning to think they might be right. Do you remember me telling you about my boyfriend last night?"

When I nodded, she continued.

"He's a country boy who will take over his father's ranch some day. I really love him, and it's not such a bad way to live. But I have always wanted more than raising alfalfa and babies. I want to use all the talents I've been given."

"That's not such an unreasonable desire, and making the right career choice can be a challenge."

"Especially now that he's asked me to marry him. I always thought I would know what I wanted when the time came. But I'll be graduating in December, and he expects my answer in time to make plans for a winter wedding. I know he won't wait forever, but I'm just not sure I'll be really happy spending the rest of my life in Iowa."

The air suddenly felt so heavy I could hardly breath.

"Are you all right, Miss Sloan?" she asked. "You look kinda pale."

"I'm fine. You just reminded me that people need to take advantage of opportunities when they come. Do you really want to know what I think?"

"I wouldn't have asked if I didn't."

"Then I'll give it to you straight. If you really love this boy, don't shut him out of your life because simply you're afraid. Things have a way of working out, and I've come to the bitter conclusion that it isn't a specific occupation that makes life worth living. It's who you share your life with that really matters."

"Did you walk away from Professor Fowler?"

Her question was a more than presumptuous for a student, but it still deserved an answer. "We walked away from each other and have both lived to regret it."

"But he made it sound like none of the magic was gone last night when he sang that song to you."

"The feelings may still be there, but sometimes too much water has gone under the proverbial bridge to make a new start realistic."

Amber lowered her head. "I'm sorry, Miss Sloan. I just thought the gesture was romantic."

"It was! But building a relationship that works for a lifetime is hard, and statistics prove that over half of the most well-intentioned marriages fail. That's why I can't tell you what to do. You're the only one who knows if what you have is worth fighting for."

Amber smiled for the first time that day. "I think I'll call Austin as soon as I get to somewhere quiet. He really is too terrific to lose."

"Sounds like you've decided on wedding bells."

"I guess I have. If nothing more, I can always make clothes for my family. They'll be the best dressed people in the county."

"I'm sure they'll appreciate your expertise, but you don't have to give up all your professional dreams."

She gave me a confused look. "Have you ever been to Iowa, Miss Sloan? All we have are rolling fields and small towns. No one is interested in fashion when all they wear are jeans."

"I think you might be surprised. I've read half a dozen accounts of women opening boutiques in very unlikely places and becoming very successful entrepreneurs. One of them even started out making custom-designed prom dresses on her sewing machine at home. She now submits her designs to a big fashion house and gets paid handsomely without ever setting foot in a city."

"Are you trying to tell me that where there's a will there's always a way?"

"Not exactly, but I do believe dreams can be fulfilled in a number of ways. Sometimes we just have to get out of the way so someone else can move a few mountains for us."

"Is that what you're hoping will happen with Professor Fowler?" she asked. "I feel silly calling him by his first name in front of you, even though all the girls on campus call him Brett."

"I'm sure he doesn't mind the informality outside of the classroom, but I really have to be going. I'm actually having dinner at his place. He's doing the cooking."

"How exciting. I'll be rooting for both of you. We need you here at Bentley, and I've never seen Professor Fowler look happier than he did last night."

"In that case, I'll tell you how it goes, provided you promise me something in return," I replied, not wanting my private life, or his, broadcast around campus.

"Anything, Miss Sloan. I just want you to be as happy as I am."

"Then don't tell anyone what you know. If I was even to look into the job you mentioned, my reputation would have to be above reproach."

"My lips are sealed. That's why I don't talk about Austin, unless it's with someone I trust. What we have is special, and I don't want anyone making light of it."

"I'm with you on that. Is there anything I can help you with before I head back to the cottage to change? No one else seems to need my assistance."

"That's because you covered everything so well. All any of us need now is time to work. And I know exactly what I'm going to finish for you to look at. I was always afraid it would be too simple and unimaginative for a class project, but for some reason it seems right for this."

"Simplicity is the bread and butter of the fashion world," I replied. "All that fluff and extravagance never really sells. It just makes a few headlines."

She walked away, and I continued on down the vine-covered pathway that led to Whitman Cottage. Maybe teaching wouldn't be such a bad idea. Having plenty of money was great—and I certainly enjoyed the things I had been able to buy—but not one of them could take away the pain in my heart.

I needed love desperately, and if I didn't have a family soon it might be too late. It might already be that way after what I had been through, but I didn't want to think about my other great sorrow right now. I wanted to believe that miracles could still happen for someone like me.

Hurrying through the foyer on my way to the stairs made me feel like an outcast since I could hear happy voices coming from the assembly room where dinner was being served. But I didn't slow my steps. I would be eating with the man I loved, and Annabelle would forgive my lack of congeniality if I could tell her that she was not the only to find something truly special during her stay at Bentley.

Perhaps that was I dressed with such care for my evening with Brett. He hadn't tried to contact me all day. Several times I had reached for my phone to get in touch with him, but all the insecurities of my youth kept me from touching the screen where his name came up as the last person to make contact with me.

That thought brought tears to my eyes because I knew just how dispensable I was to everyone in the life I had made for myself in a city that never seemed to sleep. My boss hadn't checked to see how things were going, and my assistant had only sent a quick text or two when she needed an answer to a decision she didn't feel qualified to make on her own. I really could do my job remotely, except for the critical weeks right before a show. That gave me even more reason for contemplation after my rather bizarre conversation with Amber. Maybe taking my own advice about grabbing what truly meant the most to me wasn't be such a bad idea.

It wasn't long until I was locking my bedroom door, but I took the service elevator instead of the main stairs to the ground floor so I wouldn't run into anyone who might question where I was going. The looks I got from staff members when I stepped into the housekeeping department were bad enough, but I simply smiled apologetically as I located the outdoor exit and made my way quickly towards it. I had parked the van near the back of the building so no one would see me leave.

The clock on the dashboard of the van said it was almost seven-thirty when I pulled to the curb in front of Brett's attic apartment—one that he always referred to as a loft since there was plenty of light and the main living area was open and large. I felt as if I had literally stepped back in time as I crossed the small expanse of grass leading to the sidewalk where I had stood with his arms wrapped around me a number of times in the past.

Everything on the street where he lived looked exactly as I remembered it. The same houses and trees, the same dented garbage cans waiting for the trash truck and the same red door at the top of the outside staircase. I couldn't hold back a smile as I ran my hand across the wooden railing before taking the first step upwards. Maybe tonight I would have the courage to accept one of his much-wanted kisses.

But while that thought brought glorious possibilities, it filled me with a certain amount of anxiety and dread because I knew my reasons for coming were not as pristine and altruistic as I wanted to believe.

"Dear Father," I silently prayed as I stood on the landing before announcing my presence. "I don't know if what I'm doing is right. I certainly don't want to bring more confusion or heartache into my life, but I love Brett. I always have. I just wish I knew if a relationship with him stands the slightest chance of success. I'm tired of being alone but don't want to make another catastrophic mistake. I'm not sure my heart could take being broken again."

I opened my eyes when I had finished and filled my lungs with some of the sweet-smelling night air. For all its beauty, San Francisco could never compare to the stillness and peace of a small town where God's presence could so easily be felt.

"Anybody there?" I called out as I rapped on the door, still wondering if I was doing the right thing.

"Come on in. It's open," I heard Brett say.

The next moment, I was stepping into a pleasant and inviting room that faced west. The pink glow coming in though a bank of floor to ceiling windows gave it a surreal feeling. I had never imagined being in his home again. He was standing in front of the stove with his back to me.

"Something smells delicious," I said, trying to fill the awkward silence as I walked towards the kitchen area with its tall cupboards, stainless steel appliances and island where he could see outside while washing dishes. "You didn't open a bottle of Rao's Homemade Marinara Sauce did you?"

"Not on your life, young lady. This is one of my mother's secret recipes."

"How is she doing?" I asked. Giselle Fowler had been in poor health for as long as I had known Brett, but he had never invited me to go with him so I could meet her.

"She's doing okay for a woman who is seventy-plus years young. I haven't seen her for a few months, but I call every day or two just to make sure nothing has changed. Lupus is a nasty disease. I wouldn't wish it on my worst enemy."

"Nor would I. Why don't you go home more often? It's not that far."

"That's a question I ask myself quite often," he responded. "I'm too busy during the week to do it, and Saturdays are always chaotic. But I could make the trip easily enough on a Sunday afternoon. Maybe I'm just tired of her always quizzing me about the girl I let slip through my fingers. I'm thirty-seven, and she's pretty much given up on her baby boy adding to the family tree. Between them, my sisters have given her five grandchildren, but she still wants someone to carry on the family name."

"A regular *old maid*," I chided to hide the fact that his honest emotions were chipping away at the fortress I had built around my heart. "But I guess none of us are going to stay young forever."

He reduced the heat on the burner and turned to face me. "You seem to be doing quite well in that department. You're even more beautiful than I remember, J."

"And you're still a smooth-talker who can turn any girl's head," I replied. "I wish I had met your mother, but we never seemed to get around to it."

My own admission made me suddenly self-conscious, so I crossed the room to the window and looked down on the street below. Brett followed me.

"I wish we had taken the time to do a great many things, but while the past can't be altered, there is no reason we can't do better in the future. I know my mother still wants to meet you."

"How can you be so sure of that?" I asked.

"Because she still reminds me that if we had made that trip she would have convinced both of us us that we were better off together than we would ever be apart."

"That's quite an assumption to make."

"Not for my mother. She claims to be half-gypsy, even though our linage shows no such connection. I think she's just overly astute when it comes to her family. She told me from the time I was a small boy that I would never be happy with some flashy, self-centered girl who was always worried about what other people thought because the competition would be too great for either of us to handle. I needed someone with a level-head, strong values and the patience of Job because my impulsiveness, and lack of self-restraint, were not a qualities to be admired."

"Ouch! That must have hurt."

"Only because it was true. I was never satisfied with anything for long. Even new toys for Christmas were soon forgotten because someone else had something I thought looked better. Those undesirable traits carried over into adulthood. How many musicians do you know of who aren't full of themselves—always believing that their needs come before those of anyone else? I used to tell myself that playing the field was just part of the game I needed to master so true success would be mine, but the truth is, I wanted the attention. Hooking up with different girls gave me the high I so desired and kept me from taking illegal drugs."

I swallowed back some very disturbing thoughts and feelings before responding. "I'm not sure what you expect me to say after that admission."

"You don't have to say anything, J. What age hasn't resolved, in-depth sessions with a therapist has."

"Then why bring it up?"

"Because I need you trust me, and I know that has to be earned after all the shenanigans I've pulled in the past. You were never one who liked surprises."

"Still don't," I admitted.

"Then if there's anything else you need to know, ask it now. I want you to believe in me and know you still have reservations or you would have allowed me to kiss you last night."

"There were many reasons for me not wanting to move too swiftly, Brett, and all of them don't involve you. They don't even involve the lifestyle you've lived. I've spent the last eight years working my tail off to build a life where I can function without falling apart every time I have to deal with something unpleasant. If I let myself go, and we can't make it work, I could lose everything."

"Are you telling me that you've decided you don't even want to try?"

I shook my head. "I wouldn't be here if that was the case, but some of the scars you left me with run deep. I guess I never fully understood all the pressure you were under, or what drove you to act like you did."

"I was a very confused man back then. I had been around the world but was still afraid I might miss something."

"Have you done everything you wanted to do now?" I asked.

"Everything I wanted to do alone."

My hands were in his, and the tone of his voice let me know that he was serious, but I wasn't quite ready to succumb to his charms. There were still a few things he needed to know about me and telling him wouldn't be easy.

"Don't you need to check on the food?" I said as he tried to pull me into his arms. "Lunch was hours ago, and I'm starved."

His sigh was heavy, and I knew my evasiveness was getting old, but he had promised to give me the time I needed.

"Just give me five minutes," he said, making his way into the kitchen again.

He had indeed turned into a master chef. He had even learned how to set an attractive table. The sauce he served was divine and the French bread soft as a cloud on the inside and crisp to perfection on the outside. I ate every morsel of food on my plate—including a side salad—as light, cheerful banter about nothing of consequence filled the air. But when he asked if I was ready for dessert, I laughed.

"You really expect me to eat anything more? My plate is so clean you don't even have to wash it."

His look was filled with mirth.

"Not that I'm afraid you have anything contagious to spread, but I doubt anyone would consider that sanitary. I have a dishwasher. It's one of those modern conveniences no home should be without. Certainly you've heard of them."

"I have one myself, although I rarely use it. Most of my meals are eaten at my office, and all the takeout places in the area know exactly where to find me."

"That doesn't sound like the girl I used to know who was always cooking for everyone else. Your brownies and jelly rolls are practically legendary."

"Times change!" I responded as my eyes sought comfort in a centerpiece of freshly-cut flowers. "My life has revolved around work for so long that heating something up in the microwave is about as domestic as I have time to get."

"Does that mean you have a maid or a housekeeper?"

"Don't judge me, Brett Fowler. I've paid my dues. Lexie comes in once a week to make sure my place of residence hasn't become infested with things that either crawl or slither."

He involuntarily grimaced. "I didn't mean to imply that you had become a snob or a slob."

I leaned back in my chair and allowed a smile to form. It seemed like forever since I had enjoyed a pleasant evening when I wasn't by myself.

"You might not be too far off if you had," I reluctantly admitted. "I seem to have closed myself off from most everyone over the years. But that's my problem, not yours."

"I like to think of our problems as being shared. You used to feel like you could confide in me about most anything."

"That was a different time and place."

"Maybe, but some things never change—like my feelings for you."

I bristled as my smile faded. "You promised you wouldn't push."

Before responding, Brett reached across the table and took my hands. I felt gooseflesh cover my arms as our fingers intertwined.

"I'm trying very hard to do just that, but the time we have together is so limited. I wish I could capture each moment and hold it tight to my heart because I know there's a very real possibility that these few days may be all we ever have."

"There's no reason to believe that."

"Why not, J? You have yet to give me any indication that my feelings are more than one-sided."

"Because it's not fair," I responded as a frown formed, but I didn't pull my hands away from his as my head told me to do. "I told you how I felt when we were on the staircase, but I can't help having a few reservations.

It's not like we've had any contact the past few years, and we've already admitted that we're hardly the same people. Can't we just enjoy an evening together without having it turn into a battle of wills?"

"Is that what you really want?"

"Yes, Brett, it is. I don't want us to get ahead of ourselves and do something foolish just because we're afraid time is running out. If what we have is real and right, it will still be that way when all the heady emotions have settled enough for us to think straight. I need to take things slow so I won't become overwhelmed and run again. Unlike you, I haven't spent much time exploring my feelings. I've been burying them as deep as I could just to survive in a very challenging world."

"I didn't mean to minimize what you've been through. I just don't want to lose you again. I've felt more alive the past two days than I have in the past two years."

"Me too," I said as the pressure of his fingers increased. "And thank you for inviting me into your home for such a sumptuous meal. Next time I want to eat something that doesn't come from a takeout box I'll know exactly where to come."

"Just promise that you won't run away again."

I forced myself to really look at him for the first time that evening. "I don't want to be distant and cold, Brett. I've dreamed every way possible of seeing you again, but I never dared imagine we would be spending any time under this roof. There are so many memories here."

"They aren't all bad, are they?"

"No. That's just the problem. They were all good, and I'm afraid I might allow myself to slip into believing that we can recapture the past simply by willing it to be so, rather than dealing with our present reality."

"And just what do you think that realty is?"

"I'm not sure. But whatever it is, I hope that when all is said and done we will still be friends."

"I don't want to be just friends, J."

He released my hand and rose to his feet. "I need to put the leftovers in the fridge. Everything else can wait until morning."

The loss of physical contact left me feeling more abandoned than ever, and I wished I had it within me to throw every worry aside and literally take what I had wanted for so many years.

"Then I'll help you," I replied, reaching for my plate. But he stopped my hand in mid-air.

"You don't have to do that. You're my guest."

"Who's acting distant now?" I asked.

"I am," he responded. "I was really hoping that a few barriers would come down once we were alone together, but just the opposite seems to be happening. I'm not asking for a lifelong commitment, but I sure as hell hate feeling like I'm going to come out on the losing end again."

"The rest of our story has yet to be written," I countered. "I wish you could believe that."

"Then give me something that will help me feel like I haven't lost the entire war. Every time I say something personal you pull away."

His look was so intent that I couldn't meet it, so I looked down at the floor.

"You're right! My instincts for survival are in overdrive, but that's only because I know the power you still hold over me. If I was to give you what you want tonight, where's the guarantee that you wouldn't be over me come morning? I'm not exactly experienced in the art of lovemaking."

"Thank you for finally being honest," he responded. "While my track record with women leaves a lot to be desired, it doesn't mean I'm a totally lost cause. Why don't we leave the rest of dishes on the table and go into the living room where we can have a real talk, minus any expectations?"

"We can talk while we clean up," I said, not wanting to leave the security of the kitchen where I would have something to do with my hands, other than fight the desire to touch him.

"I want your undivided attention, J. What we still have to say to each other is important."

He took me by the hand and led me away from the table, the food that needed to be put away and the dishes that had already been used.

"Do you remember these drapes?" he asked, crossing to a window that served as a backdrop to the small recording studio he had made in one corner of the large, open room. It was separated from the main living area by a white brick fireplace. A spacious master bedroom and bath were at the end of a short hall.

"Of course I do. I wasn't sure I would ever get them finished. They were the first drapes I ever made." I took a piece of fabric in my hand and pleated it between my fingers. "They look like they've held up quite well."

Brett was now standing behind me with his hands on my shoulders. I could feel their warmth searing my flesh. "Do you remember the sales lady who sold us the material?"

"The one who kept asking us about the honeymoon cottage we were decorating?" I asked.

"She smelled just like my great-grandmother. If I remember correctly, you did nothing to set her straight."

"I didn't see any reason to. It was fun doing homey things together, and I kinda liked the idea of her thinking we were newlyweds. I used to dream about moving into this loft as your wife."

"That's the way it should have happened, J."

He took my hand again and led me to the sofa that sat in front of the fireplace. It was the end of July, and despite the central air, I felt as warm as I once had sitting in front of a raging fire.

"You know, Brett, I really am surprised that you're still living here."

"Me too. While I've thought about buying a home many times, it never seemed all that important after you left. My memories of you were here, so I put any leftover money in the bank and let it collect interest."

I felt my bottom lip begin to quiver. Maybe he really was ready to settle down, but was I ready to forget how badly we had already hurt each other so we could try again?

"What kind of a place do you live in?" he asked, stretching his legs out. "It's not all glass and chrome, is it?"

I laughed. "I had my fill of that the first couple of years I was living in the city. The home I bought is as countrified as I could find. There are lots of mature trees, a small stream, flowers and a big patio for entertaining—which I never do."

"What about the inside?"

"It's not so different than this room. I have overstuffed chairs, nicknacks that make me happy, a place to work, handmade quilts on the beds and lots of light in every room."

"Sounds ideal!"

"It is, for now. I'm just not sure that I want to live anywhere near a big city for the rest of my life. I'll always be a country girl at heart. Why didn't you move to some exotic place? Hanging around Bentley must be dull after all the places you've traveled."

"I guess I just got tired of sleeping in a different bed every night or two, and this place isn't so bad. It's quiet and peaceful most of the time, and there's a reasonably-sized city an hour away if I want more excitement."

"There's a lot to be said for that," I admitted.

"I take it that San Francisco doesn't always agree with you. If you remember, it was my hometown until my dad died. Then my mom felt the need to move away."

"I remember," I said. "And it's still an action-packed city if you're into things like that."

"And you're not?"

"When one's private life is a mess being successful professionally doesn't seem to matter much."

"So why did you stay there after you and Greg broke up? You could have gone some place else or even come back here."

My eyes flew open. "And let everyone know what a big loser I was? I didn't want anyone feeling sorry for me or saying *I told you so*."

"I doubt anyone would have done that. Most people are just trying to make it the best they know how. Maybe I could have helped you recover."

The heat rushed to my cheeks again. It was impossible to keep a conversation from becoming personal when two people had shared as much as we had.

"That would have been nice, but I've become very self-reliant. Trying to make it in a very demanding field does that to a girl. If I let people think I'm weak, even for a moment, they'll walk all over me. Sometimes I wonder if I've lost all my sensitivity. I literally have panic attacks whenever I think about letting someone get close to me."

"Even me?" Brett asked.

"That's an unfair question since you weren't there during all those challenging years."

"But I should have been. I should have protected you."

"From who? Myself?"

"If necessary," he responded. "I fell in love with an innocent, vulnerable girl straight from the country. It didn't matter to me what her family was like. If anything, it made me love her more because she tried so hard to act sophisticated and confident, but the guilelessness always showed through."

The tears were welling in my eyes, and I tried to make them stop. I could no longer remember what it felt like to be accepted and loved, and Brett knew just how to evoke feelings I was terrified to acknowledge.

"I didn't mean to make you cry," he said, brushing a tear from my cheek. "You were a victim of circumstances."

"Only because I didn't understand that I wasn't responsible for anything that happened during my youth."

"My beautiful, J," he replied, turning his entire body so he could see me more clearly. "Why couldn't we have just loved each other while we had the chance, instead of making everything so complicated?"

I let a few more tears drop off the end of my nose. "Maybe we had too many lessons to learn. I still believe that Heavenly Father wants us to be happy."

"And yet we seem to fight him every step of the way in the truly important matters because we think we know more than he does."

"That was certainly the case with me. I married a man I didn't love in the right way because he said he needed me and risking being alone for the rest of my life was too terrifying."

"And I stayed a confirmed bachelor because telling myself that someone better would come along eventually was easier than making a commitment I might live to regret."

Without really thinking, I took his hand and lifted his fingers to my lips. It was an odd thing to do since physical contact with anyone made me uncomfortable, but I could no longer deny that he had a few regrets of his own. "Despite all the pain, I really did wish the best for you, Brett. I wanted you to have an amazing wife and lots of kids."

"And I wanted you to be loved, even if it wasn't by me. Would you have stayed with Greg if he had given you even a portion of what you needed?"

"Probably, but he wasn't even around when our baby died."

Brett's hand dropped to his lap and mine went over my lips. I had never mentioned that incomprehensible part of my life to anyone.

"I didn't know you lost a baby, J. I am so sorry."

"Me too," I said, forcing a tearful smile as my mind rushed back to the morning when I felt the most intense pain imaginable and found myself standing in a pool of blood. "Greg didn't know until after the fact since we never lived together as husband and wife. But I must have gotten pregnant on our one-night honeymoon. He didn't even tell me he was sorry or ask if there was something he could do when I told him. So I tried to pretend that it hadn't happened too, but a part of me died when our baby did."

"But what about the doctor? Didn't your husband care that you had been in the hospital?"

"There wasn't a doctor, and I didn't go to the hospital. I didn't even miss a day of work."

"But why? You could have died!"

"I suppose that's true, but I didn't give it much thought at the time. I just wanted my baby. I needed someone to love so desperately. All I have is the ultrasound that was taken a week before he or she died."

"That means you were more than a few weeks along."

"Almost four months. I knew I felt different but kept thinking it was just nerves because I was under so much stress with my work and my very unconventional marriage. Besides Greg not wanting to tell his family about us, I was beginning to notice other behaviors that had me concerned."

"Surely there was someone you could have turned to if your husband was going to be such a jerk?"

"Not really. I had just started at the firm, and most of the women I worked with had chosen their careers over having a family. They knew even less about childbirth than I did."

"So you decided to do everything on your own. No wonder you have so little confidence in men. But I can assure you that not all of them are like the one you married, or me either. They actually prove by their actions that they care about the women in their lives."

My eyes were focused on the indentations between the bricks that made up the surface of the fireplace. It was easier than trying to look at him. He might be saying all the right things, but he would never know how it felt to have a child ripped from the womb without warning. It had left me wondering if I would ever feel whole again.

"I'm sure that's true, but some things happen so fast there isn't time to think clearly. Besides, it wasn't all Greg's fault. I could have told him I wasn't ready for marriage before we tied the knot, or even that I thought I might be pregnant."

"But you were basically forced into doing those things because I took the coward's way out. No wonder you're scared to get involved with me again."

While it was important for Brett to understand where I was coming from, too much information would put me at a real disadvantage. That's why I didn't tell him what my former husband had said when I came to him as an innocent, virgin bride or some of the truths I had learned about him before the annulment papers were signed. I didn't want what I continued to share with my lost baby ruined. The ultrasound I had been given stood in a frame on my dresser back home. I talked to it every day and wanted the reunion I envisioned us having to be one of joy. My child may not have been conceived under the best circumstances, but my love for him or her was never-ending.

"I was a big girl, Brett. I made an unfortunate decision and have lived with the consequences."

"But a life without love and tenderness? You should never have settled for that."

"Had I known how things were going to turn out, I would have chosen a different path to get over you. But I'm glad you now understand why I'm a little skittish."

"I was a fool back then, and you scared the hell out of me because you were the marrying kind of girl—not one who would ever settle for a one night stand."

"Is that your way of saying that I was unenlightened and boring?"

"Hardly! You had more layers than any girl I have ever known. What was the matter with us back then? We had the real thing and were too scared to do anything about it."

"Like I just said, we had a lot to learn. I didn't know how to love anyone, especially myself, and I'm not much better at it now."

"How could you be after all the things you've gone through?"

"Those things make up the almost impenetrable wall I've been living behind since the day my father died. It was easier than opening my heart to more pain, but that seemed to come anyway. I'm sorry I laid so much on you when this was supposed to be a pleasant evening."

"Not me! There's a lot we still need to learn about each other, but I've never quit believing that something would bring you back to me."

"I guess something did." I replied, leaning my head back until it touched the sofa.

"Are you saying that you could give up all the fame and fortune of being a renown clothing designer to come back here and see what might happen between us? Your lifestyle certainly outclasses mine."

"Money and glory had never really mattered to me, but who said I would be the one doing the moving?"

"Still, you have thought about it the past few days?"

His question touched my soul just as he knew it would.

"I want to believe in the magic of falling in love for real, but what if there really aren't any happy endings?"

"Then the world, as we know it, would end," he promptly responded. "Love is the most powerful force in the universe. With it, even the coldest hearts can melt. I know you're hesitant to discuss the future, but you have to know by now that I would stand by your side no matter what this time around."

"Even if I couldn't give you a family?"

"Is that a possibility?" he asked.

"I don't know. The doctor was never able to figure out what caused my first miscarriage. He only said it could happen again."

"Then we'll cross that bridge when, or if, it ever happens. I just want to love you."

My eyes filled with tears again, only for a very different reason.

"Do you really mean that, Brett?"

"I do, and something tells me that deep inside you feel the same way."

I wanted to believe in a selfless love that could weather the storms of time, but nothing about my past made that kind of permanence seem possible. Everyone I had ever let into my heart was gone, including my precious child.

"You know I do since we've discussed my reservations, personal issues and hopes for the future at nauseating length since I got here."

"That may be true, but we've discovered a lot of truths about each other in the process since I haven't exactly been quiet about mine. Isn't it about time some of our fantasies come true? Neither of us is getting any younger."

"Stop it," I said, sitting upright so I could get a better look at his face. "Age is no reason to enter into a relationship. Besides, you still have your boyish charm and all of your hair."

"Thank heavens!" he declared. "It would be impossible to convince you to try it with me again if I was bald."

The sun was gone now, but the soft light in his loft made it impossible not to see how utterly attractive and masculine he was. Thirty-seven wasn't all that old to be starting a family. Famous men did it all the time, even when they were well over sixty.

"Your hair—as much as I have always loved running my hands through it—isn't the only thing that attracted me. I fell in love with your hands."

"My hands," Brett's tone showed his surprise. "What kind of a romantic are you."

"I'm not sure since I've always considered myself more of a pragmatist. But your hands are strong and capable of doing so many things. When we were together, I always knew I would be safe since they were incapable of violence."

"Wow! That's the last thing I expected to hear. Did the same thing apply to Greg?"

"Not at all! His fingers were long and tapered. My hands were even fatter than his."

"Heaven help us," he said, abruptly reaching for mine. "Maybe we had better check this hand thing out. I don't want you running away again because mine have changed."

We placed our palms together. They were still a perfect fit.

"You're crazy," he said as our fingers wrapped around each others. "Are there any other rather bizarre things that I need to know?"

"I hate caviar, sushi and rollercoasters, and I'm afraid to swim in the ocean because I can't see what's underneath the surface."

"Anything else?"

"I hate clutter. Everything has to be in its assigned place before I crawl into bed. And then I have trouble sleeping because I can never get my mind to shut off."

"I think I could help with that," he said with a smile that made my toes curl. Making love to him had always been part of my fantasies.

"What about you?" I asked to keep my mind from straying too far away from the present.

"I love surfing and snorkeling, but I can't even swallow a runny egg. And never ask me to set foot on a farm. There's something sinister about cows, pigs and chickens whose only function in life is to give all they have to the very people who are supposed to be taking care of them."

"You do know that farmers are the backbone of our nation since they produce most of what we eat?"

"Right you are, J. See what fun we could have spending the rest of our lives finding out new things about each other and other bits of trivia."

"You make it sound easy."

"Not easy, but doable if it's what we both want. I stopped taking student groups abroad last year. Five days a week, I'm a stuffy old German professor—who will always have an eye for pretty young things—but who just doesn't need them anymore."

"And your music?"

"It's an important part of who I am, but it doesn't have to be the most important part. I've finally reached a point where I'm ready to move on to the next phase of living."

"And what that be?"

"To be loved by one woman who will accept my faults and go on loving me in spite of them. Do you know anyone who might qualify?"

"I might," I said, giving myself permission to take down a few more of the boulders that were surrounding my heart. "I've always accepted you just the way you are, and I've never stopped loving you."

"You're not just saying that in the heat of the moment?"

"While it's plenty warm in here for reasons you are well aware of because the air conditioning is working just fine, I've never seen anything more clearly. But that doesn't mean I'm not scared."

"And for good reason, J. But I promise never to intentionally hurt you again."

I let the air out of my lungs very slowly. My emotions had bounced from one end of the spectrum to the other during the past couple of hours, but I had never been more sure of one thing. I belonged with Brett, and I was ready to give what we had another chance.

"So where do we go from here, Brett Fowler?"

"My hormones say the closest justice of the peace so I can show you just how serious I am about committing to one woman for the rest of this life and whatever God grants us in the one to come. But you've already been that route, and I want you to have the kind of wedding you've always dreamed of—fancy dress, bridesmaids, flowers and all the trimmings."

"A simple ceremony with family and a few close friends is all I've ever really wanted. Even then, I'm afraid my part of the guest list will be very small. I've lost track of everyone I used to know and haven't seen my brother in over two years. But aren't we getting a little ahead of ourselves?"

"Probably, since I know how you feel about taking things slow. I'm just excited that we're starting to make some headway."

"We've determined that we want to be together, but we've built very different lives. That means one of us will have to make some mighty big adjustments."

"Like your life or mine?" Brett asked.

The smile, brought about by visions of what had always been little more than a dream, quickly faded. I had worked hard to get where I was, but my career had never been anything more than a bandage trying to heal a broken heart.

"Despite my rather caustic remark a few moments ago when I basically told you that I wasn't open to compromise, I want whatever life will make you happy, Brett."

The tables had definitely turned, and he gave me a look that was impossible to read. "You can't answer that quickly, J. You're practically a celebrity."

"Only in a very small circle. I belong where you are, and if that's here, then here is where I want to be."

"But what about your career? I can put a roof over your head but that's hardly providing the kind of life you've grown accustomed to."

"I don't need more material things, and I could work another fifty years and never feel the same high I did the night of my first showing. I thought you, of all people, would understand that."

"I do, J. But asking you to give up everything hardly seems fair."

"Only if you're not being straight with me. I can submit designs from anywhere in the word if I want to, but people rise and fall in the clothing industry on an almost daily basis. Maybe it's time to put my charcoals and pastels away and give some other young designer a chance. I really do want a family before it's too late."

"No regrets later on?"

"Not the kind you're implying."

He laughed. "I guess that holds true for both of us since I have no idea what kind of husband I will be. I've never had to answer to anyone other than myself."

"Neither have I, unless it's about work. I understand there might be an opening in the school of design right here. Do you think there's any chance I could get it?"

"You would be a shoe-in. Fate definitely seems to be working in our favor for once. I just wish you didn't have to go back to Whitman Cottage tonight."

"No one is doing bed-checks, but if I stay, we both know what will happen."

"Nothing would make me happier," he said, pulling me to my feet and into his arms. "I've never wanted you more."

I felt like a giddy teenager who had just discovered what it meant to be falling in love for real, but with that feeling all the moral values that had been instilled in me as a child came back too. I didn't want to play house without a wedding ring on my finger. When I made love to Brett for the first time, it would be as his wife.

"Would you settle for a few kisses?" I asked, daring myself not to look away from his him.

"If that's what you're offering, I'll accept them with gladness. We have the rest of our lives to explore everything else."

And then his lips found mine. His kisses were far from plutonic, but I would have been sorely disappointed if they weren't. In return, I gave him every ounce of tenderness and passion I could without crossing the invisible line that would destroy everything we hoped to build.

It was nearly midnight when he escorted me to his front door. We were both a little breathless, and I knew my lips might even be bruised. They were unused to doing anything more making expressions or forming words.

"You do know how hard it is to let you go," he said as the red door opened and he pulled me into his arms again. A cool breeze wafted over my shoulders. "I'm afraid I'll wake up in the morning only to find out that tonight was some illusive figment of my over-active imagination."

On impulse, I rose to my tiptoes and pressed my lips against his once more. "No, mirage, Brett. Lady Luck couldn't be that cruel. Will I see you again in a few hours?"

"You could be seeing me until the light of dawn if you would just say the word. I promise we wouldn't have to do anything more than snuggle."

"On that note, I'm leaving because we both know that would never happen. You've taken me too close to the edge as it is, and despite my resolves, I am not made of stone."

"That's for sure," he replied with a sensual smile. "Our bodies have never fit so perfectly together."

I hurried down the staircase and was sitting in the van with the door locked before I dared look in his direction again. He had his elbows resting on the railing. It took every ounce of resolve I had left not to rejoin him.

Chapter 7

I figured it would be impossible to sleep with the feel of Brett's lips so powerfully seared into mine, but my eyes closed almost the moment my head hit the pillow. I must have slept deeply because I wasn't aware of anything—not even a fanciful dream—until the sunlight was streaming in through my bedroom window. I had forgotten to set my alarm and would have to skip breakfast again if I was going to make it to class on time. I had scheduled thirty minutes private sessions with each of my students to see where they were at, offer suggestions and make sure they had what they needed to complete their projects within the next twenty-eight hours.

The grand finale Bethany had set in motion for late Friday afternoon had me concerned, but I had made it abundantly clear to the people who had been in on the original plans that I would leave the details to them. As a last-minute replacement for a woman who enjoyed elaborate and unrealistic festivities, I had my hands full making sure my students were ready.

What I had asked them to do was huge, but they had been made aware that a final project was required when being selected to participate in the seminar. And from what I had observed during the past three days, most of them had begun working long before my arrival on designs they hoped would only require a few doable tweaks. That kind of initiative was what separated the sheep from the goats, so to speak, and precisely why I had been given a chance to work at *Wide World of Design* before even meeting my benefactor. The fact that they were required to use some of the fabric I brought kept them from completely recycling, or even using, something that had been critiqued before. I needed to see how they reacted under both stress and duress.

But my time with them was almost over, and while I was exited to see their finished creations, award the cash prize, and perhaps even extend an internship to the student I felt most deserving, it also meant that I would no longer have a bonafide reason to remain at Bentley.

After the fashion show on Friday, all that remained was an uncomfortable meeting on Saturday morning with the program directors and the rest of the guest lecturers to discuss the pros and cons of our experience and offer suggestions as to what might make the program better. And then I was expected to pack up and head for home so Whitman Cottage would be ready for its next batch of guests.

I left the building shortly before eight and didn't run into anyone I knew. That wasn't particularity noteworthy since Annabelle and Professor Price—I still couldn't bring myself to call him by his first name unless he was facing me—were the only people I had spoken to, other than a polite hello in passing. I was glad they seemed to be doing so well. Annabelle's transformation was the most miraculous I had ever seen. In one night, she had made the transition from an ugly duckling, who was barely able to look in man's direction, into a graceful swam who finally knew what it was like to be loved.

I almost envied what had come so easily and naturally to them and hoped it wasn't trying to tell me something about my relationship with Brett. We wanted to be together, but it would be an uphill battle until all the trust that had been lost was restored.

My footsteps took me as rapidly as they could along pebble-filled pathways from the wooded area where the cottage was located to the main part of the campus. Bentley was a small university and while most of the classroom buildings stood conspicuously close together and were over a century old, they had been undated so the asbestos was rendered harmless and the plumbing and electrical wiring was up to code. I loved the feeling of antiquity that seemed to cry out to me from the smooth, stone surfaces of the buildings to the tall, thick-branched trees that made finding large patches of sunlight nearly impossible.

It was far different from the high-rise dormitories and modern gymnasium that had been constructed as new land became available—mostly from the estates of former patrons and faculty members who had given all they had so my generation could live in the kind of luxury and excess they knew nothing about.

A bird cried out overhead, and I stopped walking long enough to look upward. Beads of perspiration had pooled on my forehead and neck. It was going to be anther warm, sunshiny day, but that wasn't why I felt compelled to take a moment for myself before confronting my students with what I hoped would be useful and well-received advice.

Without the kind of thought I had learned to give to impactful decisions, I had made a huge commitment to Brett, and it was hard not to worry about the potential fallout. While I truly believed that the reawakening of love we both felt was real, if I followed through my entire life would be rearranged. Could I really walk away from a successful career and be happy standing in front of a bunch of students day after day? There was still so much I wanted to accomplish in my professional life before handing the torch to someone else.

My fall line would be the best one yet, and my boss would be furious when I told him what I was planning to do after all the time and resources he had invested in me. What if he demanded reparation and had me blackballed from ever working in the field again? It would certainly be within his rights and starting over would be impossible without his blessing.

In addition to that sobering reality, there was little reason to believe that I would ever be given a faculty position with no additional formal education and very limited experience in the classroom, especially when I hadn't made the best impression on the people who had invited me here. It wouldn't have hurt to me to act interested in the plans that had been made to ensure we had a good time, but I couldn't be bothered with people who held no interest for me. I hadn't even tried to get to know Annabelle better because I was so focused on coming to terms with the past.

The students with the first scheduled appointments were already fidgeting in their desks when I walked into the classroom. I apologized for my tardiness since I knew they had a great deal to accomplish before morning and then called the first person into the back room where supplies were stored for a consultation. I had scheduled an hour break for lunch since I knew I would need it. I wanted my comments to sound fresh, personal and non-rehearsed. That wasn't easy since there was only so much that could be said about any design.

Amber was already there for her one o'clock appointment when the lunch hour arrived. I knew she had come early so I could give her a rundown of my evening with Brett. But my stomach was growling, and I felt like I was going to explode since he hadn't tried to contact me since our date ended. I knew he was busy, but it took less than a minute to send a text, and I needed to know that he still cared. So I told her to wait where she was, and I would be back as soon as possible.

I practically sprinted to the student union building for a quick salad or sandwich and was standing in line waiting to pay my bill when I saw Brett sitting alone in a booth. My heart began to race as it always did in his presence, but he looked so lost in thought that I contemplated leaving without saying hello. He might be having some doubts of his own, but he looked up and saw me. I waved and he smiled back.

"This is a surprise," he said when I was standing next to him. "I was going to call first thing this morning but got off to a late start. How is you class going?"

I felt my knees go weak. This wasn't the enamored and light-hearted man I had left standing by the railing the night before. Something was really bothering him.

"Good, and yours?"

"Can't complain, but the department head has called a mandatory faculty meeting for seven this evening. I was planning on spending that time with you."

"No worries," I said, sliding into the seat across the table from him, even though I had not been invited to sit down. "I really should eat at least one meal with the rest of my colleagues and find out how things are going. I haven't made a very good show at being a team-player."

"And most of that is my fault. I am sorry for keeping you away from your responsibilities."

I leaned back and frowned. "Come on, Brett. What's really going on? I've never seen you like this before."

"That's because I'm usually very good at hiding what I'm feeling, especially when I'm singing in front of a crowd or involved in something else I find equally as enjoyable."

"Are you having doubts about us?" I asked as my jaw seemed to lock.

"Never," he responded, grabbing my hand as it lay almost lifeless on the table. "But I feel just awful about you making all the concessions if this relationship is going to work. You're the one with the bright future, not me."

"Come on, Brett. You've done very well for yourself."

"Not from where I'm sitting. I made a couple of cd's, but instead of pushing harder to see if I had what it takes to make it big, I came right back to Bentley and took up where I left off. You could become really famous, J. But if you give up your career for me, you'll never know."

I bit down on my bottom lip before responding. "I'll admit that there are a lot of logistics to work through, and I could burn some valuable bridges. But despite some very real fears, I think being with you is worth it."

I was digging an even deeper hole for myself and knew it, but if I walked away without giving us a genuine chance the regrets would be far more debilitating than anything I had lived through thus far.

"You say that now because everything is so new. What if you wake up some morning and resent me for destroying your life?"

"I could say the same thing to you, Brett. What we're contemplating won't be easy. We're both very set in our ways and used to being on our own. That's why I think it' so important for us to take things slow."

"But we've only got two more nights until you leave. Once you go back to the city, you won't even have time to think about me."

"Not true," I replied, placing my free hand on his cheek. It was soft, warm and comforting. "We each have the same amount of minutes in the day, but I'm suspecting now isn't the best time to talk anything through."

"My next class does start in a few minutes."

"Then you had better be going."

"True, but not until you give me a kiss. I can't stop thinking about the ones we shared last night."

I glanced around at the large number of people in the cafeteria—not all of which were busy eating. "Are you sure that's advisable? I wouldn't want to ruin your image."

"People can think what they like, J. I've waited forever to have you back in my life," he responded, rising to his feet and picking up his tray. "Would it be okay if I called after I got out of my meeting? I'm not sure how long it will last."

"I seldom get to bed before midnight. Maybe we could take another walk."

"Maybe," he said, bending down and pressing his lips to mine. The kiss wasn't long or passionate, but it let me know that he hadn't changed his mind about us. He was just considering possible ramifications, much like I had been doing all morning.

I ate what I could of my salad before heading back to the classroom through throngs of students whose lives were still filled with so much expectancy and hope. Amber was waiting for me, but instead of giving her an opportunity to ask any personal questions I began our consultation.

She appeared to be almost as distracted as me, and the garment bag she opened made me wonder what she had been doing all week.

"I'm sorry, Miss Sloan," she said. "I spent most of night on the phone with my boyfriend ironing out a few details about what we both wanted in regardless to our future together and when certain plans could be made, but I promise it will be done by morning."

"That's good because I would really like to see it finished. The programs for the show have already been printed and explaining a gap would be unprofessional."

"I won't let you down, Miss Sloan, but I already know I won't be getting the prize."

"How could you possibly know that?" I responded. "I haven't made up my mind about anything yet."

"Because you're looking for someone who doesn't mind not having a personal life, and I've always been more interested in becoming a wife and a mother than building a career."

I left it at that. Censuring her was futile since I actually admired her ability to make a very difficult decision when what the world viewed as the start of a successful life could be right at her fingertips.

The rest of the afternoon went by much as anticipated, and I was excited about what most of my students had been able to create in such a short period of time. But I was more confused than ever about offering an internship when I didn't know where may own future lay. That's why I wasn't too concerned about dressing for dinner. I just wanted to be sitting at a table when Annabelle and Professor Price arrived. Coming up with a reasonable explanation regarding my overt lack of interest in socializing with my colleagues—without giving anything of a personal nature away—would take a little thought. But the fact that it was unlikely I would see any of them again come Saturday made stretching the truth a little more palatable.

Still, I felt bad for basically ignoring Annabelle. She had proven her desire for friendship, but I had never anticipated my own life taking such a drastic turn. I wanted to believe that faith alone would knock down some of the barriers between Brett and me but was perceptive enough to know that our relationship was going to take work. That meant I needed to put aside some of my fears about being too aggressive, or making any demands, and start acting like I really cared.

For that reason, I took my cell phone from my purse as I sat at a corner table in the fading sunlight and sipped at a glass of ice water while waiting for Annabelle and Professor Price. Brett had not told me the reason an emergency meeting of the foreign language department had been called, but I knew it must be serious or he would have blown it off to spend more time with me.

My breath was labored as I tried to decide what to say. It seemed absolutely bizarre that someone in my position would be at a loss for words when I had dozens of people working for and with me, but I had never held a personal relationship together for more than a few months. And despite my strong feelings for Brett, I didn't know if I was capable of maintaining one now.

"*Just thinking about you,*" I typed. "*Your touch is like the warm embers of a fire. Give me a call when you get through with your meeting. I'll be waiting by my phone and . . . .*"

"You look like you have something important on your mind," Annabelle said as my fingers stopped in midair. "I am really surprised to see you here."

I felt the heat rise to my cheeks as I glanced up. Professor Price was by her side, and they appeared to be getting along exceptionally well.

"Just thought I should show up for at least one meal," I said, dropping my phone into my purse after hitting the send button. The noise that let me know it was on its way seemed unusually loud.

"Well, it's good to see you again. I was just telling Russell that I felt like you have been avoiding me. If I' have done anything to upset you, I'm sorry."

She looked so contrite that I felt some of my resolve about keeping my personal affairs private start to waver.

"Please sit down, and I'll try to explain. I haven't been avoiding anyone on purpose. I've just had a million things going on."

Professor Price held out a chair for her and then sat down in the adjoining one. He still looked very stiff, formal and unapproachable, but Annabelle must have broken through some of that veneer because they seemed to be very comfortable around each other.

"I hope my spending time with Annabelle hasn't been the cause of your staying away, Miss Sloan," he said. "I recognize that I am not a very sociable or even likable man. I am much too crusty and set in my ways. But until I met Annabelle, I never felt the need to think about anything other than my work. That is why I have decided to name my latest discovery after her."

"No kidding," I replied as I watched her eyes dance. "Any woman would be thrilled having an orchid named after her, and my absence from the cottage has nothing to do with either of you."

"I knew it," Annabelle said, looking slightly embarrassed by her newfound ability to speak what was on her mind. "I heard you come in last night. That evening with an old friend has turned into something more."

I waited until green salads had been brought to the table before responding. "In a manner of speaking, but I don't want to make any conjectures since we couldn't make things work the first time around."

"Always best to be cautious," Professor Price said, but I noticed that he had no difficulty squeezing Annabelle's hand. "You are young and have plenty of time to take things slow."

"I suppose. He has a meeting at seven, but we plan on getting together afterwards."

"You have no idea how happy that makes me!" Annabelle exclaimed, nearly dropping her fork. "Perhaps if he gets through early enough he could come here. It would be lovely sitting together in the lobby and getting to know each other."

"Don't push, Annie," Professor Price chided. "I am sure that spending time with us is the last thing they want to do with what remains of their evening."

I nearly choked on a piece of lettuce at his clear understanding of what was really going on.

"Not at all, sir. We would both enjoy the experience, but I can't make any promises. He's a very busy man."

"So are you," Annabelle interjected.

It was hard to keep a frown from forming. "I guess that's part of the problem. His life is here and mine is in San Francisco."

"Nonsense," Professor Price said. "Compromises have to be made for any relationship to work. Annie has already agreed that moving to Texas isn't an unrealistic expectation since most men still want to be considered the head of their households when it comes to providing for their families. Isn't that right, my dear?"

She looked at him and smiled. "I would go anywhere if it meant being with you, Russell. But Jada is young and just starting out. I have already made a name for myself and find the possibility of helping you create beautiful things a real honor and a privilege."

"Never negate the powerful impact your work has had on a healthier society, Annie. Your company will not be happy I am taking you away."

"But I have never discovered anything on my own like you have, Russell. Your new species of orchid is going to make history if everything you say about it is true."

"All of my research looks promising, my dear. But so far, I only have one, delicately-shaded plant, with perfect flecks of gold, that is unlike anything that has ever been developed before. There is always a chance I might not be able to replicate the formula."

"You said you had already written a paper, and from the pictures I've seen it is the most amazing flower ever. I'm just sorry your students couldn't see it."

"So am I, but Miss Annabelle Little can't be moved. She's locked inside a climatized vault at the university. Not even the graduate student who helped in its development can get inside without the code and believe me, he has tried. While what we do might not be earthshakingly monumental in how the world views success, once this discovery has been perfected my name will be listed amongst the greatest botanists this country has ever produced. Unimaginable doors will be opened, and the revenue I bring to the university will ensure that my legacy continues long after I have left this earthy sphere."

"It's all so mysterious and exciting, don't you think, Jada?" Annabelle asked as her face literally seemed to glow. "I can hardly wait to see my namesake and add what I can to its further development."

"Let's not get ahead of ourselves," Professor Price cautioned. "My paper hasn't been submitted my paper for publication yet. I figured I needed to know if a single cutting would be enough to produce another plant or if the process had to be duplicated from scratch. It's all a very time-consuming and laborious process, and one never knows what the outcome might be."

"But you said with my background I would be an invaluable help. I could even take the place of your intern."

"That's all very true but nothing goes as smoothly as expected. I am sorry for speaking out of turn, Miss Sloan. I know your concerns are real. Annie and I are just at a different place in our lives. I feel like she has become my muse. She has already expressed some tremendous insight when it comes to my article."

"What you have is truly awe-inspiring," I said as the entree was served. "And maybe things will work out for Brett and me."

"Brett?" Annabelle questioned. "Isn't that the name of the lead singer in the band we listened to on Monday night?"

"I do believe it is," Professor Price said as I sat without moving a muscle. The cat was about to come out of the bag, and I was far from ready for it. "And now that you mention it, I could have sworn that I saw Miss Sloan standing directly in front of him right before she disappeared."

Annabelle turned her attention to me far sooner than anticipated. "Is he right, Jada? Has a musician captured your heart?"

"He's not just a musician. He's also a German professor, and I've known him for over a decade."

"I didn't mean to sound snobbish, but even someone as sheltered as I have been knows the kind of reputation men behind microphones have."

"Fortunately for both of us, he's grown past the need for constant adoration. I wouldn't wish the kind of regrets we have on anyone. At least you have a clean slate to work from."

"And we're both very grateful for that," Professor Price said. "Annie and I have waited our entire lives to find each other, and there are no skeletons in either of our closets that will make a union between us less than ideal. If you would like me to set your young man straight about a few things, I would be more than happy to oblige. Annie has become quite fond of you."

"As I have of her, but Brett and I have to work through this together."

Annabelle's brows came together. "And you don't need us interfering. I am sorry for sticking my nose where it doesn't belong, but you feel like the little sister I have always longed for. I just want to make sure you're going to be okay."

"None of us know what tomorrow will bring, but I have never loved anyone the way I do Brett Fowler. I think I owe it to both of us to see if we can make it this time."

There was no more talk of romance during the remainder of the meal— just pleasant, light-hearted conversation. I wanted the kind of open and grounded relationship Annabelle and Professor Price seemed to be building, but that wasn't in the cards for Brett and me. Some of our issues would not be easily resolved, but at least we were both willing to try this time around.

It was after nine-thirty. My new friends had gone on a tour of the campus. Since I had spent four years there, I felt it would be best if I went to my room to ponder the evaluations of the day. I needed to decide which of my students was truly worthy of the money Mr. Fredericton had allocated as a prize. But giving away an internship when my own life was up in the air didn't seem either fair or wise.

I wanted to followthrough on the verbal commitment I had made to Brett, but since he hadn't replied to my text, my insecurities were going into overdrive. I understood that the major reason men did not respond to a prompt was because their interest lay elsewhere, but I was proud of myself for having taken a risk. It meant I was finally growing away from some of the trauma of the past. I had even promised Annabelle that I would join her and Professor Price for breakfast the next morning. I was certain it seemed like a small concession to them, but for me it was huge.

They might know about Brett now, but I didn't want them asking about my extended family. Talking about my father's death and my brother's lack of interest were difficult enough, but the fact that my mother was still in an institution raised a lot of eyebrows. Mental illness was still grossly misunderstood and a had a huge stigma attached to it.

I was about to call it a night when the face of my phone lit up, and I saw Brett's name. I let the tone sound several times before answering.

"How was your meeting?" I asked, hoping my voice didn't betray any of the emotions I had been trying so hard to suppress. He was an adult, and I had no claim on him yet.

"Much longer than anticipated, but there was a lot to discuss."

"Really," I replied, pushing my notes to one side so I could lay down on the bed. "I thought most faculty meetings were nothing short of boring."

"Not this one," he responded. "The dean of the department has been removed from his position pending a full investigation into certain allegations of inappropriate conduct."

He had my full attention now. "That sounds serious."

"It is, but we live in a political climate where certain people take great pleasure in destroying someone else's reputation and career."

"So you think all the claims are false?"

"No idea, but I've worked with the guy for nearly fifteen years. As far as I knew, he was an upstanding, married guy with three kids. There has never been a word of scandal about him until now."

"Maybe it will blow over. I always thought of Bentley as being the perfect place for young people to gain a higher education. There was never a word of impropriety while I was here."

"We live in a different world, J. That's why I quit taking student groups abroad. An innocent comment can easily be turned into a federal case. I won't even hold a simple meeting with anyone unless the door to my office is left ajar."

"That doesn't sound like a very effective way to help students. Maybe I should have been more cautious today. I took each of mine into the back room and gave them a thorough critique of their work. I'm sure a couple of them weren't entirely pleased with what I had to say."

"I'm sure you'll be fine, but teachers have to protect themselves."

"So what's going to happen to your department?"

He took a long, deep breath before responding. "There's nothing much any of us can do to help Donaldson, but a decision had to be made about who should take over until a replacement is named. Unfortunately, until that time comes, you're talking to the head of Bentley's Foreign Language Department."

"Wow!" I replied. "I don't know what to say except congratulations. I know you'll do a great job."

"It's not something I lobbied for, J. In fact, I offered every reason I could come up with as to why I was the last person who should fill the position, even for a short period of time. Besides not having the time, the fact that I spend most of my nights on stage should sound a few major alarms."

"Maybe they figured you already knew how to handle difficult situations since you've been in the limelight for years.'

"That's just it. I might know how to keep everything aboveboard now, but that wasn't always the case. I don't want anyone looking into my background too closely. I've done a few things I'm not overly proud of."

"Anything I should know about?" I asked as a lump seemed to settle in my throat.

"I thought you didn't want details about my numerous escapades? They're all in the past anyway."

"But there are things that could be used against you?"

"I would be lying if I said there weren't, but despite how it may appear to some people if certain facts become public knowledge, I wasn't completely indiscriminate when it came to the women I invited into my bed. They all came willingly, were legally of age and not a current student."

"Is that supposed to make me feel better?" I asked.

"Hardly, I would imagine, but I promised to be honest. That's why I was so late getting back to you. Admitting my mistakes has never been easy."

"I'm not judging, Brett. But if you have so many concerns, why did you say you would do it?"

"Because someone had to, and my past can't be erased. I hope you're still with me."

"You know I am. In fact, I'm very proud of the man you've become."

"Who's the sweet-talker now? I know it's getting late, but I still want to see you tonight. Do you feel like going uptown for some ice cream? We could even drive out to the lake. I understand it's very beautiful at night."

"Ice cream sounds fine, but I'm not sure about the lake. Neither of us needs to be questioned by the police."

"See why I need you so much," he responded "You were always my voice of reason, even when I didn't want to listen. Why don't I swing by in about fifteen minutes?"

"I'll meet you out front."

"What, no coming to your door?"

"I'm not sure that would be wise, unless you're ready to answer a lot of personal questions."

"So people are beginning to notice our rather strong bond?"

My sudden lightheartedness surprised me. "I guess you could say that since I've been acting like some giddy teenager the past couple of days. But I'm not complaining. I never really believed we would be given a second chance until you found me sitting in my accustomed place on that staircase."

"Some things are impossible to forget," he responded. "I'll see you in a few."

I left my room almost the moment we stopped talking since there was no reason to stay inside. The night was dark but mostly silent, and I loved the feel of freedom and peace of mind being away from the city brought. Back home, every noise reminded me that someone—guilty of criminal activity or simply a victim of the base desires or carelessness of others—was in trouble. The sound of sirens seemed endless, and I had given up watching the news because all it did was make me sad.

Not that I didn't believe there was much good to be found in the world, but those in positions of power had fallen into such a state of corruption that it was hard convincing myself that people who were trying to keep the

Ten Commandments, or even something as simplistic as following the Golden Rule, stood a chance.

No one was in the lobby when I hurried down the staircase. I momentarily wondered where Annabelle and Professor Price were since the tour was over at nine, but that thought flew away on the cool evening breeze the moment I was standing underneath a virtual blanket of stars. The scent of roses and Jasmine was particularly strong.

I wanted to give Brett and me every chance to put our most critical issues to rest before I left Bentley in that cumbersome, white van. It hardly seemed possible that only one full day of my commitment remained, but the idea of staying longer was a pipe-dream I couldn't afford to seriously entertain. My staff was counting on me, and I needed to get the fall line finished before approaching my boss. There had to be some way of keeping my foot in the door of the fashion industry without reneging on my promise about being willing to relocate. Maybe Amber and Annabelle were both right about just walking away from everything familiar for love, but I needed a safety net so I wouldn't fall so completely on my face if things did not go as planned.

While my misgivings were great, my smile was bright when Brett pulled to a stop in front of the cottage. But instead of climbing into the passenger seat like I had always done, I forced myself to wait on the edge of the gravel driveway until he walked around the front of the car and opened the door for me. I had learned, mostly through trail and error, that if I wanted to be treated like a lady, I had to act like one.

"My carriage awaits," he said with a bow. "While it's not as fancy as the limos I'm sure you're used to riding in, it's the best I can offer."

"I don't mind. I've never needed champagne and caviar to be happy."

"Good to know because those items never show up on my grocery list. By the way, you look ravishing as always."

I was in jeans, a light, collared shirt and wedged sandals—not at all the type of outfit I was used to wearing—but it felt good to be noticed as a woman whose purpose was more than just making other people a whole lot of money.

"Thanks! But maybe I should have dressed more carefully for the occasion since it's not every day I get to celebrate a promotion with the man I love."

"It's not exactly a promotion, J," he countered. "It's more like a trail by fire. But if I can pull it off, the department head position comes with a sizable raise. I don't ever want you to feel that you've become involved with some lowlife who can't even put a decent roof over your head."

"That thought has never crossed my mind."

"Well, it's crossed mine. I did a little sleuthing today and managed to find the house you call home. It's hardly the country cottage you described."

"So I didn't mention all the perks. I bought it as an investment and have the mortgage payments to prove it. Why all the interest in my lifestyle? I've already told you I'm willing to walk away from everything for the right reason."

He slammed the car door shut without responding. I watched him walk to the driver's side and wondered if we would ever get past our preconceived notions. Our time together was almost over, and we had yet to make it through one evening without having a disagreement. That had to tell us something. Youthful infatuation, or even grownup love, wasn't meant to be easy.

"I'm sorry for being irritable, J. Maybe I should have waited until tomorrow to see you, but we have so little time left. I'm just feeling a little insecure because you've made a real name for yourself, and I'm still doing what I've always done."

I reached for his hand as his fingers tightened around the gear shift. "Never apologize for being human. I used to feel insecure around you all the time and still do."

"Why?" he asked, looking at me from one corner of his eye. "You're the one who is living your dream."

"Only the easiest one to capture, Brett. Have you forgotten what I told you about Greg and our disastrous non-marriage? If I hadn't been able to come up with a few solid designs, along with convincing my boss that I had what it takes to create my own line, I could just as easily have ended up living on the streets. Since you're not living on them either, I can only assume that we have both proven our capability in doing some pretty amazing things. Just imagine what we could accomplish if we were working towards more of our goals together."

"So you really meant it when you said you were ready to celebrate with the man you loved tonight? I've been worried ever since we talked that my careless comments had made the chasm between us even wider than it already is."

"Our problems won't be resolved overnight, Brett. We're complicated people with challenging lives, but the fact that we're still talking gives me hope. I never remember having so much as a single disagreement when we were spending time together before."

"That's because we were both so adept at running."

"Then let's make a pack never to do that again without having a serious heart-to-heart first. I know what we have is too special to throw away a second time without giving it everything we've got."

He leaned over the console and kissed me. "I'm with you on that, J. I was so worried about the meeting tonight I couldn't eat anything earlier, and I'm starved."

We drove to a local diner—a small Mom and Pop establishment that was trying to stay afloat in a very difficult economy. He ordered a hamburger and fries, and I sipped on a chocolate milkshake while he ate. We didn't say anything of much consequence. I think we both needed a sense of normalcy before another deep conversation began.

I wiped some ketchup that managed to slip out of his burger away from his carefully trimmed goatee. He smiled and told me thanks. It was a simple thing that made me feel like we really belonged to each other. I studied his face while hoping he wouldn't question my motives. I wanted to remember with exactness every feature when I was back on my own turf trying to set some very difficult business transactions in order.

It was closing time when we left the diner, but he didn't seem in any hurry to take me back to Whitman Cottage. I longed for the freedom to feel right about suggesting we go to his place. Exploring every possible aspect of our relationship was cruelly enticing since we were both consenting adults, and I wasn't entirely unskilled when it came to lovemaking. In my own unenlightened way, I had tried to make my marriage work, but the backlash of giving in to my baser needs without that gold band on my finger would completely destroy what we were trying to build. And the fact that Brett had been involved with so many different women still bothered me.

When we were in the car, he gave me a very thought-provoking look. "I know it's late, but I'm not ready to take you back to your room."

"What did you have in mind?" I asked as my lips began to tremble. Some of my resolves stood a very good chance of crumbling if he said the right words.

"I think you know exactly what I would like to do, but I promised to behave until you were ready for more. I love you, J. I always have, but I know it's going to take time for you to believe I really am a reformed man."

The fact that he could so easily read my thoughts was disconcerting.

"I don't want to get into another heavy discussion, Brett. I will trust that you have changed as long as you don't give me a reason to believe otherwise. In return, I hope you will be patient with me. I haven't been involved with anyone since Greg. I'm not sure what that says about me, but I could't risk another heartbreak. You were my first, and only, real love."

He ran his hands down the sides of my cheeks as his eyes bored into mine. "Then I would be the biggest fool on the planet if I didn't give you the space you need. I think the term that is often used to describe what you've gone through is being re-virginized. I'm sure it's not in any dictionary, but I think it's sexy as hell."

"Stop it," I said. "You're making me blush."

He laughed, and it was music to my ears. "You have no idea how many memories this brings back, J. When I look at you, I still see that beautiful, innocent and desirable girl I sent such a ridiculous note to all those years ago."

"If your note was ridiculous, my response was straight from Hicksville. I figured you would never speak to me again."

"Want to know the truth?" he asked.

"Only if it won't destroy what is left of my fragile ego."

"I would have followed you around like a puppy until I got that formal introduction, but I allowed my friends to influence most of my decisions back then. They said to leave you alone until you were dry behind the ears because there were plenty of willing young women who were ready to show how much they wanted a man."

"Wow!" I responded, glad that he was no longer doing anything more than holding my hand. "I don't mean to sound naive, but are all guys like that?"

"Every one that I've ever met. They only think with their heads when it's absolutely necessary. Other than that, it's all about satisfying primal needs."

"And yet you want me to believe you've changed?"

He laughed again. "While I will always appreciate a pretty girl, I'm ready for a lasting relationship. I'm only sorry it took half my life to figure that out."

"I hope you plan on living well into your nineties because I don't want to lose you one second before I have to."

"So you're not sorry that you fell in love with an older man?"

"Seven years is nothing. I just read about a seventy-five year old celebrity who is dating a girl barely out of her teens. Granted, he has both fame and fortune on his side, but I would say we have nothing to worry about."

After that, we drove to the town square. The sidewalks were empty since it was a weeknight, but the streetlights high above our heads were bright, and the evening was still warm enough that there was no need for anything more than what we were wearing. Since a curfew had not been imposed anywhere, except campus, we decided to look at window displays. It was fun talking about fashions neither of us would ever wear, sneakers that were supposed to make feet feel like the person wearing them was walking on air and new skin products that claimed to reduce all wrinkles and signs of aging.

We lingered a little too long in front of the jewelry store. I knew Brett was thinking about making our verbal commitments more binding, but it was too soon to be picking out a ring. I would treasure whatever he selected when the time was right. He had excellent taste in everything and knew exactly what I would like.

It was with fond memories that we stopped in front of the round, marble fountain whose shooting water sparkled as it disappeared into the sky and cast small droplets for several feet in every direction when it came down. I would never forget watching children play beside it during the hot, summer months while their mothers sat on the benches—strategically placed around the courtyard—talking with friends. Brett took some coins from his pocket and handed one of them to me.

"You do know that we can't leave until we've both made a wish."

I looked up at him and sighed with complete contentment. "I already have everything I could ever want."

"So do I," he replied, giving my upturned cheek a kiss. "But I would hate to disappoint the townsfolk who drop something into the water every time they pass by. It's a great way to increase city revenue—if the homeless don't get to it first—and I have yet to hear anyone say that their wishes haven't come true in one way or another."

"Then let's give it a try."

I closed my eyes and allowed the lines between my eyes to deepened as I tried to determine what my greatest wish at this very moment would be. I already had a beautiful home and a good job that allowed me to use my innate creativity and well-honed educational skills. My health was excellent so far as I knew, and there had been no indication that I had inherited any of the bad family genes when it came to heart disease or severe mental illness like my parents. I had all the money I needed for a comfortable life, if I paid attention to details, and a firm belief that we had been sent to earth as part of a magnificent plan that was unfolding before my very eyes.

All I had ever wanted—other than what I already had—was someone who could take away some of the loneliness. And now it appeared that God, in his goodness and mercy, was about to grant my last fervent and heartfelt desire.

So what could I ask for that would not seem remiss? I let the warmth of the evening sink into every fiber of my being as I tried to decide. Maybe all I really needed was the wisdom to make the right decision when it came to Brett. Four days was long enough to discover that our feelings for each other had not diminished. But the adjustments and struggles were just beginning if we truly planned on building a life together.

I tossed the coin outward but didn't open my eyes until I heard it hit the water. Brett's arms went around my waist immediately.

"I won't ask what you wished for. I can only hope it was something good about us. I really do wish you didn't have to leave at all but know you have things to take care of back home. Just don't forget me while you're gone."

"No chance of that happening," I replied, placing my hands over his. "I'm afraid you're stuck with me now."

He leaned down and nuzzled my neck before responding. His show of affection and desire made me almost wish we weren't in such a public place.

"Couldn't ask for anything more, other than wishing all of our dreams could come true a little sooner. I've never been a patient man. Have you decided which of your students is going to walk away with the prizes?"

"I have a good idea who will get the cash, but I'm not sure awarding an internship would be fair since I might not be around to follow though."

"So this really is going to happen?"

"It certainly looks like it. I just hope I can work something out with my boss. While being a full-time teacher would definitely have its perks—like the two of us meeting for lunch every so often—I'm not sure my application would even be considered. And I'm not ready to join the ranks of the unemployed quite yet, even for love."

"You do know that I would never let you go hungry."

"I'm used to missing an occasional meal, but I'm a very driven woman and being idle drives me crazy."

"But couldn't the designs for the coming season be sketched anywhere?" he asked.

I turned in his arms. "They could, but I need to be in the office for the few weeks leading up to the unveiling."

"I can live with that, J. In fact, I would be more than delighted to accompany you every chance I get. I've never given up writing music, and a change in location always makes the creative juices flow. We could have the perfect life jet-setting from one city to another."

"What about children?" I asked.

"They would go with us. Just think about the valuable education they would get away from the classroom? I've always believed that the family who plays and works together stays together."

"It does sound rather ideal."

"Then keep that in mind when any doubts arise. We only have one life to live, and it's up to us to make sure it isn't completely wasted."

He dropped me off in front of the cottage a few minutes later, but the possibilities running around in my head made it impossible to sleep. I was still glancing at my cell phone at four in the morning and wishing I had the nerve to see if he was still awake.

I had asked him to join me for breakfast with Annabelle and Professor Price. He said he would like nothing more—even if he would feel a little out-of-place—but he had already made arrangements to meet with the rest of his staff to discuss strategies in how to best handle the news of the department chairman's fall from grace. He wanted a seamless transition so the rumor mill would have less fodder to play with.

Chapter 8

No one was waiting when I got to my classroom the next morning, but that was hardly surprising. The fashion show was scheduled for four, and I knew that most, if not all, of my students had been up until the early hours of the morning finishing their projects. I was excited to see the completed creations but was a little worried too. I could not in good conscience offer an internship until I knew how my boss would take my news.

Obviously, he would be upset when I told him that I was going to marry my first and only love and move back to Bentley—possibly even angry. After all, he had given me Bethany's line when she proved so completely unreliable. I had taken it in a younger and more widely-appreciated direction and was beginning to receive part of the acclaim that had always been hers. I had even seen some of my work on the pages of the most prestigious fashion magazines, and that translated into increased revenue for Mr. Fredericton. I wasn't exactly a cash-cow yet, but I was the closest thing he had to one, and that meant he would not let me go without a fight.

But I did not want to end up like my predecessor. While I respected her accomplishments and appreciated the things she had taught me when I first started out, I wasn't at all envious when it came to where she had ended up. She might be living in a spacious villa in the south of France, but she had never married or had any children. And the people she spent most of her time with only stuck around because she could provide things they were unable to attain on their own.

I pulled a stack of papers from my briefcase and sat down at the desk to review the plans for the rest of the day. Bethany may have bailed at the last minute again, but it seemed unlikely that she had done so with much forethought. I would have held a fashion show within the department that was open to any interested students or community members. But she had made sure that the auditorium was reserved and suitably decorated and that the local media, in addition to reporters from the university press, would be there to report the results. An after-event reception with hors d'oeuvres, champagne and photo opts had also been planned.

It was just the kind of event that had Bethany Kilpatrick's name written all over it— a monument to herself that seemed totally unnecessary, and even a little tacky, since she had opted not to come. Maybe that was why I hadn't volunteered to help with any of the physical arrangements. Besides not being my style, I wanted to distance myself from her as much as possible so my own actions would not seem like such a betrayal.

A run-through of the show had been scheduled for eleven, but that was two-hours away. So instead of pacing like I usually did when I was nervous, I began loading everything that would no longer be needed in the back of the van. I didn't want to wait until morning to do it since Brett would only volunteer to help and seeing another side to him would make leaving even harder. I wasn't sure how I could drive underneath that decades-old arch now when I might not see him again for months.

I needed him more than ever, but I would be re-entering a world where I had known great satisfaction as I pushed myself closer to the top. What if I wasn't able to call it quits if it came to that? Mr. Fredericton was a very persuasive man. That was precisely the reason I was here when I had vowed never to re-visit my past.

All of the mannequins had been secured when another disturbing thought surfaced. I had brought a change of clothing and could repair my hair and makeup in the teacher's lounge, but I wasn't ready to get on that stage in a few hours and announce the cash recipient in front of a live audience while cameras were rolling. And I definitely wasn't ready to offer an internship that might cause one of my students to lose faith in the power of dreams because I might not be around to do my part.

Some of the young people I had worked with during the week were truly amazing and would find great success once their niche was secured, but others would not be so lucky. That was why I had been so meticulous when giving them an accurate representation of what I believed the world was really like in the industry we had all chosen to pursue. Was it fair of me to pull the rug out from underneath someone who deserved the same chance I had been given simply because I wanted something different now?

I pondered that dilemma while packing boxes with leftover supplies and debating the advisability of texting Brett to see how his morning had gone. I truly believed he would make an excellent department head, but dealing with the fallout from a scandal wouldn't be easy. I had heard more about it than I wanted to at breakfast. Apparently, the former dean had been led away from campus in handcuffs and potential victims were coming out of the woodwork with charges of sexual misconduct dating back nearly two decades. There was even a report of possible embezzlement.

I wiped the back of one hand across my sodden brow after taking another load to the van. I couldn't afford to let my mind wander to such unsavory thoughts when there was still so much to be done before the day was over. It would hamper my ability to complete some distasteful tasks of my own. While Brett had been both careless and casual when it came to past personal involvements, as far as I knew, he had always played by the rules when it came to his current students. And he would never take anything that did not belong to him.

Perhaps I would be making a huge mistake if I was ever offered a position on the staff at Bentley and took it. I liked working mostly alone and having to account to no one but my boss. Worrying about the things Brett had to from formulating lesson plans and motivating unengaged students to writing grants and advocating for programs that would bring additional revenue into the school were certainly not within my range of comfort. And the administrative tasks his promotion entailed would make him feel like he was living in a fish bowl. Other than being alone, I rather enjoyed the life I had built for myself. It suited my temperament and made it relatively easy for me to remain in control.

The door to the classroom opened just as I was finishing up in the back room. I hoped the lesson I had planned would be beneficial to my students before we left for the auditorium. I didn't want any surprises from someone tripping on the runway to a clothing malfunction and knew that not everyone would be wearing his or her own creations since I had given them the option of using a model.

"Miss Sloan," Amber called out. She was carrying a large, garment bag, and the smile on her face let me know that her project was finished. "I thought I would be the last one here."

"Quite the opposite," I responded, running my hands over my jeans to help dislodge any leftover dirt. "I was just making sure the dividers were up so there would be a little more privacy."

"You don't have to worry about that, Miss Sloan. We've been dressing in front of each other for the last two years. Wasn't it like that when you were here?"

"Pretty much, but I was always a little self-conscious."

"I suppose most of us are—at least in the beginning—but your expertise has given us us so much to think about. I'm glad you were the one to come instead of Miss Kilpatrick. She may be a legend around this school, but she's too old understand what young people today are facing when they strike out on their own."

My arms crossed in front of my chest. "Some things in the business world will always remain the same, but I'm glad you enjoyed the experience. I just worry that I may have been too forceful in some of my opinions. It was never my intention to turn anyone against a career in the fashion industry."

"My decision was basically made before you got here. I just needed a little reassurance that my sacrifice in earning a degree wasn't an all or nothing situation. I talked to my boyfriend this morning about starting my own business once we're married. He thinks it's a great idea. All he's ever really wanted was for me to be happy."

"It sounds like you've found a keeper."

"Oh, I have, Miss Sloan. He said he would even build a special workplace for me where I could store all my supplies. We both know it won't be easy considering where we will be living, but I was hoping I could submit a few designs to you along the way and see what happens."

"You already have my phone number," I said, not wanting to say or do anything that would take away from the triumph or excitement of the day. My students deserved their brief moments in the spotlight because it was all some of them would ever have.

Amber suddenly looked perplexed. "I don't mean to speak out-of-turn, Miss Sloan, but I am worried about some of my classmates. They have put everything into this one competition and might not take the outcome well."

That thought had been running around in my head too, but learning to handle disappointment was just as important as reveling in success.

"That's why I let everyone know upfront what the requirements were and that only one cash prize would be awarded. The opportunity for an internship was never a given."

"I know, but you haven't seen how truly competitive some of them are. Between Ted, Aisha and Clarice, I'm afraid there might be a few fireworks. They've clashed since day one."

"I thought Clarice was thinking about switching majors," I said with a frown of my own.

"She just made that comment to get a laugh. Everyone knows she believes she was born to design clothing for the rich and famous, and she already knows how to wrap people around her little finger."

"I'm not sure that's aways a plus since this industry is built on teamwork. I have yet to design an item of clothing that couldn't be improved by listening to others."

"Please forgive my lack of understanding," she said with a look of complete remorse. "It was never my intention to cause waves. I just wanted you to be prepared for a possible explosion."

"Apology accepted because I've seen a few of those over the years. But believe me when I say that causing commotions or making unnecessary enemies is never a good idea. Life offers opportunities but few guarantees. Not everyone is going to find the desired level of success, but happiness is available to those who know how to adjust."

"Is that what you and Professor Fowler are doing? I heard through the campus grapevine this morning that he has been named interim chairman of the foreign language department."

I let the air out of my lungs slowly. "It was an unexpected honor, Amber, but hardly one we should be discussing. Why don't you take this time to change. I'm sure everyone else will be here soon."

The next hour reminded me of my runway debut when I had become so nervous I went into the ladies' restroom to throw up. Since I didn't want that to happen today, I sat everyone down after a semi-successful run-through and tried to calm a few very unsettled nerves.

I began by explaining how grateful I was at being given the opportunity to work with such talented and competent students. Then I added to what Amber and I had discussed about how one award would not automatically determine success or failure. My opinion, while valid for the company where I worked, would not be the consensus of everyone in the fashion industry.

"But that's what we're here for," Clarice said. "If we don't win, what was the point?"

"It's a legitimate question," I said as I noticed a few uncomfortable looks. "Having one's work recognized is important, but real life isn't like it was on the playground where everyone who participated got a trophy just so he or she wouldn't feel bad. While I have no doubt that all of you will see a fulfillment of dreams once you find the right fit, my job today is to give an unbiased opinion as to which of your designs most accurately reflects our company's goal."

"So we really are going to be penalized for being too creative?"

I knew exactly what Clarice was worried about now. While impressive in conception and completion, the creation she had assembled had an undeniable edginess that would only appeal to some of the designers I had met over the years but hardly to most members of the middle class.

"I'll tell you what, Clarice. I am more than willing to help you, and anyone else in this room, get their designs to someone in the right part of the industry, but I'm going to ask something in return."

"What's that," she pouted.

"That everyone here tries to enjoy the afternoon—come what might. A lot of time, energy and money has gone into making this event memorable. Reporters from both print and televised media will be at the reception to hear your stories. And the planned photo op—using photographers who know what they're doing—will provide high quality glossies that can be submitted to any fashion house you desire. Not many soon-to-be graduates are given an opportunity like this, but what is done with it is an individual matter."

"Well said," Ted Atherton interjected. "None of us, besides you, are professionals yet, even if we choose to believe otherwise. I would personally like to thank the powers that be for even sponsoring this program. I know I've spent more time in my head this past week than I should have, but I won't forget the sound advice Miss Sloan has offered. As the only male in this program at the present time, I've had my share of moments when I have felt undervalued, judged and even totally out-of-place, but I'm not willing to give up my dreams just because someone looks at me with derision or doesn't see things the way I do. I plan on giving everything I've got to my chosen career, and a few setbacks aren't going to stop me. I'll pay my dues, find my place and keep on learning."

"Thank you, Ted," I responded as some the tension I had felt earlier seemed to dissipate. "That was the perfect ending for our classroom experience. I can only say best wishes for a lifetime of happiness and self-fulfillment. You have been awesome to work with, and if I can ever be of assistance, you know how to reach me."

I was about to dismiss them—knowing they were mature and wise enough to show up at the auditorium on time—when someone knocked on the door.

"Do you want to me get it?" Amber asked, jumping to her feet almost immediately.

I nodded but felt a moment of foreboding. No one had interrupted one of our classes before. But when she turned to face us, I knew our visitor hadn't come bearing any unwanted news.

"It's for you, Miss Sloan," she said with a bright smile that made my face flush. "But the handsome gentleman would like to speak to you in private."

"Have you been holding out on us?" Clarice asked as her eyes narrowed. She no longer appeared to be overly upset, but that could change at any moment. "I wasn't aware that you had other acquaintances on campus."

"It's an old friend, Clarice," I said after clearing my throat. "I won't be long."

"Take your time," she responded. "We don't have to be at the auditorium for over an hour, and I'm sure none of us feel much like eating."

Keeping my legs steady was far from easy as I walked to the back of the room. No one, but Amber, knew about my relationship with Bret, and I wanted to keep it that way for now. That's why I slipped through the door and closed it behind me, but not before hearing the sound of muffled laughter. Brett heard it too because he immediately extended a wrapped box in my direction. There was a picnic basket at his feet.

"I'm sorry for interrupting, J. I know how busy you are, but I couldn't wait until tonight to see you. At least I'm hoping you don't have plans that will take the entire evening. I know I should have contacted you before leaving my loft to wish you good luck, but to tell you the truth, my mind was elsewhere. I had no idea what my reception would be when I made it to the office."

"But everything is okay, isn't it?"

He made sure I accepted his gift before answering. "Nothing I can't deal with. What I cannot get used to is the idea of you leaving."

"Hopefully, it won't be for long," I replied as the beginning of another frown stole across my forehead. As delighted as I was to see him, I really didn't have the time for a prolonged conversation that would cause me to lose focus. "What's in the box? I haven't done anything to deserve a gift."

"Just something we saw in a shop window last night."

"When did you have time to go shopping? I thought you would be in meetings all morning."

He brushed away a tear that was threatening to run down my cheek. Despite a great many uncertainties, I couldn't bear the thought of being away from him either, and we had less than twenty-four hours until I was on my way back to California.

"I was, but one of the perks to my new position is having a secretary. I had her do a little shopping. And when she got back, I asked if she could get one of the grad students to take my afternoon class because I needed some time to think. Could you spare a few minutes and play hooky with me?"

I glanced down at the picnic basket at our feet. "I wish I could, but I'm not even dressed for the afternoon and have students who need me."

"They're not the only ones," he said, pulling me into his arms. But our kiss didn't last long. "I knew you likely wouldn't have time for me with all the upcoming festivities, but I had to give it a shot. While I'm much too old to be running around like some love-struck young stud, it's how you make me feel. I could walk away from everything right now and still be the happiest man alive."

I smiled and brushed his lips with my fingertips.

"But you won't because you've worked too hard to get where you are, just as I have. Will I see you at the reception?"

"That's the plan. I have an unavoidable meeting with all the other departments heads at three, but it shouldn't take more than an hour. Howard made everything look so easy, but the paperwork alone has me terrified. I'm really not any good at sitting behind a desk."

"You'll adjust, and please don't jeopardize your new appointment to spend time with me. I promise to stop by your loft when I'm finished if you aren't able to make it."

"What about the lunch I brought?" he asked.

"I guess we'll just have to save it for when we have time to sit down and relax."

"That must be my my cue to go, but I would like to say hello to your students first. I'm sure they would be interested in learning who was at the door since it was impossible not to hear what was said."

"You're crazy," I responded. "It would be like a lamb walking into a lioness's den since I only have one male student. They'll just bombard you with questions."

"I have no trouble telling them that I'm over the moon in love with their visiting professor and hope she feels the same way about me."

When I looked in his eyes, I saw nothing but love and complete devotion. "She does, but I'm not sure making some grand announcement would be the best thing for your career right now."

"Let me worry about that. I think everyone involved would be overjoyed to know that I'm finally ready to take myself off the market and settle down. Come on, J. Just a quick hello and I'll go."

"Promise? They need to stay focused on the show."

"Cross my heart," he said, reaching for the doorknob. "I refuse to let you leave town before someone knows how I feel about you."

"You're really ready to make a commitment like that?"

"Just give me one minute, and you'll see how ready I am."

The door swung towards us, and I heard the movement of bodies and the sound of voices as Brett stepped into my classroom. I might have stayed where I was, but my hand was in his as he pulled me along behind him. The picnic basket remained on the floor in the hall, but I held the gift he had given me as tightly as I might have gripped a lifeline on a sinking boat in the middle of a vast and turbulent ocean.

Falling in love with him for a second time had been scary enough, but announcing what we were feeling meant permanence. My students would know before their runway debuts that I might not be as committed to my career as I had led them to believe.

"Class," he said when we were standing in front of the room. "I won't take much of your time, but I want you to know that I have been in love with your Miss Sloan since the day I first saw her on campus nearly twelve years ago. She scared the hell out of me because she was different than any girl I had met before. She was bright, beautiful, sassy, principled and determined not to be swayed from accomplishing any of her goals. I'm just sorry I let my own ambitions get in the way of telling her how much she meant to me back then, but I won't make that mistake again."

"You go, girl," someone shouted as applause filled the room.

"Oh, Miss Sloan," Amber practically cooed when an individual voice could be heard again. "I knew he had it bad when I saw the two of you dancing the other night. This is going to upset a lot of girls because he is by far the sexiest professor on campus, but I couldn't be happier for you."

"He is one classy man to be desired," Clarice added as she sat upright in her desk and tossed her shiny hair away from her face. "If you don't want him, Miss Sloan, I would be more than happy to take him off your hands."

It was my turn to say something, but I was at a complete loss for words. Regardless of how old Brett became, women would always find him desirable, especially when he was singing songs filled with sensuality and passion. If I was still too insecure to live with that, I should have let him know before he made such a fervent declaration that was bound to be repeated around campus.

"Professor Fowler knows how I feel about him," I managed to utter while the eyes in the room shifted from his face to mine. "I haven't been able to forget about him either."

"Does that mean what I think it does?" Amber asked.

Brett gave her a captivating smile. "My days of being included among the single professors on campus are over. That is, if Miss Sloan will have me."

My knees buckled as the air around me became so heavy it was hard to breath, but Brett's strong arm around my waist kept me from falling.

"What are you doing?" I whispered, unable to look in his direction.

"I'm asking you to marry me, J. This wasn't the way I envisioned doing it. I know you hate surprises, and I don't even have a ring. But if it's something you want even a portion as much as I do, I hope you won't refuse."

I glanced around at the expectancy on the faces of my students. Some of them had tears in their eyes. He had taken a huge risk popping the question in front of a group of strangers who would make sure the word got out before the afternoon was over. Perhaps he had an underlying reason for doing it that way, but I suspected that his honest expression of love was as much a shock to him as it was to me. And any dalliance on my part would only make him believe I had doubts about his sincerely or my true feelings for him.

"Yes, Brett," I said, placing the gift he had given me on the desk so I could place both of my hands in his. "You know there's nothing I want more, but . . . . "

He silenced what he knew would only be my fear talking with a kiss. "We don't have to decide any of the details right now. I know you and your class have a busy afternoon. We'll talk more over candlelight and soft music when you've finished. Good luck to everyone. I know you've enjoyed your experience this week. As for me, I can only tell you that I never thought I would be lucky enough to have the woman of my dreams come home to me."

I watched him take long, confident strides towards the door and felt like my heart would explode with a new kind of belonging and happiness. If we were together a million years, he would never stop astonishing me.

"Wow!" Amber said when he was gone. "I thought Bryan's proposal was romantic, but Professor Fowler's was practically earth-shattering. Does this mean you'll be staying at Bentley?"

I leaned against the desk for support. Now that Brett was no longer by my side, I would have to come clean about a few more things since my life seemed to be as much up-in-the-air as anyone else's in the room.

"You have just witnessed one of the truisms of life," I said with a sigh that could be felt to the tips of my toes. "The direction one is heading can change in a heartbeat. That's why it is so important to prioritize wants and desires but never become so rigid that a change of plans causes an emotional, metal or physical meltdown. Giving up a successful career—that I've loved and hope doesn't have to end—never crossed my mind before coming back. But my accomplishments have meant very little because there has never been anyone to share them with before. Seeing Professor Fowler again made me realize that there is more to life than making money or chasing fame. All we can take with us when we die are our experiences and relationships with others. In many ways, I'm in the same boat most of you are right now, but I will follow through on the promises I have made."

"Does that include an internship?" Clarice asked. "I know I won't be getting it, but someone should. After all, it was mentioned as a possibility."

"My boss is the one in charge of hiring. All I was asked to do was present the seminar, award the cash prize and return the winning design for him to look at."

"But surely he expects you to tell him what you thought of your students."

"I can assure you that he will get an honest appraisal of everyone in class, Clarice. But after what you have just witnessed, I am not sure my word is going to carry much weight. He's a very driven man who dislikes surprises even more than I do."

"But you did know that you might see Professor Fowler again when you agreed to come. He's a pretty hard man to miss."

It was now or never if I wanted to redeem myself as a professional.

"The assignment came at the last minute, and I wasn't in a position to refuse. But I think we have more important things to do right now than discuss my personal life. You need to be at the auditorium, dressed for a rehearsal, in a very short amount of time. I'll meet you there, unless someone needs a ride since I have my own preparations to make."

I pulled open the drawer where my purse had been stored, but most everyone was already heading out by the time I was standing upright. I smiled to myself as I watched them leave. Brett's proposal would be forgotten as soon as they walked backstage where last minute arrangements and unadulterated excitement would keep their minds occupied until the entire event was over.

It wouldn't be quite that easy for me. I already knew that few things were more nerve-wracking than being in front of audience with cameras recording every possible mistake and knowing that people would ether like, hate or be totally indifferent to what had been so lovingly created.

But before getting my dress from the backroom so I could change, I wrote the name of the student I felt most-deserving of the monetary award on the check and certificate that been previously prepared and sealed them in an envelope with the *Wide World of Design* logo printed on it. I would stop by the classroom again before returning to the cottage for the few things that still needed to be collected before the drive home.

The program director—a woman approximately twenty-years older than me who was wearing stiletto heels and a fashionably-cut suit—greeted me when I walked through the back door of the auditorium.

"I hope you approve of the arrangements. Ms. Kilpatrick was very specific in her requests, and we've done our best to make sure everything is just as she desired since she's paying the bill. We'll be streaming the program to her villa in France, and she plans on making a few televised closing remarks."

"That's only right," I said as we stepped into the bright lights and I saw the large and flashy banner that read: *Bethany Kilpatrick presents some of the brightest rising stars*. A stage manager was calling out last minute instructions, but everything appeared to be in order. "She's more than welcome to announce the winner. I'm only here because she was unable to attend."

"She wants you to take care of that, Miss Sloan. I hope you're not disappointed that you weren't our first choice, but Ms. Kilpatrick has been on our board of directors for over three decades. Her contributions have been invaluable in keeping our program alive."

"She believes very strongly in supporting the rising generation of designers."

"If I remember what I've been told correctly, she took you under her wing as a new Bentley graduate. That must have been an amazing experience. I've never know anyone truly famous myself."

"I wouldn't be where I am today without her," I responded, not wishing to express the fact that I hadn't spoken to my former boss for over two years. She considered me a traitor to her generosity for accepting the invitation to produce my own line after her ill-timed disappearance.

"Well, we're just glad you're here, Miss Sloan. Is there anything you feel needs to be changed or adjusted before we let anyone through the front doors? People have been lining up for the past hour. There should be a good crowd. I didn't know what standard protocol for an event like this was, other than what Ms Kilpatrick said, but I told the reporters that no one would have access to the designers or models until after the show. I hope that was okay."

"That was precisely the right approach. We're not dealing with professionals who understand how to handle the press, just talented young people who are excited about having their work seen. Now why don't we have that run-through? I gave my students all the help I could in the classroom, but it's nothing like taking that walk under the bright lights."

I was suddenly feeling more than nervous. I should have boycotted the idea of such an elaborate extravaganza the moment I arrived, but I had let private matters override common sense. If even one of my students had a bad experience, I would hold myself personally accountable as I tried to undo what could be some very bad press.

Bethany Kilpatrick's name and list of accomplishments appeared on every piece of information I had read about the event, and no retractions or changes had been made. That left me to take the fall from the slightest mishap to the biggest fiasco while she walked away like the injured party because I had accepted the responsibility of representing her and had failed.

As I followed the program director behind the curtain so the models could take center stage, it abruptly occurred to me that Bethany might truly enjoy watching me fail. Perhaps that was part of the plan from its inception since she knew I seldom concerned myself with the bigger picture. But with just over an hour before the curtain rose there was little I could do besides trust that I had given my students what they needed.

"Are you okay?" Amber asked when I walked up to the mirror where she was applying additional mascara. "You look white as a sheet. Are you having second thoughts about Professor Fowler's proposal?"

I put one hand on her shoulder. "Not at all. He's made me the happiest woman alive, next to you. I just wish I could have done more to prepare everyone for this moment."

"Please don't worry about us, Miss Sloan. You've been a wonderful teacher, and it's not like the entire world will be watching us try to strut across the stage without making a fool of ourselves. A few kind words in the community newspaper, or a possible glimpse of our work on the local television news, is all any of us are really hoping for. We're just grateful for your words of wisdom. You made everything real so we could decide for ourselves if the career we had chosen was what we really want."

"You should be a diplomat," I responded.

"And you should quit worrying about things that can't be controlled. The flowers on the stage are lovely and the runway well-lighted so we won't have to worry about where we are going. Besides, like you said, we won't be able to see anyone in the audience so unless there is a complete lack of applause we just have to carry ourselves with our shoulders back and our head's erect. Some of us have even been practicing the comments you told us were effective with reporters who ask difficult or overly personal questions."

"I did all that, did I?"

"Yes, Miss Sloan. You showed us that being true to one's convictions is more important than fame or fortune. Maybe that isn't important to everyone, but it certainly is to me."

Amber's kind remarks put many of my fears to rest so I could end the experience on a positive note. Bethany Kilpatrick could not hurt me unless I allowed it, and that was something I had no intention of doing.

I called my students, and the models of the ones who had chosen to use them, together after turns had been taken walking across the stage in a pace where the spotlight could easily stay focused and expressed my gratitude for what working with them had taught me. Then I wished them good luck as they formed a line in the order they would present their creations to an already assembled audience. The entire production would take little more than an hour, and I would watch from the wings and be ready when my turn to present the award came.

Notwithstanding my desire to remain in the background as much as possible when it came to promoting my work, I had been to many such affairs where audience acceptance could make or break a designer. That was why I had spent so much time the past few days talking about the value of knowing how to impress prospective buyers, even when things did not appear to be going well. Success truly was as much about attitude and delivery as talent and ability.

But when the master of ceremony took center stage and the clapping began, I had to take a deep breath to steady my nerves. I did that by thinking about the gift Brett had given me. It lay unopened on the passenger seat of the van with a jacket thrown over it. The square box was a little over a foot in diameter and quite heavy. I had spent every quiet moment since he had placed it in my hands trying to recall what we had seen the night before that I had expressed an overt amount of interest in but kept drawing blanks. I would open it before I saw him again but felt bad because I had nothing for him.

Clarice was the first one to walk down the runway. She looked like a pro in shimmering gold and black silk that clung to her body in a very provocative way. I had no doubt that I would see her name in lights once she found the right niche. Her avant-garde approach to fashion would definitely be appreciated by the young and wealthy who spent most of their time going to the gym and partying. The deafening applause let me know that the audience was going to be both receptive and appreciative.

It was quite surprised that I didn't question my choice as to the winner as I listened to the reactions my students got as they crossed the stage. Each ensemble was unique and expressed the personality of the designer from evening dresses to casual wear and what could be worn to the office. Ted's business suit for an aspiring young executive was a great hit, and the white, satin wedding dress with its sleek, smooth lines that Amber had completed for her own wedding drew massive shouts of delight.

But when Bethany Kilpatrick's live feed from her villa in the south of France came up on a screen that had to be lowered into place, the audience went silent. I stepped closer to the front of the curtain where I could see at least a portion of what they did. The image was distorted when looking at it from such an awkward angle, but I would recognize the woman who had given me my start anywhere. She was standing in front of a marble fireplace in a flowing gown with jewels at her neck and wrists. The entire setting radiated the kind of opulence she was known for. I had no doubt that everyone in the audience would be suitably impressed.

"My dear friends," she began. "It pains me greatly that I am unable to attend such a truly spectacular celebration, but alas, age and time away from America soil have given me a slightly different way of viewing life. I am thrilled with the quality of work that has been presented this afternoon and wish I could be there to congratulate the winners. But I trust that my former colleague and friend will do justice to the young talents whose futures—I am certain—will be exceptionally bright under the right tutelage. I love Bentley University from the spreading lawns to the rustic buildings that were once my home. I hope to return again one day but only time will tell. Please enjoy the reception that has been planned in everyone's honor and know that my thoughts are with you."

That was it! The screen went dark and applause began again. Once it ended, the master of ceremonies would call my name. I gripped the envelope in my hand more tightly than was necessary. Bethany's remark about me being a former colleague and friend had not missed its mark. She had hoped I would fail so she could say something truly disparaging while cloaking it in an attitude of charity, but she had underestimated the drive and tenacity of the students who had been invited to participate in the program.

My stiletto heels made a loud, clicking sound as I moved into the spotlight after the introduction about my accomplishments had been read. It paled in comparison to what had been written about my nemesis, but I no longer feared that my life would end up much as hers had—minus all the excess. Brett was giving me the chance to have what I really wanted. I felt the tears come as my eyes found a safe spot on the back wall so I wouldn't become overly emotional as I gave my few remarks.

"It has been a real honor and pleasure to work with these talented and amazing students the past few days. What you have seen is just a prelude to what the entire world will see as they begin their chosen life's work. I wish each of them much success and happiness in both their personal and professional lives. I know they're going to do some amazing things."

Without conscious thought, I turned my head and smiled at them before continuing. Despite their outward composure, I knew just how anxious they were feeling inside.

"While I would like to be handing each one of them an award, my boss was very specific about what he was looking for since the winning design will be featured in one of his fall lines."

I slid my finger underneath the sealed flap on the envelope and took a deep breath. I could say so much more about my time here but feared I might let something slip that needed to remain private until Brett and I had decided exactly what we were going to do.

"And the winner is . . . . " I took what I thought was an appropriate pause. "Karen Landing."

The deafening scream that came from behind made me feel as if my heart had literally skipped a beat. Karen's name had come to me most unexpectedly as I watched my students retreat from the classroom for the last time. We had never exchanged anything of a personal nature, but she knew how to ask thoughtful questions, take suggestions and follow instructions. That's why her design was so perfect for Mr. Fredericton's company. It showed creativity while still being something the middle class, American woman—with only so much money to spend on clothing—would eagerly wear.

She threw her arms around my neck before I was able to place the check in her hands.

"Oh, thank you, Miss Sloan. I never dreamed I would be the recipient. I thought you would pick someone much more outgoing than me."

I stepped to one side while she took her bow and then moved behind the curtain while she received the congratulations of her classmates. It was hard not to notice a few looks of surprise, and even one or two of disbelief, but I had stayed true to my convictions by selecting the recipient I felt most deserving. Karen had the ability to make any employer proud, and I knew if for any reason I was asked to work with her there would be no friction. I sensed in her some of the same characteristics others had seen in me. She would fight for what she wanted, but she would never back down when it came to her convictions—whatever they might be.

I had hoped to see Brett at the reception and kept scanning the parameters of the room to see if I could catch a glimpse of his handsome face, but apparently his meeting had taken longer than anticipated. So I chatted amicably with anyone who approached as I held a water glass in one hand. I was much too anxious to eat any of the finger-food that had been prepared.

Several of my students introduced me to family members. I could see the disappointment in their eyes but no one said anything disrespectful or condemning over the decision I had made. I gave whatever feed back I felt was appropriate to the reporters who asked for my input. But I mostly stayed to myself and watched my students mingle. They were loving every moment of being in the spotlight.

It was nearly six when I went back to the classroom and loaded the few things that remained into the van. I would try to get an early start the next afternoon but dreaded saying goodbye to Brett. It might be months before I saw him again and texting and video-chatting wasn't the same as being with him in person.

Our few short encounters had left me with a newfound hope for the future that I didn't want to delay any longer than necessary, but it would take time to complete my commitments, settle personal affairs and move forward into an exciting but unsettled future. I just hoped Mr. Fredericton would agree to some of the proposals that were churning around in my head. They seemed more than workable to me.

Annabelle and Professor Price were coming down the staircase when I got back to the cottage. She had her hand in his and from the way they were dressed, I knew they had special plans for the evening.

"We just saw you on television," she said, giving me a warm smile as the skirt of the black dress she had worn on Monday swirled around her ankles. "Why didn't you tell us about the fashion show? Russell and I would have been there to support you. It was a much more elaborate send-off than the ones we had. We simply finished our lectures and left."

I returned her smile as they joined me in the lobby. "The pageantry wasn't my idea. Plans for it had already been made before I arrived."

"So I gathered from some of the comments the reporter made, but it still looked like everyone had fun. Was your friend, Professor Brett Fowler, able to join you? I'm assuming he had a very busy day after all the hubbub concerning his department chair. It was all over the news as well, including an interview with him. I'm supposing congratulations are in order."

"What exactly did he say?" I asked as the blood rushed to my head.

"Nothing of a personal nature, and he had no comments about the allegations made against his boss. He merely stated that it was his intention to make sure that everything went smoothly in the department during the transition. I knew he could control an audience when he was singing, but I had no idea he felt so passionately about his teaching. He said that all of the students under his leadership deserved the best education possible, and he was going to make sure they got it. Russell said he believes that young man has a very bright future."

"Did he now," I responded.

Professor Price raised an eyebrow before speaking. "Are we making assumptions about the two of you when we shouldn't, Miss Sloan?"

"Most everything about our lives is up in the air at the moment. I didn't even know he was being interviewed."

"But you will be seeing him tonight?" Annabelle asked, staring at the package in my hands as if she had just noticed it.

"No definite plans have been made, but I'm sure we'll talk."

"You could always come to the movie with us. We won't be out late, and it isn't right for you to be alone on your last night here. We're stopping for ice cream later."

"While that sounds delightful, I really don't mind being alone if it turns out that way. It's been a long day, and I have lengthy drive waiting for me tomorrow."

The look in Annabelle's eyes let me know that she had hoped things were going as well for me as they were for her and Professor Price. But Brett and I had a complicated history, and if we were going to make a new relationship work there were more things to consider than just liking each other and deciding that we were better off together than we would ever be apart.

"If you're sure," she said, placing her free hand on my arm. "I know there hasn't been much time for getting better acquainted, but I would hate to lose track of you. Russell and I wouldn't be together if you had not attended that first party with me. I will never be able to thank you enough for helping me see beyond my outward appearance so I felt capable of taking a risk. I never knew I could be so happy."

"Your happiness shows, but all I did was support a friend. And we will definitely keep in touch. I'll want to know all about your trip to Texas. I really am excited for both of you. I have always heard about love at first sight, but you make it look more like a magical fairytale."

"We are not wide-eyed, innocent children any longer who believe in fairytales," Professor Price replied. "We simply recognized a good thing and decided to make it work. Few people like spending their lives alone. It is not why the human race was created. But some of us got so caught up in our work that we were unable to see the value of anything else. From this point on, Annie and I are partners in everything. We will take the good with the bad and enjoy every moment of it."

"Do I hear wedding bells?" I asked.

"Officially, no!" he responded. "But I intend to take care of that as soon as I get mother's approval. She is not as young as she used to be and has always wanted me to find a suitable, intelligent, level-headed woman who knows how to be supportive when it comes to her husband's work. Annie fits all of those qualifications perfectly."

It wasn't how I would want my future husband to describe me, but Annabelle didn't seem to have a problem with it. Maybe companionship and shared goals were sufficient for them at this stage of life, but I still wanted it all.

"Then you do have cause for celebration. That's why I will tell you goodnight. I'm sure there will be more time to talk in the morning before everyone scatters."

"You will come to the wedding, won't you?" she asked. "I want you to be standing there with me when we say our vows. I know it might be an imposition since you live such a busy, fulfilling life, but it would mean the world to me. It's going to be a small affair because, like Russell, I was too busy doing other things to develop any close friendships until I came here. I have never expected much when it comes to really living, but this trip has changed everything for me."

Her openness tugged at my heart. I had never imagined that one small act of kindness could produce such dramatic results.

"It would be my honor, Annabelle," I responded, trying to give her a hug without hitting her with the box I was carrying. "Any idea when the nuptials will take place?"

Mentioning Brett's impromptu proposal, and what it could mean when making personal commitments elsewhere right now, would be cruel. She deserved her one true moment in the sun.

"As soon as arrangements can be made. We can't see delaying the wedding when it's what we both want. I have already contacted the company I work for to tell them I will not be coming back."

"That was a very brave thing to do."

"Not at all," Professor Price broke in. "Annie and I know what we're doing, even if other people disagree."

"I'm not disagreeing. I think what you've found is wonderful. I'm just not sure I would have the courage to quit my job without having another one lined up."

"Under the right circumstances anything is possible, Miss Sloan. Now, we really must be going if we don't want to miss the previews of future films. We will see you at the debriefing in the morning if you are unable to make it to breakfast."

"See you then," I responded as Professor Price led Annabelle out the front door. My head was spinning, but for the first time all week it was over something totally unrelated to me.

When I got to my room, I kicked off my shoes and sat down on the edge of the bed. Brett hadn't tried to reach me, but that wasn't all bad because I needed to see what he had given me before we spoke to each other again. None of his former gifts had been purchased at a store. They were just small and tender things like a flower picked from someone's garden, a cd of songs he had burned or a card he had made from scratch.

My fingers were practically shaking when I removed the wrapping paper from the box. A note fell to the floor almost immediately. I reached down to retrieve it before removing the tape that kept the lid shut.

"*Dear J,*" it read. "*I don't even know what to say about how much my life has changed the past few days, but you have to know by now that I'm serious when I say that I love you and want us to spend the rest of our lives together. I keep having to pinch myself to see if I'm awake or dreaming, but I felt something quite moving when our eyes focused on this at the same time last night. It was almost as if an inanimate object was telling me that it needed to be in our home as started our new life together. I can't tell you how excited I am for that to happen. I know a lot of concessions will have to be made, but I'm ready to do my part. I will even leave Bentley and start over with you in San Francisco if relocating is giving you any concern. I just want to hold you in my arms, kiss those glorious lips and know that we never have to spend another night apart—once I have made you my wife. I love you with all my heart and nothing will ever change that.*"

I rubbed the back of my neck as the note drifted towards the bedspread. Oh, how I wanted to be like Annabelle and take the leap of faith into the unknown without any reservations, but I had seen too much of life to believe that bad things couldn't happen to good people. I just hoped she and Professor Price would be as happy as they thought they would be.

Inside the box was a candleholder. I turned in around in my hands, awestruck by its unique beauty. Part of it was made from worn, metal pieces of pipe about three inches in length that looked as if they had been cut in half by a blowtorch. The rough, variegated edges—some of which looked as if they were in various stages of rusting—had surfaces that were not overly smooth to the touch. They were held together—with the inside of the pipes turned outward—by heavy, metal meshing. Each of the four pieces was easily describable from the others with spots where welds had been made, differences in color that ranged anywhere from black to gray and gold, and uneven holes in unusual places. It was truly the most remarkable piece of sculpture I had ever seen, and I immediately knew it would look perfect on my mantel back home or on the mantel in Brett's lost. The combination of artistry and forethought was astounding.

My phone was next to my ear before I even knew what I was going to say. But the note of weariness in Brett's voice let me know that his day had been far less pleasant than mine, despite our brief get-together in my classroom.

"You sound like you've been through the wringer. Did I call at a bad time?"

"It's never a bad time with you, J. I'm sorry I couldn't make it to the reception."

"I heard about your interview with the press. I guess we've both had our fill of the media, for the time being anyway."

"That's an understatement. I used to enjoy talking to them about my music, but politics is an entirely different story. I'm not so sure they want to uncover the truth. They just want a story that will boost their ratings."

"One of the ills of modern society," I responded. "People seem to enjoy the afflictions and difficulties of others."

"Not his guy. I like to see a happy ending once in a while. Have you had time to open my gift?"

"That's why I'm calling. It's absolutely incredible."

"So I wasn't wrong in assuming that it spoke to me? I could see us laying close to it in the flickering light of a candle. I'm sure I don't have to describe what we would be doing."

My smile was voluntary. "I guess great minds really do think alike because I was imagining the same thing when I saw it. You have very good taste."

"I'm glad you like it. Is it too late to ask if there's still time for us to get together tonight? I know you have a busy day tomorrow, but I still wish you could just stay here. I'm starting to miss you already."

"Same here, but I can't avoid the inevitable forever. Do you still have that picnic lunch? I'm starving. I've been too tense to eat anything since breakfast."

"I can have a meal on the table in fifteen minutes."

"Give me an hour and I'll be there. I need to take a quick shower. It's hot underneath the bright lights, and I'm not a dainty little thing when it comes to sweating. That must come from spending my most formative years in the country when there was always something outside my grandmother needed help doing."

"You could shower here. I promise to give you adequate privacy."

I smiled again. "Maybe another time. I think we both know what would happen tonight if I did. You think you're going to miss me, but I'm not sure how I will be able to get in that van and drive away from here. You have become my life, Brett Fowler, and I'm not leaving because I want to. There are just some things that can only be taken care of in person. I really hope you understand."

"I do, but that doesn't keep me from wishing things could be otherwise. We've been such fools. Just look at all the time we've wasted chasing dreams that were never meant to last forever."

"We promised each other there would be no regrets. All that matters is the present, but if I don't get off the phone, I'm going to cry. I can't believe this is the last night we have in who knows how long. There are no guarantee that my boss will work with me, and I still have a fall line to get out."

"Let's not talk about that until we have to. This night is for us, and I want to make sure every moment counts."

I was knocking on his apartment door sixty-nine minutes later. My emotions were all over the place. Giving in to my desire to be with him completely would be a dream come true because I had never wanted anything more. I could feel his lips on mine and his hands wandering with impassioned purpose to places that he knew would bring me the most excitement and pleasure. My knees felt weak just knowing what could be awaiting me inside.

After all, it wouldn't be like I was taking any real chance, except with personal beliefs that few people felt had any merit in the twenty-first century where satisfying every desire without considering the consequences ran rampant. He had already asked me to marry him in front of witnesses who were unlikely to forget his earnest declarations of love and fidelity. Their observations might already be circulating around campus now that all the pageantry surrounding the runway show was over. Perhaps he had even told someone what he was planning to do, albeit not quite so spontaneously.

His new secretary had to know he had strong feelings for someone since he had sent her to purchase such an incredible gift for me.

These thoughts, along with some I couldn't even admit to myself as having, were swirling around in my head as I listened to his footsteps approach the door. I wished I was carrying something I could hold between us when he pulled it open because I wasn't sure I had the willpower to control my own rising desires. By this time tomorrow night, I would be part of the way home. All I would have to keep me going until we saw each other again were the memories we made while I was here. The painful ones from our past had almost been forgotten.

"Hey there," Brett said, pulling me into his arms as our eyes met. His lips found mine as the fading sunlight cast a dreamlike feeling over the beginning of our last evening together.

I wanted to get lost in his embrace because nothing had ever felt so right before. I'm not sure how many moments passed before our kiss ended, but I allowed myself to enjoy the feel of his heart beating close to mine and the softness of the skin on the back of his neck. He was the most incredible man I had ever met, and I no longer cared who saw us together. I just wanted what we had found to last forever.

"I was beginning to think you had decided not to come," he said as I literally clung to his arms. Breaking physical contact made the inevitability of my leaving in a few hours far too real. "I know you don't want to mess anything up by crossing into the glorious world of lovemaking until the time is right, but you sure do make it hard for a man by looking so incredible."

"Maybe I should have worn jeans," I responded.

"That would only make your delicious curves more evident. I'm afraid most every thought I have of you needs to be followed with a cold shower. Can't you just stay here tonight? I promise to be good."

"Not after what you've just said."

"And why not?" he asked, trailing a finger down the curve of my neck.

"Because I've never wanted anything more than to give myself to you both body and soul, but . . . ."

"I know, J," he interrupted. "You would regret it the moment we were through, even if you pretended not to. That's one of the things I love most about you. You've never been afraid to stand up for your convictions, even when everyone around you was giving in to some of life's greatest pleasures. I can wait until you're ready."

"Are you sure?" I asked, leaning against the wooden railing that looked as if it had been recently painted. "I'm not sure I could survive a phone call, or text, where you say that you got tired of waiting for me to grow up and found someone else with far fewer hangups."

"Not going to happen," he said, nibbling on my ear. "I am yours forever. No one has ever made me feel the way you do, and I'm finally smart enough to accept the fact that I have always been my own worse enemy when it comes to having relationships that are doomed to failure. I'm through with all the games. You are my first, my last and my only true love."

My hands found their way to his cheeks. "Promise? I never thought God would bring you back to me, but now that he has, I can't bear the thought of losing you again."

"You're not the only one with fears," he admitted as his eyes lost some of their playfulness. "I'm scared to death that the minute you get back to your glamorous life in the city that what I have to offer won't be nearly enough."

"That glamorous life as you call it has never been what I really wanted. It just gave me something to do while I waited for real living to begin."

"But you can't just walk away from everything you've built, J."

"Hopefully, I won't have to. Other people get to have it all. Why shouldn't we?"

"On that note, perhaps we should eat," he responded, and the huskiness in his voice was clear. He needed reassurance every bit as much as I did because the commitment we had made to each other was huge. "You said you were starving and so am I."

I followed him inside. His table had already been set with white, expensive-looking plates, sparkling silverware, long-stemmed crystal goblets and linen napkins. There was a bouquet of red roses and dainty Baby's Breath sitting in the center and soft music playing in the background. Lighted candles were everywhere. It was the perfect setting for a seduction.

"Don't get the wrong idea," he said pulling out a chair so I could sit down. "I may have gone a little overboard, but I couldn't seem to help myself. I needed you to know just how much I'm going to miss you and what you can expect when you come back to me for good."

"I've always known you were a romantic, Brett. It was clearly evident when you were singing."

"But I never let that side out when we were together in any other setting. I took you for granted, J, always believing that you would be waiting when my wandering days were over."

"So did I, but fate—or perhaps divine intervention—knew we would never make it all those years ago. Fortunately, time apart has helped level the playing field. I may never really like all the attention you pay to other women, but I am finally secure enough to understand that couples in love don't have to be joined at the hip. I married Greg because I was afraid no one else would ever want me, and I wasn't sure I could survive on my own. After that unfortunate relationship ended, I closed off my heart because I didn't want to feel the pain of rejection or loss again. But I'm no longer quite so afraid of things that can't be controlled. I know I can make it on my own, but I also know that the journey doesn't have to be made alone. I love you, Brett, and I want what we have to work. You don't have to worry about me. Nothing will keep me from coming back."

"Whew!" he said after kissing the top of my head. "You do know how to make a man feel loved."

"So your extemporaneous proposal today was genuine?"

"How could you doubt my sincerity?" he asked as he sat down across the table from me and reached for my left hand. "I have more than a dozen witnesses. I just wish I had a ring to slip on that finger so everyone knows that you're finally mine."

"I don't need a ring for people to know that. I plan on announcing my intention to marry the man of my dream the moment I get home. My boss might as well know that I won't be around to design another season of clothing unless he agrees to certain stipulations."

"You really think he'll agree to unwanted demands? He's used to having you on the premises."

"I think he's always known I'm not like Bethany Kilpatrick, regardless of the fact that I've practically lived at my easel the past few years. She was perfectly happy devoting her life to her career because she never wanted a husband and family. She was content languishing in adoration, having numerous lovers and making bucketloads of money so she could buy anything she wanted. I believe that underneath his often arrogant facade he likes the fact that I'm not a glory-hound. I show up for the required events but let him decide on marketing strategies."

"And you're not worried that he'll just find someone to replace you?"

"He might try, but he hates training new people and has learned that I will fight for my rights. Bad publicity is his worst nightmare because he wants his firm known as one of the most stable, and profitable, in the business."

"You really have changed during the past few years."

"Only in certain areas. I still prefer working behind the scenes, but it's quite liberating knowing I can butt heads with the best of them and still maintain my dignity. Nonetheless, I will never forget where I came from or the fact that my family of origin leaves much to be desired. Perhaps that's one of the reasons I've purposely stayed away from the press. I don't want anyone doing an expose on my life. The fact that my mother has spent most of her life in a mental institution won't garner much sympathy. People are afraid of what they don't understand and would always be waiting for me to crack up like she did."

"You do know that the chances of that happening are slim. You're the most together person I know."

"Not always," I interjected. "I've spent plenty of nights berating myself for things I can do nothing about. Aren't you afraid I might be carrying some of her genes?"

"Not the ones that would lead to something like that. My family has its own share of issues, but life is too short to spend it looking for potential problems. I want people to accept me on my own merits."

We ate cold chicken, potato salad and fresh rolls. He had my favorite kosher dill pickles and sea salt chips on the side, and there was a wonderful parfait filled with my favorite granola, yogurt and fruit for dessert.

"You do know you're spoiling me," I said as we cleared the table.

This time, he didn't overreact. He simply let me rinse off the plates and put them in the dishwasher while he took care of the leftover food. I had never felt so content. It made going back to the city seem like drudgery, but

I was too practical to throw everything I had worked for away. If my boss didn't agree with my proposal to do my creative work at Bentley and return to the city as needed, I might have to make other plans.

"Dance with me," he said when we went into the living room where dozens of candles were still burning. "I need you in my arms, and I'm not sure I can control my actions if we're sitting on my sofa or anywhere else."

"So you've been in that situation before," I said without thinking.

His sigh was one of regret and sorrow. "You know I have, J, but even bad boys can change. I won't disappoint you again."

"What if I disappoint you?" I asked.

He swept me into his arms where I rested my head on his shoulder.

"We've had this discussion before. I'm not afraid of the past and you shouldn't be either. We're going to make it this time. The stars have finally aligned in our favor."

He hummed along with the song that was playing as I allowed my mind to drift to a future that now seemed very real. I would come back to Bentley as often as I could, and he would come to see me in California while I made preparations to leave. Selling my home wouldn't be a problem. The renovations that had been made would assure me of getting a good price once it was on the market, and then we could decide where we were going to live as a married couple. While I loved his loft, living there wasn't an option. Not only was it too small to hold all things I would be bringing, but it also held vivid visualizations of his past relationships with other women.

We would find a place we both loved where we could grow old together and raise our family. I didn't know how many children he wanted since he was approaching forty, but I wanted at least two—a girl for him and a boy for me. I was so lost in my dreams for a happy future that a knock on the door made me jump.

"Don't get it," I whispered. "I want this moment to last forever."

"I'm not going anywhere," he said, kissing my lips. "But I really need to see who it is. "I've been waiting for a contract that needs my signature so the band can record another commercial. I get to do one of my original songs so it's a pretty big deal to me."

"How will you ever find the time to do everything you want to with your new promotion?" I asked as he broke our embrace.

"No worries on that front, J. I've never felt more alive or energized."

I moved towards the large window overlooking the street while he answered the door. A car that had not been there when I arrived was sitting in front of the house. I didn't think much about it until I heard him gasp.

"What are you doing here?" he asked the person standing outside my line of vision. "I thought you had left town for good."

"What a silly you are," a female voice responded, and I felt my entire world start to crumble. "I said I needed a few days to think. Well, I've done that, and I'm ready with my decision. But I would prefer not delivering it in your doorway. Why don't you just invite me in? It's not like this is the first time I've shown up at your place unannounced."

"Now isn't a good time," Brett told her as the knot in the pit of my stomach rose to my throat. "Why don't you come back tomorrow night. We'll have plenty of time to talk then."

"But I want to talk now."

I felt rooted to the floor as a girl—young, blonde and beautiful—threw herself into Brett's arms, smothering him with passionate kisses.

"I told you I've made my decision," she breathlessly said when their lips parted. "I will marry you. I couldn't decide for the longest time because of the difference in our ages, but I know you'll be good for me. I couldn't bear to go through this experience alone."

I felt my hand on the cool, glass surface even knowing that it would leave a mark. What was the girl talking about? Marriage? Commitment? Brett had already made those promises to me.

"Who's that?" she suddenly demanded as her cold, green eyes shot like a laser through me.

I had never known Brett to be at a loss for words, but he looked helplessly at me before turning his attention back to the girl who looked as if her fingernails would leave scars on his arms they were so deeply imbedded in his flesh.

"Listen, Shelley, we need to talk, but not right now."

"You can't do this to me," she almost snarled. "I leave for ten days and when I come back, happy as lark over making a decision I know both of us really want, I find you here with another woman. How could you do this to me?"

"None of this was planned. You have to believe that."

"I don't have to believe a word you say, and I'm not going without a fight. You made a promise to me, and you will make good on it. She's not even your type. She's years older than me."

By now my world had quite spinning quite so rapidly, but I couldn't stay were I was and let the humiliation continue.

"I really need to be going," I heard myself say as I walked towards the sofa and picked up my purse. "It was good to see you again after all these years, Brett, and thank you for the celebratory dinner. I'm glad I was able to be part of a program where so many students got to see at least part of their dreams fulfilled. But it's back to the real world for me. I'll see myself out."

I was on my way down the steps, hoping I wouldn't trip over something in the dark before he made it to the door.

How could I have been so blind? Leopards couldn't change their spots, and girls like me always ended up alone because we wanted to believe the best about others.

Chapter 9

My eyes were dry as I pulled away from the curb in the rental van. The car belonging to the woman who was now standing in Brett's apartment where I had just been was parked directly behind me. It was something most any college student would drive—an older model sedan with a large dent on the driver's door. I could see why he had been attracted to her. She was exactly the kind of girl who had always stood right in front of him as he performed. But the joke was on me for thinking he could ever really care about a girl who had enough self-respect not to fall all over him. I had been nothing more than a diversion while the woman he really loved was trying to make up her mind about marrying him.

But I would berate myself for the stupidity I had shown by falling so completely under his charms again once I was away from Bentley. Right now, all I could to preserve my dignity and keep from falling completely apart was to put as much distance as possible between us. The day that had begun with such promise had turned into the worst one of my life, and I wasn't sure I would ever recover. But thank heavens I would never have to see anyone involved with my folly again if I could make it out of town before anyone tried to stop me.

I didn't care what people thought or said after I was gone. I didn't even care if my boss fired me for not following through with my commitment and attending the closing at ten the next morning where I was expected to give a report about the experience I'd had during the week. In fact, it might be better if he did. I could change my number and disappear.

Maybe I would even follow Bethany to France. As much as she resented, and possibly even hated, me, I knew I would be able to convince her to let me work with her again. She needed what I had to offer to make a comeback, and if I proposed a deal where she could take all the credit and I would remain in the background for good, I might never have to set foot on American soil again.

I could become a recluse who took up painting and never left my room —much as mother had been doing since I was a child. Perhaps I wasn't as different from her as I had always believed. Neither of us seemed to be any good at handling loss, and I didn't have the strength left to move forward on my own again.

Few lights were visible as I drove down the lane leading to Whitman Cottage. It was after midnight, and it wouldn't take long for me to pack my suitcase and be on my way. I would leave a note on the front desk telling the program director that something unexpected had come up at work, and I needed to return to the city as quickly as possible. I would thank her for the experience and offer my assistance in the future. It was the polite thing to do, even though I knew I would never come back. The part of my life that had to do with Bentley University was over for good.

I parked the van in front of the building and hurried up the stairs. I could be gone in less than thirty minutes, as long as I didn't spend much time writing my notes. I couldn't exactly leave without giving Annabelle a reason. She expected me to be at her wedding, but that was impossible now. I would simply tell her that things with Brett had disintegrated to the point that I couldn't take the chance of seeing him again. The damage done to my heart was already more then I might ever be able to bear. Besides, she and Professor Price Price didn't need me hanging around on what was supposed to be the most glorious day of their lives. My presence would only bring everyone down.

Since driving such a long distance in a dress and heels wasn't practical, I changed into some jeans and a light shirt as soon as I had closed the bedroom door. Then I pulled clothing from the closet and drawers as rapidly as possible. There was no need to take care with my packing. Everything would need to be washed or sent to the dry cleaners once I got home anyway. Perhaps I would even burn most of it. I didn't need reminders of what I had worn while spending time with Brett, especially when he was asking me to marry him. And I certainly didn't need the gift he had placed in my hands. I would attach a note to it and leave it in front of Annabelle's door as a wedding gift. Even if she didn't like it, there was no way I could take it with me.

I pulled my suitcase down the carpeted hallway, but carried it down the stairs so the noise of it thumping against the wooden risers would not awaken anyone. I thought I heard voices coming from Professor Price's room, but perhaps he and Annabelle were discussing future plans. At least someone had an amazingly, heartwarming story to tell. My experience at Bentley had turned into an incident from hell.

The night was dark and eerily silent as I slid the side door open and hefted my personal belongings inside. It wouldn't take long to write my notes, and then I would be gone. I almost pulled the van to the side where Brett would not see it if he happened to come looking for me. But I needed my escape to be quick, and I doubted his paramour, Shelley, would allow him to leave. Something about what she had said bothered me, but I couldn't take the time to try to decipher what it was right now. The adrenaline I was running on now wouldn't last forever. I would crash, and I needed to be miles away when I did.

Writing anything of a personal nature had never come easy for me. I hated expressing feelings that made me appear weak or vulnerable. The note to Mrs. Tracy was easy. I had only talked to her once and seen her a few times in passing, but with Annabelle it was different. I had never believed I would become even remotely attached to the mousy-looking woman who had come to my room before turning into a swan. How she had managed to capture the man of her dreams in less than five days would always remain a mystery. I had known Brett for over twelve years, and we still didn't know how to make each other anything less than miserable. Although I doubted he was feeling much pain now, except perhaps from cruelly misleading me.

My notes were written rapidly. Even the one to Annabelle was more impersonal than I wished it could be, but if I allowed my emotions to surface the crying might never stop. I would put the candle in front of her door, and then return for my purse and computer before heading down the staircase for the last time.

There were still no lights visible in the hallway, except for a small patch of amber shinning out from underneath Professor Price's door at the end of the hall. I had just stood upright after delivering my gift when loud, angry voices reached me. I had no intention of eavesdropping, but it was impossible to ignore what being said.

"You lousy, rotten, old codger. How dare you use me like this? I've been by your side every step of the way in the development of that orchid, and now I learn from the department head that not only are you taking complete credit, but you're firing me so some lady you met just days ago can take my place. Well, I'm telling you right now that's not going to happen."

"Calm down," an unruffled voice that I knew belonged to Professor Price said. His wooden-toned verbalizations were impossible to mistake for someone else's. "It's not as simple as you might wish to believe, Wally. I am not excluding you from anything. The paper has yet to be released, and I have mentioned your contributions in it. As for you being replaced, I have given you as much guidance as I possibly can. It's time for you to strike out on your own and see what kind of a name you can make for yourself."

"But I need the money coming from our discovery to get a new start. No one is going to give me a chance if I can't bring something tangible to the table. You would never have discovered the exact formula if it wasn't for me."

"We're still not sure it can be replicated, Wally. Don't you want something that is completely your own?"

"I want my fair share for what I've already done."

"Now listen here, young man! I agreed to let you internship with me so you could gain some experience in horticultural research. I have paid you a decent wage and cited your contributions in the footnotes of my paper. That is all I ever promised to do."

"But you could rake in millions with our discovery."

Professor Price laughed as I moved closer to his door. If he needed my help in standing up to some clown who had been in his employ, I would give it. I owed that to Annabelle since I wouldn't be attending their wedding.

"Not likely! Only the people in our field are really going to care. Do you have any idea how many plants we would have to sell to make a million dollars? It could take the rest of my lifetime. I create different varieties of flowers because it is what I most enjoy doing. I have never cared about being rich."

"Well, I do," the man name Wally announced. "I happen to know people who would be very interested in the genetic engineering we did to make those gold flecks so pronounced."

"You must be mad if you think I would ever sell my formula to the highest bidder. It belongs to the university anyway because they funded the research. What you are asking is impossible."

"Only if you're still alive to stop me."

The door was ajar, and I could easily see into the room by leaning forward. Professor Price was sitting on the bed, a look of total disbelief and despair on his face. A man stood in front of him. He was enormous when compared to Professor Price. Not fat, just big like a football player with broad shoulders and heavy arms. He was wearing a crumpled shirt and soiled jeans. A girl stood by his side. She couldn't be much over five feet tall, although most anyone would look dwarfed standing by such a big man. I couldn't seem to move as the argument continued.

"Look, you old fool. Just had over your briefcase and the combination to the lock on the security vault back at the university, and I'll leave without hurting anyone. If you don't, I have a little friend here that might help you make up your mind." He pulled a gun from behind his back and pointed it at Professor Price's head.

I clapped my hand over my mouth to keep from screaming. I had to do something before the big man carried through with his threat. But there were only a few people in the cottage this time of night—mainly older men and Annabelle Little—and I had left my cell phone in my room.

"Go ahead and shoot," Professor Price calmly returned. "You'll never get away with it. Besides, I don't think you have it in you to be violent."

"Oh, you don't," Wally said. "Then you don't know me as well as you thought. I'm very capable of killing someone. I've done it before. You forget, I was in Iraq."

"But that was an entirely different situation."

"Maybe, but I would suggest you think twice before calling my bluff."

"Let's just go, Wally," the girl with him said. "I didn't sign on for murder."

"But you didn't sign on for poverty either, Myra. Don't you see that Professor Price holds our futures in his hands?"

"We'll find another way to get what we want. It won't do either of us any good if you end up in prison."

"I'm not going to prison. Professor Price is going to listen to reason, aren't you, old man?"

"You're not going to pull the trigger," he replied. "An investigation would lead right back to you."

"It might, but I'll be long gone before anyone can figure out what really happened. My contacts are about as far away from Texas as anyone can get, and with Myra to back me up, no one will be able to prove anything."

"Flight records are easy to pull, and when the orchid goes missing everyone will know exactly who took it."

"Quit tempting me to pull the trigger. I'm not stupid. I know how to cover my tracks. Now, what's it going to be?"

Professor Price rose to his feet. "I guess you'll just have to do what you must because I am not going to budge. I have spent my entire life trying to create something truly beautiful, and you have only been working with me for a few months. Your contributions, at best, were minimal."

The big man shook the gun in front of Professor Price's face. "You give yourself too much credit, old man. Maybe I'll just make you disappear. Then I'll be able to go back to the university and take over without any fuss. After all, I'm the best choice they have if they want to keep your research going. Once I have access to all your records, there's nothing to stop me."

"Only your greed and ambition," Professor Price countered. "Won't it look rather strange for me to disappear right before your name is put on my discovery?"

"I'll let you take most of the credit, and no one is going to question a suicide, especially with a note saying why you did it."

"I won't write anything."

"Oh, I think you will. Myra, look around for some paper and then see if you can open than damned briefcase. His notes have to in it since he didn't leave them in the lab or at his house."

"You've broken into my home?" Professor Price asked.

"It couldn't be helped, but no one will suspect anything other than a robbery. I helped myself to your coin collection and a few other miscellaneous things in your safe. They should bring a sizable amount of money once I feel secure enough to get rid of them."

"You're crazy, Wally. You need professional help."

The big man laughed. It was a totally diabolical sound.

"I'm not going to be locked up, and you're going to cooperate. See this attachment to my gun? It's a silencer. No noise! No fuss! No witnesses! Just a dead, old fool who couldn't live with himself because he could no longer take credit for something he didn't do."

"No one will ever believe I took my own life. I have never even owned a gun"

"So you stole mine. You see that all the time in detective movies."

Professor Price put out his hand. "Give me the gun, Wally. You're not thinking clearly. You could be the next one to come up with a new variety of orchid all on your own."

"If you think I'm going to believe that you won't turn me in then you're crazier than I am. Have you found anything for him to write on yet, Myra?"

The girl shook her head.

"Then we'll go with plan two. Get something to tie him up and we'll drag him to the car. There should be plenty of places around here to hide a body."

"Please, Wally," she pleaded. "Can't we just run away? With what you got from his house we should be able to make it to a place where no one will ever think to look."

"Your girlfriend is right, Wally. There is no need for violence."

The big man was sweating. "Both of you be quiet! I need to think."

Myna opened a drawer and pulled out a necktie. I knew I should do something, but I was unarmed. And if I ran back to my room to get my phone and call the police, Wally and Myra might be gone by the time I got back and Professor Price might be dead. I needed to do something to distract them while there was still time for both of us to get away.

I watched in complete horror as Myra tied Professor Price's arms behind his back and Wally told him to turn around. The gun with the silencer was thrust into his back, and then they were moving towards the door. There was no time for me to get out of their way, so I did the only thing I could. I let out a scream and ran. But before I made it to the top of the staircase I heard a heavy thump on the floor.

"You didn't have to kill him," Myra was shouting as they exited the room after me.

"Shut up you fool," he responded. "We have bigger concerns right now if you don't want to end up in prison with me. We need to find who saw us."

I was reaching for the knob on the front door by the time they made it to the top of the stairs, but I had lost one of my sandals before reaching the lobby. My pursuers might not have seen my face, but they knew exactly what I looked like from behind. And with only one shoe I would have difficulty making it anywhere in the dark. Thick, prickly undergrowth was everywhere, and I had left the keys to the van on my bed. But I had one advantage they didn't. I knew my way around campus and where I could most likely find help in the middle of the night.

For that very reason, I headed off to my left instead of following the gravel road. I could get to the main part of campus by foot, although it might not be easy. It was impossible to believe they had killed Professor Price to come after me, but I was the only thing that stood between them and continued freedom since I could give accurate physical descriptions and make positive identifications in a lineup.

If they were smart, they would get in their vehicle and leave town immediately. Someone had to be with Professor Price by now, unless they had closed the door so their crime would not be discovered until morning. A scream could have come from anywhere, and most people didn't want to become involved with anything that didn't directly concern them.

There was a full moon and the parking lot was lit up like a lantern. I ducked behind a hedge of red roses just as Wally and Myra came into view. They spent a moment talking, but it was impossible to hear what was being said because my heart was pounding so hard. I had to get away, and I had to get help for Professor Price. I should have made a move sooner, but I had been given no indication that violence would erupt until I saw the gun, and by then it was too late.

While I was still casting blame where none was deserved, they parted. Myra was looking carefully behind and underneath each car, but Wally was heading directly towards me.

My only hope was to run, straight up the hill and onto the campus. One foot moved in front of the other as I began the assent, trying to stay hidden in the shadows of the trees and bushes while the pain in my bare foot increased. I must have stepped on something that cut it deeply because every time my foot touched the ground I wanted to scream.

I tried to push prickly vines away from my face as I made my way up the side of the hill through underbrush that I knew was filled with animal and insect life that I didn't even want to think about. Coyotes and snakes— not all of them harmless—along with squirrels, raccoons and skunks made their homes in the bullrushes around the streams. I had even seen deer and an occasional fox as I walked its borders as a student.

It was hard to believe I was running for my life after just having had my heart broken, but it somehow seemed a fitting end to my time at Bentley. I should never have come back. The past could never be recaptured, and the present was good as it ever got.

The tears were freely flowing, but I couldn't worry about them any more than I could spend time wondering what Brett was doing with Shelley. I was very conscious of twigs snapping and knew my pursuers were still coming after me. I stopped running only once when I slid down the embankment but managed to hang onto a tree branch to catch my breath before continuing.

"I've got her in sight," I heard Wally shout through the ominous darkness. "Just try to keep up, Myra. We'll make sure she's out of the way and be on our way. I really am sorry things had to turn out this way."

"Me too," Myra panted. "You promised everything would be okay."

"Stop complaining. She's just a few feet ahead, and we're almost out of this stinking underbrush. Once she's in the open, I can get off a clear shot."

I knew what my fate most likely would be, but I wasn't willing to give up and wait for death to take me any further into the unknown. There would be someone to help if I could just make it to the central part of campus. While none of the buildings would be unlocked, I knew where a key to the rear door of foreign language building had once been hidden. Brett had used it one night when he needed something from his office. He explained that he hadn't been the one to put it there, but it had come in handy a time or two. Perhaps he would make sure it was removed now that he was in charge, but I hoped for my sake that it was still there.

The man and the girl were closing in when I got to the top of the hill. My fall had given them time to catch up. I could hear their heavy breathing and Wally's continual oaths that he wouldn't stop looking until I was dead. I knew I could easily increase the distance between us again if given half a chance, but I couldn't outrun a bullet. I just wished the moon would disappear behind a cloud for a few moments. That was all I needed to make it through a short clearing and disappear into the thick vegetation that surrounded nearly every building.

I had just stepped into the open when I heard a muffled whooshing sound and something pinched my arm right below the shoulder. A stinging pain rippled through my body, and I fell to my knees. I had been shot!

Dizziness and nauseous came instantly, but I struggled to control the sinking sensations. I grabbed my arm and forced myself to my feet. The Foreign Language Building was to my right, and I knew the approximate location of the key Brett had once used in my presence. It was underneath a broken brick on the ledge of the window closest to the back door. Finding it, and getting inside, was the only hope I had left. Warm, thick blood was oozing through my fingers and streaming down my arm. It wouldn't be long until I lost consciousness.

I half-crawled and half-ran towards the cluster of buildings—where I hope to find safety—staying as close to the shadows as possible. But I knew the exact moment when Wally and Myra cleared the crest of the hill.

"There she is," he shouted as his footsteps hurried in my direction. I rounded the corner of a building before he could get off another shot.

If I could keep my wits intact until I reached my destination it would be a miracle, but for some bizarre reason I almost felt I deserved one after what I had been through. Not that living seemed like such a blessing since I would never have what I truly wanted, but it was better than facing a complete unknown.

The bursting rush of adrenaline that had keep me moving since leaving Brett's loft was being replaced with the desire to fall to the ground and let oblivion sweep me away. But if I gave in to my fears, or the trauma my body was going through, no one would ever find the man who had killed Professor Price. I was the only one who knew what had happened in his room and could see that both Wally and Myra were held accountable.

I glanced up in time to see a dim light peaking out from between the slats in a drawn blind on the second floor of the building I needed to enter without being seen. Maybe I would even be able to find a phone so the police could be notified that they had more than a campus rapist to worry about tonight.

Wally and Myra would not give up until they found me and were just yards away when I touched the cool, brick wall that was covered with ivy and started to make my way around to the back. If they would just concentrate their search elsewhere until I had time to find the key and let myself inside . . . .

"You check out the building next to this one," I heard Wally shout as their heavy footfalls ended. "She has to be close. I know I hit her."

"Can't we just go," the girl pleaded. "There was no reason to shoot Professor Price. He was just a harmless, old man."

"A harmless, old man who would never give in to our demands. Do you want to be poor forever?"

"It's better to be poor than spent the rest of our lives in prison."

"No one is going to get caught. We hid the car halfway down the lane. It will take the authorities hours to find it, and by then, we'll be back at the university and no one will ever be able to prove that we even left town. Things are working out even better than I thought they would. We just have to find that girl so she can't tell anyone what she saw or heard."

"But nothing tonight has gone the way you promised, Wally. I'm scared. I just wanted to have a real family."

"Then help me finish this. You're just as guilty as I am now."

I felt sorry for the girl but hoped she would keep the conversation going. If Wally came around the building, he would find me. I had to be in the open to unlock the door, if I ever managed to find the key.

"Oh, please let it be there," I prayed as I got shakily on the tips of my toes and reached above my head for a brick I hoped was still loose after nearly ten years.

I needed something to stand on, but there wasn't even a large rock in sight. Both my feet and my arm throbbed but giving up wasn't an option if I wanted to live. Stretching out as far as I could, I managed to grasp the lower edge of the window ledge. I felt to both the right and the left but not a single brick moved.

Panic gripped my soul, but as I gulped in as much air as I dared, a voice seemed to whisper in my mind. "Push up from the bottom."

I didn't need to be told a second time. My knuckles moved against each brick, but it wasn't until I got to the last one that I felt anything move. I wrestled with it for what seemed like forever until it shifted and almost went crashing to the ground. I slid it to the side before reaching up again. The key was soon under my fingertips, and I gripped it tightly as I lowered myself back to the ground.

The couple on the other side of the building was still arguing. I couldn't hear every word since my mind was definitely elsewhere, but it appeared as if Myra was ready to call everything quits.

"I didn't pull he trigger, Wally. I could never hurt anyone."

"You might not get the gas chair, but you'll definitely spend time in jail. Now quit complaining and find that girl. I'll put a slug in her head, and then we'll throw her into that damned ravine that nearly tore off some of my appendages. Her body will never be found intact."

I didn't listen to anything more. I simply hurried to the back door and slid the key into the lock, but it wouldn't turn to the right as it should have done. For a moment I thought the lock had been changed.

"Don't panic," I told second or two before Wally put that bullet in my head as he had promised to do. I could hear his feet pounding on the ground as he came closer. A wave of relief washed over me as I felt the door move inward. I stepped over the threshold and slammed it shut behind me. I had just turned the lock and moved to the side when I saw something come through it. The door was old and sturdy, but it was still made of wood.

"You aren't going to get away from me that easily," I heard Wally shout as his booted foot slammed into it.

But something told me he would never get inside. He had already used most of his bullets, and he would never be able to kick the door in. I leaned into the rock wall as I heard Myra's voice.

"Why all the shouting? I thought you didn't want to get caught."

"I don't, but all your complaining allowed her to get inside this building. I don't know how we're going to get at her now unless we can find some other way in."

He rattled the door knob. Instinctively, I moved further away from it.

"We can't do anything about that, Wally. Let's just go. Our backs were towards the door the entire time. She couldn't have gotten a good look at us."

"The door should never have been left open—not even a crack. She knows our first names, and we have no idea how much of the conversation she overheard."

"I'm sorry," the girl sobbed. "Maybe she'll bleed out."

"You better hope that's the case, but I thought you were against anyone getting killed?"

"Don't make me the bad guy in any of this. I only came along because you promised no one would get hurt."

Wally hefted his weight against the door, but it remained firm. "You do know that we can't go back to the university now. Our only chance is to make it across the border into Mexico and never come back."

"I can live with that," Myra said. "I know how to speak Spanish and can get a job."

"Well, it better be a good one because I'm not fond of getting involved with one of the cartels just to make a reasonable living. That could shorten my life span considerably."

I listened intently as their footsteps died away and then tore a length of fabric from the bottom of my shirt and wrapped it around my upper arm. I wanted to allow myself to slip into oblivion. Wally and Myra would not be coming back, but I knew that time was not on my side. The bullet in my arm may not have hit an artery, but I was still losing blood and needed to get help before I was unable to tell anyone what I knew.

Quite suddenly, I remembered the light on the second floor. Someone, other than me, had to be in the building—a night custodian, a security officer or even someone working late in his or her office.

I hugged the wall as I moved in the direction of the staircase. I was cold, colder than I had been in my entire life. That meant I was going into shock, but I had to concentrate on finding help first. I pulled myself up the flight of stairs using my left hand. My right arm hung limply at my side. I was tempted to stop on the main level to see if anyone was around, but it was the next one up where I had seen a light so I kept going.

I had entered through the basement since the building had been constructed on a slight incline. Perhaps that was why Brett had felt that leaving the key under the brick wasn't such a bad idea. Few people ever used that door, except delivery persons or someone on the janitorial staff.

Wondering what he would think when he learned that the brick had been moved and there were bullet holes in the door gave me the incentive to keep moving. Maybe he would even feel bad for having deceived me if he found out I was injured or even dead.

It was as dark and foreboding on the second floor as it had been in the basement, but at least I was safe. And Professor Price might still be alive if the bullet Wally had fired in his direction had missed vital organs. With what little strength I had left, I prayed that that was the case. Annabelle deserved her happily-ever-after.

My knee hit something tall and cold before my body did. It had to be a statue or an exhibit of something. All I had to do was work my way around it. My good arm slid easily around the obstruction, and I was on my way back down the hall with the light at the end guiding me.

"Help me," my mind shouted as I stumbled the last few feet. I wasn't sure if the words even came out, but I still managed to hit the door with my fist before sliding to a heap on the floor.

The last thing I remember was a glorious flood of light.

Chapter 10

"Miss Sloan."

The voice was very near, and I tried to unfold my eyelids, but I was too tired to make even that slight effort. It was a strange kind of tired—a complete numbness of both body and mind—and I wanted it to remain. Coming back to a world filled with nothing but sorrow was just too much after what I had endured, but I knew my desires were not a real consideration for anyone right now. People needed my help, and I couldn't give it if I wasn't fully awake.

The voice speaking to me was unfamiliar, but it seemed so incessant in its desire to get a response that I tried to focus my semi-conscious mind on it now that I was no longer running from people who wanted to kill me, just as they had done Professor Price.

That thought alone should have been enough to bring me back to full consciousness, but if I allowed that to happen, I would also have to remember Brett's betrayal.

"Miss Sloan, I need you to wake up now. You've been asleep long enough, and I have to check your vitals."

I tried once again to focus. The room was dark, except for some filtered light that was spewing in from the hallway and from somewhere behind my head. A woman dressed in pink scrubs stood beside my bed. She had a stethoscope around her neck and one of those little finger things that checked how much oxygen I was getting in her hand.

"Where am I?" I mumbled.

My mouth felt as if it was filled with a thousand, dry cotton balls.

"You're in the hospital," the woman said in a tone I knew she had practiced to help patients feel less afraid. "Do you remember anything that happened?"

"Most of it, I think," I responded, feeling uncomfortably out-of-control. I tried to push myself upright so I could get a better look at my surroundings, but a dagger of pain ripped through my upper arm forcing a stifled scream of pain.

"Just lay still, Miss Sloan. Your shoulder is going to hurt for a few days, but it will feel much better if you don't move around. The doctor was able to remove the bullet and said that no major damage had been done. I can give you something more for the pain if you like."

"Thank you," I said, much too bewildered to protest.

There were so many questions I needed to ask, but I settled for laying back on the pillow and inhaling deeply. I hoped that a few deep breaths would stop the darkness from descending again, but I wasn't sure the pounding in my head or the nausea in my stomach would quit any time soon. I needed to know if Professor Price was still alive and if our assailants had been caught so I asked one more question as she inserted a needle into my I.V.

"Can you tell me what's been going on since I was brought here? The last thing I remember is knocking on someone's door."

"Unfortunately, I can't be of any help when it comes to that. I'm just a nurse in the intensive care unit, but I can tell you that the police have been here and want to talk to you. I told them they would have to come back later."

"But I need to speak with them as soon as possible," I objected. "Someone's life could depend on it."

"There isn't anything you can do about that right now. The doctor said to make sure you got some rest."

My eyes closed, and when I opened them again it was light outside and a cleaning lady was running a damp mop over the floor near my bed.

"Good morning," I whispered, blinking several times. "Can you tell me what time it is?"

"A little after five. I didn't mean to wake you."

The lines between my eyes deepened as another sharp pain brought the nausea to my lips. "You didn't, but I need something because I'm going to throw up."

She handed me an amber-colored, plastic bowl. "Just let it come. I can always get someone to help with the cleanup."

Everything remaining in my stomach was gone before I was able to speak again. "I'm sorry you had to witness that. Can you tell me when the doctor will be here? I really need to speak to someone."

"Can't say for sure," the woman responded. "They usually check on their patients first thing in the morning. I can try to find out if you give me his or her name."

"I don't know what it is," I said as a heavy weight settled on my heart again.

I had lost part of my life, and even walking backwards through my mind wouldn't help. Everything was a complete blank after I had slipped to the floor in the Foreign Language building. I could barely recall speaking to the night nurse.

"Then I'm afraid the best I can do is call a nurse."

I could do that myself, but if the authorities were aware of what had happened, and our assailants were still at large, uniformed officers would be close so they could offer protection. That was one thing I had learned from hours of viewing police and FBI dramas during my many evenings alone.

"What about men outside my door?" I asked.

She gave me a look of complete frustration. "There is someone, but I didn't speak to him. We were told go about our duties unless instructed to do otherwise."

"Could you get him for me? I have information the authorities need. Without it, two cold-blooded killers might never be caught."

That seemed to capture her full attention, and a moment later a young man in a blue, police person's uniform entered my room. The cleaning lady did not return with him.

"Glad to see you're finally awake, Miss Sloan. Some of our detectives have been more than anxious to speak with you. I'll have them here in a jiffy. They just went to the cafeteria for some coffee. It's not often we have a night like this around here."

"That would be much appreciated," I replied.

I could have plied him with questions but knew I needed to conserve my strength. Since everyone at the hospital, that I'd had any contact with, seemed to know my name, at least part of my night's adventure was already common knowledge. That meant the detectives assigned to case could give me some of the answers I needed. My job was to fill in where I could. Professor Price might not be one of my biggest fans, but Annabelle loved him. I would do whatever I could to help her through this.

The officer left me alone, and I used that time to quiet my mind and order my thoughts. A hysterical woman wouldn't be of any value in an investigation, and I needed to relate what I knew with exactness. If Wally and Myra were found, I would be the only one who could put them away.

My shoulder was still throbbing, but I couldn't see anything more than the abrasions on my hands and lower part of my left arm. The entire upper part of my body was encased in a sort of sheath that was designed to keep me from further injuring myself. I was surprised I hadn't noticed it before.

I waited with nothing short of dread until the door opened again, and a man and a woman in street clothing approached the bed. They looked businesslike, confident and professional. The woman smiled as she spoke to me.

"We've been in hospital for several hours hoping you would soon be able to tell us what happened last night, Miss Sloan. We're sorry for what you've been through, but the doctor tells us that you're going to be okay."

"Good to know," I replied. "I haven't seen him yet, at least not when I was conscious. I want to tell you what I know so I can get out of here as quickly as possible. I have urgent work waiting for me in San Francisco."

"We'll see what we can do to expedite that," she replied while taking her phone from her pocket.

The tall man in a two-piece, dark suit took a step backwards. Quite obviously, he must have decided that it would be easier if a woman questioned me. What he didn't know was that I had been around men all my adult life and had no problem being questioned by them.

"I'm Detective Davidson, and this is my partner, Detective Reaves," the woman dressed completely in black continued. Like me, she wasn't wearing a wedding ring, but the man was. "Can you tell us, in your own words, exactly what happened? We'll be recording the conversation so there will be no difficulties later on."

"That's fine with me, but I need something from you first," I responded, knowing that I was way out of line to be asking anything of them.

She gave her partner a quick, almost desperate, glance. "We'll do what we can to answer your questions, but that's not why we're here."

"I'm well aware of that, Detective Davidson, but I need to know about Professor Price. I was standing outside his door when one of his colleagues by the name of Wally shot him."

"So you are an eye witness to what transpired."

"Most of it, but I need to know if he's alive before I continue."

"I can only tell you that he's in surgery. He was found in his room after he didn't come down for breakfast. Now, can you tell us what happened so we can find the perp? We were unaware of how closely the two cases were connected until now."

"That's too bad," I said, feeling my pulse begin to race much too fast again. If they didn't have Wally and Myra in custody by now it was unlikely they ever would. "I'm sure you'll find that the bullets came from the same gun. Wally was using a silencer. I thought I made enough noice trying to draw them away from his room to awaken everyone at the cottage."

"Some of our people have interviewed most everyone there. No one saw or heard anything."

"Then how did you figure out who I was?"

Detective Reaves cleared his throat before breaking into the interrogation his partner was trying to conduct. 'Your van was parked in front of the building, and you seemed to have disappeared."

"Are you saying I was a potential suspect?"

"Everyone has to be ruled out in a case like this, Miss Sloan. Now please answer Detective Davidson's questions. We can't help either you or Professor Price if you don't tell us everything you know."

"I basically know very little," I replied.

"But you got caught in the crossfire, Miss Sloan. That didn't happen by accident."

"No, it happened because I let my curiosity get the best of me. I was leaving a gift in front of Miss Little's room when I heard some loud voices coming from further down the hall."

"And you didn't think to alert anyone else?"

"It didn't seemed important at the time. I could have gone back to my room, but Professor Price and Annabelle Little have become personal friends during the week we've been here. I wanted to see if there was anything I could do to help."

"And was there?"

"Hardy, Detective Reaves. Professor Price and the man he addressed as Wally were having a huge argument over who should get the credit for some orchid that was grown at the university where the man was the professor's assistant."

"And that conversation escalated to violence."

"Quite rapidly, actually. I don't know much about horticulture, but I'm not sure the reason behind the disagreement is all that important right now. The man you want was heading for the Mexican border with a woman by the name of Myra."

"Did you get a good look at them?"

"Enough to pick them from a lineup. They broke into Professor Price's home in Texas and stole a coin collection and a few pieces of jewelry they were hoping to fence for the money they needed to get where they were planning to go."

"And you have no idea where that is?"

"I can write down everything I remember, but most of it won't help you right now. One of them said they left whatever they were driving in the lane leading to the cottage so it wouldn't been seen if something went wrong. I think Wally was just trying to force Professor Price's hand, but he wouldn't back down. The next thing I knew, he had a gun in his hand. I thought I could stop him from firing it if I screamed. But my diversion backfired. He fired it anyway and then came after me."

"What happened next?"

"I ran as fast as I could. I contemplated going back to my room because that's where my cell phone was but didn't want to put anyone else in danger."

"You most likely saved a few lives by doing that, but please go on."

"I headed up the hill towards the main part of campus. I knew the way because I was a student here once. I thought that gave me an advantage, but I underestimated the man who knew I could identify him."

"Can you tell me when you were shot?"

"Just after I made it to the crest of the hill. There was a clear stretch, and I wasn't fast enough."

"But you still managed to get away."

"Only because I remembered what a friend once told me about a hidden key to the building that houses the foreign language department."

"So you used that to get inside. It sounds like you're one lucky woman," Officer Davidson said.

"I guess I am. All I can say is that the man with the gun didn't want me around."

"What about the girl?"

"She was scared! I don't think she was really involved. She kept saying that it wasn't what she had signed on for."

"Well, I suppose we have plenty of time to determine her extent of involvement," Detective Reaves said. "Right now we need to find them. Is there anything else you can think of that might help us establish the route they took to the border?"

I shook my head. "I can't even tell you if that's the way they'll end up going. But if I was in their shoes, I know I would get out of the country as fast as I could. Wally talked about not wanting to becoming involved with one of the cartels, and Myra said she knew enough Spanish to get a job south of the border. They were hoping I would bleed out since they couldn't finish me off, but they have to be smart enough to know that if either Professor Price or I survive we know enough to help put them behind bars."

"We'll start looking into it immediately, Miss Sloan, and thanks for both your candor and help. I'm sure we'll be in touch again soon. There will be someone stationed at your door until you leave the hospital, and then we'll arrange for you to be in protective custody until they're caught."

"That won't be necessary," I replied. "They never got a look at my face and once I'm gone there's very little chance of them ever finding me."

"Let me be the judge of that, Miss Sloan. Desperate people do desperate things."

I knew he was right, but I couldn't live my life in fear. Nor could I stay where I was any longer than absolutely necessary. I didn't want to see Brett again. He had ruined everything.

"Could I ask you one more thing before you leave, Detective Reaves?" I asked to stop my mind from going elsewhere. "How soon will word get out about what happened?"

"I'm afraid the press is already hounding us for a statement, Miss Sloan, but we will keep your name out of it since you're a material witness in an ongoing investigation."

"Thank you, sir. I work in a high profile field, and my picture was on the news last night."

"I thought I recognized you," Detective Davidson said. "You're that designer from San Francisco."

"Guilty as charged. I suppose it wouldn't be that hard to figure out who I was if someone really wanted to know."

"We'll make sure you're protected," she responded. "But I have to warn you that I might ask for an autograph. You're the first really famous person I've ever met."

"I'm not that famous, but I suppose it wouldn't hurt to be cautious until you find Wally and Myra. I just wish there was more I could do to help."

"You've given us more leads than we ever expected to have. Now try to rest. We'll keep you updated."

I watched them leave and wished I could do just that, but my head was spinning faster than it ever had before. I could not go into protective custody for an undetermined length of time while two people I didn't know were caught and prosecuted. I was just an everyday person who had never done anything out of the ordinary, except for being in the wrong place at the wrong time twice in one night.

Maybe that's why I felt as if I was finally living one of my childhood nightmares   where—though no fault of my own—everything was in a complete state of turmoil. The reason behind my feelings of hopelessness and despair were never quite the same, but I always tried to find a way back to a place of peace and safety until the emotional trauma became too great.

And then I would simply give in to the spiraling, circular motion of an underground cavern where the darkness would take me beyond being able to feel anything. It was like free-falling into a state of oblivion where the only reason I knew I was still alive was waking up—covered with sweat and screaming.

I needed to be in familiar surroundings now where I could immerse myself in my work while putting Brett's deception and being shot behind me. If I allowed myself to think about the cost of those two actions before I was a safe distance away from where they had happened, I would never survive.

Perhaps what I had already told the two detectives would allow them to capture the man who had tried to kill both Professor Price and me before I was even released from the hospital. From what I had seen of Wally and Myra, they would disappear and never resurface. They were cowards in the truest sense of the word. They wanted something for nothing and blamed everyone, but themselves, for the things they did that were wrong.

It was ten-thirty before a Dr. Brennen walked into my room. I had already eaten what breakfast I could and felt as if every nerve ending in my body was on fire. I was a woman of action and being confined to one place, with a pain in my shoulder that even the best drugs could not entirely remove, was driving me crazy. He was a short, thin man with horn-rimmed glasses who looked so incredibly tired that I almost felt sorry for him.

"How are you doing, Miss Sloan?" he asked, taking a deep breath before approaching the side of my bed where I would not have to move while we talked. "I'm sorry I wasn't able to get here sooner, but it's been a very busy night."

I managed a half-hearted smile. "I've been better, but it looks like you're not in much better shape than I am."

His smile caught me off guard. "Let's just say that I'm not used to doing back-to-back surgeries. This is a very small hospital, and there wasn't time to move anyone to the city."

My mind was telling me to ply him with questions. But the oath he had taken, along with all the laws regarding patient confidentiality, would keep him from answering most of them.

"I appreciate what you did to help me, Dr. Brennen."

"All part of the job for a surgeon. Now let's take a look at that shoulder. You're a very lucky young woman. The bullet didn't hit anything major, just a little tissue and muscle. You'll be up and about in a couple of days and some concentrated therapy will help you regain full movement within the next two months."

"Two months," I said. "I use my right arm everyday in my work. I can't design anything without it."

"Then perhaps that incentive will push you to a quicker recovery. My wife was at the fashion show yesterday. She admires your work greatly."

"Then you understand why I can't be laid up with a bum arm. My fall line has to be ready by the first of September."

"The body is an amazing thing, but it can only be pushed so far."

"What about possible infection?" I asked to keep a distasteful setback from overshadowing what I really needed to learn before he left.

"You've been treated for that, and we'll keep a close eye on you while you are here. It's a good thing one of the custodians was still in the building or you might have bleed to death. We had to give you several pints of blood."

"I suppose that's fairly common."

"It is with gunshot wounds, but having two in one night is a first for us. This has always been such a safe, pleasant little town."

He had given me the segue I needed. "So you did operate on Professor Price?"

His look was one of surprise. "You do understand that I can't discuss my patients without their consent."

"I am well aware of hospital rules, Dr. Brennen, but I was there when he was shot. I even tried to get the man away before he pulled the trigger, but that didn't work out so well either. I think that gives me a vested interest in his condition."

"So it does," he responded. "The patient in question took a bullet to the stomach, but he made it through a very difficult surgery, compounded by the fact that he lost even more blood than you did by the time we got him on the table."

"But he's going to be okay?"

"It's too soon to make a call like that, but we're doing everything we can. He'll be kept in the I.C.U. until it's safe to move him elsewhere."

"So he's under protection too."

Dr. Brennan smiled. "You don't pull any punches, do you?"

"I've always been a firm believer that the squeakiest wheel gets the most grease. It might not be the most endearing quality, but it usually gets results. Will you let me know if anything changes, or at least ask someone if his fiancé, Annabelle Little, can come to my room? She needs to hear what happened from me."

"No promises, Miss Sloan, but I'll see what I can do. The detectives in charge decide who goes in and out of your rooms."

"But I already told them there was little reason to believe that we would be in any further danger. The man who did this will want to get as far away from here as possible before anyone is able to put the pieces together."

"That's certainly what I would do as a felon. But right now, you need to rest. I'll check back later this afternoon. And no more heroics! I don't want to see you on my operating table again."

"No, sir," I replied. "I want to go home as soon as possible. This trip has been far from what I expected."

That wasn't entirely true, I had to admit after he left me alone. I had wanted to see Brett again, but why would he make such a point of declaring his love for me in front of my students when he had already made the same commitment to someone else?

Maybe in time I could give him the benefit of the doubt, but right now, I needed to be angry. It was the the only way I could stay focused as I tried to recall everything that had happened during the past eleven hours. Even the simplest comment Wally or Myra had made could help the police find them.

But after I had gone over everything I could remember for the third and forth time, I realized that I had given the detectives every shred of information I possessed. It would be up to them to contact the university and follow up on any leads they found. And with the level of technology available, along with the expertise of the analysts the government employed, it shouldn't take them long to find out exactly what Wally was driving, if there had been any movement on his credit cards or if he, or Myra, had family or friends south of the border.

At least I certainly hoped that would be the case. I needed to be back in my own bed before my name was released to the public. Not that Brett wouldn't be able to connect me to what had happened before then. He was certainly smart enough, but I couldn't listen to an apology or any words of remorse or pity. Hating him for the rest of my life was far preferable to being pulled back into his web of deceit.

I tried to sleep after eating what I could of a very bland lunch, but my mind wouldn't let me. I even asked the nurse who came every hour to check my vitals if there had been any word on when I might be able to talk to Annabelle Little. I knew she was in the hospital. She would never leave the man she loved alone. Perhaps she had even been able to see him. If that was the case, I needed to know what he had been able to tell her so we could compare notes. It was after four when I heard her voice outside my door.

"Thank goodness you're okay," she said, rushing to the side of my bed. Her eyes were large and filled with fight. "I've been demanding to see you since early this morning, but no one would let me near your door. I can't believe this has happened. I knew something was wrong last night when I heard your scream, but when I opened the door the hallway was empty. That's when I saw your gift. Were you really going to leave without telling me goodbye?"

"I suppose I was, but fate obviously had something else in mind. How is Professor Price? I really thought that man had killed him."

"Oh, Jada," she said, practically falling into the nearest chair. "When I saw him lying in that pool of blood with barely any pulse, I thought my own life was over. I have never loved anyone the way I do him. All I could think about was never getting to experience being his wife. Is that awful of me?"

"It's a very human reaction," I replied, wishing I could sit more erect without causing more pain. "Have you been able to see him?"

"Only for a moment," she said with a shake of her head. "He was too weak to talk, but he squeezed my hand. That's why I know he's going to be okay. He wants to be married as much as I do. You've got to tell me what happened. Two detectives grilled me this morning, but I had no answers to any of their questions. Russell and I didn't discuss our work. We figured there would be plenty of time for that after we were married. We just wanted to get to know each other better. But what I really don't understand is why you were involved."

"It's a complicated story."

"I've got nothing but time. Russell is the best man I've ever known. I can't imagine anyone wanting to hurt him."

Responding to her request would be easy. Every event, up to the time I had lost consciousness myself, was deeply embedded in my brain. But it would mean at least mentioning what had happened with Brett, and I wasn't ready to go down that rabbit hole yet.

"Please, Jada," she pleaded. "The detectives told me that if you hadn't gotten that awful man away, Russell wouldn't be alive."

"I'm not sure that's true, but I'll tell you what I can. I was loading things into the van when I heard an argument. In retrospect, I should have called for help, but I had no idea it would turn violent. From what I heard through the crack in the door, Professor Price's assistant—a man by the name of Wally—wanted more credit for the discovery of the black orchid that was named after you."

"That's absurd! All he did was help out around the lab. Russell was the one who did all the work."

"Be that as it may, he said he broke into Professor Price's home to look for the formula since it wasn't at work. When he couldn't find it, he stole a coin collection and a few other things. But what really set him off was finding out that he was being dismissed from his position."

"Are you saying this is my fault because Russell wants us to work together?"

"No, Annabelle," I responded, wishing I could offer her physical comfort without putting myself in excruciating pain. "The man was clearly deranged and wanted something for nothing. When he found out he couldn't get it, he decided to get rid of the competition. With Professor Price out of the way, he thought he could take over the lab and claim the discovery as his own."

"But everyone knows that isn't the truth."

"That's why I said he was insane. I just hope the authorities catch up with him before he makes it out of the country."

"They told me he wasn't alone."

"He had a woman named Myra with him. I'm not sure of their relationship, but they seemed close. I've already told the detectives everything I know. They promised to get back to me as soon as they had some news. I was hoping you might have something to add."

"I wish I did," she replied, brushing her hands up the sides of her hair. "Nothing they told me sounds promising since that monster has such a big head-start. I was told that Russell will be in protective custody until they are caught. Does the same thing apply to you?"

"Unfortunately, yes. I had hoped to be well over halfway home by now."

"But why?" she asked. "Does it have something to do with Professor Fowler? I saw him in the hallway just now, and he looks just awful."

"You really saw him here?" I asked as the color heightened in my scratched and bruised cheeks. I had looked at my reflection in the spoon I had used for eating. "I thought the names of the people involved had yet to be released."

"No one has been mentioned by name, but both shootings are all over the news. Besides, I saw him at the cottage earlier this morning. He was asking everyone if they had seen you since your van was sitting out front and your room was empty."

"Did you talk to him?" I asked.

"Only in passing. I was on my way to find Russell, but he seemed genuinely distraught. I can only surmise that things did not go well on your final evening together.   That's the only explanation I have for why you would leave without saying goodbye. I know we're not bosom-buddies, but I thought at least we were friends."

"We are, by my involvement with Brett is complex. I thought we were truly in love this time around, but I was wrong."

"Not from what I observed."

"You've got to leave this alone, Annabelle," I said as forcefully as I could without becoming overly agitated. "I can't deal with him right now."

"But you'll have to eventually."

I shook my head. "No one is allowed in my room without having it cleared first, and I won't give my permission. Promise me that you will not talk to him again. The less he knows about me the better."

"You can't run away for your past, Jada. I know from experience that it will follow wherever you go."

"Let me worry about that. You have Russell to take care of."

"But who's going to take care of you?"

"I don't need anyone to do that. I'm perfectly capable of taking care of myself. I've been doing it since I was a child."

"Maybe you have, but no one should be alone at a time like this. You've been shot, and it's going to be a long recovery. At least let me tell that young man that you're going to be okay. I've never seen anyone look quite so upset."

"He's not worried about me. He just wants to ease his conscience. But if you feel the need to say something, just tell him that he doesn't need to waste any more of his valuable time on me. I was leaving before a bullet hit my shoulder, and I won't be coming back."

"You sound so bitter. That isn't the least bit like you."

I looked at her as if she had bitten me. What had happened to that retiring soul of a few days ago—the one who had apologized for asking me to help her?

"I know you think I'm being insensitive," she continued as she wrung her hands together. "But you have to give him a chance to explain. If you don't, you will spend the rest of your life wishing you had."

"Why would you think that when you know close to nothing about me?"

"Because I've always been intuitive, besides having a very high I.Q. I just never had the courage to tell people what I think or how I feel until I met Russell and you."

"While I applaud your newfound freedom of expression, I'm afraid you've only seen the side I show to the public until now. I'm completely filled with wounds that will never heal."

"You're too young to be so disillusioned with life, but I won't push any more right now. You need your strength to get better."

"That's what the doctor said. I truly don't mean to sound churlish, but if I give in to what you're suggesting, there might not be any coming back for me."

She didn't respond, she merely rose to her feet and placed a kiss on my forehead.

"I need to be getting back to Russell, but I would like to visit you again. I promise not to pry into your personal life again without asking clearance to do so first."

"Then you're welcome to come back any time you like. I know I sound unreasonable, but it's how I survive."

"We all do what we must. But you need to understand that you're no longer alone, unless it's what you really want. I feel like I've finally a family, and I don't want to lose it."

"You won't," I said. "I just need some time to get back to a better place in my head. Tell the professor I'm praying for him."

"As we will be doing for you. Thank you for distracting his assailant. I am convinced it's what kept that bullet from taking him away from me."

I couldn't stop thinking about Brett after Annabelle left. I wanted to believe that he really loved me and had a logical explanation for why some young, blonde girl said she had decided to accept his proposal. He had looked genuinely shocked when she walked into his living room and saw me standing at the window, but he hadn't come running after me. He had stayed behind to take care of her needs. Perhaps that was the real reason I was so upset.

Tears stung my nostrils as I recalled his endless games from the past. There had always been one more young woman to meet and romance, and I had been a fool to believe he had changed. Still, it was hard not hearing his side to what must be a very enlightening story. It might give me some of the closure I needed so I wouldn't feel quite so disfigured inside.

The night was endlessly long. The only people I saw were the nurses who came to check my vitals and the girl who brought my dinner and wanted to know if I would like a snack before trying to sleep. I should have asked Annabelle if she would make sure my personal belongings at Whitman Cottage were secure since they had been left in an unlocked room, but she hadn't come back to see me. I just hoped it had more to do with her need to be with Professor Price than my churlish attitude. She wasn't responsible for anything that had happened in my pitiful life.

I did, however, get permission to call my boss from one of the hospital phones and tell him why I wouldn't be home as planned. Despite the chaos I was feeling inside, I could at least be grateful that I had not made any bold declarations about having fallen in love and leaving my job like Annabelle had done. It might be all I ever had to keep my fragile sanity intact.

"This is a surprise," Mr. Fredericton said when his secretary put me through to his office. It was late Saturday afternoon, but he generally worked six, or even seven, days a week like most everyone else at the firm. It was considered a necessity unless vacation or family emergency time was involved, and I had never minded because it gave me something constructive to do so my mind had little time to wander. "I'm supposing all went well and you're on your way home. But why the call now? You haven't given me an update since you left."

I took a deep breath to help calm my nerves, but the pain shooting through my shoulder let me know that I was far from being recovered.

"Everything was going great until last night, sir, but I'm afraid there's been a little hiccup in my plan for getting back."

"Nothing serious, I hope."

"That depends on how one looks at it. I'm in the hospital but will be fine in a few days."

"Don't leave me in suspense, girl. You do know that we have a fall line to get out."

"That's why I'm calling. Lacy knows what to do until I get back, and I promise that everything will be ready on time."

"What about you? No one ends up in the hospital by choice, unless cosmetic surgery is being done."

"It's nothing life threatening, just a little inconvenient. I was shot in the shoulder last night while trying to help one of my colleagues. It's a long story, but the police seem to think I may need someone watching my back until the assailant is caught since I can identify him."

I could almost hear the gears in his brain grinding during the prolonged pause before he responded. "I am sorry to hear about such an unfortunate occurrence, but we have qualified security personnel on the payroll that I trust far more than some stranger to keep you safe until the scoundrel is behind bars. And Miss Hampton can start checking into licensed and trustworthy physical therapists as soon as our conversation ends. I refuse to have you secreted away in some back-woodsy town where you are left to the care of the locals—who may, or may not, know what they're doing. Any idea when you will be released? I can have a plane ticket waiting, along with someone from my personal security detail. You will not be left alone until I have a guarantee of your continued safety."

His show of concern made me feel not quite so alone. "No word yet, sir, but you don't have to go to all that trouble."

"Yes, I do. I take care of my people, especially those who have shown such loyalty to me. Is there anything I can do from here?"

"You could send someone to get the van. It has mostly mannequins and fabric inside, but I think it would be worth the effort."

"Then consider it done. I am surprised I haven't heard anything about an altercation at Bentley on the news. The networks are usually all over it when someone gets shot."

"Not when white people are involved," I responded, knowing I might be speaking out of turn since I had no idea about his political affiliation, only that he had always lived in a blue state and appeared to be a very liberal thinker. "We don't seem to matter much any more as long as we're paying our taxes and keeping our mouths shut."

"We do agree on that," he replied. "I have my own beliefs about most everything, but I definitely miss the days when people tried to get along and certain folks weren't offended by everything. What caused the argument, if you're free to tell me?"

"It was a dispute over a new variety of orchid. The assistance who worked with the professor who created it wanted the credit."

"Not exactly what I expected to hear, but then I guess you are in the world of academia. I hope the inventor wasn't killed. That could make for a lot of nasty legal entanglements if you were a witness to what happened."

"I'm afraid I overheard most everything, but the doctor is hopefully optimistic that the professor will survive a bullet to the abdomen. I told the detectives everything I know but have no idea how long it might take for the shooter to be apprehended. He sounded as if he might be heading straight to Mexico."

"A good place for him to stay if he's willing to kill someone and doesn't want to get caught, but that's beside the point. Please keep me updated about your condition and when you might be ready to come back."

JS Ririe

"You'll be the first one I call. I just wanted you to know that I wouldn't be back in my office on Monday morning."

"I appreciate the heads-up. Take care of yourself, Jada. You have a very bright future here, and I would hate to see anything cut it short."

My feelings were mixed when I hung up the phone. I liked knowing my job was secure after what had happened with Brett, but it would be an uphill battle to keep my broken heart from impacting my work. Creativity was directly affected by emotions.

The nurse gave me something to help me sleep about midnight. I had fought taking another sedative because I could remember with vivid clarity what they had done to my mother before she disappeared from my life. Her zombie-like demeanor had been terrifying because I was never sure if she actually heard what I was trying to say. She just moved through the house in a medicinally-induced trance never allowing any emotions to surface. Perhaps that was why I had always been so afraid of my own. If I allowed them to take control, I could end up exactly where she was.

Besides, I didn't want to relive my flight to safety through one of the nightmares I was bound to have. Even with my eyes wide open, I could see myself running across sharp rocks, through deep crevices and up steep inclines in the dark. I could feel my flesh being torn as I slipped more times than I could count and fell into barbed shrubbery, piles of rotting leaves and unknown debris. I could sense the terror of watching Professor Price slump to the floor and being hunted, much like an animal, by people I didn't know who wanted me dead because I had witnessed their crime.

But wondering if I could have avoided being shot by not stopping for that brief moment of contemplation and rest at the top of the hill was the hardest. The sound of that bullet whisking through the air and the indescribable pain that came when it ripped through the flesh of my arm would stay with me until the day I died. I hadn't asked the doctor about having scar but was fairly certain there would be some round, pink and fleshy remembrance that would let me know just how lucky I should consider myself that I was even alive.

The clear, blue morning sky was visible when I opened my eyes again. I had no idea what time it was, but a bird was chirping in the pine tree that rubbed against the window, and a small brown squirrel was running across the narrow ledge outside the glass. There was only one floor to the hospital, but as far as I knew, no unwanted felons had come anywhere near it while I was sleeping.

The doctor stopped by not long after breakfast had been served—a horrid compilation of bland, cooked mush, apple juice, dry toast and strawberry-flavored yogurt. After giving me a brief examination, he said he had no problem releasing me the next morning—as long as I continued to improve and followed up with my own doctor, and a physical therapist, back home. Of course, he couldn't be sure if the detectives investigating the case would object, and they had the final say since I was an eye-witness to a crime.

I wanted to believe I could convince them that I was no longer in any danger and would willingly come back to testify at a trial. I needed to get away from Bentley before another chance encounter set my world reeling again.

"Is there anything I should know about my recovery that hasn't already been covered?" I asked as he was getting ready to leave. I figured I was a prime candidate for a good case of PTSD. My past had been no picnic, but I had never been shot before.

His smile was not quite as forced as it had been the day before. "I guess we should talk about what you can expect besides a very sore arm and several weeks of physical therapy. No tendons were involved, but there was considerable muscle damage. That will have to be rebuilt, and it's going to take time. You might also consider talking to someone who deals with trauma. I could suggest a good psychologist if you were going to stick around for a few weeks."

"That's impossible, Dr. Brennen, but I will keep it in mind," I responded. If, or when, I needed mental health services, I would take care of it on my own. "Anything else?"

"From a surgical standpoint everything went routinely. Naturally, you will need to keep the area dry until the stitches come out, and contact a doctor if you suspect an infection. All post-operative instructions will be included in your discharge papers. However, I would recommend using the prescribed painkillers for as long as you need them. I understand that you had a slight altercations with one of the nurses about doing so last night. Are there any addiction issues I should have been made aware of?"

I leaned back and sighed. "No, Dr. Brennen. I just don't like taking medication. The list of possible side-effects far outweighs the benefits."

"Not if they're used in the prescribed manner. But the length of your recovery will depend mostly on you, Miss Sloan. This has been a sad year for our small town since most everyone relies on the university to keep their businesses running. Two rapes on campus and now this. The media is already casting blame everywhere they can."

"There's no one to blame but the perpetrators. They are the only ones who should be punished."

"I agree, but criminals survive on societies' understanding, and the media always portrays them as being victims of past injustice instead of holding them accountable for deplorable acts. I'm just glad my children are past their public school years. I would likely face jail-time myself for being too vocal about all the proposed curriculum that doesn't mesh with my beliefs."

"You're not alone in that," I responded, surprised by his willingness to talk when I knew I wasn't the only patient under his care. But then I was in a small town where people were more concerned about what went on around them than they were in a big city where violent crimes were an everyday occurrence.

"Is there anything else?" he asked, taking a step towards the door.

"Yes, Dr. Brennen," I said. "Do you foresee any problem with me traveling right after I leave the hospital. Not by car, of course. My boss will be sending an airline ticket and a traveling companion."

"Then you should be okay," he replied. "Just try to take it as easy as you can. Whether or not you want to admit it, your body has been through an ordeal."

"Not like the one Professor Price's body has been through. Would it be possible for me to see him before I leave? I know I'm not family, and his injuries are far more extensive than mine, but I feel it's important for us to talk."

"He's quite heavily sedated, and I can't risk having him upset. I hope you understand."

"How about tomorrow?"

"You find it hard taking no for an answer, don't you, Miss Sloan?"

"I suppose I do, but I have become very fond of both him and Annabelle this past week. She even invited me to their wedding."

"That's hardly a reason for me to break hospital protocol. However, these circumstances are highly unusual so I will see how he feels later on today and possibly bring it up. His full recovery is my biggest concern."

"As it should be, but I do hope he will feel like speaking to me. I think we could both use it."

Once he had gone, my mind began scrambling for things I might be able to say that wouldn't cause a setback. Talking details seemed unwise since Wally and Myra might never be caught. But at least I could express wishes for a speedy recovery. Despite our lack of commonalities, we both cared a great deal about Annabelle. Perhaps my willingness to talk to him would undo some of the damage my surliness from the day before had caused.

The two detectives working the case stopped by mid-morning. I could tell nothing about what might be going on from their countenances, but at least I was sitting up in bed and felt much better than I had the day before.

"I hope you come bearing good news," I said before they had time to ask if I had thought of anything else.

"We don't have them in custody, but the pickup truck they were driving was found not far from the university in Texas late last night. Apparently, they figured they had enough time to pick up a few things from home and switch vehicles before continuing. Their pictures have been released to all law enforcement agencies, along with a description of the vehicle we assume they are driving. It belongs to a Myra Banks who has been living with Wally Cummings for the past three years. From what we've been able to discover, this isn't the first time Mr. Cummings has had a run-in with the law."

"But you have every reason to believe they will soon be caught."

"We have some strong leads and will let you know as soon as we have them in custody."

"Does that mean I'm free to leave town once I've been released from the hospital? The doctor said it could be as early as tomorrow morning."

"While we can't force you to accept our protection, Miss Sloan, we would highly recommend that you don't take this situation lightly. As long as they are at large, there is always the possibility that they will come after you again."

"I'm willing to take my chances. I've already spoken to my boss. He said some of his security people can keep an eye on me, and as long as my name isn't released to the public, I should be in the clear until they're captured and brought to trial. I promise I'll be here to testify."

"It's good to know that you understand your civic duty, but why don't we see what happens during the next twenty-four hours," Detective Reaves said. "This was a courtesy visit. We'll have a guard stationed at your door until you leave the hospital and no one will be allowed into your room without clearance. I hope you don't have a problem with that."

"No, sir," I responded. "Getting shot wasn't a pleasant experience. I just wish there was more I could do to help."

"Never underestimate what you've already contributed to this case," he continued. "Without your input, we would still be gathering background information. In fact, we probably wouldn't even know who they were. There were no prints left in the room, and you appear to be the only one who saw them. Professor Price couldn't tell us much when we spoke to him after surgery."

"What about today?" I asked.

"We're on our way to his room now. The doctor said he is much more coherent this morning. Perhaps he will be able to add to what we already know. If the suspects are on their way to the border as you suggested, someone will see them and let us know."

I certainly hoped that would be the case. I needed a return to my own kind of normalcy before I could even think about all the massive changes a few days at my alma-mater had brought.

Chapter 11

I was unaware of having fallen asleep until lunch was brought to my room. But it wasn't the sound of the tray being placed on the bedside table that awakened me or even the soft noise of shuffling feet. It was the resonance of voices in the hallway that made the hair on my arms stand erect. I listened as intently as I could while my brow furrowed and my lips turned into an unflattering frown. While I couldn't make out exactly what was being said, the voices sounded suspiciously like those of Annabelle and Brett.

My compassionate and tolerant new friend had promised not to speak to him, and I had hoped that my former, unofficial fiancé would stay away from the hospital once he had been made aware of the fact that I never wanted to see him again. But I had my suspicions that I was in for at least one more disagreeable confrontation. Brett was every bit as stubborn as me.

"Can you tell me what's going on in the hall?" I asked the young woman as I tried to push myself a little more upright in bed.

She looked at me and smiled. "The man outside your door—who doesn't have a gun at his side—has been here since you got out of surgery. I thought he would leave in as much as visitors aren't allowed, but he seems determined to see you the moment it's allowed."

"You're sure he's been here that long? It's been a day and a half since I was brought in."

"I can only tell you that he was here when I left last night and was sitting in the same chair when I arrived this morning. Since he's still wearing the same clothes and looks like he hasn't slept for a couple of days, it seems safe to assume that he hasn't been home. You must mean a lot to him."

"We have a complicated history," I responded as she situated the arm of the table over my body so I could eat what had been brought.

"I suppose that could be said of most every relationship during these times of uncertainty and unrest. I know I'm having trouble deciding if it's fair to bring a child into this world. My husband says I'm being unreasonable because things will get better, but I'm not so sure of that."

"He's right in believing that hope is important."

"You really believe that, even after being shot?"

"What happened to me was an unwanted twist of fate. If I hadn't been packing a van in the middle of the night so I could leave town sooner, I would never have overheard the argument that got me here."

"I guess no one can really plan on anything, other than taxes and death, as my parents used to tell me."

"I heard the same old adage when I was young but prefer to think that it's what goes on between those events that really matters. We can't exactly take anything with us when we die."

"So you do believe in an afterlife."

"I also believe in God, the divinity and mission of his son, and the gift of agency. We might not know what's going to happen as we take this mortal journey, but I would hate to miss any of it because it's making me a much stronger person . . . ."

My words drifted off as I realized what I was truly saying. I was furious with Brett for having hurt me again, but I would never heal without giving him the chance to explain.

"I guess I feel the same way, Miss Sloan," she said. "I would have loved to be in attendance at the fashion show you hosted but had to work. I understand from some of my friends that it was the most elaborate production of its kind every presented on that stage."

"Does everyone in the hospital know I'm here?" I asked, not wanting to get caught up in trying to explain the mechanics of something I knew relatively little about, other than getting the fashions on the runway.

"Not everyone," she replied with a knowing smile. "I only recognized who you were because I saw your face on TV. Those of us with assignments in this wing were told to keep quiet. That hasn't been overly hard since this is the first time I ever remember seeing guards at any of the patient's door. I'm just glad everyone is going to be okay."

"Me too," I said. "But you could tell me the name of the woman talking to the man in the hall, couldn't you?"

She glanced quickly over her shoulder. "I don't know her name, Miss Sloan. The charts only have initials on them. But she has been spending a lot of time with the man who was brought in not long after you were. Would you like me to see if she's still there?"

My head moved back and forth of its own volition. "That won't be necessary. You have work to do, and I'm sure she'll stop by when she has the time."

"What about the man?"

"He shouldn't even be here."

She looked down at the floor, and I felt bad about being crotchety again.

"Please don't take anything I say too seriously. I'm not any good when it comes to dealing with pain."

"Do you need me to get a nurse?" she asked.

"No! I just need to eat my lunch and try to relax. I don't know how you handle working in a hospital. I'm much too queasy around bodily fluids and lack the patience to be around peevish people. You have my admiration."

My attempt at making amends must have worked because she left with a smile on her face. I just hoped I could keep my tongue in check when my next visitor came to call. In a few hours, I would be on my way back to my home in northern California were I could continue basking in my misery without making anyone else feel bad.

It was three o'clock before Annabelle came back. She looked as if she had been crying.

"What's wrong?" I asked when the door closed behind her. I was in a private room so we could talk frankly and freely without worrying about being overhead. "Has something happened to Professor Price."

"I wish you felt like you could call him Russell," she replied. "I know he can be a little intense, but he's a wonderful man with a very kind heart."

"I'm sure that's true, Annabelle, and I am sorry for not trying harder to become friends. But I have never been any good at letting other people in. I suppose that comes from growing up in a very unstable home."

"We haven't talked much about either of our childhoods, but they should not be allowed to define who we are now."

"That's easier said than done for some of us since the past has a nasty habit of repeating itself."

"Only if we let it," she countered. "I tried to stop by earlier to tell you that Russell is doing much better and will be moved out of the ICU later today but had an interesting encounter before I could knock on your door."

"Is that why you've been crying?" I asked, hoping to deflect her away from what I knew she was planning to say. Brett had an uncanny knack for getting women to believe anything he said, but I wasn't going to fall under his spell again. For my own survival, I had to keep an emotional distance from most everyone right now.

"Maybe," she admitted. "I want you to be as happy as I am and feel like you might be throwing something quite wonderful away because you don't have all the facts."

"Then enlighten me," I responded as my heart began to beat more rapidly and loudly than it should if I didn't want the nurse checking on me before making her scheduled rounds.

"I'm afraid I can't do that because I didn't ask him the nature of your most recent difficulties. Russell told me to leave it alone, but I'm pretty good at reading people. And that young man who has been waiting for over thirty-six hours to see you is totally crushed."

"Perhaps he should have thought about the consequences of his actions before making promises he couldn't keep."

"I don't want to get into another battle of wills with you, Jada. I would only lose because I'm not any good at conflict resolution, but I really think you should give him a chance. He said he would stay right where he is until you were released if he had to. I really don't see where that would do either of you any good. If there is anything I have learned the past few days, it's that loving someone is messy but definitely worth it."

"So Russell really is going to be okay."

She smiled when I said his name and some of the softness returned to her eyes. "That's what the doctor said when he made his rounds this morning. Russell told me the whole story about Wally, the orchid and why his former grad student felt so betrayed. I get why he feels partially responsible for the attacks. He knew Wally had some grandiose ideas and that a showdown was coming the minute word got out that the assistant position was being given to someone else. The dean promised to keep it under-wraps until he got back, but somebody dropped the ball. What really gets me is the fact that he refuses to press charges."

"I'm not sure that will be up to him. Attempted murder is a criminal act."

"That's what I told him, and I guess you could say that our first argument ensued. I feel just awful about it because he's supposed to be recovering from a very serious operation."

I reached for her hand that was busy twisting the cuff of the blouse she was wearing. "It is a little mind-boggling that he contacted his boss almost the moment you met. How could he even know where things might lead?"

"He said he had been praying for me all his life and wasn't about to let me get away when we walked back to the cottage that first night. Since I felt the same way about him, we decided not to wait to get the proverbial ball rolling."

My eyes suddenly became very large. "Weren't you even slightly concerned making such a huge commitment to a complete stranger?"

"Russell never felt like a stranger. That's why I came to your room to ask for help. I knew I would regret it for the rest of my life if I didn't take a bold move to get what I really wanted."

"But what if he was married or involved with someone else? Men have a bad habit of withholding the truth."

"I had to trust my heart, Jada. That's what people in love do because everyone makes mistakes. Maybe it really is just a matter of deciding between being with a person who isn't perfect or being alone."

"So logic and science are no longer the determining factors in how you live your life?"

"I will admit that they are much easier than taking a religious or spiritual approach, but I have always believed in a higher power, despite the brutality my father often showed. Russell came from a similar background and said he felt the same way I did until he met me."

"So you really have spent some quality time talking."

"Maybe age has something to do with it. Russell will be sixty-one this year, and I'll be fifty-four. Waiting around just because others might find fault with what we are doing seems like a horrid waste of time. But I really need to go. I promised to hurry, and Russell says he feels so much better when I'm in the room with him."

"Then I won't keep you. Give him my best. I really am glad that he is doing so well."

"I will, but what about that young man in the hall? He has been waiting an awfully long time."

Annabelle's observations about life and love had given me something new to think about since I couldn't exactly judge anyone for bad behavior when my own was not above reproach. But I wasn't ready to face Brett again. His actions had hurt me deeply.

"Tell him I'm doing okay, and we will talk later. I can't give him any more than that right now."

"Just don't wait too long. Right now is all any of us really have."

She said we would talk again before I left the hospital. I was tempted to ask if she knew what was going on at the cottage. My computer, cell phone and sketching tablet all contained vital information that I did not want getting into the wrong hands, but I couldn't concern her with any more of my problems. I had to assume that my belongings would be safe until I could collect them and leave town.

Now, more than ever, I wanted it to be soon. When I thought about Brett, my true feelings were no clearer than they had been when I saw the woman he had proposed to before me walk into his loft. I knew I still loved him. Most likely a part of me always would, but he had broken my heart for what seemed like the millionth time and, while I knew I could eventually forgive him, forgetting would be much harder.

My stomach was growling when dinner was brought to my room, but the mounting anxiety I felt knowing that he might still waiting outside my door made it nearly impossible to swallow the smallest mouthful. I knew my actions were no kinder than his had been, and all the self-justification in the world would not change anything. I could either spend the night obsessing over what would happen when we faced each other again or take my stand now so the healing could begin.

That's why I asked the young woman collecting the food trays to tell the guard that he had my permission to let Brett in. Then I bit down on my thumb as I waited to see what would happen. There was no need to worry about my appearance since I wasn't allowed to get out of bed on my own. And I was well aware that my hair was tangled, my breath smelled horrid and unsightly abrasions and bruises covered most of my body. But maybe it was better that way. If he saw me at my worst, it might make our final goodbye easier for both of us.

I was staring at the closed door when I heard a soft knock. But before I could say anything it swung open, and I was looking at Brett's face. He appeared tired, miserable and lost, and I felt a flutter of something I couldn't quite describe because he hadn't left me alone for even the amount of time it would take to shower and change.

"How are you feeling?" he asked as he took a few stiff steps in my direction, but I was mostly listening to the door knob click shut.

"Like someone who has been shot," I retorted while pulling the sheet closer to my chin with my good arm. Now that we were alone together, I almost resented my impulsiveness. I hadn't even decided what I was going to say to him yet. "I'm sorry you felt like you needed to keep vigil at the hospital. I know how busy you are."

"Where else would I be when someone I care deeply about is in trouble? When I got to the cottage two mornings ago and saw the police scouring the place, I felt like my world was about to end. And when I figured out it was you that had been shot, I knew it was all my fault for letting you leave my loft. I should have gone after you the moment Shelley unloaded her bombshell, but I was in a state of complete shock. I still can't believe you remembered where that old key was hidden."

"I suppose you could say it saved my life. Thank you for not removing it."

"Quite frankly, I had forgotten it was still there. Why didn't you call me for help?"

My jaw seemed to lock of its own volition, and it was hard to get the next words out. "Even if there had been time, or the means to make a call, I think you know the answer to that."

"So it is true that you were loading your van to leave in the dark of the night? Your friend, Annabelle told me about the note and the gift you left at her door."

"I didn't see any reason to keep the candleholder since we would never be using it."

He was standing beside me now, and I could feel the sorrow, guilt and fear just beneath his mostly-calm exterior.

"I don't care about the damned candleholder! I only care that you were shot trying to get away from me. I don't need some police report to tell me that you would never have been in that hallway to overhear some threat if you had been sleeping peacefully in your own room."

"Your assumptions are accurate, but if I hadn't been listening at Professor Price's door, he would have been killed. Those people meant business. I'm just sorry I didn't come up with a diversion sooner. It might have kept him from nearly losing his life."

"What about your life?" Brett demanded.

"I was reacting to the situation at hand. But in retrospect, while I wasn't ready to die, I didn't feel as if my life had much value either. Most anyone with a little creativity and some formal training can design a line of clothing. But the real kicker is that my mother doesn't recognize me, I have no real friends in San Francisco and it has been over two years since my brother returned one of my texts."

"And I suppose Shelley's abrupt announcement led you to believe I had just been playing one of my endless games?"

"She merely confirmed suspicions that had never been completely put to rest. I may have let my guard down for a few days, but I'm not a complete fool, Brett. There was only one way to take what she said. You were using me as a rebound to get over what you thought you had lost with her."

His look was one of misery and disillusionment that almost equaled my own.

"It's not what you think, J?"

"I've tried not to think about it at all. Of course, getting shot helped, although it did keep me from leaving as planned. It was crazy to think we stood a chance, especially the second time around."

"Not crazy," he said, running his hand through his thick, blonde hair and looking at me with pain-filled eyes. "Our circumstances may have changed, but our feelings for each other were as real as the day we met. Emotions that deep can't be faked. I love you, J, and I always will."

I felt the blood rush my head and closed my eyes against the dizzying feeling. Brett sounded sincere, but he had duped me before.

"Aren't you going to say something?" he asked after a few moments of anguished silence. "I know I should have told you how I much I loved you years ago, but I was too focused on building my recording career. Sadly, I never made it to the big-time like you did and have never had anyone permanent in my life."

"That's not fair!" I almost shouted. "You know why I married Greg, and you have someone now. By the way, congratulations on your upcoming marriage. I hope you will both be very happy."

"There's not going to be a wedding. Shelley might be pregnant but . . . ."

His words trailed off as my breath caught in my throat. I wished unconsciousness would take me from this moment of utter agony like it had done after I was shot, but apparently I had recovered too much for that.

"It's not my baby," he continued while my eyes remained closed. If I looked at him, I would explode. "Her boyfriend walked out on her when he found out. She was one of my German students last year. We became friends—never romantically involved—but she was easy to talk to. Being around her, and listening to her problems, made me feel less alone. Haven't you ever felt that way?"

My eyes flew open, and I knew they were shooting little flames of near contempt. "Of course, I have. But I would never marry someone I didn't love."

Brett gave me a scathing look. "How can you be so self-righteous, unless you weren't telling me the truth when you said you were never really in love with Greg?"

"We're not talking about me, and I did love Greg in my own immature, self-serving and impetuous way. But you are right, I have no room to judge you or what you have done. We have both been doing things our own way for a very long time."

He ignored my half-hearted apology. "Shelley was in a bind. She didn't want to get an abortion, and she wasn't ready to raise a child on her own."

"What about her family?"

"They told her she was ruining her life by taking on the responsibility of parenthood when she wasn't even twenty. Besides, I've always wanted a family, and she had no qualms about the difference in our ages. We decided together that there were worse things in life than being married to a friend."

"If you had already decided to get married, why did she leave?"

He sat down on the chair next to the bed and rested his elbows on his knees. "Because no matter how many times I told her I didn't care about campus gossip, she knew that marrying a student half my age could ruin both my reputation and my career, especially since she was already five months pregnant when we came to our decision. She needed time to decide if she could live with that."

"But she made that decision, and I ruined it."

"Your presence only corroborated what we both knew in our hearts. Marriage to each other might solve a few pressings problems, but in the long run, it would only create so many more."

"Are you saying she saw through my charade at making a dignified exit?" I asked, trying to shift my body into a more comfortable position. Every part of it hurt since I wasn't any more used to strenuous activity than I was to laying in one place for an extended period of time.

His snort of laughter was hollow. "I'm sure the look on my face told her that you weren't just an old friend who stopped by for a visit. What we planned to do seemed reasonable at the time. But after seeing you again— holding you and kissing you—I knew I couldn't marry her. Shelley might be young, but she was very much in love with her baby's father. The first words out of her mouth after you left were, *you've fallen in love with someone, haven't you?*"

"I'm sorry. I know she was counting on you."

"We spent most of the night talking. That's why I didn't follow you back to Whitman Cottage like I should have done. I figured I had to work things out with her before you would even listen to me."

"You were right. I actually feel sorry for both of you."

"Don't be like that," he said. "A child deserves to be raised by parents who love each other. She's talking about putting the baby up for adoption. That way, she can finish her schooling and eventually find the right guy. She said this whole thing has taught her that abstinence really is the best form of birth control, and it doesn't leave a trail of tears and broken hearts."

"I guess it is better to learn something late than never learn it at all. Are you really sure she's not in love with you?"

"No more than I am with her, but that doesn't mean we're not still friends. I told her I would help out any way I could."

The truth behind his words cut deeply. He was going to stick by her when all he had ever done was run away from me.

"I'm sure she appreciates the continued concern for her well-being and happiness, Professor Fowler."

He shifted uncomfortably in his chair. "Is that your way less-than-direct way of saying it's over with us?

I took the time to let some of my disillusionment settle before responding. "I have loved you my entire adult life, but it appears that complete honesty continues to elude us. Why didn't you tell me you were unofficially engaged instead of letting me believe that I was the first girl you had ever proposed to?"

"Because I never considered it an actual proposal. It was more of an arrangement between friends who could offer what the other one lacked."

"But you would have gone through with the marriage if I hadn't come back?"

"I suppose. I'm tired of being alone. I want all those things I used to avoid, but I knew when Shelley left that she was having second thoughts. I figured I would eventually get a call saying she had found someone else. It's not like she isn't a very desirable young woman, despite her present circumstances. Most any man would be happy to have her in his life."

Unwittingly, flashbacks of the baby I had lost started to surface. I would have given anything the world had to offer to raise him or her—even on my own—but that option had been taken away from me like everything else when it came to being part of a real family.

"Still, she chose to be with you, and leaving her stranded so she even has to consider given her child away seems heartless and unfair."

"What about life is truly fair? he countered. "Those with the most money and influence rule. The rest of us are left to make it the best way we can. Shelley agreed to marry me because she wanted someone to take care of her like her parents refused to do any longer, but I believe she is starting to feel more confident about standing on her own."

"Aren't you afraid she will grow to hate you one day for going back on your promise? Having a baby is a big deal for most women."

"Is this about her, or you, now?" he asked.

"Maybe a little of both," I replied as I struggled to maintain composure. "I know what it's like to lose a child. I also know what it's like to be left on my own. Making the wrong decision under any duress is incredibly easy."

The hard line of his jaw let me know that at least part of what I said was sinking in. "Most everyone is afraid of making poor decisions, especially these days, J. It's not an easy world to live in, but marrying someone for the wrong reason isn't the answer either. Especially when the woman I have loved for over a decade has come back. I never want to let her go again, unless she refuses to have me. But I am hoping she knows that I never meant for any of this to happen."

He was starting to wear me down, as he had always been able to do, but I wasn't ready to forgive and forget.

"A few days ago, I felt like we had a fighting chance. But the past hours have left me wondering if anything we've ever had was real. We never went through good and bad times together, had a fight, learned anything more about each other than the obvious, sacrificed one thing of importance so we could spend more time together or even tried to resolve anything without running away. We were like two ships passing in the night without anchors or moorings, and I can't see where anything has really changed. Our entire time together has been nothing more than some out-of-reach dream."

Brett just stared at me with pain-filled eyes for the longest time as if he was trying to think of a plausible rebuttal. But there was nothing he could say to change the past. What we had shared was little more than an illusion we had been trying to recapture.

"You're right, J," he finally said. "We never gave ourselves a chance, and it was mostly my fault. In addition to my other faults, I was addicted to the rush of finding new conquests so I wouldn't have to worry about making a commitment I might not want to keep in a week or two, but those days have been over for a long time. That's why I told Shelley I would be there to give her child a last name and a stable home environment. While my undertaking may have been a little irrational, my heart was in the right place. I was ready to make a promise and keep it."

It was my turn to say something, but there was no going back to the time when I had started to believe in happy endings. He had hurt me deeply, albeit unintentionally.

"I wish the week had ended differently, Brett, but maybe it ended the only way it could. Some things really aren't meant to be."

He reached for my hand. Maybe I was simply too physically and emotionally exhausted to resist, but I allowed his fingers to slide between mine.

"I can't begin to imagine the trauma you've been through after what happened at my place and then being hunted down and shot. I would take away every moment of agony if I could but know that I'm to blame for most of them. I just hope you can find it in your heart to forgive me one day. I know that's asking a lot because all I've ever done is hurt and disappoint you, but I want a chance at redemption. If you truly feel I'm not worth the effort any longer, I will walk out that door and never bother you again."

My heavy sigh expressed just how confused I still was, but I knew that Brett was finally at a place where he would sacrifice his owns wants for the needs of someone else.

"I promise to give what you've said some thought, but that's the best I can do right now."

He rose to his feet immediately and placed a kiss on my forehead. "That's all I'm asking, J. Would it be presumptuous to ask if I could stop by again before you leave?"

"If there are no setbacks, Dr. Bennett said I would be released in the morning," I told him before closing my eyes. Provided he truly believed we belonged together, he would be back. If not, I would simply go on with my prearranged plans. "Now, I really need to rest. It's been a very long day."

He left, and I dozed on and off until I sensed that someone was watching me.

"Hey, sleepy head," Annabelle said. "I've been waiting for you to wake up so I could give you an update. Not that you've been napping all that long since it's only a few minutes after seven, but Russell will be in the hospital for at least a week—hooked up to all kinds of awful looking equipment. The doctor said he should make a full recovery."

"That's wonderful, Annabelle," I responded. There were tears in her eyes, and I knew how incredibly happy she was. "You're a very lucky woman to have found the man of your dreams."

"Don't I know it," she replied. "I always thought that finding love only happened to beautiful people like you."

"I'm not beautiful, and my love life isn't exactly going anywhere."

"But I know you talked to Professor Fowler. I saw him leaving the hospital when I came back from the cottage, and he looked like a much happier man. Russell wanted me to make sure all of his belongings were accounted for."

"If I had known you were going, I would have had you check on mine," I said to keep her from asking any personal questions.

"I did that anyway. The entire floor has been sealed off and everyone, but us, is gone. Someone even moved the van to the back parking lot since it was sitting right outside the front door, and the director said that everyone's values had been secured. All we have to do is show up in person to get them."

"Then I suppose we have nothing to worry about."

"I wouldn't say that since the man who shot both Russell and you has yet to be caught, but we do need to treat each day as the treasure it is."

"You definitely sound like a woman in love."

She blushed most becomingly. "That's because the part of me that was always missing has finally been found. I'm going to take care of him when he gets out of the hospital and for as long after that as God allows. But instead of going to meet his mother right now, he's coming home with me. I've already called the university and explained what the authorities hadn't told them. They've put him on paid leave until he's completely recovered and made sure the *Annabelle Little Orchid* is safe. I still can't believe how much trouble a simple flower has cost."

"Neither can I," was my reply. "But I was under the impression that the detectives in charge want us to remain in protective custody until Wally and Myra are caught."

"I don't know you can call two thugs by their first names. What they did was unconscionable."

"Maybe it's because I had a front-row seat. At least the girl had a conscience. I'm not sure the same thing could be said about the man."

"And Russell is very upset about even hiring him. He said it has made him reevaluate his desire to do the Christian thing. Some people simply do not deserve the generosity of others."

"Perhaps," I responded. "But you haven't answered my question about being under constant surveillance until they are both behind bars. I think it's far from necessary."

"Russell feels the same way, but I told him it wasn't a big deal as long as we could be together. It truly is a miracle that we found each other. I just want the same thing for you."

"I'm not saying it will never happen, Annabelle, but I'm going back to San Francisco as soon as I'm released. I need time to recover from a great many things."

"But you will still come to our wedding, even if it can't happen for awhile?"

"I wouldn't miss it. Is Russell going back to his old job when all of this is over?"

"Nothing would keep him away. Like I told you earlier, he feels partially responsible, but there is something else I need to tell you."

She looked so concerned I almost laughed. "And what might that be?"

"Would you mind having another visitor? That young man we met at the party is in the waiting room."

My hands seemed to flail in the air. "T.R. is here? I thought our names had been kept out of it."

"Apparently, he has connections inside the police department. I think it might do you good to talk to someone who isn't personally involved."

"Not in my condition," I countered. "I've never looked worse."

"He'll see you as a battered angel for saving someone's life. Besides, he has flowers. What girl can resist a kind gesture like that?"

"One who isn't very bright, I suppose."

She was gone almost immediately, and I ran my fingers through my hair in a vane attempt to look more presentable. But Timothy Russell didn't give me much of a chance. The door hadn't even closed behind her when I saw a huge bouquet of pink, purple and maroon flowers and a young man with smile that made feel almost glad to be alive.

"Hey, beautiful," he said, putting the clear, crystal vase on the nightstand near my bed. "What some women won't do for a little attention."

"Like I asked for this," I replied. "How did you even know I was involved?"

"Because I listen to the news and know how to draw simple conclusions. They're only saying that a young woman, not officially affiliated with the university, was shot, along with a visiting professor. It scared the living daylights out of me so I went to the cottage to check things out. When I saw all the hubbub going on I came straight to the hospital, but the security was so tight no one could even get near this wing. That's when I called my cousin. She's a dispatcher at the police station. She said she couldn't tell me anything, but she didn't deny my suppositions. I really wish I had been wrong. You could have been killed."

"Thankfully, no one was. I'm not really sure the man involved wanted to hurt anyone. He just backed himself into a corner and didn't know how to get out."

"He was carrying a gun. That shows premeditation, but how the hell did you get involved? The last thing I knew, you were handing out a prize at the fashion show."

"You were there?" I asked.

"Sitting in the second row. I wanted to come to the reception to tell you how much I enjoyed it—and see if you would give me your telephone number so we could keep in touch—but I couldn't miss another chemistry class if I wanted the credits."

"I would definitely have given you my number, but you should not be skipping classes if you want to graduate."

"That's what my counselor keeps telling me, but I'll only be young and carefree once."

"Never underestimate the power of a single decision. Here I've spent nearly eight years in San Francisco where violent crimes are a daily occurrence, and I have to come back to Bentley to get shot. There must be some kind of poetic justice in that."

"Maybe you were supposed to come back to meet me so I could take care of you."

"Oh, I'm sure that's the reason," I said with a smile of my own. "An attractive, virile college student would be just thrilled to take care of an older woman who seems to have an aptitude for being in the wrong place at the wrong time."

"Hey, I'm game," he said. "Besides, I'm really not that much younger. I'll be graduating next spring."

"So that makes you all of what, twenty-one?"

"I'll be twenty-two when I graduate."

"And I'll be thirty. We'll be in different decades."

"I wouldn't mind, but I think there's a certain someone who has already captured your heart. Professor Fowler has been in the waiting room every time I've come to see if I could get in to see you."

I felt a ripple of uncertainty travel up my arms. "I knew him when I was a student here."

"But he's here. That means you must have had a pleasant reunion."

"Our history is complicated, just like our present, but I really don't want to talk about him. Tell me what you've been up to. I know it's Sunday evening, but you must have more important things to do than hanging out with me."

"There's always plenty of homework, but I didn't feel like doing it. My head has been in a different place since meeting you."

"Your flattery is endearing, but we both know that as soon as I am released, I will be on my way home. And there will be no looking back this time."

"What about Professor Fowler?"

"I already told you that our relationship is complicated."

"Most are!" he exclaimed. "But the truth is that you either love someone or you don't. That's just the way it is with matters of the heart."

"What if I'm tired of getting my heart broken?"

"Then I suppose you play it safe, even if you end up spending the rest of your life alone. In many ways, I am a lot like Professor Fowler. I play the field because it's fun, but I really don't want to graduate unattached."

"Then do something about it. This campus is filled with beautiful, young women who would enjoy spending time with you."

"I've known my share of lovely, young things who enjoy having a good time, but they all seem rather shallow after meeting you."

"Come on," I said. "Most of them will surpass me in every way by the time they're my age."

"I don't know how you can say that. We might not know each other very well, but I can tell that you're a fighter who has overcome some pretty tough things."

He reached for my hand like Brett had done earlier, but I wouldn't let him take it.

"We don't know each other at all, T.R. We're simply two individuals who felt a certain connection, but that's no reason to think we can become anything more than friends since I don't see us ever crossing paths again."

"You'll have to come back and testify once the man who tried to kill you is caught."

"Professor Price isn't going to press charges. He believes there are two sides to every story."

"But you will see that he gets what he deserves."

"While I certainly don't think he should be free to hurt anyone else, I'm not going to hold my breath. There's a very good chance he'll get away with everything. He had a head start and a plan."

"That sucks," T.R. said.

"Yes it does, and being shot isn't a lot of fun either. But I just want to get on with my life."

"I wish you felt like I could be part of it."

"I'm not saying you can't. Everyone needs friends. I just don't want you to have unrealistic expectations."

His brow furrowed, and I knew he understood exactly what I was saying. Flirtations might offer a fun diversion, but there was rarely anything lasting about them.

"Can I still have your number? That connection you were talking about is very real to me. You are the most beautiful woman I have ever met, and you have the most amazing eyes. A guy could easily get lost in them."

I shook my head. "Now I know you're playing with me, but I will give you my number simply because I would like to know how you're doing."

He entered the ten digits I gave him into his phone since mine was still at the cottage, and then we chatted for a few minutes more. I would miss him, but it wouldn't be long until what we had shared was just a pleasant memory.

Visiting hours were over when he left. The thought crossed my mind that I should tell my brother what had happened, but we were really little more than strangers now.

Chapter 12

Doctor Bennett came in just as I was finishing another bland meal the next morning.

"Are you ready to be released later today, Miss Sloan? I have informed the authorities that there is no reason for you to stay any longer, unless they need you here for safety reasons."

I put my fork down on the tray and pushed it away. "They know how I feel about unnecessary protection. And since no one has made a move against ether the professor or me, I have to believe we are in the clear."

"While I tend to agree that another confrontation is unlikely, it will be up to them to make the final call. Right now, I would like to see what you're capable of doing with your arm."

"So soon?" I asked as he began undoing the strap that held it in place.

"Muscles atrophy if they're not used. That's why we get heart patients out of bed as soon as possible after bypass surgery. If you can't get around on your own, then you won't be able to leave."

I gave him an unpleasant frown. Apparently, two or three walks up and down the hall with a nurse's help didn't count as being independent when there had never been anything wrong with my legs besides a number of hideous bruises and lacerations.

"Okay, doctor. Just tell me what you need me to do."

"First, I want to check the incisions and then I want you to raise you arm as high as you can. Do you think you can do that."

"Piece of cake," I replied in a less-than-convinced tone. "But you have to know that I'm not a great fan of pain."

"That's why I want you to take the prescribed medication for as long as you need it. We'll take it slow, but I would like to schedule your first physical therapy session before you leave. You will find someone to work with when you get back? I can't express too strongly how important that is."

"My boss has it covered," I replied as he undid the bandage and took a studied look at my arm. "I'm sorry for being such a difficult and demanding patient. I really am grateful that my injury wasn't worse."

"Hey, it's not easy being shot or being in the hospital," he responded without looking directly at me. "You're a smart young woman, and I know you would never take any unnecessary chances, but sometimes it's easy to overlook warning signs. Now let's see how far you can move that arm."

I shot him a *you've got to be kidding* look and then proceeded to lift my arm. Two inches in the air and I had to quit. It fell lifelessly back to my side.

"So what now," I asked as I bit down on my bottom lip as hard as I could without drawing blood. "Will I have to stay in this room until I can move it all the way up?"

"No," he said. "But my job is done. The rest is up to you."

"That won't be a problem," I told him.

He gave me an unexpected smile. "In that case, I'll see you around four. I'll have one of the nurses take you on another walk before therapy, but I have to caution you about not trying to drive until your shoulder is healed, therapy is complete and you are no longer on any pain meds."

"Most of my work can be done from home, Dr. Bennett, and my boss will make sure all of my needs are met. That includes following up with my regular physician and seeing a physical therapist. This injury will not keep me down."

"Then I don't foresee any problems. Is there anyone who can take you home from the hospital and look after you for a few days? I really wouldn't recommend flying right now."

"I can do that," Brett said to my utter astonishment. He had come into my room unexpectedly while we were talking. "I'm a friend from the university, and Jada can stay at my place for as long as she likes. I'll even make sure she isn't alone when I have to be at work."

"You don't have to do that," I replied as my heart seemed to miss a beat. "I'm sure I can stay at Whitman Cottage until my flight leaves. No one will come looking for me there. After all, it is a crime scene."

"Precisely the reason you shouldn't be there. I know this past week has been unsettling, but we have known each other for nearly twelve years. I'm offering as a friend. You need a place to stay and someone to make sure you're okay. I have the room, along with a vested interest in your welfare. It's the perfect solution if you don't want to stay here. Isn't that right, doctor?"

"I would prefer it if you weren't alone for next couple of days."

"Then it's settled," Brett interjected. "What time can I pick her up?"

I hated having anything decided for me. I just wanted my own life back —that safe, compartmentalized life I had known since my divorce from Greg. But my options were limited until Mr. Fredericton sent someone to accompany me home, so I clenched my teeth as the tears formed. No matter what I did, the next few days were going to be awful.

"While it sounds like the best thing for now, I will leave it up to my patient to decide where she's going to stay." Dr. Brennen was saying when I forced my mind back to ongoing conversation. "I'm not even sure the detectives will agree to having her released before their investigation is finished. I just hate having her lay around the hospital when there's no medical reason for it. Most patients do much better once they're away from here."

"So what's your answer going to be?" Brett asked, looking directly at me. "I have a class to teach at nine, but I can make arrangements to have the rest of the day free."

When I saw the both the love and compassion in his eyes, I knew there was only one decision I could make. He would not make any demands, or cause me to feel ill-at-ease unless I provoked it. He just wanted to make good on his promise.

"I would be very grateful for a place to stay, but I need to pick up my personal belongings. My boss has already agreed to send someone to drive the van back. It's packed and ready to go, but a little makeup and a change of clothes would be nice."

"Done," Brett said. "I'll be back by eleven."

"No rush," the doctor told him. "She won't be ready for discharge until closer to five, and that's not a given."

"It will be once I have done a little finagling," Brett said with a cheerful smile. "I've gotten to know the detectives quite well the past few days, and they know Jada will be safe under my watchful care, even if I have to hire a personal bodyguard. I'll even stop by Whitman Cottage. There's no reason to go back there."

"What if I need closure?" I asked.

"Then I'll take you, but you need a little pampering first."

I was about to say something that would give away the real nature of our relationship but decided the doctor didn't need to know everything. "I'm sure all I really need is a place to sleep, a warm shower and something to eat. It would only be for a couple of days. My boss is securing a plane ticket and finding a traveling companion for me. He's very anxious to get me back since our fall deadline is only a few weeks away."

Brett gave me a knowing look. "I'll take what time I can get. Thank you for your excellent care, Dr. Brennen. Students on campus are quite upset by what happened and will be glad to know that our visiting guests are expected to fully recover."

"Just glad I was here to help. I'll see to the paperwork once I've finished my rounds while you talk to the local authorities. But I have to caution both of you about getting too excited just yet."

"No worries on this front," I replied. "But I need to know if you have given any thought to the request I made yesterday about paying a visit to Professor Price?"

The doctor cleared his throat as people always seemed to do when they needed a few moments to collect their thoughts. "I have no objections since he seems to be doing much better this morning. Just make it a short visit because he still tires easily."

"I promise not to stay long, and I won't ask any direct questions. I just need to see for myself that he's going to be okay."

Brett stood by the side of my bed after he had gone. The fact that we would be spending a few nights under the same roof suddenly didn't seem like such a great idea. His actions had hurt me profoundly but understanding why he had asked someone else to marry him had taken some of the sting away. Still, I knew that if I allowed myself to forgive him before leaving town I might not be able to control where things went.

"Nice flowers," he said to break the uncomfortable silence as he looked at them instead of me. "Who sent them."

I felt myself bristle. "A young man I met the day I got here who made me feel like I still belonged."

"You must have made quite an impression on him, but then there's always been something pretty incredible about you. I knew that the first time our eyes met, only I was too full of myself to make the right moves."

"Please, Brett. If this is going to work we can't go back there. We both had walls around our hearts that were pretty much impenetrable."

"I know, but it was nice to see some of them start to come down."

"Only because we've both learned a few things during our years apart. You were the only man who ever tugged at my heart, and my grandmother never prepared me for having feelings like that."

"I wish I could have met her."

The curve upward that came to my lips was purely spontaneous. "I'm not sure you would have liked each other much. She was very strict, and holding hands was all she thought appropriate before the wedding night."

"Maybe that's what I found so refreshing about you. Most of the girls I knew had been around the block a time or two. I never really wanted you to know that I was the kind of man who enjoyed one-night stands and was afraid if we spent too much time together I would do the same thing to you."

"I'm glad that didn't happen," I said, looking at him with more tenderness than I thought I had left. "It really would have destroyed everything."

"I finally get that," he responded. "Maybe that's why I asked Shelley to marry me. I have often wondered if I ever left a girl pregnant and in pain, and if some other guy is raising my kid. Perhaps it was my subconscious way of paying penitence for living such a wayward life. How many men do you know of who are my age and have never married or had children?"

"Not many, "I admitted while wondering if he did have a child somewhere who would want to be part of his life one day. "But then I have lived in San Francisco for almost a decade, and in my line of work, I don't meet many men who are interested in having traditional families anyway."

"Gotcha," he said. "It must be hard spending so much time around people who don't share the same values."

"My boss knows the kind of work I do, and while he thinks what I believe is archaic, he respects what I stand for. He's actually gotten quite adept at making excuses as to why I'm not in attendance at all the cocktail parties we host."

"I'm surprised," Brett admitted. "I thought your presence at things like that were crucial in building your career."

"I guess it would be if I was on the runway. But since I'm a designer, not a model, I'm more like a back-seat driver. I can tell a person what to do and how to get somewhere, but I don't actually have to do all the driving."

"You really are an amazing woman. I don't know of anyone who has been so true to herself or to what she believes."

"No one is immune to making mistakes or having heartache. That's why we're here."

"I know, but some of us weren't smart enough to walk away, even when we knew what we were doing was wrong."

"You've already explained your past, Brett. I'm not going to hold it against you."

"Do you really mean that, J?"

"I wouldn't be a very good Christian if I didn't. I'm glad you feel like you're on a better path."

"It hasn't been easy, but I haven't slipped up since I made the decision to change. I know it's what I need to do with, or without you, in my life."

"So, no regrets for giving up your former way of living?"

"There are always regrets, but not in the way you mean. I'm sorry I hurt so many girls. Maybe some of them didn't care, but I know some of them did. While I can't make amends the way I wish I could, at least I can make sure I never use anyone that way again."

"If you feel that strongly about it, you won't. Even back in college I knew you weren't out to do me any harm."

"I just wish I hadn't made your life harder. You were young and innocent and didn't deserve to be treated so poorly. I ran because I was a coward and wasn't ready to be caught."

"We're quite a pair," I said, looking at him with a wane smile. "It's probably a good thing nothing ever happened between us back then."

"What about now?" he asked. "I don't expect your complete forgiveness any time soon, but I do love you, and I would like a chance to prove that I am a man you can be proud of."

"Is that why you asked if I would stay with you?"

He let the air our of his lungs slowly as the morning light coming in through the window danced around his shoulders. I liked the man standing before me. He was still full of surprises, and I might never know everything about him, but at least he was willing to make amends for past mistakes.

"Subconsciously, most likely, but I don't want you to ever feel alone again," he said. "Even if things between us don't work out the way I'm still hoping they will, I will be there for you in any capacity you need. But if I don't leave now, my students will wonder where I am. I wish you had your phone so I could call and check on you, but I'll be back later to spring you from this joint."

He placed a kiss on my forehead like he had done the night before and left. I felt a sort of calm knowing I would see him again, but there was still a lot I needed to accomplish before then. I was ready to see Professor Price but had no idea which room he was in. That issue was resolved a few minutes later when Annabelle showed up at my door.

"I just heard a rumor that you're being released and thought you could use something to wear," she said as she placed a rather bulky, pale blue bundle in my arms. "It's just a robe, scrubs and some heavy socks. That's all they had in the gift shop, but I figured you wouldn't want to wear the clothes you had on when you were brought in, and I didn't want to leave the hospital again to see if I could get the things you left at the cottage. Being away from Russell for more than a few minutes at a time makes me nervous. He says he likes seeing my face when he opens his eyes. Have you figured out what you're going to do?"

Her comments and questions made my head tired they were delivered so rapidly, but I knew they were coming from a place of trust and friendship.

"Thank you, Annabelle, but I haven't heard anything specific. Dr. Brennan is all for it, but the detectives have final say in just about everything, unless we're ready to make a run for it."

She giggled. "Leave it to you to say something absurd like that. They aren't going to have a problem as long as they can reach you by phone. When they stopped by our room earlier today, they said that Myra's car was spotted crossing the border into Mexico, but the authorities were too busy worrying about all the people coming into our country illegally to stop it in time. For all intents and purposes, it is unlikely that anyone will see them again."

"How do you feel about that?" I asked as a feeling of sheer solace swept over me. If I didn't have to worry about them, I could get on with my life without any huge curtailments.

"I'm mostly relieved since I don't like the idea of looking over my shoulder, but I think they should pay for what they did to both Russell and you. It seems like few people get prosecuted for crimes these days, unless it's something the media can use to further some mandated agenda. It boggles my mind that there are so many different news stations, but they're all controlled by the same two or three companies so we never get the true story abut anything."

"There are a few outlets that give a more accurate description of what is going on."

"I know, but someone is always trying to silence them."

"Do I detect some discontent?"

"Maybe with the outside world. I've never been happier personally, but now that Russell is staring to feel better he wants to get back to work. He's not a very good patient."

"Few men are. They just want to fix things."

"I'm beginning to understand that. I love him with all my heart but know we've barely begun the adjustment process. How are things going with you and Professor Fowler? I know you still have reservations."

"He's ask me to stay at his place until I can go home. It will only be for a few days since I'm anxious to get back to work as well."

"And you feel okay about doing that? I'm sure you could stay at the cottage. That's what Russell and I plan on doing until he's well enough to travel. The university will cover all of our expenses."

"That's very generous, but Brett doesn't think I should be alone. Apparently, the doctor doesn't either."

"Then I'm happy for you. It will give you time to talk."

"We've been doing far more of that than anticipated the past few hours. He's a very complicated man."

"But so cute," she quickly added. "We could have a double wedding."

"That would be pushing it," I said, intrigued by her charming idea. "We're still trying to decide if we can be friends."

"Maybe someday you will feel like telling me what really happened between you. But for now, I'll be content just knowing that you're trying to move forward."

"So it would seen since I have agreed to his kind offer. But I would really like to see Russell before I leave . . . . "

"That's actually why I came," she cut in. "He wants to see you too. He knows he wouldn't be alive without your quick and selfless intervention. He wants to thank you for saving his life."

"There's no need for that. He would have done the same thing for me."

"I know," she said, nodding her head. "He considers you family, just as I do, but he still wants to thank you personally. We could go now, if you have the time."

"As far as I know, I have nothing but time until someone tells me when I have to meet with the physical therapist. But I'm afraid you might have to walk with me since I have yet to be given permission to leave the room by myself."

"I can do that, but maybe we should clear it with a nurse first. I would hate for you to have a relapse."

"They would not be talking about releasing me if there was any danger of that," I assured her. "But I can't go anywhere in this nightgown."

She helped me out of bed and then waited while I went into the bathroom to change, but when I got a good look at myself in the mirror, I wished I hadn't been quite so bold. The scratches on my body were covered with scabs and the bruises had turned horrid shades of purple, yellow and brown. The hospital had furnished me with a comb and a toothbrush, but that did little to improve my appearance. And it didn't help that I had absolutely no undergarments. I managed to get the bottom part of the scrubs over my feet and up my legs with one arm, but maneuvering the top part over my head was impossible. So I settled for tying the robe securely around my waist.

I frowned as I opened the door. There was nothing in my suitcase I would be able to put on without help and asking Brett for assistance wasn't going to happen. Maybe I had been a little hasty in believing I was ready to be released from the hospital.

"I forgot all about your shoulder," Annabelle said when she saw the top of the scrubs still in my hands. "How are you going to manage around a man?"

"That is a rather perplexing question. Perhaps I should go back to the cottage and see if a nurse could be hired to help me until I can move a little more freely on my own. How are you and Russell going to manage?"

She blushed quite becomingly. "I've never seen a man naked before, but Russell assures me that he will be able to do most things himself. However, we have discussed getting married even earlier than planned. He doesn't want me to ever be uncomfortable around him."

"You would really do that?" I asked.

"Why not? It could be done right here in the hospital before we leave. That way you wouldn't have to worry about making another trip in the next few weeks. I know you have a big deadline waiting for you at home."

"And you wouldn't care about not having a real wedding?"

"It would be a small affair anyway. I don't mind how or when it happens, I just want to be his wife for better or worse."

"You do realize that it's only been a week since you met," I said as she took my good arm and ushered me towards the door.

"I'm not going to change my mind. We want to be together. Would you still be willing to stand by my side if we did it in the next few days?"

The hallway was nearly empty and very quiet. The guard outside my door did little more than nod his head as we passed by. That's when I knew that all restrictions would soon be lifted.

"You know I will, but what about a dress, rings and flowers. Every bride should have those."

"I kinda like the idea of having a very simple wedding, much like the one my grandparents had at the beginning of World War II. They had only known each other a few weeks before he got his orders to ship out. There wasn't time to make elaborate plans, so they got married at the courthouse in front of a justice of the peace. My grandmother wore her best suit and carried a small bouquet of flowers and my grandfather used part of the wrapper that came off a cigar for a ring. They were happily married for sixty-five years."

"That's quite a romantic story."

"I think so, and it only goes to show that long engagements aren't necessary. If two people really love each other, time isn't going to change anything. It just means they'll be apart longer, especially if they aren't willing to accept living together as most people do now days. Not being able to make a real commitment seems like a copout to me."

"To me as well," I replied as she pushed open a closed door that was only half a hallway from mine.

Professor Price was still attached to numerous machines and tubes. His face was white, and he didn't look that great to me, but then I hadn't seen him since the night we were both shot.

"How are you doing?" I asked as the door closed behind us. Annabelle led me towards one of bedside chairs so I wouldn't have to stand up while we talked.

"I've seen better days, young lady," he replied in his usual distant tone. "But the doctor tells me I will be fine in a few weeks. I am sorry you got mixed up in all this nonsense. It was rather late for you to be up and around."

"I was just packing the van so I would be ready to leave."

"That is not exactly the way Annie told it, but far be it from me to pry. I just want you to know that I am grateful for your intervention. I knew Wally was unstable but never thought of him as being capable of violence."

"I suppose anyone can be driven to a breaking point. I only wish I hadn't been so slow in doing something."

"Nonsense! It was my problem. I had no idea anyone else would get caught in the crossfire when I started badgering him. I figured he would eventually listen to reason since he didn't have a legal leg to stand on, but some people simply don't know when to quit. I suppose living in a foreign country with no chance of coming home will give him some time to think about what his foolishness cost both him and Myra. She was a good girl. That's why I am surprised she went with him willingly."

"Maybe she felt like she didn't have much of an option."

"Why not? They may have been young and in love, but some things are just wrong. He wanted a free ride like so many other people in this country today. When did working for what was wanted become such a bad thing?"

"It's okay, Russell," Annabelle said, taking his hand and kissing his fingertips. "You did what you thought was right. I told Jada that we might move up the wedding to as soon as the end of the week. I hope that's okay?"

"Nothing would make me happier than having you for my wife. I just wish mother could be here, but she's deathly afraid of flying. I spoke to her while you were gone. She wants you to have her diamond ring. It has been in the family for generations."

"So she isn't disappointed by our plans?"

"She wishes us nothing but happiness and can hardly wait to meet you. I told her we would be there as soon as we could but not about being shot. She is just shy of her ninety-fifth birthday, and I did not want her to worry."

When I caught the look of love and understanding that passed between them, I knew I had little to worry about when it came to their relationship. I only wished I felt the same way about Brett and me. Being alone together for an extended period of time might do nothing more than prolong an already unhealthy bond.

"I am still hoping she will consent to living with us once we are settled," Annabelle was saying when my mind floated back to the present. "I just wish we had met sooner so I could give you a family."

"Now, Annie," Professor Price told her. "We have already discussed that. While children would be nice, we will have each other, and that is far more than either of us ever thought we would have."

"You're right, my dear," Annabelle said, squeezing the hand she still held so tightly. "I am not going to dwell on what might have been. How would you feel about adding a small apartment to the back of your house if your mother wants more privacy? From what you said, there is plenty of room for a guest house."

"I think that is an excellent idea and one we can propose to mother when we see her, but right now we have a wedding to plan. Are you sure you don't want something more elaborate than what I can offer until I have fully recovered? I know propriety is a great concern to you, but how we choose to live is no one's business. We can do whatever we like behind the closed doors of our own home."

"What other people think has never been a major concern to me, Russell, but I want to start this out right," Annabelle responded as the lines between her eyes contorted into the only frown I had seen on her face. "I am too old to play house. I want the real thing or nothing at all."

Professor Price laughed. "Then that is exactly what you will have, my dear. I am sure Miss Sloan will help out since she was a major contributor to our newfound happiness."

I could feel the tears coming again but letting them fall would be unwise since my emotions were still pretty much all over the place.

"All I did was offer a little support. You and fate did the rest, but I will do anything I can to make sure your day is perfect. We could shop for a dress and flowers once I'm released—which I am hoping will be in a few hours.""

"Maybe we could go tomorrow, if you're feeling up to it. Are you still going to stay with Professor Fowler until you're ready to travel?"

The look that passed between them made me wince. I trusted Brett, but if I went home with him, Annabelle might think the worst of me. And I had fought too long and too hard to make sure my actions did not betray my beliefs.

"I am having second thoughts about that rather rash decision, but not because anything might happen between us. I just can't see him helping me with some of the personal needs I am unable to take care of on my own right now. Maybe I should find a motel room and see if the the doctor could help me locate someone who is trained to help people shower and dress until I am better able to do it on my own."

"A motel room sounds like a much better idea," Annabelle said with what I knew was a sigh of relief. "Just walking down the hallway at the cottage yesterday gave me the chills, and I wasn't even part of what happened. But you don't need to hire someone. I would be honored to offer my assistance for as long as you need it."

Her willingness tugged at my heart, but her plate was full enough.

"I can't ask you to do that. You have a wedding to plan."

"Thank you for not including me in her list of growing responsibilities," Professor Price broke in, giving me one of his looks that made me feel like a child. "But I am with Annie on this. There is no way of adequately repaying you for saving my life, and the care around here is more than adequate. Besides, my lovely bride needs time away from watching me sleep. She hasn't left my side since I was allowed to have her in my room."

"That is what people in love do," Annabelle replied.

"And you have made me feel like the luckiest man alive, but I have a few plans of my own to make when I am not dozing. Maybe you should get a room at the motel too—one with a connecting door would be perfect. You have been sleeping in a chair the past few nights, and I want you fully rested and awake for our wedding since it is the only one I plan on having."

The conversation ended soon after that, and Annabelle walked me back to my room.

"I hope you don't feel like we're being overprotective, but Russell and I only want what is best for you," she said as I was getting back into bed.

"Not at all, and I think we should get connecting rooms at a decent motel within walking distance of the hospital. You need to be with Russell, and I have already been told that therapy is necessary if I want full movement in my shoulder again. Brett will be bringing my things from the cottage a little later today, and then we can make the arrangements. It has been very strange not having my phone, or the contents of my purse, when I need them."

"Do you think he will be upset when you tell him there has been a change in plans?"

"Only if he doesn't want what is best for me. He knows how I feel about cohabitation. He just wants to make sure I'm okay. Thank you for being my friend. I haven't had a real one for more years than I can recall."

She placed a kiss on my forehead. "And I have never had one at all. Now try to rest while you can. I will make sure we have the rooms we need, and we can work out the details later. I was thinking about a nice, tailored suit for the wedding. I'm a little too old for something fluffy and white."

My first therapy session was less than pleasant, but I endured all the painful pushing and prodding without screaming. I knew after returning to my room that I would be able to put on a button-up shirt when it was time to leave. I had one of them in my suitcase. I would just have to ask Brett to get it for me.

Detectives Davidson and Reaves were not happy about my refusal of protection when I left the confines of the hospital, but with Wally and Myra in Mexico it really was a waste of taxpayer dollars. Besides, they already had my personal information and knew I would be back if the case ever went to trial.

Unlike Professor Price, I did not feel like I had a hand in what had transpired on Friday night. Wally would have killed me given the chance. That kind of rage could not be controlled forever. I worried about what would happen to Myra if she ever truly crossed him. From what I had overheard of their conversations, he was an abusive man with a very short fuse.

The signed discharge papers were sitting on the moveable tray in front of me when Brett came back. It was after four, and I wished I had known how to contact him so he would not have wasted the better part of his day preparing for a houseguest that wasn't coming.

"How are you feeling after your first therapy session?" he asked as he approached my bedside with something small clasp tightly in one hand and my purse and briefcase in the other. "I would have been here sooner, but I want you to feel comfortable staying with me for as long as you feel you can."

I brought my left arm in front of my body and slid my feet to the floor as I listened to the briefcase hit the floor. He was just so handsome, sensual and appealing that I almost changed my mind again, but Annabelle had already secured rooms for us at the Medford Inn.

"What's in your hand?" I asked, wanting to delay another debate for as long as possible.

"Something one of the detectives gave me earlier. It might seem a little odd, but it reminds me of just how close I came to losing you again."

My eyes opened a little wider than normal. "Now you do have my interest. Can I see it?"

His palm opened. A small, silver object that was sorely misshapen lay inside. I felt my breath catch in my throat. "Is that what I think it is?"

"The one and only," he replied.

I took it in my own hand and looked at it with morbid curiosity. "Isn't it considered evidence?"

"I think you've watched too many police dramas on television. Things like this are usually disposed of unless a death has occurred, which fortunately, it didn't."

"But why would they give it to you?"

"Because I asked them if I could have it."

"And they didn't question your sanity?"

"I suppose they may have. But from the number of intense conversations we shared while I was waiting to see you, they knew how deep my feelings ran. Would you like to have it?"

My head went back and forth quite forcefully. "Not really! The doctor says I'll have a nice scar to remind me of being shot. It's hard to believe something so small and harmless could kill someone."

"It's anything but harmless, J. I don't know what I would have done if it had taken you from me."

"But it didn't," I said, giving the bullet back to him. He put it in his shirt pocket. "I'm going to make a full recovery. I just hope the same thing happens for Professor Price. He didn't deserve to get shot over an orchid."

"It's a little more complicated than that."

"I know," I replied as the air left my lungs. "There's a lot of recognition involved, but Wally and Myra will be on the run for the rest of their lives. That seems like a high price to pay for trying to claim something that never belonged to either of them."

"People do crazy things, but I would much rather get you home before we have another philosophical conversation. The nurse should be here any minute with your wheelchair. I've changed the sheets on my bed so you can have some privacy and am more than happy to sleep on the sofa. I just want you to be comfortable."

"About that," I said, glancing at the floor since I couldn't bear to see the disappointment when I told him my latest plans. "Annabelle and Professor Price are getting married before I head back to San Francisco. She wants me to help her with the arrangements and felt we could get more done if we were staying at the same place. She's booked rooms at the Medford Inn. We can still spend time together, but it will save you from having to help me shower and get dressed. I won't be able to do that on my own for a few days."

It seemed like forever until he spoke. "While I was afraid you might change your mind about staying with me, I still hoped you knew you could trust me."

"This has nothing to do with trust, Brett. I hadn't fully considered my limitations this morning. It's not like I just need a little bed rest. I can't even put on my clothes without help."

"And you don't want me to see you like that? I would never take advantage of you in such a heartless way."

"But you would see me at my worst. When the time comes for us to be together in that special way, I want it to be romantic."

"So this isn't just another way of blowing me off?"

"Hardly! If I didn't think we still stood a chance, I wouldn't care. I would give you all kinds of awful jobs as punishment for hurting me."

"I would do anything you asked."

"And I would enjoy watching you grovel, but that's not who I am."

"I guess that works in my favor, but I still can't believe your friends are getting married. Didn't they just meet?"

"They had spoken only briefly until the night I saw you. She wanted Professor Price to see her in a different light and asked me to accompany her to the party as a buffer. I had no intention of leaving my room, but she can be a very persuasive woman."

His frowned was instantaneous and caused one of my own. "Are you saying that if she hadn't asked you to go with her we might never have seen each other again?"

"More than likely! I must have looked at the phone book a dozen times the night I arrived but didn't want to go through the pain of having my worst fears confirmed."

"And what were they?" he asked.

"That you had moved on and had a wife and family of your own."

"I guess I can understand that," he said, shifting uncomfortably on his feet. "It wasn't a picnic coming back from Germany and finding out that you had left town with another man."

I leaned into the bed for support since I felt very much like collapsing in a heap on the floor, but that would only delay my departure.

"We've both made so many mistakes that could have been avoided if we had only been willing to talk. While I wish I had never become involved with Greg, I do know that I have grown as a person because of what we went through. I hope you don't think that surrendering some of my self-perceived control over to God makes me weak."

"Not at all, J. In fact, I've come to the same conclusion. Humility has never been easy for me, but I am trying."

We didn't have time to finish our conversation, or for me to change into something better than the robe and scrub bottoms I had been wearing for most of the day. The nurse brought the wheelchair and, before I was able to make any requests, had me sitting in it with the flower arrangement T.R. had given me the night before sitting in my lap.

I was glad to be leaving the hospital, but my worries were far from being over. Brett had found the strength and the courage to face his demons and change, but what if I wasn't able to do do the same?

Could I really walk away from my work, my home, my personal freedom, and the prestige I had earned in the fashion industry? While my life was far from perfect, it was safe and relatively painless. Would I grow to resent being asked to leave everything behind to become the wife of a German professor and musician? Answering that question right now was impossible, but we would remain in our current state of limbo until I did.

Chapter 13

Brett didn't say anything as we drove the two blocks to the Medford Inn—a recently constructed commercial property made of white bricks with pillars out front, tall stately trees in the back and blue trim around the doors and windows. There were cement pots filled with colorful flowers underneath the front portico. That's where he stopped so I could get to my room as quickly as possible. Annabelle had told me to go to the front desk for a key since she wasn't sure what time she would be arriving.

I pulled the robe more tightly around my body as Brett took my hand and pulled me to my feet. Sunglasses covered my eyes since he had brought my purse to the room I had occupied in the hospital. I appreciated his thoughtfulness since I might be required to show identification, but I still hoped that few people would see me with my left arm in a sling and socks on my feet. My appearance was a dead giveaway to any reporter who wanted an inside story as to what had happened the night two people had been shot on campus.

"Try not to worry," Brett said as he put his arm around my waist and led me inside to a nearly empty lobby. "We weren't followed."

I looked up at him and frowned. "Do you think I made a mistake coming to a public place so soon? I was just trying to do the right thing."

"So was I, but I can't protect you here," he responded. "Not that I think you have anything to fear from Wally or Myra, but the press is a different story. Right now, your story is on the front page of every newspaper in the state and is the lead on every news broadcast. If anyone finds out you're here . . . . Well, let's just say that it will be impossible for you to avoid a massive invasion of privacy."

"I guess I wasn't thinking as clearly as I thought."

"You could still stay at my place. I'm sure your friends would understand."

"If Annabelle hadn't already made the arrangements, I would be tempted to do just that. But I think she's a little nervous about being on her own too since she's the fiancé of the man Wally originally came after. I'm sure we'll be fine if we don't open our doors to anyone we don't recognize. Butt you need to know that I do feel much safer when you're around."

He leaned over and kissed the top of my head. "I'll always be there for you, J, any time, any place. All you have to do is call."

His declaration was still ringing in my ears as he got the key from man at the desk and then led me to the elevator. It was a short assent to the third floor, and my room was surprisingly comfortable with a kingsized bed, a sofa in front of a huge window that faced east and a brightly lit bathroom. He left me sitting on the edge of the bed while he returned to the ground floor for my suitcase and carryon bag. I would need them before I could shower and hopefully change into something that was not too difficult to put on.

The pain pills I had been given were doing their job with great efficiency, but I didn't want to become dependent on them. I had seen too many of the models I worked with addicted to both prescription and illegal drugs, along with massive amounts of alcohol. While most of them were still able to function, I knew the day of reckoning was coming when their vitality, youth and drive would be gone. That's when they would either seek help, die from an overdose or remain in a life of confusion, self-justification and pain. But then people seldom wanted to do what was best for them, even when they knew what lay ahead if they didn't.

I thrust those unwelcome thoughts aside as I listened to Brett's footsteps disappear down the carpeted hallway. But once my mind was free, I felt a deep, engulfing tiredness enter every cell of my body. It had been an emotionally intense day with difficult decisions to make, but I didn't regret striking out on my own without a backup plan or someone around to protect me. I needed my life to return to a normal I was capable of handling, and that would never happen as long as I felt afraid. Wally and Myra were gone, and I could handle any question some nosey reporter might ask. After all, I had done it numerous times in the past.

But I didn't want anyone associating me with what had happened at Bentley. It was a part of my life I needed to forget because flashbacks were already keeping me awake at night and making me question if everyone I saw was a potential friend or a foe. That was not the way I chose to live and was quite possibly the real reason I had decided not to stay with Brett. I wanted him to see me as a strong, competent, fearless woman; not some sniveling, needy parasite who no longer felt capable of standing on her own.

I lay back on the bed. But before I could close my eyes, there was a soft knock on the connecting door and Annabelle poked her head into my room.

"I hope I'm not disturbing you, but I heard voices and wanted to know if you were ready for a nice, relaxing bath. I know you can't get your shoulder wet, but between the two of us we should be able to get you in and out of the tub without any mishaps. We just have to avoid the incision for a couple of days."

"That seems like asking a lot. I'm sure I can survive with another spit-bath."

She folded her arms in front of her chest and gave me a very determined look. "The doctor said you needed to start using your arm more. I know it hurts and having me help you is uncomfortable, but I was a nurse's aid while going to college. I know exactly what to do, and I promise not to drop you. Now, where's your suitcase? I want to see if you have something that can be worn without modification. I can go to the store in the morning, but everything around here closes at five. I'm not sure I could ever live in such a back-woodsy place again. It brings back too many memories of a very abusive childhood.'

"Brett is bringing it up, and this town isn't that bad," I replied. "But wouldn't you rather be at the hospital with Russell?"

"I promised to come back and sit with him once you were settled in for the night. I'm sure you must be exhausted."

"I am, but you don't have to rearrange your life around mine."

"That is not what I'm doing. You risk your life to save the man I love. That is something I will never forget. Besides, we're sisters now. At least that's what you said a few hours ago, and family sticks together no matter what."

I felt my nose tickle with more unwanted tears. Annabelle was the first person I had felt even a mild kinship with since the day my grandmother died. Even my brother and my mother no longer felt like family. We were more like distant acquaintances who had nothing to say, even if we found a few minutes to spend with each other.

"All right, Annabelle, you win. I just wish I had time to design a dress for your wedding."

"While that would be lovely, I really don't mind wearing something off the rack. I just want to be Russell's wife. I shudder every time I think about how close I came to losing him. If you have even the slightest belief that Professor Fowler could be the man for you, I think you need to give him a chance."

I was saved from making a reply by Brett's fortuitous knock on the door. Annabelle let him in.

"Thank you for bringing Jada's things and for being agreeable to a change in plans. I know you had no reservations about taking care of her, but some women are a little old-fashioned when it comes to wanting to avoid even the appearance of evil. I am sure there will be plenty of time for you to be together before our wedding on Friday. Russell and I would like you to be there. If you are agreeable, he would even like you to be one of our witnesses. It will be a small, but important, event."

Brett's look of confused amazement matched my own. "It would be my honor. Is there anything else I can do to help? There isn't much time between now and then."

"Just take care of Jada during my absence. I will make sure she is bathed and ready for bed, but she will need something nutritious to eat. Perhaps you could bring her favorite take-out meal around seven. I told Russell I would sit with him for a couple of hours but don't like the idea of her being alone. While she is perfectly capable of taking care of herself, she needs to know there are people in her life who really care."

"No one cares more about her than I do, Miss Little," he said. "I don't know what she's told you about our rather tumultuous past, but I want a future with her and will do whatever is necessary to prove to her that I am a changed man."

"Words are for the weak!" Annabelle declared. "Actions are what really matter. Now, we need some privacy. We will be ready to open the door at seven."

Brett swallowed hard but didn't try to approach the bed where I was having a hard time keeping a straight face. "I guess that means I'll see you a little later. Is there something you would like me to get?"

"Anything, as long as it isn't sushi. You know how I feel about raw fish."

He left, and Annabelle helped me undress and into a tub of warm, wonderful-feeling water. My bruised and battered body welcomed the heat as I leaned my head back and closed my eyes. My new sister and friend would make sure I had something presentable to wear when I got out.

Brett came back as promised. I was propped up in bed wearing a tank top and pajama bottoms, but at least my hair was clean and there was no longer any residual dirt stuck to my body. He waited until she was gone to push the bouquet of flowers T. R. had given me to the center of the table and put a large bag of something that smelled wonderful next to it.

"I got Chinese. I thought Mexican might be a little hard on your stomach."

"That's perfect," I replied. "I hope you weren't upset by anything Annabelle said. She is being a little over-protective."

"As she should. You are a real heroine in her eyes."

"I mostly acted without thinking like I usually do. I was scared half out of my mind running up that hill while a crazy man with a gun came after me. He was shouting out oaths I never thought I would hear."

"You haven't told me much about that night, only that you broke into the building where I work to get away."

"And I don't want to talk about it now. I just want to eat. The food at the hospital was awful."

"Well, this isn't. I got it at your favorite place."

We talked while we ate, but it wasn't long until the subject turned to us. However, it was in an rather unexpected way.

"Do you want to know what I've been thinking about the past few hours?" he asked while tossing the remains of a mostly-eaten meal in the trash.

"Not if it's it's something too serious," I replied. "I just want to enjoy a pleasant evening."

"Me too! It has been a long time coming. Still, it's hard not to reflect on what might have been. I didn't have much when we first met, but you would never have been homeless. Maybe barefoot and pregnant but never without the necessities of life."

He was looking at me with such intensity that I laughed.

"So you think that's funny, do you?"

"Only mildly! I was picturing myself in that condition wearing a lose-flowing sundress and running barefoot through the wildflowers. It sounds like a Hallmark moment, and something I have always wanted to do."

"So you don't think I'm crazy for bringing up something like that when you just got out of the hospital?"

"Come here," I said, motioning him towards me. He took my lead, and when he got close enough I sat upright, put my right hand on his cheek and then kissed his lips.

"What was that for?" he asked with surprise when I had finished, but he didn't back back away as I half expected him to do. Instead, he put his own hands on my cheeks as I sank back on the pillow and returned my kiss.

I allowed myself to get caught up in the moment, hoping he would know when things became too intense for me. The fact that my left arm was still in a sling helped.

"We really have been given something special," he continued after our much longer kiss ended. "But you're still not sure about us, are you?"

"My heart says I am, but my head tells me we're far from being out of the woods yet."

"In what way?" he asked, sitting down on the bed beside me. "I promise to be truthful, so fire away!"

I looked down at the light tan blanket that was covering me from the waist down instead of his face. "Maybe I'm more worried about me than I am about you right now. I have no idea how to make all the changes necessary for us to be together. I love my job, but I know I love you more. I love my house, but without you there it will always be lonely. I love life in the big city but know I will always be a country girl at heart. And while I love being independent and making it on my own, I know I will never learn what it means to be a real wife if I stay single forever. Everything has happened much too fast for me."

"It sounds like you've already answered most of your questions without any input from me, J. And where is it written that you have to be the one who makes all the concessions? I could look for a job at Berkley or some other college in the bay area. I still have some distant relatives there."

"Then why haven't you done that before?"

"Because I kept hoping that the woman of my dreams would find her way back to me somehow, and I wanted to make sure she didn't have any trouble finding me."

I let out a giant sob, and he took my good hand in his. "But there is still another reason I've stayed here. I don't want to raise children in a big city. I want them to feel safe enough to go to the park or ride their bikes up the road without being afraid that some stranger with unconscionable desires is going to approach them. Oh, I know there are risks here too, especially after what happened to you and Professor Price, but I've grown very fond of Bentley. I really have no desire to leave, unless you decide you don't want to marry me. Then it won't matter much where I live."

"But what if we find out a year or two down the road that it simply isn't working? I don't want to be a two-time loser."

"You've never been a loser," he said, putting his finger underneath my chin and forcing my head up so I would have to look at him. "You're one of the most amazing women I have ever known—right up there with my mom. I can't promise you that we will never have disagreements, or that life will even go smoothly most of the time, but I can guarantee you that I will never pull away like I did before. And I won't get upset if you burn the dinner, forget to do the laundry or even wreck my car. I just want to grow old with you."

"I'm not sure you know what you're saying. What if I end up being an awful wife? I messed up so horridly before."

"Because I have no preconceptions of what married life should be. I figured we could learn together."

"You really think that would work?"

He was wearing away at my defenses, but then I no longer felt like putting up much of a fight. Maybe we could have a happy ending. I knew that I wanted to share everything with him, and when I died, I wanted his eyes to be the last ones I saw. Being with him was what eternity meant to me.

"I do," he said. "I've never wanted anything more."

"But what if I can't give you a family?"

"Just because you lost one baby doesn't mean you'll lose another one. And even if we never have children, I'll still have the woman who was meant for me. Besides, I happen to believe that life goes on forever, and the day will come when every righteous desire of our hearts will be realized."

I finally let the tears flow and buried my head in his shoulder. I had lived my life alone for as long as I could remember and had learned how to handle loss. But during the past seven days I had been given two chances to let people into my heart. There were risks no matter what I did, but the choice was mine to make. I took the time my soul needed to feel relief. It was the most cleansing experience of my life.

"I'm sorry for falling apart," I told Brett quite some time later as he continued to hold me. The room had turned dark except for the lamp beside the bed, but I was no longer afraid of the dancing shadows on the wall. "If I was wearing makeup your shirt would be ruined."

"They're easily replaced," he responded, brushing the hair away from my eyes before sliding off the bed and kneeling before me. I felt like I was living in some dream and if I even breathed the spell would be broken. But he simply cleared his throat before continuing. "I know this isn't any more romantic than the first time I tried it in front of your students, and I still don't have a ring, but I can't risk losing what we have again. And I am deathly afraid that our feelings are going to get swallowed up in another couple's happiness if I don't say something now. I should have done it years ago when we spent that night in some farmer's field. It had been on the tip of my tongue all evening because I knew it was right, but I chose the familiar over the unknown. I won't make that mistake again. Will you marry me, Jada Sloan? I know I am no great prize and you could do so much better, but I promise to make you laugh at least once every day for the rest of our lives."

I felt gooseflesh cover my entire body. There was still so much I didn't know, but everyone else seemed to be right about at least one thing. Today was all we had. Tomorrow would always be unknown, and the past could never be undone.

"Yes, Brett Fowler, I will marry you," I said as the warmth of his love made me feel like I had finally arrived at the only place I had ever wanted to be.

"You really mean that?" he asked.

"Of course I do! I have always loved you, even when I was young, foolish and afraid to admit it."

"I can't believe this is really happening," he said. "Maybe you should pinch me so I will know I'm not dreaming."

"No way, future husband," I responded, loving the ease with which the words slipped off my tongue. "Our lives will only get better with each passing year because we're finally old, and smart, enough to recognize what we could have had all along."

"I wish I could slip a ring on your finger right now so the entire world will know that you've finally consented to be mine, but I do have a dynamite dessert if you're ready for it."

"I don't need a ring," I said. "All I need is you."

"But you'll have one anyway and soon. Now, how about some chocolate covered strawberries and whipped cream? I couldn't seem to resist them."

We must have fallen asleep talking because the next thing I became aware of was sunlight peaking in from around the window curtains and the connecting door being opened. Brett was laying in the bed next to me, fully clothed as I was, but I still felt a surge of wrongdoing.

"Don't mind me," Annabelle whispered since it was obvious that Brett was still asleep. "I just wanted to make sure you were okay. It looks as if we all fell asleep a little sooner than planned last night. I was going to see if you needed anything but heard voices when I got back. I can see now that Professor Fowler had everything covered."

"Nothing happened," I said, forgetting for a moment that I was now an engaged woman too.

"I'm not accusing you of anything. I'm just glad the two of you are finally working through a few of your issues. For what it's worth, I think he's the genuine deal."

"So do I, but we can talk later. It looks like you're ready to leave."

"I told Russell I wanted to be there when the doctor came for his rounds, but I shouldn't be gone long. We have a lot of planning to do because I know he's going to be released soon. He told me last night that he's practically good as new."

Her easy smile was contagious, and I found myself looking intently at the man I had committed to marry after she left us alone. Even one day earlier, I would have been horrified to awaken with him so near. But the truth was that I had never slept so soundly. His soft, rhythmic breathing, along with the way all the tension in his body seemed to relax, made me feel as if I was seeing the real him for the very first time. I longed to brush my hand over the contour of his face and kiss his sensual lips, but he would only wake up if I did. So I lay back on my pillow and continued to watch him sleep.

My life had certainly come full circle, and I wanted this peaceful moment to last. But when Annabelle closed the outside door to her room, I saw his eyelids flutter.

"What time is it?" he asked, stretching lazily before rolling onto his side and placing his hand on my good arm. "I was having the most amazing dream about what we'll be doing on a morning like this in the not-so - distant future."

I glanced at my cell phone instead of looking at him. He was used to waking up with a woman, but I had slept alone since long before my marriage to Greg ended. If I allowed myself to look his way while being consumed with the love and tenderness he aroused something I was sure to regret would happen.

"A little after seven," I responded. "I'm assuming you have an early morning class."

"Not until ten. There's still plenty of time."

His fingers were now tracing a seductive path up my neck, and I involuntarily shivered. "But you will need to go home so you can shower and change."

"That I will," he replied with a heavy sigh as his hand dropped to his side. "Are you having buyer's remorse already? I'm sorry for falling asleep, but you have to know by now that I only want to love and protect you."

"I do," I replied, giving myself permission to face him. "I'm just being silly because this is all so new, and I have never had a man in my bed before. Greg doesn't count because he was my husband and what we had was never real anyway."

"Then I suggest we have a short engagement like your friends because I like waking up next to you. Now please give me a kiss. I promise to be gentle because I know your shoulder must be killing you. Unless I slept through it, you haven't had a pain pill in over eight hours."

"And I am not sure I need one now. You are all the medicine I need for a complete recovery."

He pulled me into his arms, and I didn't even flinch. "Then you wouldn't be opposed to me coming back in a few hours? I know you and Annabelle have plenty to do."

"Our shopping won't take long, unless we can't find something for her to wear. Any idea where we should go to find something appropriate for a wedding? She doesn't want a tradition dress, just a nice suit. If there was more time, I could design something she would really like."

"From what I've seen of your friend, style means nothing to her. She just wants to be with the man she loves. I think there's a lesson for us in how they're navigating a potentially stressful time, unless you want an elaborate wedding."

I shook my head before kissing him. "And just who would I invite? I have been too afraid of opening my heart until now."

"Only because you've never known what it's like to be truly loved. Your dad died before you really knew him, and your mother and brother are missing an extraordinary gift by excluding you from their lives. You are the most loving, forgiving and courageous woman I have ever known, and I feel truly blessed to be holding the key to your heart. But I suppose I should be going. I wouldn't want Annabelle to get the wrong idea."

"She already knows you didn't go home last night. She wanted to make sure I hadn't had a relapse before heading to the hospital."

"That must have been uncomfortable and the perfect trigger for confusion and self-doubt. Did you give her our big news?"

I reached for his hand. "She needs her moment in the sun. I'm perfectly content with things the way they are now. Once people find out, it won't be the same."

"I suppose not," he replied as the feel of his touch made the butterflies dance in my stomach. "Just don't wait too long. I think she will be thrilled for us. She might even suggest a double wedding. I kinda like the idea of getting married before you leave. Then I will know that you're coming back."

"You have me now and for always, Brett Fowler. I don't need a ring or a piece of paper to tell me that we belong together."

"Then there is a place I want to take you this afternoon, if you feel up to it after a morning of shopping. I will be through by four and we could spend the evening together."

"Are you going to give me hint so I will know what to wear?"

"Anything, other than what you're wearing right now. Despite a few bruises and abrasions, I find you—hands down—the sexiest woman in the world. I don't want other men ogling you, or I might have to defend your honor."

"You're crazy," I said with a smile. "I just hope you feel that way in forty or fifty years. I have no idea how I am going to age."

I spent the day with Annabelle. She was driving the car Professor Price had rented when he arrived for the conference. Our first stop was at the florists where she picked pink roses, rather than orchids, for her wedding bouquet. I thought it a wise choice under the circumstances but knew she would overcome her aversion to the flower that had nearly cost her fiancé his life once they were working in his lab together. He had already called the courthouse and arranged for a justice of the peace to be at the hospital at six on Thursday evening where the wedding would be conducted in the chapel. He was being released the following morning and wanted Annabelle to feel comfortable since she would be providing whatever care he still needed.

I almost envied their clarity when it came to seizing the moment and letting all the details take care of themselves. I was still too focused on what needed to be done before I took the plunge to even relax. My boss had called while I was eating a breakfast muffin to say that he had purchased a ticket for my return to the city on Sunday afternoon. I would tell Brett about it when I saw him later, but he had to know I couldn't just abandon the life I had built for myself because I now wanted something else now. People depended on me, and I needed to make sure their livelihoods were secure before pulling any rugs out from underneath them.

After an hour in Macy's department store, Annabelle declared a beige suit with a classic cut as what she wanted to be married in and then found some shoes to go with it. But when I suggested that we look at lingerie, her entire countenance changed. "I can't do that, Jada. I have plenty of nightgowns to wear."

I knew she had never worn anything even remotely sexy, but she needed something soft and becoming for the first time she made love. "I'm not talking about the skimpy stuff you see in catalogues. I would be hesitant to wear most of them myself, but I would like to give you something for your wedding night as a gift."

"But you've already given me a candle holder. It is quite the most unique one I have ever seen."

"This will be in leu of a bridal shower where you would likely get a great many things that would make you blush. I was thinking about something silky and floor length."

"And black," she quickly added. "It's what I look best in."

"Then black it is," I said. "I have a date with Brett later today. I hope that won't be a problem."

She gave me the brightest smile before sliding her hand into the crook of my right elbow. "I knew things were heading in the right direction when you didn't send him packing last night. I hope I will be invited to the wedding."

"You will be at the very top of the list, but the next three days are about you. I was thinking we should stop at a bakery. We don't have to get a large cake but we need a few things to focus on while taking pictures. Will Russell be wearing a suit."

"He said he could manage an open-collar shirt and some pants. Should we get some non-alcoholic bubbly since neither of us drink the hard stuff?"

I was back in my room by three. But my shoulder was throbbing, and I felt the need to take something for the pain before Brett arrived. His mysterious date was intriguing, and I had purchased a light sundress that was easy to get on for the occasion. There was a wrap in my suitcase I could take along in case the evening turned cool.

But Instead of heading to an exclusive, and most likely very expensive, restaurant, we drove to one of the newest sub-divisions in town. Brett stopped in front of a two-story house at the end of a lane. It had been framed in and was ready for bricks and siding. Boxes of shingles for the roof were sitting in the driveway.

"What are we doing here?" I asked. I had been thinking about how much I wanted to kiss him, along with my home and job in the city while we were driving. I liked the idea of being successful, and I loved the home I had created for myself. But I belonged with Brett, and wherever he wanted to be was okay with me.

"I can't expect my future bride to live in my loft. We need a real home, and I thought we should get an idea of what's available. It's not like we are kids any longer who have to watch our pennies. Bill Hanks is the best contractor in the area, and he happens to be a very good friend. I know he would do right by us."

"Sounds to me like you have been doing some serious thinking."

"I just needed the right motivation to get off my hind end, and please don't mention Shelley. We never talked about anything other than giving her child a name."

"That thought never crossed my mind, but buying a house is a huge step."

"So is getting married, and I am ready for both.

He led me up some concrete steps and through an open doorway but didn't stop on the ground floor to show me around. Boards had been put in place to form the base of a circular staircase leading to the second level, and he practically sprinted up them.

"You've got to see this," he said as we side-stepped sheet rock, insulation, screws and chunks of 2X4's. "It's really the most amazing part of the house."

I was confused since most houses were basically the same, but his enthusiasm was contagious. We passed by several doorways until we came to a large room over the triple-car garage. There were floor to ceiling windows along the wall that faced north, a fireplace in one corner and a mammoth walk-in storage area that seemed rather out-of-place.

"Is this supposed to be the master bedroom?" I asked.

"That's the crazy thing about it. The master suite is at the other end of the hall, and it's amazing too. There are also three other bedrooms on this floor. This is supposed to be a bonus room, but all I could think of when I saw the blueprints was that it would make a perfect studio for you. The light is great, and there is plenty of storage space for all the stuff you'll need. I don't want you to give up your career to marry me. I know your work is important. That's why you're so good at it. You could create some amazing things right here and still be home for me and the kids."

This time I couldn't resist, and I kissed him long and hard. When I stepped back, he was smiling.

"So it wasn't a mistake to bring you here? I was afraid I might be moving too fast."

"I think we're way past that now, Brett. I need to go back on Sunday. My boss has already made the arrangements, but I won't be there for any longer than I have to. I've been trying to figure out how to make the transition from one life to another as easy as possible on everyone involved, but seeing this room helps see more clearly how it can actually be done. I can design clothing from anywhere, but I've always needed a place to call my own. Having you recognize that need means the world to me."

"Does that mean we've made it through our first big hurdle?"

"It's a great start, but my boss has to agree. Most of my business is conducted over the internet anyway, but there would be frequent trips back to the city for consultations, fittings and runway shows. The good thing is that it's just an hour flight once the plane takes off. And even if he decides he doesn't want the hassle, I might be lucky enough to get a faculty position at Bentley, or even another school close by. I really can't see me without a job, even with a house filled with children. I hope that doesn't disappoint you."

"I have always known you were a very self-sufficient woman, and I would never presume to tell you what to do. We will make adjustments as necessary when the time comes. But right now, I want to know how you feel about this house. The couple who signed the contract have decided to take a job overseas. It's on the market, but it won't last long."

"I think I love it, but I would like to see the rest of it before making a final decision. And we need to determine if we can afford it. This is a prestigious neighborhood, and I want everything to be perfect this time around. You know how much I hate unpleasant surprises."

He took my hand and led me on a tour of the upper level. It was so much more practical than the home I had purchased in San Francisco with all the glass and chrome. Little fingerprints would be a nightmare to deal with there, but this house was different. It was made for a family, my family, from the bedrooms to the main living area to the basement and huge back yard that could be easily fenced. And if those weren't enough to make me want to live in it, there was a church a block away and a grade school right outside the sub-division gates.

"How about it?" Brett asked as he stood behind me with his arms wrapped snuggly around my waist and his chin resting on my uninjured shoulder. We were standing where the great room would be in a few short weeks. The sun was beginning to set, and we had the perfect view of the mountains. "Should I make an offer?"

"It's perfect, but I don't know what I will get out of my house."

"You don't have to worry about that," he teased. "I haven't been living in that upstairs sauna all these years just because I love it."

"And here I thought you stayed there because there were so many memories of me. I did make curtains for all the windows that needed them, along with the throw pillows on the bed and sofa. I can't believe you still have them after all these years."

"How could I get rid of them, even when they started to fray? They were the only part of you I had left."

I turned in his arms. "And you said you weren't a romantic, except in your songs. I never want you to stop writing or singing. It's part of who you are, and you need a place of your own too. Maybe we could share the bonus room."

"I have another idea, with your approval, of course. That big empty space in the basement has recording studio written on all over it. While most background sound is produced digitally now, I still need a place where I won't be disturbing the neighbors, or our children when they have homework to do. So how about it, J? Do you think you could grow old with me in this house?"

"Nothing would make me happier," I said giving him another kiss. "But we're in this together now, and I don't want any badgering about using whatever money I have to help pay the mortgage. It isn't easy for any family to make ends meet in this economy."

Chapter 14

With only four days until I was scheduled to return to the city, and Annabelle's wedding a major priority, I was left to wonder how Brett and I would ever find the time necessary to discuss relevant details regarding our own life changes. He had classes to teach and his new responsibilities as department chairman to learn and administer, and I had therapy sessions that were far from pleasant and multiple zoom conferences with people from work.

Now that my boss knew I was going to survive, it was back to normal for him. He was not a family man, lived for his career, and made no pretense of his dislike for organized religion. That had never bothered me before, but I didn't want to burn any bridges when I was forced to announce my plans to marry and move to the middle of the continent where the largest city in the state was over an hour away. And If Mr. Fredericton decided to let me go, I would have to come up with a game plan I could live with. That would most likely include starting at the bottom again—something that didn't sit well with me—but I had come too far to back down.

That's why I called Brett the moment I woke up on Wednesday morning and told him to make an offer on the house we had looked at the night before. It had been our main topic of conversation during dinner, but we had decided to sleep on it before making a final decision. Another house might come on the market that we liked even more.

"You're sure?" he asked after I had stated every reason I could think of to move forward in what might be considered a rather reckless way by people who didn't know our history. "We could lose the money we put down if we change our minds."

"Thank you for not saying it might be months before we can actually move in since I have no idea what's going to happen in California. Property isn't moving nearly as fast as it is here, and we could end up with double mortgage payments until I can find a buyer for mine."

"I'm not worried, J. Things have a way of working out. Besides, watching the construction progress, and taking care of any little issues that might arise, will give me something to think about, other than missing you. I wish you felt less conflicted about staying with me the next few nights. I hate sleeping alone and doubt Annabelle would mind if you checked out of the motel a few days early. I promise not to do anything more than hold you, and I can't imagine her wanting you on the other side of a very thin wall when she spends her first night with the distinguished professor."

I laughed. "Since he still has a long recovery, it's unlikely they will do much more than share a few kisses and sleep, but I get your point. They deserve complete privacy on their wedding night. Are you still going to pick me up from therapy? Annabelle and the professor are in the midst of negotiations of their own, and she would rather spent the evening with him than go out to dinner with me."

"I'll be there, but please don't let her lack of interest in anything that even resembles a bridal shower bother you. She opted for a very unconventional wedding without any of the fanfare."

"Much like we're going to do?" I interjected. "But I'm sure your friends will give you the most elaborate bachelor party ever."

"Undoubtedly, and I deserve it. After all, I have held out longer than anyone else I know to tie the proverbial knot. But I can assure that it won't be traditional either. No strippers, booze or overindulgence in anything for me. I want a clear head, and conscience, when I say my vows."

I liked that idea. And while Annabelle and I were having lunch in a small bistro on the main street of town, she gave me some news that took away my concerns about staying where I was until Sunday.

"I hope it won't be upsetting to you since I promised to be there when you needed me, but you were doing so well I changed my accommodations to the bridal suite. I thought Russell and I deserved something special."

My smile came straight from my heart. I had been part of many weddings parties during college, but I had never seen such a calm and collected bride. "So are you ready for your big day? You have less than twenty-eight hours to go."

"I've been ready since I was a teenager, but even my parents thought I would spend my life alone. I suppose that's why they left me their house. They wanted me to have a place to live if I couldn't keep a job. My brain worked just fine, but I couldn't carry on a conversation with anyone."

"But you've done very well for yourself."

"I was lucky to find a job where social skills were not relevant to earning a living. My boss thinks I'm crazy for quitting my job to marry some man I just met. He told me quite plainly that I was an easy target for a con artist who wanted what I have. When you are a spinster with only a cat for a friend, people see you differently. They confuse marital status with the ability to reason, think or even understand."

"I happen to believe you are very bright and very strong woman. Some people are just mean-spirited."

"While that may be true, they would claim that they are simply realists and no one could love a woman like me."

"Then they would be crazy. I admire you for taking a chance with love."

"What else could I do?" she asked, giving me one of her endearingly shy smiles. "I need love as much as anyone else, and although I have never seen one of Russell's bank statements and still know relatively little about his personal life, I have read sufficient about his career to know that he is an honorable and trustworthy man. I just wish we had met sooner because we don't know how many years we will have together."

"No one does."

"But I was never afraid of dying before I met Russell. And now it seems like such a waste of love since the marriage vow itself says *until death do you part*. That sounds pretty final to me."

"Only in terms of mortality," I replied, hoping I wasn't being insensitive to either her beliefs or her needs. "I truly believe this life isn't all there is."

She took a sip of ice water before responding. "My father was a very strict Christian minister who gave fiery speeches about hellfire and damnation if we didn't follow certain rules but never said much about ever having a happy life either here or later. I suppose that's why science was so appealing to me. Cause and effect made sense because the outcome was visible to even the most disbelieving eyes. But I don't want to talk about things like that anymore. This is the only time in my life when I've been truly excited about what tomorrow was going to bring. Do you think the hotel would mind if I lit a few candles in the bridal suite? I know we won't be able to consummate our marriage until Russell has completely healed, but I do want things to be perfect."

The way Annabelle spoke still made me smile. Most people used crude vulgarities when talking about something that had always been special and sacred to me. Perhaps that was one of the reasons we felt such a kinship. We were certainly very different otherwise.

"Open flames might be a problem, but I'm sure we can find something that will help create the desired ambiance," I told her. "And there's nothing wrong with being held all night. There's something very fulfilling about being loved that way."

We made a few additional purchases before she took me back to my room. I wasn't afraid to bathe and dress on my own any longer. I took pain pills when I felt the need, but mostly I was doing much better than ever imagined. I had to believe that the love I felt from so many sources was the reason.

Brett was waiting when I finished therapy. He looked thoroughly relaxed and gave me both a hug and a kiss in front of everyone in the waiting room.

"Are you ready for some really good news?" he asked when I was sitting in the car next to him. We hadn't spoken since morning because we both had so much to do.

"You bet I am," I replied, deciding that telling him I would be staying at the motel could wait until later.

"Then hold onto your hat because we have a new home. Bill called an hour ago to say that our offer has been accepted. We just have to fill out the paperwork if you're not too tired for that."

"Never!" I replied, leaning across the gear shift column to place a kiss on his lips. "But I haven't given you my share."

"You can do that when your house sells. I've got you covered, and you never have to worry about making it on your own again because I'm going to be right by your side for as long as God allows."

My face contorted as the tears came, but I didn't fight them as I was in the habit of doing. Brett was continually surprising me by his depth of understanding, and I felt like the luckiest girl alive.

We had takeout pizza at his loft, filled out what we could on a housing loan application and then watched a movie. I was no longer worried about things happening too fast. I was much too exited about being part of his life permanently.

It was nearly midnight when he took me back to the motel. He supported my decision to stay where I was and told me he would pick me up for the wedding since he knew I would be busy helping Annabelle get ready most of the day. He wasn't wrong about that. I had booked us a day at the spa. She didn't complain about not being with Russell because she was a southern girl, deeply steeped in tradition, who believed it was bad luck for the groom to see his bride on their wedding day.

I worried until early afternoon about what to tell her regarding Brett because she was far too astute not to notice subtle changes in our body language when she saw us together again.

We were laying on tables with cool, cucumber slices on our eyes when I decided to broach the subject.

"Are you enjoying yourself, Annabelle?" I asked.

"More than I thought I would," she responded. "Thank you for giving me such a treat. I don't know what I would be doing with myself otherwise. I am so excited I feel like I'm going to crawl out of my skin."

"You deserve a day that's all about you."

"Is that why you haven't told me what's really going on between you and Professor Fowler? Even a blind person could tell that you're head-over-heels in love. I've been dying to know every detail but didn't want to spoil your happiness now that I know how rare it is to feel truly important to someone."

"You're a much better friend than I am."

"Not true, Jada. Without you, I would be sitting back in my parent's old house with my cat instead of getting married in a few hours. I owe everything to your willingness to go with me to that party and then stepping back when you thought I could handle it on my own."

"I know you feel that way, but all I did was let you know what a truly remarkable woman you are."

"That's just it! No one had even seen anything remarkable about me before. I was just a wallflower who knew her way around a lab. Do I hear wedding bells in your future too?"

It was now or never, and I decided to go for broke. "Loud and clear! In fact, we have already found a house under construction we like and made an offer."

"Why didn't you tell me sooner," she said with just a pinch of sadness. "We could have had a double wedding."

"We're not quite ready for that. Unlike you and your beloved, we share a complicated past, and last week didn't turn out quite the way either of us thought it would."

"I truly am sorry you had to get caught up in our problems, but things seem to be better for all of us now?"

"I would say they are pretty close to perfect, except that I don't know if I'm going to have a job once I talk to my boss. And I have a home that won't be easy to sell in this economy. People are moving away from California in droves."

"But you have to know that everything is going to be okay. People who love each other should be together, no matter what it takes. I will be invited to the wedding, won't I?"

"Absolutely! I'm hoping you'll be my matron of honor."

"Nothing would make me happier, but what about all your other friends?"

"That's just it. I don't have other friends, just acquaintance from work. I know you feel like you've been an outcast your entire life, but so have I. My father died when I was very young, my mother has spent most of her life in a mental institution and my brother cast me aside when he went away to college."

"Why didn't you tell me that before? We could have commiserated over our equally tough childhoods."

"Because I never talk about my past."

"But I would never judge."

"I know that now, Annabelle," I said, sitting upright and allowing my cucumber slices to fall where they may. "That's why I'm going to tell you that when Brett and I knew each other before, he was too busy romancing every girl who caught his eye to spend any quality time with me. He left town my senior year without saying goodbye, so I married a man I didn't love just so I wouldn't be alone. When that fell apart, I gave my life to my career. I hadn't been on a date in over four years when I came here. Like you, I pretty much figured my life was over when it came to finding love."

"I am so sorry," she said, sitting upright too but keeping her cucumber slices in her hands.

"Don't be! I've worked hard to create the illusion of being a hardworking, competent and composed woman, but it crippled me to the point that I wasn't even sure I could have a normal relationship. These past eleven days have shown me that it's okay to be human and let my weaknesses show because everyone has them—along with a lot of self-doubt and lack of clarity when it comes to what this life is really about. Thank you for being part of that journey. If you hadn't come to me with a simple request, I might have returned home without even seeing Brett."

"So we really do have a few things in common."

"I think we are far more alike than we are different. I just hope we won't let our newfound happiness with the perfect men keep us from getting to know each other better. I believe there is a great deal you could teach me."

The conversation ended when the women who had been taking care of us returned for our scheduled deep tissue massages. Mine had to be careful because of my shoulder, but I still felt more of the tension I had carried around for years work its way to the surface. I had prayed often, long and with real intent that my heart would soften so I could feel more than jealously, anger and self-contempt while I was busy judging others. But apparently I was meant to learn the hard way that every life story was tailored so the one living it could learn the greatest lessons.

I was ready to move beyond all the clutter and debris of the past into a much brighter future, and a plain-spoken, retiring spinster—with a heart of gold—had shown me the way.

Annabelle made a lovely bride, and Professor Price looked far less austere than usual as they stood before the judge and promised to love, honor and cherish each other in sickness and health until that great equalizer called death came calling. The hospital chapel was small and plain, but the fading sunlight coming in through the west window cast a rosy glow over the happy couple. The doctor and nurses who had helped with his recovery were there, as was the guard who stood at his door and the two detectives that would keep looking for Wally and Myra until every lead ran cold.

It was an odd assortment of guests, but the entire affair seemed fitting. We had come together through very unusual circumstances, but I knew it was all part of God's plan, or he would have intervened before anyone got hurt.

Brett looked amazing in a suit and tie, and I couldn't keep myself from looking in his direction. I had loved him for twelve long years, but never more than I did at the moment when when his eyes found mine, and I could see eternity written in them.

He would come to California as soon as the summer semester ended and help me pack for my return trip to Bentley. I would show him what I was leaving behind, but none of that seemed important any longer. And even if life didn't give us all we hoped for, it had already given us more than we ever believed we would have.

Love—given from the heart and without any restraints—was a most glorious gift. It was the essence of the message the Savior had given during his earthy ministry, and one I would never forget. Despite all its trials, life was definitely good.

Other Titles From Jan Hill Books:

Kismet Finds a Way

Rivers of Rage

Beyond the Glass Doors

Final Allegiance - Reagan Sinclair, FBI
Resilience - Reagan Sinclair, FBI - Book 2

Safe Haven - Reagan Sinclair, FBI - Book 3

Unsheltered - Reagan Sinclair, FBI - Book 4

Welcome Redemption - Reagan Sinclair, FBI - Book 5

Indecision's Flame
Lost - Indecision's Flame - Book 2

Exposed - Indecision's Flame - Book 3

Betrayal - Indecision's Flame - Book 4

Reawakening - Indecision's Flame - Book 5

Unraveling - Indecision's Flame - Book 6

Destiny - Indecision's Flame - Book 7

About the Author

JS Ririe is the pen name for Jan Hill who spent her youth in the country where she learned to appreciate solitude, making her own fun, and reading romance novels from some of the masters like the Bronte sisters, Louisa May Alcott, Victoria Holt and Phyllis Whitney. She penned her first novel as a teenager but never pursued what is now her greatest passion until becoming the lead witness in a federal case brought against the school district where she taught broadcasting and journalism. She has written two series: Indecision's Flame and Reagan Sinclair - FBI, along with four stand-alone novels. She lives in Utah and has two children and two living grandchildren who bring meaning and joy to her life.

A Note From Jan

Thank you so much for reading this novel. I'd love to stay in touch with you. Please consider joining my MAILING LIST so I can send you periodic newsletters about upcoming book releases, special offers and more. The link to sign up is: http://eepurl.com/dCPYVf . I promise not to spam you or sell your email information to anyone. It will be treated with care.

One last favor: Your rating/review of this book helps promote my work and encourages me to keep writing. A short, but honest review would mean a lot. It shouldn't take more than a minute or two. You can reach the page directly at http://bit.ly/IFReview

Thank you again.
JS Ririe

www.JanHillBooks.com
For contacting the author: JSRirie@JanHillBooks.com